Ac...
RAND...

D1561579

"It's a rare delight to come across a new writer with a distinctive and captivating voice . . . P.I. Sydney Sloane is a honey—if she doesn't mind me saying so."
Donald E. Westlake

"Randye Lordon's lesbian p.i. is a brave young woman with an outsider's witty voice and an insider's penchant for secrets."
Justin Scott, author of *Stonedust*

"It's great to have Sydney Sloane, p.i., with her gritty New York pizzazz and humor, back on a new case."
Annette Meyers, author of *Murder: The Musical*

"The world needs more heroes like Sydney Sloane— and more mystery writers like Randye Lordon."
Tom Savage, author of *Valentine*

"Good writing, engaging characters, irreverent humor, and an intriguing plot all combine to make this another Randye-Lordon-can't-put-it-down mystery!"
Joan Drury, author of *Silent Words*, on *Mother May I*

"[An] excellent series."
The Purloined Letter

Other Sydney Sloane Mysteries by
Randye Lordon
from Avon Twilight

FATHER FORGIVE ME
MOTHER MAY I

Avon Books are available at special quantity discounts for bulk purchases for sales promotions, premiums, fund raising or educational use. Special books, or book excerpts, can also be created to fit specific needs.

For details write or telephone the office of the Director of Special Markets, Avon Books, Inc., Dept. FP, 1350 Avenue of the Americas, New York, New York 10019, 1-800-238-0658.

SAY UNCLE

a
sydney sloane
mystery

R A N D Y E
L O R D O N

AVON

TWILIGHT

This is a work of fiction. Names, characters, places, and incidents either are the product of the author's imagination or are used fictitiously. Any resemblance to actual events, locales, organizations, or persons, living or dead, is entirely coincidental and beyond the intent of either the author or the publisher.

AVON BOOKS, INC.
1350 Avenue of the Americas
New York, New York 10019

Copyright © 1999 by Randye Lordon
Published by arrangement with the author
Visit our website at **http://www.AvonBooks.com/Twilight**
Library of Congress Catalog Card Number: 98-93312
ISBN: 0-380-79167-6

All rights reserved, which includes the right to reproduce this book or portions thereof in any form whatsoever except as provided by the U.S. Copyright Law. For information address Avon Books, Inc.

First Avon Twilight Printing: January 1999

AVON TWILIGHT TRADEMARK REG. U.S. PAT. OFF. AND IN OTHER COUNTRIES, MARCA REGISTRADA, HECHO EN U.S.A.

Printed in the U.S.A.

WCD 10 9 8 7 6 5 4 3 2 1

If you purchased this book without a cover, you should be aware that this book is stolen property. It was reported as "unsold and destroyed" to the publisher, and neither the author nor the publisher has received any payment for this "stripped book."

For U.B., A.R.,
and
purple flowers

Acknowledgments

I would like to thank the following people for their generous assistance in helping me with this book: one of New York's Bravest and all-around good guys, Bob Davidson; legal eagles Cynthia and Al Osterweil; Fred Padula at the New York Division of Labor Standards; Mike Donovan and Liz Jones at UNITE; E.W. Count; Janice Greer; Julie Landsman; Marji Danilow; Clare Hutton; Scott Lazarus; Dr. Cynthia Ligenza; all of my cohorts on DL who know a drug when they take one; Leonardo Michaelangelo Leocumlovitch, who understands time; and Joanne Spina, who has helped more than she might even know; and @.

It is impossible to write about the *shmatte* business without a healthy smattering of Yiddish. When in doubt, check the glossary at the back of the book.

*Families are nothing other than
the idolatry of duty.*

Ann Oakley (b. 1944),
British sociologist and author

Bullshit!

Olga Annamacher Tinklepaugh,
fellow traveler and spiritual guide on the M104 bus

One

You wouldn't think oatmeal could kill a gal, but—thanks to a fast-thinking, large-breasted waitress by the name of Polly—I'm here to tell you anything is possible.

It was like this: I was sitting at a booth for two, reading the morning paper, minding my own business. I was vaguely aware that a couple had walked toward my table, but I didn't look up, because I assumed they were being seated at the booth across the aisle. I had just put a spoonful of oatmeal with a strawberry and maple syrup into my mouth when I heard my name, looked up, and saw my cousins, Elly and Mark, cousins I hadn't seen in years. I was stunned. And that's when it happened. I opened my mouth to voice my surprise, and the strawberry slid into my throat and jammed.

What would have been, in the best of situations, an uncomfortable reunion was rapidly turning into dangerous farce, and bizarrely, I was the only one conscious of that fact. It felt as if I had suddenly sprouted an Adam's apple and the strawberry was literally expanding in my throat. Clearly my cousins didn't know what was going on. Elly, always the peacekeeper, smiled tensely at me and nodded, while her older brother, Mark, grimaced what he might have thought was a smile, but fell way short. He moved a half step away from the table. No doubt I looked agog, stunned by their sudden appearance—which indeed I was—but, in fact, I knew if I didn't get help, these two people would be my last vision of the world. This alone was enough to make me pound on my chest to dislodge the damned berry. I watched in a panic as Elly's smile slowly faded and her upper lip inched up, exposing her gums. She squinted uncomprehendingly at me. Mark just looked embarrassed.

Fortunately, at that very moment, dear, sweet, maternal Polly came rushing past my cousins and screamed into my face, "Can you talk?"

I threw my head from side to side, grabbing out to her for help. Everything was a blur around me. The people at the counter turned from their coffee to watch, little old ladies looked up from their poached eggs (half of which they would wear home on their chins), and the entire establishment was caught in a suspended moment of disbelief as the very exciting prospect of watching a patron die at booth twelve loomed before them.

Polly seized me by the waist and spun me around. She braced my torso against her left arm and smacked my back with her right. Nothing. I was feeling light-headed, ready to give in to the stupid piece of fruit. Again she smacked my back, her arm feeling more like a two-by-four than an appendage of a sixty-odd-year-old woman. Nothing happened. I was unable to inhale or exhale, and it felt as if it was about to burst. She wrapped her arms around me from behind, pressed her massive breasts against my back, uttered some words of reassurance, and then, as hard as she could, jabbed her fists just under my sternum and practically pulled me up off the ground.

It was a glorious moment. I watched the oatmeal-covered strawberry sail in slow motion, a perfect arch, glistening in the overhead light as it landed smack dab in the middle of Mark's forehead.

My body went limp in Polly's embrace as she lowered me back onto the red vinyl seat. I took several deep gulps of air before I was finally able to clear my now raw throat and thank her. Polly, also shaken from the event, squeezed my shoulder and said, "I couldn't lose you, kid, you tip too well."

She looked up at the useless gaping duo and handed Mark a napkin.

Without a note of thanks, he took it from her, dipped it in a glass of water, and wiped his brow.

"Bull's-eye," she muttered, as she straightened up and gently patted my back. "You okay now?"

"I'm fine, thanks to you."

"Remember, kid, *chew*." Polly sauntered over to another table and loudly warned the elderly stooped woman, "Careful, now, Annie, that's what happens when you don't gum things enough."

In less than five minutes life was back to normal. The busboy had cleared away my breakfast dishes, as well as the offending strawberry, and Elly and Mark were sitting across from me with water and coffee. Aside from one last remaining piece of oatmeal plastered to Mark's forehead, you never would have known that I had almost died just moments earlier. Mark lowered his penetrating eyes, green like mine, and lifted his coffee cup.

"Wow." Elly opened two packets of artificial sweetener and poured them into her coffee. "That was pretty intense." My younger cousin is a pretty woman whose round face and straight, straight brown hair make it clear that she's her father's daughter. In the yellowish coffee shop light, I could see that hairline wrinkles had only recently started to grace her eyes. "I knew you'd get choked up when you saw us, but I never expected *that*." She looked up at me from her coffee and smiled with her eyes, picking up where we had left off, years earlier. The drift with Elly had been something I'd never really understood, since my "falling out," if you could call it that, had been with her father. Seeing her now made me realize how much I had missed her.

I reached beyond the divide. "Didn't think I'd be so *berry* surprised, eh?"

Mark, who is three years my junior and three years older than Elly (placing him somewhere near forty), let out an exasperated sigh and glared at his sister. "You want to entertain each other or get to the point?"

I hadn't remembered Mark as being such an ass, but a lot can happen in four years. The last time I'd seen anyone from my mom's side of the family was when my brother, David, had died four years earlier. Mark had attended David's funeral but couldn't make it to the cemetery because, as he had told my sister, Nora, he had a *very* important business meeting. He never even said good-bye to me that day—not that I dwell on that sort of thing—but it struck me as just a little tacky.

I stared at my good-looking self-important cousin. Family dynamics have always baffled me. I mean, what is family, really? Should DNA be the guideline by which we define family, or should it be a matter of love, respect, and trust? There is no question that Mark and I share some similar genetic coding, but we are as different as cantaloupes and scissors.

No longer the nice little girl in need of my family's approval, and not about to put up with his attitude, I cut to the chase. "Obviously you want something, Mark. What is it?" He squinted but didn't say anything. Feeling provoked, I continued. "I can only assume that this meeting—which is neither at my home nor my office, but in the coffee shop where I *was* having a nice, leisurely breakfast—I can only assume that this meeting was not happenstance and you have gone to some trouble to track me down on this cold, gray day." Through the picture window behind him, pedestrians with umbrellas struggled against a February rainstorm. "So why don't you get to the point?"

Elly added half the pitcher of milk to her coffee and Mark contemplated his hands. Good-looking hands, actually: large, strong, with dark hair and a gold-and-sapphire pinkie ring on his left hand. Still no wedding band. The only imperfection was a cut between his thumb and index finger on his right hand.

I stirred sugar into my coffee and felt hungry, despite my recent brush with death. I waited for Mark to pick up the slack.

Finally, Elly turned her dark brown eyes to me and said, "We went to your office and your secretary told us where we could find you. We have a problem, Sydney." She paused. "It's Daddy. He's been arrested for—"

"*Arrested*?" I echoed softly.

Before she could complete her sentence, Mark interrupted. "*Was* arrested. He's not in jail *now*."

I looked blankly at Mark, turned back to Elly, and muttered, "Go on."

Her whole body seemed to inflate when she took a deep breath. "Two months ago Dad was arrested for arson and murder—"

"*What?*" It felt as if I had been hit in the head with a sledge hammer. Uncle Mitch? Arrested for murder? It was impossible. A thousand thoughts crammed into my head at the same time. Who would he have murdered, and why? "Arson? Murder?" I felt my face pull into a deep scowl.

Elly nodded. "His ex-partner's factory was torched and a woman died in the fire."

"*Ex*-partner?" I interrupted again, feeling more and more like a stranger to these two people with whom I'd shared a childhood full of sleepovers, baths, and secrets. As far back as I could remember, Uncle Mitch and Jake Aronson had been bickering partners in Harriman's, a dress manufacturing business. It seemed impossible that something as monumental as the dissolution of their partnership would have happened without someone having told me.

"Oh yeah. Daddy bought Jake out over a year ago. You didn't know that?" She, too, seemed surprised by my ignorance.

"Over a year ago?" My hands were resting on the tabletop, palms up as if pleading. I curled my fingers in and shook my head.

"Oh, God, Sydney, I'm sorry," Elly said as if she meant it. "Anyway, Jake may be Mom's cousin, but he and Daddy have always hated each other. Tell me, do you still know anything about the *shmatte* business? Because it's nothing like it used to be when we were kids."

When I was four, Uncle Mitch started bringing me to work with him at least once a month, a routine that lasted about three years. He'd show me off to his employees and set me up at a desk in his office where I would do very important business. After work he would buy me a hot dog, a Cel-Ray, and an ice cream sandwich. Back then I had every intention of growing up to be Joan Crawford, taking over the family business and turning it into a zillion-dollar enterprise. I had it all figured out; I'd smoke cigarettes and click around on high heels, all the while snapping orders at people who respected me because I was tough, but not too tough.

"Ninety-nine percent of the manufacturing is done overseas now. Cheap labor. It makes sense." Elly shrugged. "Anyway, after thirty years of being in business together and hating each other, Dad and Jake finally decided to call it quits. Jake's crazy son, Danny—remember him?—well, he went after Dad with a box-knife . . . that's when Dad decided *genug iz genug*.

"They were very smart about how they handled the settlement. You see, they both agreed that they had to dissolve the partnership, but they didn't decide who would take the business until *after* they drew up an agreement. Get it?''

"Sure. But why?''

"Because this way no one would think they were getting screwed. They negotiated an agreement not knowing who was going to retire, or who was going to take the business. That way, they both felt confident that whichever side they were on, they were getting a fair deal. After all the papers were drawn up and everything was agreed upon, they went to their lawyer's office and flipped a coin.

"Depending on how you look at it, Dad won the coin toss, which he should have because he genuinely loves the business and Jake's always complained about it. Anyway, when Jake lost the toss, he said he planned to retire." Elly picked up her coffee and looked at me over the rim of her cup.

"I take it he didn't," I said.

Elly blinked. "Nope. Instead, the *goniff* opened a new shop within a year and a half." She brought the cup to her lips.

"The son of a bitch had signed a noncompete clause, it was part of the agreement." Mark tapped on the tabletop with his index finger. "But then, to make matters *worse*, the *schmuck* tried to steal Dad's clients by offering them a forty-percent discount."

"Jake had to be doing something dirty because the cost of manufacturing in the States is now prohibitive," Elly said, when Mark took a breath. "I mean, he made excellent money when he and Dad ended their partnership, but not enough to bankroll a whole new operation, especially in the States."

If it hadn't been for the surrealistic fact that we were discussing Uncle Mitch's future, it might have felt like old times, the three of us huddled over afternoon coffee. The only things missing were a haze of cigarette smoke and the kind of connection that comes with intimacy. I don't know what I missed more at that moment, the cigarettes or the connection to my family.

"Jesus, how's your mom taking all this?" I asked, knowing that Jake was Aunt Maddy's first cousin, which probably put her smack dab in the middle of everything.

Elly's shoulders fell. "It's been hard on her, but we all know the truth."

"Okay. So Jake's business was torched and Uncle Mitch was arrested. Do they have any evidence?"

Elly and Mark looked askance at one another before Mark took a deep breath and told the palms of his hands, "On the surface it really doesn't look good. I mean, a grand jury has already ruled against him." He looked up at me and clamped his hands shut. "Apart from the fact that Dad threatened Jake in front of about a hundred and fifty people, the investigators found something in Dad's garage that they say was used at the fire."

"What?" I asked.

He shrugged and studied the restaurant behind me. Then, very softly, he said, "I don't know, a crowbar." He clicked his tongue against his teeth and looked almost angry, but I knew it was pain he was feeling, not rage. "His fingerprints were on it." His voice cracked, but he quickly continued. "Someone planted it in his garage. It was placed on the hood of his car, and his fingerprints got on it when he picked it up and tossed it off to the side." He rested his chin in his hand, hiding his mouth behind his fingers.

"Let's start at the top. Tell me about the fire." As much as it disturbed me that this was the first I was hearing about all this, I had to take a deep breath and remind myself that this wasn't about me. It was about Mitch. My uncle. A man who used to be my friend. A second father who had loved me unconditionally . . . until he learned I was gay.

Elly clutched her coffee cup and asked, "Will you help us?"

That she would even think to ask the question hurt me, after all, we're family. Then again, I was looking across the table at two virtual strangers. I knew less about them than I did about Mrs. Jensen, a little old crackpot in my building, who has actually won a soft spot in my heart after all these years.

"Of course I will." My words came out sounding husky, almost gruff, which masked what I was really feeling; apprehension bordering on fear. This wasn't an unknown client coming in and hiring me to pick through their dirty laundry . . . this was my family, and whether I wanted to admit it or not, it made a difference. A good investigator needs to rely on his objectivity, which is something I usually pride myself on, but this was a different kettle of fish altogether. How could I be objective with my family, especially since there had been years of silence weighing us down? It was a challenge I wasn't sure we could all rise to.

TWO

I arranged to meet with the family at Elly's the next day, and left my cousins at Mark's car, which was parked just outside the restaurant. The three-block walk between the coffee shop and my office wasn't nearly enough time to assess my feelings. The conversation with my cousins had brought to light the painful reality that Uncle Mitch didn't want my help. When Mark suggested that I conduct the investigation without letting Mitch know I was on the case, I pointed out, as calmly as I could, that it would be strategically, physically, and emotionally impossible. Mark hadn't stopped there. He had actually had the audacity to suggest that my business partner, Max, take on the case. That's when I lost my patience.

"Max is away on his honeymoon for the next few weeks. However, if you like, Mark, I can give you the name of a straight white very macho detective by the name of Hogan. Granted, he's not nearly as good as I am, but I'm sure he'll meet all your other criteria."

"Oh please, Sydney, don't tell me you're still sensitive about that."

Elly had interceded before I could respond. "We wanted to make sure you'd agree to help us before we said anything to Dad. It may not be the best way to reconcile your differences with him, but right now at least it's a doorway. Besides, there doesn't seem to be much choice. Please. We need your help. Dad didn't set that fire, Sydney, and I won't let him go to jail just because he's so damned stubborn.''

I was sandwiched between anger and loyalty. On the one hand I felt good that my family knew they could turn to me in a time of need. On the other, I was incredibly hurt that they would contact me only *when* they needed me. I didn't know if I was a hero or a sucker, but the fact is, I was committed because this was about family. And if what Elly and Mark had told me was true, Uncle Mitch was in a peck of trouble and needed all the help he could get.

Family. I shook my head as I bound up the steps to my second-floor office.

When I opened the door to my agency (Cabe Sloane Investigations), I was greeted not only by Kerry Norman, my friend and secretary, but my ten-month-old puppy, Auggie, who raced from my office, skidded into a turn on the wooden floor, and slid the rest of the way to me on her fanny. You'd have to be either miserable or dead not to respond to the unrestrained enthusiasm of a puppy greeting.

"Hey, did your cousins find you?" Kerry looked up from the book she was reading.

"Yes," I said, wiping puppy kisses off my cheek. "You know, they might not have been my cousins." I slipped out of my wet raincoat and hung it on the coatrack.

"Of course they were your cousins, you guys could practically be twins, especially the guy, what's his name?"

"Mark."

"Mark. Very cute."

"Oh yeah, adorable," I said with muffled sarcasm. I draped my wet scarf next to the raincoat.

"Besides, Sydolium, you have to trust me. I've been in this business long enough to know when something's kosher or not. I knew they weren't evil."

"Really?" I lifted a brow. "For your information, those two nearly killed me just now."

She flattened her hands on the desk top. "No-way-

you're-lying," she said, as if the sentence was one word. I
noticed her shapely fingernails were painted a florescent
shade of lime green.

"Of course I'm lying." I sailed past her desk into my
office and continued talking. "But you should always warn
me before I have family visitors." As soon as I entered the
room, I saw that Auggie had been busy filing in my absence. Her job is to take all the papers out of my wastebasket, tear them apart, and pile them under my desk, which
is actually her private office. Kerry followed me with a
stack of mail in hand. "There I was having a perfectly
lovely breakfast and the next thing I know, I'm choking to
death," I said over my shoulder, as I pulled open the canvas
window covering as far as it would go. Usually sunlight
pours into my office, and even on overcast days light man-
ages to fill the large arched windows that face east, looking
out on Broadway, but there was no light. It was a gray,
cold, and uninviting day; the kind where you want to stay
in bed until spring.

"They choked you?" she asked, tossing the mail onto
my desk and trashing Auggie's filing efforts.

"No. But a big strawberry did." I turned away from the
street and went to check the mail. The door to my partner
Max's office was open, and I had a wave of missing him.
He was in St. Bart for several weeks, with his new bride.

"Really?" She grew wide-eyed with anticipation of a
story. I imagine that when Kerry was in kindergarten, she
was probably the first to position herself, cross-legged, on
the floor in preparation to hear a story read or told. "Tell
me what happened." She flopped down onto the sofa at the
far end of the room and hiked her feet onto the coffee table.

I settled behind my desk, quickly flipped through the
envelopes and catalogs, and handed Auggie an *occupant*
letter to file. "Okay. I was eating oatmeal—"

"With strawberries?" Kerry interrupted.

"Yes. With strawberries."

"Oatmeal should only have, like, raisins or bananas."

"I've learned that the hard way. I looked up, saw Mark, and the next thing I knew, I was turning blue." I tossed the catalogs into the garbage, knowing there would be doubles at home, and found four interesting bits of mail. Two checks from happy clients, a wedding invitation from my friend, Lyle, in Texas, and an envelope from a law firm.

"He didn't help you?" She was incredulous.

"He didn't know."

"What is he, stupid? You can't tell when a person is choking?"

"Well, fortunately Polly did. She saved my life, for which I will always be indebted to her."

"I hope you tipped her well."

"Of course I did. I mean, really, what's my life worth?"

"More than sixteen percent, I hope."

I opened the letter from the law firm and scanned its contents. A long time ago, a musician friend of mine, Ned, and I quit smoking together on a bet. Neither of us was allowed to touch a cigarette for five years. If we did, we owed the other person $5,000. Six months after we quit smoking, Ned died of cancer. However, always a gentleman, true to his word, he had arranged, in his will, that if I stayed smoke-free, I was to receive the $5,000 along with his trumpet. If not, the money would go to the American Cancer Society and the trumpet was to be tossed into the Hudson. I had received the money several years earlier, which I donated to research in Ned's name, but the trumpet was another story. The trumpet had been misplaced, and the attorney handling the estate had thought I would simply say, okay, no big deal. But it *was* a big deal. It was Ned's. It was a Mount Vernon Bach. And it would make a great gift for an aspiring young musician. Apparently, after years of letters back and forth, the law firm was writing to say that the trumpet had finally been recovered.

"Listen," I said, tossing the letter onto the desk and leaning back into my squeaking chair, "we have a lot of work ahead of us." I put my feet up on the end of the desk and let Auggie up onto my lap. At forty pounds and still growing, this wasn't a habit that she and I would continue for long, but I like having her near. "My uncle has been arrested for arson and murder, and from what my cousins tell me, the evidence does not point favorably in his direction."

"Jeez." She twisted a lock of red hair around her finger. The color clashed with the lime green nail polish. Kerry is by nature a beautiful woman—with a magnificent mane of hair, a trim, compact body covered with porcelain skin, and a smile to die for. There's only one small problem; ever since she started dating Patrick—a Soho artist—her style of dress makes one wonder what the hell is going on inside her head. At that very moment she was wearing skin-tight canary yellow pants patterned with clown heads, a shapeless fuzzy sweater of hot pink with purple stars, and enormous plastic earrings sporting Howdy Doody on the left ear and Clarabelle on the right, and to top off the ensemble she wore scuffed platform black military boots tied with lime green laces, no doubt to match her nail polish. It's hard to imagine that a woman who looks like that could be as organized as she is, but she is.

"He's a clothing manufacturer," I said, pulling my gaze away from her costume and setting Auggie back on the floor. "He and his partner of about a zillion years terminated their association and the partner—Jake—was going to retire. But he didn't. Instead, he opened his own business—the same business—and tried to steal Uncle Mitch's customers. Uncle Mitch has always had a temper. He saw Jake at a family bar mitzvah where he threatened him loudly and in front of many people. A week later, Jake's place was torched. A cleaning woman was killed in the fire, but she still hasn't been positively identified, which is pathetic, I mean, here it is close to four months after the fact and she's still at the morgue.''

"They still have her?" Kerry asked, adding ''*eeesch*,'' which interpreted meant ''totally gross.''

"That's one of the things we should find out. The woman may have been ID'd during the last month, unbeknownst to Elly or Mark, or maybe she was given a Jane Doe burial, I don't know.''

"Cause of death?" Kerry asked.

"Elly said the woman died as a result of the fire, but who knows? That's another thing to add to the list.''

"Didn't your uncle have an alibi?" Kerry poked her fingers into her massive head of hair and wiggled through the tangles. "I mean, he's got to be an old man, right? Old men don't start fires, do they?''

I shrugged. ''I think that's like assuming a woman will never hurt her children simply because she's a woman and therefore maternal. People are just people, and some of them are really weird.''

"Is your uncle really weird?" She clicked the toes of her army boots together. Her arms were raised over her head with the ends of her hair pinched between her fingertips, making her look as if she had an electrical current charging through her body.

"I don't know. I don't think so,'' I answered honestly. Once upon a time I would have jumped to his defense and assured her in no uncertain terms that he was a man above reproach. But that was when I knew him. Things seemed different now.

" 'I don't think so'? What does that mean?" She stopped clicking her toes together and dropped her hair, which fell gently over her shoulders.

"It means that I can't imagine my uncle would do anything like that, but the fact is I don't know. I am going to find out, though, or I should say, we are."

"Which uncle is this?" Kerry asked, lifting her feet off the table and sitting upright. She reached out for Auggie, who was shaking the daylights out of a rope toy.

"My mom's brother." It's not as if I have a large family to keep track of. In my immediate family, there is only my sister, Nora, left, and of course, my Aunt Minnie, who, at eighty-we're-not-allowed-to-count-anymore, is one of my best friends and closest relations. Other than Min, almost everyone on my Dad's side is gone, including Dad who died in '87.

On Mom's side, the only remaining siblings are Uncle Mitch and an aunt, Kate, who was estranged from the family since before my mom died, when I was nineteen. I met Kate once, when I was around six, and remember that she lived on a ranch with horses, had leathery skin, and called me "partner," and I liked her. A lot. There was something both mysterious and engaging about Mom's younger sister whom everyone talked about in hushed tones. She was one of the few adults who talked to us kids as if we were real people.

"What's the status with your uncle?" Kerry asked.

"He's out on bail, pending trial. After the grand jury found the evidence against him 'compelling,' his attorney, Paul Levin—who is also my cousin Elly's husband, ergo Mitch's son-in-law—hired an investigator to get to the bottom of it."

"Who?" She grabbed one end of Auggie's toy and tried to snatch it away.

"Guy named Alfred Hickey. You know him? He's in Bayside."

"Queens? No way. I don't know *anyone* in Queens. What did he find out?"

"After what I can only guess was an abbreviated investigation, he concluded that Uncle Mitch would be well advised to plead temporary insanity and pray. Naturally, my cousins want something more substantial than that. But the fact is . . ." I linked an index finger around the pinkie of the other hand as I itemized the particulars. "A bunch of people heard him threaten Jake. They found a crowbar in his garage that not only has paint on it from the fire site, but Uncle Mitch's fingerprints as well. He has no apparent alibi, and the fire department conducted a very thorough investigation." I unlinked the four fingers I had used in my count and flattened them on my desk top. "I have a great deal of respect for city fire marshals. They're usually meticulous."

"Wow. This doesn't sound good for your uncle. What do you mean by no apparent alibi?" Auggie issued a low growl as Kerry tugged at the rope.

"He was ostensibly at home watching TV when the fire broke out, but he can't say what was on, because he fell asleep."

"And your aunt? Is there one? Can she back him up?" Kerry released the toy and Auggie tumbled back onto her fanny, barking a delighted high-pitched puppy yelp.

"She was in Detroit visiting her sister that weekend." I chewed nervously on the inside of my cheek. You didn't have to be Sherlock Holmes to understand the severity of the situation. "And to make matters worse, Uncle Mitch doesn't have a clue as to how serious his situation is."

"Maybe that's not so bad," Kerry suggested, as she planted her hands on her knees and hefted herself up off the sofa.

"Of course it is. No one's leveling with him. From what Elly says, he believes that he'll be vindicated in court because the legal system is just and fair."

Kerry took a seat in front of my desk and shook her head.

"What is *wrong* with people? Don't they understand law has nothing to do with justice?"

"I guess not."

"Okay, so where do we start?"

"First I want to find out which insurance company was covering Jake." I passed her a slip of paper with my notes from the coffee shop. "Here's the name of his business, the date of the fire, his full name . . . basic stuff. I'm going to meet with Mitch at eleven-thirty tomorrow morning, but in the meantime I'll get a copy of the investigation report from Paul, the attorney son-in-law. Also, I want to head out to what's left of the factory with Miguel. Where is he?"

Miguel Leigh is the latest addition to our staff. A street-wise smart-aleck, he clearly has a knack for the business, but there are problems. He's young and impatient, and brash bordering on arrogant, and occasionally he likes to dress up like June Cleaver. Mind you, I don't think there's anything wrong with dressing in drag, but professionally it could be a liability. Which is not to say that in some circles it couldn't be a benefit. However, as progressive as we are at CSI, we tend to discourage that sort of business apparel.

"He had to take his grandmother to the dentist. He should be here by two."

It was nearly one, which meant that I could at least start the ball rolling.

When Kerry stood up I experienced a fleeting moment of questioning fair play; why did I let her dress like that, while I insisted that Miguel steer clear of the high heels and rouge? I sighed and mumbled, "Life's not fair."

"Amen to that, girl." Kerry stepped over Auggie and headed back to the outer office. "Don't worry, Syd, we'll get to the bottom of this."

I pushed the corners of my mouth up to resemble a smile, but it only felt like a twitch. At this point, getting to the bottom of it wasn't my concern. It was what I'd find once I got there.

Three

My first call was to George Davis, a friend and fire marshal based in Manhattan. I had met George through Max many years earlier.

"Sydney, Sydney, how the hell are you?" George boomed in a thick Boston accent.

"I'm good, Georgie—yourself?"

"Nothing worth complaining about. No one would care anyway, now, would they?"

"*I* would."

"That's because you're special. Not like that *schlemiel* you work with."

"Yes, well that *schlemiel's* in St. Bart with his new bride."

"Go on. Max, married? Max Cabe? Didn't he learn better with my sister?"

"Guess not. They eloped. Very romantic."

"Sis is going to be mighty upset by this news."

"So don't tell her."

"What are you, crazy? Of course I'm going to tell her. She loves this sort of thing, it helps her lose weight. So." I could hear him shifting in his seat. "You didn't call because you've missed me, did you?"

"How did you know?"

"Because you and that nutcase you work with only call me at the office when you have trouble."

"Is that true?"

"Yup. You two have become like peas in a pod, which would concern me if I were you."

"It does. That's what happens when you spend too much time together. However, you're right, I do have a question for you."

"Shoot."

I explained the case I was working on, including the fact that my client was also my uncle. George might be a friend, but first he's a professional. I needed his help, but I respect the fact that he's not the type to simply flip open the file and let me take a gander.

"Gee, Sydney, I'm really sorry about this." He sighed. "Look, chances are the police took over the case because of the homicide, but let me check for you. This was where? Corona?"

"That's right."

"Okay. Let me see what I can do."

"Thanks, George. Oh, and by the way, thanks again for asking the guys at the firehouse in Hell's Kitchen to show my nephew around. He loved it."

"What's not to love? A dog, a pole, a fire truck, and a bunch of tough good guys; a firehouse is the best place in the world."

"Well, I think in another twenty years, Andy just might be joining your ranks."

"Excellent. We could always use a Sloane. Listen, I'll call you as soon as I have anything."

Next, I called my cousin by marriage, Paul Levin, who was representing Mitch. The first time I called, his secretary put me on hold for five minutes, which I have no tolerance for, so I hung up, called back, and asked her not to do that again. The condescending voice on the other end of the line told me that I was mistaken, that I hadn't been left on hold. Before I could respond, I was again snapped into hold, until she returned and explained coldly that, "Mr. Levin is in a meeting. May I have him call you back?'' I gave her my number and considered explaining the reason for my call, but decided that Paul knew who I was and most likely knew why I was calling.

Finding the Queens private investigator, Alfred Hickey, was easy enough. A quick computer search located him in Bayside, not far from my cousin Elly's in Great Neck, where I was scheduled to meet with my uncle and cousins the next day. I called and left a message on his machine explaining who I was, and asking if we could meet the next day at around one-thirty.

Miguel finally arrived when I was on the phone with Aunt Minnie. I indicated that I'd be on the line a while longer, so he leashed Auggie, grabbed a plastic bag, and held up five fingers. I nodded and watched the two of them, respectively, wiggle and strut toward the front door. Auggie loves Miguel. I am convinced this is because he kisses her. Literally. To my disgust (and Auggie's absolute delight), Miguel will grab her lips in his mouth and yank, or cover her big black nose with his mouth and blow, causing her cheeks to puff out. This routine always reminds me of my nephew, Andrew. When Andy was three, I would spin him around in the air like he was an airplane until he screamed for me to stop. But as soon as I did, he'd stagger right back, his face flush with laughter, and demand, ''Do it again, Auntie, do it again!''

''You're not listening to me,'' Minnie chided.

''I am. I was distracted for a second.''

''You know I never interfere,'' she continued where she had left off.

I took a deep breath. ''I know. But there's nothing I can do now. Besides, Min, I could have never said no, and you know it.''

There was a prolonged silence on the other end of the line. Finally, she sighed. ''Sydney, dear . . .'' She inhaled audibly. "I understand why you're doing this, but I cannot stress enough that involving yourself with family in this way is just courting trouble. Mark my word, ultimately you are going to be blamed for the whole damned mess. I hate to say this, but that's how Mitchell has always operated."

It was the first time I had ever heard Minnie say anything negative about my mom's side of the family. Oddly enough, instead of asking her why she would say that, I found myself defending Mitch. "Come on, you don't know Mitch anymore. I mean, when was the last time the two of you even had a conversation?" I paused, knowing that it was longer ago than she could handily remember. "At David's funeral?"

"This has nothing to do with Mitchell and *me*. This is about *you*. This is about you wanting to ride in on a white horse and make everything better. I know you, Sydney, you think if you save him now he'll *really* love you." She paused long enough to let the truth sink in and sting. "These people are desperate, elsewise they wouldn't have called you—"

"*These people* . . . listen to yourself. *These people* are my family."

"Really? And what does that mean, family?"

"No, no, I am not going to debate this with you." I fell back into my chair. It had stopped raining, though thick clouds still cast the city into one big gray shadow. "I take the cases I want, and I've accepted this one."

"Okay, fine," she said, affecting an air of indifference. "That's the last I'll say on this, but I still expect to see you and Leslie tonight at seven. I want to try a new jalapeño and cilantro sauce on you. Okay? And I want to hear what happened with her and the restaurant." As an interior decorator, Leslie is always regaling Minnie with stories of clients, one crazier than the other.

As soon as I hung up, I knew I was feeling something extreme, but I wasn't sure what it was. Once upon a time anger was the overriding emotion in my life, always at the ready and easy to identify. But as I've gotten older, that's changed. I no longer need to use my anger as a conduit to access all the other emotions.

I stood up and paced over to the windows. Seniors were trickling out of the cinema-one-too-many across the street. A tall, elderly man in a heavy parka, clutching an umbrella, shuffled to the end of the marquee overhang and extended his hand, checking for rain. All clear. He turned and offered an elbow to a round woman in orthopedic shoes and sweatpants. Her stark white hair poked out from under the earflaps of a colorful knit hat. Even from where I stood, I could see that her lipstick was freshly applied, and her smile was radiant as she linked her arm through his, and they carefully negotiated their way up Broadway.

As I watched them walk arm-in-arm, I identified what I was feeling. Anxious. Had I taken on more than I could chew? Was this Queens detective, Alfred Hickey, right in his assessment of the situation? Had I just taken on a losing battle for a man—my flesh and blood—who had trouble being in the same room with me, simply because I'm gay? Was Minnie right? Was I hoping to save Mitch so he would love me again?

"Yo Sydney, my main boss, listen up." Miguel paused at the office door and held his hands out as if he were about to conduct the Philharmonic. "What has seventeen characters, both letters and numbers, and can be—"

"Vehicle identification number, otherwise known as a VIN." I answered his random quiz before he finished the question, and tossed out my own. "In a 1987 Buick Le Sabre, the VIN number is located where?" Miguel often quizzed me to reinforce what he was learning in his studies.

"On a small, metal rectangular plate on the dashboard

by the driver's side, *or,* stamped on the engine.''

"Or?" I reached down and clasped Auggie's head in my hands and gave her a playful shake.

"Or on the transmission?" he said with less confidence. "Or?"

He stared at me, his mouth agape. I knew from experience this meant Miguel was thinking.

"Or . . . on . . . the inside of the driver's door!" He slapped his hands together and did a celebratory dance.

"Good. Or?" I asked as I returned to my desk.

"Or?" He was indignant. "What do you mean, *or?*"

"One more spot."

"Shit." He spun around in one clean movement and landed gracefully on a director's chair just opposite my desk. "Okay. Okay, I know this." He passed his fingers over his shorn head and closed his eyes. He had trimmed his newly grown goatee so that it almost looked as if it had been painted on his face.

"You want a hint?" I asked, as I sorted through the papers on my desk, preparing to leave.

"Nooo," he said the word not only with his mouth, but with his whole face, upon which every muscle was working, and his body, which he twisted and contorted like a sitting disco diva. Miguel and I had met several months earlier through an old friend of mine, Naomi Lewis, who runs a nursing home in the Village. Miguel had been on her security team, until he came to work for us. Now he's in training to be more than an operative with CSI. Both Max and I expect Miguel will ultimately get his license and become an integral part of our operation, but right now, he is learning and growing.

Several seconds passed.

"Okay, screw it, I don't know where the code would be."

"Dingdingdingdingding! Give the little man a ceegar."

"What?" He stared at me as if I was crazy.

" 'I don't know' is the correct answer."

"I don't get it." He slumped back into his chair.

"You wouldn't know where the code would be. Only the car manufacturer knows, because they change the location of the hidden VIN every year."

"Cool." He nodded as he hung his hand over the arm of the chair and tormented Auggie, the glutton for punishment, who kept coming back for more.

I glanced at my watch. It was nearly three o'clock, and Aronson Elite, Jake's now defunct business, was in an area of Queens I didn't know, which meant in all likelihood that by the time we found the place, it would be too late and too dark to see anything. I decided we'd start there first thing in the morning. In the meantime, I briefed Miguel.

As I went through the details with him, I couldn't help but wish Max were there to help with this one. Max not only knows me, but he knows all the other players in this configuration, and I knew I could trust him to be objective in a way I wasn't so sure I could expect from myself. There was no question in my mind that objectivity was going to be difficult to maintain on this case. Having worked together for as long as we have, Max and I have become like two bodies, the yin and yang, working together with one brain. As much as I love my life partner, Leslie, there is an element of wholeness I feel with Max that cannot be replicated. I was pleasantly surprised, however, when I was finished and Miguel asked, "Was your uncle pressing charges against Jake at the time of the fire?"

"Yes."

"So if he's got the guy in court, why would he torch the place?" He dropped his hands into his lap as if Mitch's innocence was as clear as the nose on my face.

"The judicial system is a slow process." Auggie curled up under my desk and put her head down with a heavy sigh. "Maybe Mitch was impatient. I mean, I know he's impatient, he's notorious for that. Maybe he couldn't take how slowly the courts were working it and decided to take the law into his own hands."

"I dunno. I have a friend who was in a very similar situation once. If you sign a noncompete agreement . . . that's it. Your uncle would know that this other guy couldn't have possibly won."

"Perhaps, but when people want to get even . . ."

"Look, he's smart enough to have had a successful business, right?" Miguel pulled at his limber legs until he was sitting in a lotus position on the director's chair. He rested his elbows on his knees and leaned forward.

"Yes," I said, not really sure where he was going with this.

"So that means he's smart enough to know you don't threaten some asshole in front of a lot of people and then think no one's gonna point a finger at you when the asshole gets torched. I mean, that's the kind of shit some dumb-ass fool pulls off. Like my cousin Chang."

"You have a cousin named Chang?" I interrupted.

"By marriage. You know Dummy Doreen?"

I nodded, having heard many a tale of Miguel's cousin, Dummy Doreen and her nasty son, Willie.

"Well, she was married for a month to this little weasel of a guy, Chang. I won't even go into it, but he would do something like that, *announce* he was gonna torch a house and then do it. I still see him when he's out, but he's stupid, man. He's always getting caught. He was even too stupid for Doreen, which is like having a minus IQ."

"Well, Mitch isn't stupid, but he does have a temper."

"You wanna know the truth, boss?"

"Always."

"I think you *think* your uncle did this thing."

At that precise moment, between his inflection, the tilt

of his head, the kindness in his eyes, and his observation, I could have been sitting across from Max. I said nothing.

"Am I right?" He rubbed the arm of his chair with his thumb, looking up at me from under his eyebrows.

I plucked a dying leaf off a small but stalwart poinsettia on my desk and tried to answer, but words wouldn't come. Finally I straightened my back and smiled. "Quite honestly, I don't know. I suppose part of me does, yes."

"So if you think this old man's guilty, that means you took on the case *only* because he's your uncle, right?"

I looked at him.

He shook his head and grimaced. "I don't buy it. It's not you. You're too professional . . . your instincts would stop you before committing to something stupid like a totally no-win situation. Even if it is for family." He shrugged. "Tell me, what is it you always tell me?" he prodded.

"Don't take a case you don't think you can win."

He gestured triumphantly and unfolded himself from the chair. "So, we're gonna assume Uncle Mitch is cool and find out who set him up, right?"

"Right." I was both amused and thrown that Miguel had hit the nail so squarely on the head.

"So. What's the drill?" he asked, rubbing his palms together in anticipation.

We spent the next forty-five minutes exploring how we would get the big picture. Primary on our list of things-to-do was to examine both the scene of the fire, as well as Mitch's garage, where evidence was discovered. Mark insisted the evidence had been planted there. If that *were* the case, it meant Mitch was deliberately framed, which meant premeditation, which meant that someone closer than a fleeting acquaintance was responsible.

We'd have to find out who Jake's insurance vendor was and what kind of coverage he had for the business. For all

I knew, the insurance investigators were still on the case or had found evidence since the grand jury that might help exonerate Mitch.

As far as the authorities were concerned, Mitch had motive, opportunity, and access. These three components have been known to convict innocent people since the judicial system was established. Miguel was right. Though my relationship with Mitch had changed over the years, I had to trust my instincts. I wouldn't have taken this on unless I believed in my uncle.

Mark had supplied a list of Aronson's employees, from a bookkeeper named Roz to a general manager called Mali. Miguel and I went over the half dozen names, speculating how we would approach each individual and what we would hope to learn from him or her.

In the middle of this exercise, Kerry came in. "The stiff's still at the morgue," she said, taking a seat across from me.

"Really?" I was surprised that they had held her for so long, but then, the coroner's office has been known to hold a John or Jane Doe for over six months.

"Yeah. They've got the space right now and want to wait until someone claims her."

"Cause of death?"

"Smoke inhalation. Apparently she died as a result of the fire. Or rather, she was still alive when the fire was started."

"So that means the fire wasn't started to cover up a murder?" When Miguel squinted, the corners of his eyes barely crinkled.

"In all likelihood, that's right," I said, making notes. I looked up and smiled at Kerry. "Thank you."

"You're welcome. Worthy of a raise?"

"Shhh." I cautioned with a sidelong glance at Miguel. "Not in front of the boy."

Miguel, who is Kerry's biggest fan, got up, took her hand, kissed it, and held it to his chest as he started to wax poetic, first in English and then accelerated Spanish, about Kerry and her beauty, both inside and out. Sensible woman that she is, she placed her hand over his mouth to literally stop the flow.

All in all, the three of us had more than enough to get us going and keep us moving at a quick pace. We agreed that Miguel and I would drive out to Queens the next morning, despite the ease of the train. Jake's factory was in an area neither of us knew particularly well, and I didn't want to get stuck out there with no means of a quick retreat. Besides, from there I would head to my meeting with Mitch and then, hopefully, on to Alfred Hickey's offices. Miguel's task would be predicated on what we learned from the investigator's report from Paul.

Just as Miguel let go of Kerry's hand, a cricketlike sound issued from my bag.

I have finally given in to the cellular phone fad. I tried a pager, but it was absolutely useless without access to a phone, and anyone who lives in Manhattan knows that despite the fact that there are usually four phones on every corner, you're lucky if one out of every four thousand works. Because of this, I was forced to get a cell phone, another New Age, potentially dangerous device meant to make our busy lives oh so much easier. I mean, aren't there enough bad drivers in this world? Do they really need the added distraction of a cell phone? And what about rumors of brain tumors from constant use of cell phones, doesn't that concern people? But worst of all, there are those fools who actually walk down the street, just chatting it up on the old cell phone. Like they can't spend ten minutes between destinations without making a call. If you ask me, modern technology has turned us all into a bunch of jerks.

I turned my back on Miguel and Kerry and answered my cell phone.

"Sydney? It's Elly." Her voice crackled against the bad connection.

"El? Can I call you back on the office phone? I can barely hear you."

"No, I'm . . . car on . . . spoke . . . later . . ." The connection kept breaking until there was silence.

I turned off the phone and stared at it in my hand. "I hate these things," I said to the world at large.

"Where do you wanna meet tomorrow, boss?" Miguel checked his watch, a Rolex knock-off he'd bought on the street for ten bucks and hasn't had a problem with in three years. "It's Valentine's Day, you know. I got a lotta stuff to do."

In fact, it had completely slipped my mind that it was Valentine's Day. I glanced at my own watch, a sporty Timex Indiglow, and saw that it was four forty-five. "So, let me get this straight; you get in at three and leave before five, is that what you consider a full day's work?" I asked, knowing perfectly well that I only paid Miguel by the hour, so it was no skin off my nose.

"Jes. Today is no easy." He accentuated his Hispanic accent (which stems only from his mother's side of the family, as his father is Welsh—ergo, Leigh), and dipped into a curtsy, complete with index finger poised at chin. "Tomorrow I'm all yours, boss, but today is about love." He took his peacoat off the back of the chair and slipped into it in one graceful movement. The man should have been a dancer, not an investigator. "Love of family . . . friends . . ." He took a chocolate Godiva heart from his pocket and gave it to Kerry. "Puppies . . ." A rawhide treat was extracted from yet another pocket and placed gently beside my sleeping beauty. "And work." With that he slipped a little box of candied hearts with messages onto my desk and winked at me. "I know you don't like Valentine's Day, but love is to be celebrated all the time." He knocked once on my desk top, which woke Auggie, who started barking like crazy and chased after Miguel, who was skipping out the door, calling back, "I'll be at your apartment tomorrow at nine, hokay?"

He didn't wait for a response.

Not knowing what Elly had been trying to tell me before, I left a message for her at her home giving her Minnie's number, where she could reach me that night.

The thought of Minnie made me consider what she had left unsaid about Mitch. This naturally made me wonder what could have happened in the past that would make her warn me to steer clear of family . . . a suggestion that was completely out of character for her, and clearly out of the question for me; after all, this was *family* we were talking about.

In all fairness, I had to admit that I was just as much to blame for the rift that had opened between me and my mother's side of the family. Uncle Mitch might have pulled away from me because I'm gay, but the truth is, I hadn't worked all that hard to try and get beyond his silly prejudice. He had hurt me, and in response, I had essentially walked away from them emotionally, thinking I'd deal with it later. Later had finally arrived. Now I was forced to deal with how my uncle's rejection had really made me feel.

I knew, however, that before I could tackle Mom's side of the family, I had something more pressing to deal with. Valentine's Day.

I bought three bunches of roses and a box of Bacci kisses for Leslie, who was wowed that I had given in to a Hallmark holiday which I find objectionable. I gave her the flowers but held the chocolate back for later. Over a glass of champagne, I told her about Mitch and my day at the office. I voiced my concerns over having taken on something so close to home. After all, if there's one thing I've learned in this business, it's that feelings will only cloud one's judgment. I didn't know if I could separate the two.

In the taxi to Minnie's, Leslie held my hand and assured me that I was doing the only thing I could, given who I am and how I operate.

She was right, of course.

The taxi cut through Central Park at Eighty-sixth Street. It was hard to see past the windows, steamed from Auggie's happy panting. Auggie knows that taxis usually mean Minnie's, and Minnie's means treats, the likes of which she never gets at home. Oh yes, a rawhide treat and a trip to Aunt Minnie's, all in the same day. Puppy heaven. I opened the window a crack, despite the renewed rain, and hugged Auggie.

"Next life, I want to be a dog," I declared.

"Okay." Leslie took out money for the driver as we approached Minnie's Park Avenue digs.

"What about you?" I asked.

"I'll be a dog, too, then." She reached past the bullet-proof divider and handed the driver a ten-dollar bill. "Two dollars back, please."

"You want to be a dog?" My voice revealed my surprise.

She shrugged as she looked lovingly at Auggie and then directly at me. "I just want to be with you again, Syd. That's all."

I said nothing as I opened the car door for a very excited Auggie, who made a beeline to her favorite doorman, Fred.

"Thank you," I whispered, as I closed the car door behind Leslie.

"For what?" she asked, her lips toying with a smile.

"For loving me," I said like an old *bobbeh*, as I linked my arm through hers and followed Auggie and Fred into the magnificent prewar building.

She leaned into me and whispered, "It's easier than you think."

I thought of my folks and how glad they would have been to know I had settled down with someone who loves me so much. Dad never gave me grief for being gay, but my mother never knew. She died before even *I* knew it. As Leslie, Auggie, and I piled into the elevator, I remembered a night many years earlier when Mitch had told me how disappointed my mother would have been had she known what I turned into. I wondered, was it then that I'd shut him out?

A tightness gripped my chest and I took a deep breath and reminded myself that in order to handle this case professionally, I had to reconcile myself to my feelings and push them to the side.

Right. And while I was at it, I could leap tall buildings in a single bound and stop bullets with my teeth.

Four

Minnie's apartment smelled like heaven, since her boyfriend, Enoch, had, for Valentine's Day, lavished her with six floral arrangements, each from a different local florist. Minnie and I liked the one from Surroundings the best, while Leslie picked the one from Twigs, and Enoch was partial to the bunch of neon colored daisies he had bought from a shopping-cart street vendor.

"I'm a romantic at heart." Enoch had laughed when we learned that he had not only supplied the flowers for Valentine's Day, but had made reservations for dinner and dancing at the Rainbow Room for the next night, when it would "be less crowded with people who think they need an occasion to celebrate love."

They make an oddly striking couple, Minnie and "Easy," as she calls him (a play off his initials, EZ, for Enoch Zarlin. She says it suits him). He is tall and elegant, with a full head of white hair and a set of choppers that would positively glow in black light. Minnie is about half his size, topping out at maybe five feet. Where he is easygoing and laid back, she is a spitfire who still smokes a pack and a half a day. She also works from her home writing cookbooks, practices Yoga daily to keep her muscles limber, walks a good three miles a day, and communicates weekly with those, near and dear, who have moved on to another plane.

Dinner was simple but inspiring. She started with a

tomato-and-onion tart, moved on to roasted sea bass with asparagus sauce and polenta, and a salad of radicchio, endive, and arugula with a light balsamic dressing, and then ended the meal with bread pudding and bourbon sauce.

In the living room, we sat with coffee and grappa. Auggie slept soundly under the coffee table, Leslie was tucked into a corner of the sofa, Enoch was selecting music, Minnie was stretched out on her chair and ottoman, and I was falling asleep on the opposite end of the sofa from Leslie. From the way the wind was banging against the windows, it was evident that a nasty storm was brewing. Neither Leslie nor I was anxious to go racing out into a cold, bleak night.

Just as *Enigma* started playing, the phone rang. Enoch, still standing, waved Minnie down and said he'd get it. I was seeing a side to my aunt I'd never seen before. The normally controlling lady was content to sit back and let Enoch answer her phone, a freedom she allows few. I couldn't help but smile.

He came back half a minute later and pointed to me. "For you, kiddo."

Minnie and I shared a glance, but said nothing.

I took the call in the kitchen, at Minnie's desk. "Hello."

"Sydney, it's Elly. Am I disturbing you?" She sounded anxious.

"No." I checked my watch. It was nearing ten. "Are you okay?"

"Yes. I just wanted to thank you." She sounded pinched and tired. "For today. I'm sorry if Mark was difficult. It's not an easy time."

I passed over her understatement and said, "I wasn't able to hear you when you called the office."

"I know. I got your message. Listen, Paul said to tell you he's sorry he didn't get back to you today."

I thought, *bullshit*, but didn't say anything.

"Did you want to talk to him?"

"Sure I did. Why else would I have called him?" I paused, knowing that she didn't need to get in the middle of this. "Sorry, El. If you mean do I want to talk to him now, no. I had wanted to get a look at the report from Hickey, but chances are I'll see Hickey tomorrow, anyway."

"Hang on." She put her hand over the receiver and relayed the information to, no doubt, Paul. "Okay . . ."

"You know, I was thinking, it would probably make more sense if we met at your dad's tomorrow, rather than at your place, because I want to take a look in his garage, anyway. That way I don't have to drive all over the place."

"Oh." She paused. "O-kay," she said haltingly.

"Is that a problem?"

Elly sighed. "Well, not for me. It's just that everyone thinks they're coming here. Between you and me, Dad and Mark really don't like things to be changed at the last minute."

"It's not last minute, El, we still have twelve hours," I pointed out, but backed off right away. I was already starting out on shaky footing with Mitch. I didn't need to rock things before we even got started. "Never mind. We'll meet at your place."

"Okay." She sounded distracted. "Do you know where I live?"

"Are you still on Laurel Drive?"

"Yeah."

"Good, then I'll see you tomorrow around eleven-thirty." I said this with far more enthusiasm that I was feeling from her.

"Sydney?"

"Yes?"

She paused.

"Elly, talk to me, I don't bite."

Clearly something was wrong, but until she opened up to me, there wasn't anything I could do about it.

Before she could answer, I heard her cover the mouthpiece and direct herself to someone else. "Sorry," she said, when she'd returned. The change in her tone told me loud and clear that she was no longer alone. Whatever it was she had wanted to tell me would apparently have to wait. "I'll see you tomorrow."

I hesitantly asked if she was okay, and she gave me a perky, "Oh, sure." She said good-bye and I listened until I heard her end click off.

When I hung up, Minnie was standing at the doorway. My elderly aunt may be petite in physical size, but she is a powerhouse in my life and always has been. She was wearing a tomato-red cowl-necked sweater and black slacks. Her hair was pulled back into a chignon, framing her face with loose strands of very white hair.

"Elly?" she asked, stepping into the room.

"Yes."

She walked toward me. It wasn't until she was practically on me that I realized she was reaching for her cigarettes behind me and not me.

"You know, I am concerned for you." She slipped an orange-filtered cigarette between her fingers and snapped open a lighter.

"I know."

She lit the end of the cigarette, squinting the smoke out of her right eye. "This whole damned thing places me in a very bad situation."

"Don't be ridiculous. This has nothing to do with you. It's about Mitch. And Jake. I'm just going to sort through it and see what I find."

"Oh, please." She exhaled a stream of blue smoke as she stepped past me and moved to the window. "Obviously I wouldn't get involved unless I thought it was necessary.

Have I ever interfered with your work before?''

"No." I perched on one of the white stools normally tucked under her work island and shook my head. "Okay. What's up?" I tried to make my voice sound casual, but in fact I was feeling a sense of foreboding creep over me.

"This is difficult for me to say, but I've never lied to you before and I don't intend to start now." She turned her back and exhaled a puff of blue smoke toward the exhaust fan over her Vulcan restaurant range.

I waited, knowing Minnie wouldn't be taking us here without a reason.

"I think you should know that this isn't the first time Mitchell was arrested. It happened once before, years ago." She kept her back to me. "Your father was able to pull a few strings so that there was never any record of it, but I thought you should know. He may well be your uncle, but he's also a prejudiced, bull-headed, mean-spirited man who thinks the sun rises and sets for him.''

I didn't see Mitch as mean-spirited. "Why was he arrested?''

Minnie turned on the cold-water tap and doused her cigarette. "If memory serves me correctly, he roughed up a fellah who made an off-colored remark about Maddy. But that's not the point." She dropped the wet tobacco into the garbage. "The point is, he did it. Which I think proves that he has an explosive personality, the kind of personality where he *would* torch his cousin's factory. I'm telling you, he'll use you, just like he used Nathan.''

"How did he use Dad?''

"Your father got that man off scot-free, without even so much as a scratch on his record. Now, what do you think he did for your father?''

"Dad wouldn't have wanted anything." Having never seen this side of her before, I was intrigued by Minnie's reaction.

"No, of course he wouldn't, but your father was struggling then. He and your mother could have used a little something to help them, but no, Mitchell acted like he was doing Nathan a big favor by letting him work on his case, as practice. Not even a thank-you."

"Really?" Considering how close my mom and my uncle were, I found this new information both surprising and disturbing, to the point where I had to question Minnie's memory. I told her how I felt.

"There's not a thing wrong with my memory, dear. Don't forget, as far as your mother was concerned, Mitchell could do no wrong. Criminy, who do you think convinced him that the sun rose and set for him? People don't just make these things up for themselves, do they?" Minnie sounded exhausted. "All the women in your mother's family coddled and babied *Mitchie,* so much that as far as I was concerned, he lost any sense of reality. Mitchie," she repeated with contempt. "I hate to say it, but it was disgusting." She rubbed her hands against her upper arms and said, "Anyway, I couldn't let you get involved in this without some forewarning. If you want my opinion, you would be well advised to steer clear of Mitchell Gerber. I know you, my friend, you're going to get hurt."

I walked around the work island and opened my arms to my aunt. "You're a good woman, Minnie."

"And you're a fool." She hugged me. "A crazy fool just like your father."

"Thank you."

Later, as Leslie got ready for bed I saw that she had placed a vase of roses in the bedroom. I put the box of Bacci kisses under her pillow and slipped my hand under my own pillow, in case there was a little token of love waiting for me. There was nothing. Not that I minded, because, after all, Valentine's Day was probably contrived by a trio of retailers experiencing the after-holiday slump: the florist, the chocolatier, and the scribe.

When the lights were off and Leslie was cuddled beside me, she turned onto her side and took her top pillow, which she stuck under her legs. That's when she felt the box under her other pillow.

"Oh . . . Sydney." In the darkness her voice turns to velvet.

"Bacci," I said, holding her hand to keep her from turning on the lights.

"Oh, Bacci." I could hear her smile, which I realized was all the present I needed. She put the chocolates on the nightstand and turned back to me, her breath warm against my cheek. She cupped my face in her hands and as she kissed me I knew, I knew that somewhere deep inside, I was probably turning soft about this Valentine thing.

Five

A storm had passed during the night, and though the morning brought clear skies, subzero temperatures had turned the streets into a sheet of thin ice. It took us an hour to find Aronson Elite, which was located in a two-story building in Corona, Queens. The neighborhood was predominantly warehouses and factories, but scattered here and there were pockets of two-story brick houses with asphalt shingled roofs. In front of most of the houses were tiny concrete yards, protected with white cyclone fences coated in graffiti.

I parked my old Volvo across the street from the building and hoped that it was too cold outside and too desolate a neighborhood for anyone to mess with my car. I've taken to bringing Auggie along when I'm investigating the preliminary stages of a case, but I feared leaving her in the car in an unknown neighborhood and knew that there were too many potential hazards at a fire site for a puppy's tender paws. Instead, she was spending the day with Leslie, who was refurbishing an apartment at Pomander Walk on West Ninety-fourth Street, a wonderful enclave of cottages built in 1923 by a restaurateur-developer named Healy. Just gazing in at the private street makes you feel as if you've left Manhattan and been transported to London—a world away from where I was at that very moment.

Miguel and I headed cautiously across the street. He was carrying a high-beam flashlight and I had a smaller one in

my pocket. In my shoulder bag I was carrying a tool kit
for making entry to stubborn places easier, along with my
gun, a Walther P5 Compact 9mm. I rarely use the gun, but
it's become part of my bag: wallet, keys, make-up case,
gun, perfume, phone, appointment book, flashlight, glasses.
I tend to travel with more baggage than other women I
know in my profession. I have never been the type who
could get by with just shoving ID and cash into my back
pocket and clipping a beeper onto my belt.

"If for some reason we can't get in now, I can probably
get George Davis to help. He's not only a fire marshal, but
also Max's ex-brother-in-law." The cold was so intense, I
was shivering from within.

"That's cool." Miguel had a blue toque pulled over his
forehead and ears, but the rest of his face, the part exposed
to the elements, was bright red. We reached the entrance
of the building, a thick metal door once painted powder
blue, but now dented and flaked, revealing the metal base.
The door was opened, but there was an intercom to the left
of it with two buzzers. One read *Aronson Elite*, the other
Warsh, Inc.

As soon as Miguel opened the door we were assailed
with the smell of old smoke, a smell that will always bring
back fond memories for me of Leroy Voyles and the sixth
grade. In May of 1964, a group of us took to playing after
school in the shell of a burnt-out building on Riverside
Drive. It was here that Leroy kissed me for the very first
time. My first kiss.

The door opened onto a concrete floor with a metal-
lipped staircase straight ahead of us. We were at one end
of the building, the far left of the building, as it were. Another metal door opened to our immediate right, or rather
folded open to our right. It looked as if someone had tried
to peel the damned thing right off its hinges. A broken
plastic sign reading *Warsh, Inc.* hung precariously from the

mangled door. Except for the daylight, which spilled in
from the entrance, the place was dark. Miguel turned on
his flashlight and the powerful beam danced into the place
that had been *Warsh, Inc.*

The windows had all been painted over with black paint,
and clearly there was water damage from the fire upstairs,
but other than that, it was impossible to determine what
Warsh, Inc. had been. Garbage left behind, no doubt used
by junkies and their pals, included several discarded mat-
tresses and what looked to be fairly new fast food containers. This gave us good reason to think the building was still
being used by more than the rats, who didn't flinch even
when we shone a light on them.

The smell emanating from *Warsh, Inc.* was human and
vile. Miguel snapped his toque off his head and covered
his mouth as he tried to close the door. ''Jesus, whoa! You
see that?'' His voice neared soprano.

''Uh-huh.'' I had already started up the stairs, inhaling
deeply the smell of old fire as if it were a perfume in con-
trast to the garbage and rat droppings.

''Those were rats, you know. Big, ugly fuckers. Those
things are disgusting, man. I knew a girl who was bit by
one when we were kids. That makes me sicker than sick,
you know what I mean?'' He followed close behind me.

I loathe rats, rodents, waterbugs, and cockroaches, and
would have normally let my fear scratch deeper than the
surface, but the fact is with most fears, when you are with
someone who is more afraid than you are, it has a strangely
calming effect.

Once on the landing, it was clear that the fire had inched
out beyond the confines of Elite. Here the walls were
charred and the paint had bubbled from the intense heat.

I tested the steps as I slowly worked my way up to the
second floor. The staircase was solid, though the linoleum
that had covered it during one incarnation was treacherous.

Why you would cover concrete steps in a building like this with linoleum was beyond me, but someone had. Maybe once upon a time someone had actually taken pride in this building in the middle of nowhere.

I had expected the doorway to be bolted, but it wasn't. Instead the door was charred black, indicating that much of the fire had been focused on the entrance of the space. I could hear Miguel breathing hard behind me, which, I had come to know, meant that he was anxious.

"It's okay," I said softly, as I paused before entering the place. I knew no one would be in there, but I always make it a point to listen before dashing into the unknown.

The door resisted when I first pulled at it, but it finally gave in and let out a mournful groan that would probably wake the dead.

"What are you doing?" Miguel hissed, as he pushed in front of me and pulled the door up slightly to release the strain on the hinges. I trained my flashlight on his face and realized that in this light he looked Mephistophelian with his dark, trimmed goatee and coal-black eyes.

As it turned out, once we were in the actual factory, we didn't need our flashlights because most of the windows along one wall had been destroyed, probably by the firemen venting the smoke and fighting the fire. The factory had taken up the entire length of the building, which was maybe nine hundred feet long. I led the way in, stepping cautiously around a badly charred section of floor, less than ten feet from the entrance. Given the amount of damage in this area, it stood to reason that this was where the fire had probably started. As my eyes adjusted, I could see the many gradations of black from the charring, black turned silver from water icing over, and the gradient of black soot covering the walls and ceiling. Scattered amid the varying shades of black were flecks of color, either bits and pieces of fabric or green linoleum peeled up from the

floor. A singed red fire extinguisher lay half-buried under
the charred skeletons of several chairs. At the far end of
the room it looked as if there were patches of wood actually untouched by the flames—a section of frame around a
door and a portion of wall and ceiling—but for the most
part it seemed that the concrete structure had become an
oven when the place was destroyed. There was a feeling of
chaos among the ruins. I slipped my flashlight back into
my pocket.

Though the fire had happened four months earlier, there
was still water, or more precisely, ice, covering the floor,
the walls, and detritus that had once been a working factory.
The ice made walking treacherous in some spots.

"What are we looking for?" Miguel whispered loudly,
his body almost crouched in anticipation.

"I'm not sure. Why are you whispering?" I whispered
back, as I moved from one pile of rubble to another, trying
to make sense out of what we saw, hoping that something
would jump out at me and scream *clue here!*

"This shit gives me the willies." He worked his way
toward the far end of the room near the windows. I forked
off and stayed closer to the left wall. "There's nothing here
to see," he said.

What we could see was that there had been many rows
of sewing tables running the length of the room, divided
by an aisle down the middle. The wooden tables were
burned but still standing, soldiers to the end, their black-
ened sewing machines still in place, like victims, the car-
casses of war. There were two other aisles on either side
of the tables, one closest to the windows, where Miguel
was walking just behind me, and one on the far left of the
room, where I was.

"What the . . . shit." I heard Miguel's voice, but when I
spun around, he was gone.

"Miguel?" I slowly slipped my hand into my bag, instinctively reaching for my gun. "Miguel? Are you okay? Say something, Mickie." I eased the gun out of my bag, and holding it with two hands at shoulder level, I aimed it in the general direction of where I had last seen Miguel.

I held my breath, listening for anything, even the sound of his breathing, but all I could hear was a truck shifting from second to third just outside. "Okay, Miguel, a joke's a joke." I knew Miguel well enough to know he wouldn't think that playing dead in a burnt-out building filled with rats was fun and games, but I wanted whoever was there with us to know one thing; my voice was steady, which meant I was calm and therefore in control. I also had two very distinct advantages; I was standing and I had a gun.

"I've got all day," I told the silent shadow, whom I felt certain was probably inches from Miguel. I heard movement, but it could have been Miguel or rodents.

I cautiously stepped over frozen patches of floor and started back to where I had last seen Miguel. It was possible that he had slipped and hit his head. I paused in the middle aisle and listened, grateful that this wasn't happening in total darkness. Something clunked at the far end of the room, and I spun around to see what it was. Halfway into the turn, I knew I had been had, but as I spun back around, my foot caught a patch of ice and I went slamming down on my back with all my weight. Fortunately, my Walther will discharge only if I pull the trigger completely through, and I was able to keep from doing that, but not without contorting my body in such a way that it felt as if my whole torso wrenched. My backpack softened the blow, if soften was the right word, what with half the bag filled with hardware. I didn't know what hurt more, my pride or my back. I heard footsteps and struggled to get up. Someone was in a hurry to get the hell out of there, and I couldn't say I blamed him.

By the time I had pulled myself up, he, or she, was racing down the stairs, so I rushed over to the windows, my Walther still in hand. I watched a man bolt across the street, his matchstick-thin body all arms and legs. Once across the street, he turned around and it was clear to see that what we had here was a man in need of a fix. He jammed something into his pocket, turned back around, skipped once, and fell into a loping, sloppy run.

I took a deep breath and felt the cold air sting my lungs. I put the gun back in my bag. Needless to say, I was chagrined with myself for having fallen for the oldest ruse in the books, tossing something in an opposite direction for distraction.

Miguel moaned. By the time I reached him, he had come to and was swearing softly in Spanish.

"Hey, you okay?" I squatted beside him and put my hand gently on his back.

"What happened?" He tentatively rubbed the back of his neck, no doubt feeling the start of a nasty headache.

"Someone got you from behind. Can you get up?" I asked with remarkable calm, considering that out of the corner of my eye I could see rats scuffling across the floor under one of the work tables.

"Yeah, I'm okay." He turned to brace himself to get up when he suddenly let out a scream that one would only expect from Ima Sumac. At the same time, he kicked his leg up, and when he did, a black object with a long tail flew through the air overhead, squealing the length of its journey. Miguel was up and moving like he was fuel injected. *"Raaaattttaaa!"* he screamed, as his body momentarily filled the doorway, then disappeared down the stairs. Whatever rats had been there, even the flying one, moved

just as quickly in the opposite direction, tucking themselves
away into the shadows.

As I hurried behind him I made a mental note: add to
Miguel's training . . . screaming in falsetto doesn't do much
to instill confidence in the professional detective.

Six

Despite his protests, I put Miguel in a taxi and arranged for Kerry to meet him at my physician's office back in Manhattan. I wasn't going to take a chance with the nasty lump swelling at the back of his head. In all probability it was nothing, but if I'd sent him to the emergency room at the hospital, he'd have been there all day. This way, if Dr. Harris felt Miguel needed special attention, she could arrange for it personally.

A quick check of Miguel's pockets proved that it was, more than likely, a junkie who had clobbered him, because his wallet was missing, along with a fifty-dollar bill he kept tucked in his front pants pocket. So, all totaled, the thief got away with seventy dollars, Miguel's driver's license, and about thirty family snapshots.

I arrived at Elly's only fifteen minutes late. By the time I got there, my back was so sore, I was walking like my neck was connected directly to my waist. Elly's greeting was warm and embracing.

Uncle Mitch sat at the kitchen table, still wearing his woolen gray overcoat, though he was sitting with a cup of coffee and a plate of danish in front of him. The second I saw him, my impulse was to race over and throw my arms around his wide shoulders, but I didn't. Maybe I was waiting for him to stand up, to show a hint of wanting to hug me, but the moment passed, and then it was too late. Before I knew it, a host of invisible little demons filled in the space between us, and the best I could offer was a nod and a little wave.

There was no question that Mitch had aged since we had last seen one another. We both had. He had less on top and more in the middle, and liver spots speckled his swollen hands. His eyes might have lost their clarity, but not the strength and humor I knew he possessed.

"Uncle Mitch."

He nodded, his mouth clamped into a tight smile. He barely parted his lips to say, "Sinda." He used my birth-name, which I had legally changed when I was eighteen.

Normally in my family, greetings are accompanied with physical contact, especially when time has passed between visits. The lack of it was as staggering as a slap in the face, yet I couldn't totally blame Mitch, because I did nothing to remedy the situation. Instead of reaching out and em-bracing him—even if it was against his will—I slipped out of my jacket as carefully as I could and took the seat across from him.

"You're usually so punctual," he said, clearing his throat.

"Well, I would have been on time, but things took a little longer at Aronson Elite than I anticipated." I grate-fully wrapped my hands around the coffee mug Elly placed before me.

"What happened?" Mitch asked in midbite of an almond strudel. An almond sliver stuck to his upper lip.

"Nothing. I went there with an associate this morning, just to check it out, get a sense of the place. It just took longer than I thought." I saw no need to explain that two professional detectives had been bested by a junkie who probably used the place downstairs as a shooting gallery. After I put Miguel in the taxi, I had gone back inside, but it took longer, and I found nothing of interest in the debris.

Mitch took another bite of strudel and chewed slowly,

as if concentrating, very hard, on every morsel. Throughout his chewing, the almond sliver remained affixed to his upper lip. Finally he said, "I don't want to offend you, Sinda, but the fact is, I think you might be pushing things here. As far as I'm concerned, Paul has everything under control, he's even hired a detective who knows all about these things. So as much as I appreciate your wanting to help, I think I'm in excellent hands."

It took a minute for what he said to register, but after a short, bewildered pause, I turned to Elly and said, "He thinks this was *my* idea?"

Elly looked just above my head and got up from the table as if she was on automatic, like a Stepford Wife.

"Who's he? Is he me? You talk about me third person, like I'm not even here?" The almond sliver flew off his lip and onto the tabletop. Uncle Mitch was always clear about respect; it was given to one's elders whether they deserved it or not. It's not a bad concept, just sometimes unwieldy.

I retrieved my coffee from his line of fire and asked, "Uncle Mitch, do you know that Mark and Elly asked me to look into this for you?"

He glowered at me, turned his gaze on Elly's back, and asked, "Is this true?" She stood at the sink, apparently holding on for dear life. No doubt she could feel his eyes burning a hole in her back. *"Is this true?"* He banged the table with his fist, making everything jump, including me and the errant almond sliver. The coffee rippled in the confines of the cups and the spoons rattled against the saucers.

Elly's fear was nearly palpable, so I decided then would be a good time to intervene. "Excuse me, if I could just say one thing here . . . I've always found it's much easier to deal with people honestly. Now, maybe it isn't my place to do this, but there are a couple of things you should probably know before you start banging tables and yelling." I held out my hand for him to stop before he interrupted me.

"Facts. First of all, you may be in excellent hands, but you are also in a great deal of trouble. The detective Paul hired to prove your innocence thinks you're guilty. Now, you may think *because* you're innocent, you'll be proved and *found* innocent, but trust me, there are no such guarantees.

"Second, Mark and Elly asked me to help because they believe you're innocent and they love you. They don't want to lose you. Prison is a very unpleasant prospect, especially for that sort of crime; it's not like you'll be sent to a country club. They also know that whether you like it or not, if anyone can help you right now, it's me. Not only am I good at what I do, but you're my family, and I will move heaven and earth because I believe in you. Because I love you.

"So now you have choices to make, Uncle Mitch. We can either have a professional relationship wherein you put your trust in me and work with me, or you can make a huge mistake, find someone you're more comfortable working with, and probably spend the next eight years behind bars. Understand, I don't care which choice you make, but if you want me to help—and again, let me make it clear that I would *like* to help you—but if I do, you're going to have to suspend your disbelief and work with the assumption that I know what I'm doing."

He studied the table top, as if memorizing the plate of half-eaten strudel, the coffee cups, a folded check, a school lunch menu, and a crumpled ten-dollar bill.

Elly still stood at the sink looking out a window framed with lace, fastened back with metal hearts.

"You sound just like your father, God rest his soul," he finally said.

"Thank you." I leaned back and thought that despite Minnie's objection to Mitch, they had both given me the same compliment, less than twelve hours apart. "So what do you want to do, Mitch?"

He raised an eyebrow and pointed a stubby finger in my direction. "I don't care how old you get, I'm *Uncle* Mitch to you, you got that?"

"Got it."

"And I don't know where you get this crazy idea I don't believe in you." He glanced at Elly, who was turning back to us. She looked as if she'd been up all night. "We're family, and family should stick together. I appreciate your concern, Sinda. I also appreciate your veracity. No one told me this *mamzer*, this Hinkle thought I was guilty. You couldn't tell me that?" he asked Elly, when she offered everyone more coffee.

The woman I had reconnected with the day before was different from the woman I saw before me now, and that disturbed me. It was as if in the presence of her father, Elly lost all sense of herself.

Finally she said, almost inaudibly, "We were waiting."

"Really? Waiting? For what? The Messiah? Or maybe my conviction?"

"Don't, Dad."

Just then the kitchen door flew open, bringing in with it a gust of cold air and Mark. "Hey Dad, El. Sydney." In one movement, he grabbed a chair, spun it around, slid his Charivari leather jacket on the back of it, and straddled the seat. His mouth was pushed to pout, a look I have often seen associated with contemplation, but on him it didn't seem to work. "Where's Mom?" He asked the room in general.

"I didn't want her here. There's no need to upset her more than she already is." Uncle Mitch lifted an eyebrow at Mark. "You couldn't tell me what that *faigeleh* Hinkey had to say about my case?" He confronted his son before he was even settled in his chair.

Mark was about to object when he seemed to remember I was there. He turned to me and said, "Did *you* tell him that? Smooth, Sydney, real smooth." He shook his head. "We were going to tell you, Dad . . ."

Mitch held up his hands. "*Genug iz genug.* I don't want to hear it. Let's just do this. I don't have much time."

"What do you mean you don't have time? What do you have to do?" Mark scowled. "I told you we were going to be planning your strategy today. That takes time."

"Really? Strategy? And what about Paul? I should strategize without my lawyer?"

Elly pulled up another chair and explained, "Paul's in court all day. It couldn't be avoided, but he figured Sydney could use this time to get some information from us . . . and he doesn't really have to be here. Dad, take off your coat, for God's sake."

"It's cold in here," he complained. "You people don't have enough money for heat, with all the help I give you?"

"Dad." Mark turned the word into a warning and just as quickly changed directions. "Help? What help? He gives you help?" he asked Elly.

"Oh please, Mark, don't go there now." The look she leveled at him would have kept me quiet, too.

Not wanting to get in the middle of what was definitely feeling like *their* family argument, I forged ahead. "Actually, Paul was right, I need to know exactly what's happened. Uncle Mitch, tell me about you and Jake."

Mark sighed loudly and Elly cupped her chin in her hand and shook her head as Mitch slapped the table top and went into a diatribe about Jake, starting back when they were young men taking over Harriman's together: Jake's father's business.

When he seemed to be running out of steam, I decided to try and fast-forward his story. "What happened at the bar mitzvah?"

"The bar mitzvah?" He finally shrugged out of his coat.

"Yes, where you threatened Jake. Tell me about the confrontation and what it was you said, exactly."

"Who knows what I said, *exactly*? I can't even remember my grandchildren's names, but I can tell you what *happened*. Maddy told me not to go, she said it would only upset me to see that weasel again, but I didn't listen to her because it was Morty's grandson's bar mitzvah. Jake shouldn't have gone, because Mort and I are such good friends, everyone knows that, but he's a selfish *mamzer* and he wanted to press all my buttons, which he did, like he's always done." Mitch's neck was turning red.

"Anyway, he started it. I was minding my business when he walks past our table and says loudly to his date, this wop bimbo no one's ever met before, with the skirt up to her privates, he says loud enough so everyone can hear, 'That's the moron I was telling you about.' I knew he was talking about me. I blew my stack."

"What did you say?"

"I told him he was making his father roll over in his grave. I told him I didn't understand how a *mentsh* like Uncle Eben could raise such a piece of *dreck* like Jake. He just stood there smiling like the smarmy son of a bitch he is. I told him if I could, I'd kill him with my bare hands."

"And everyone heard you?"

"Of course everyone heard me." His flush was working its way past his neck to his face and headed to his scalp. "And I don't regret it! Look it, one thing about me, people always know where they stand with me. If I like you, I like you, and if I don't, you know it. But then the son of a bitch shoved his chest right into me, so I pushed him away. It wasn't my fault they had to pull us apart. Ask anyone, it was his fault."

"Was it Jake's fault?" I asked Elly.

Rather than answer directly, Elly lifted her brows and

tightened her lips, but she did not say outright, "Yes, it was Jake's fault."

"What are you asking her for? Everyone knows what a loser Jake is, what a liar he is."

"Right. And over a hundred people heard you threaten him."

Mitch waved his hand as if to dismiss the thought. "Everyone knows I wouldn't hurt a fly. Would I hurt a fly?" He directed this to Elly.

"No, Dad, you wouldn't hurt a fly."

"Besides," he slapped the table again for emphasis, "I wouldn't do something cowardly like burn a building down."

It wasn't worth pointing out the holes in his logic. "Had you ever been to Elite?"

"I'd been to the building, but I couldn't get into the factory."

"When was that?"

"As soon as I heard he was open for business!" He yelled. "He couldn't do that! He had signed an agreement!"

"Calm down, Dad." Mark rubbed the table as if it would soothe his father.

It didn't.

"You bet your ass I went over there, I wanted to see the type of operation this *goniff* was running where he could manufacture at forty percent off market price. *Forty percent!* He knew what I was after. Everyone knew. The son of a bitch was running a sweatshop, and he wasn't going to be able to keep it quiet for long."

"Did you have proof?"

"Forty percent off was proof enough! Look, everyone in this business knows you can't offer that kind of discount and manufacture here in the United States unless you're doing something wrong."

"But Paul was working on it?" I asked.

"Of course Paul was working on it, but things take time. First he was going to close that piece of shit down because of the noncompete clause, and *then* he was going to have the authorities check into this illegal manufacturing."

"Okay." I took notes as I asked another question. "When did Jake open for business?"

"Maybe six months ago now?" Mitch made the statement sound like a question.

"And you had Paul on it right away?"

"Of course I did."

"Why didn't Paul have Jake slapped with a temporary restraining order?"

"He tried. But the courts were backlogged like crazy. He said the soonest we could expect any action was in a month." Mitch said this to the spoon he was bending in his hand.

There was an uncomfortable silence.

"So, what, two months later the place is torched?"

"That's about right. Two or three. Three, I think."

"While you were in litigation?"

"No, we weren't," Mitch said impatiently, but I had a feeling this had more to do with the answers than my questions.

"I thought you were suing him to cease and desist."

"We had a court date, but nothing had happened yet."

"Are you telling me that at the time of the fire, you had not yet gone to court over this?" I asked with unmasked disbelief. Mitch looked angrily at Elly, who chewed nervously on her lower lip. Mark stirred his coffee and shook his head as if he were above it all.

"Paul hadn't made any headway in shutting them down?"

"*Oi!*" Mitch slapped the table again. "The system takes time!" he boomed. "This!" He waggled an index finger in the air. "This has been my greatest frustration. Paul kept saying, 'Be patient, be patient,' but in the meantime I was getting sick over this."

In the silence that followed, all we could hear was the humming of a large refrigerator and Mark's spoon tapping the inside of his cup.

"Tell me about the night of the fire," I said.

"What's to tell?" He shrugged as he pinched off another piece of strudel.

"Tell me what you did that night," I said, knowing he would need a shove in the right direction. "For example, what time did you get home from work?"

"Well, it was a Saturday, which I normally don't work, but I was catching up on paperwork, so I went in at about one and I left at six, six-thirty."

"Was anyone else working with you? Did anyone see you leave?"

"I have a man on security. Walter. He saw me leave. He verified it already."

"I'm sure he did. What did you do then?"

He gave this some thought, though I would have assumed this was something he had repeated forty-eight thousand times over, like a memorized mantra. "I went to the grocery store. I bought some things I needed. Maddy was out of town then . . ."

"Where was she?"

"In Detroit, visiting her sister, Fanny."

"How long had she been away at this point?"

Mitch shrugged and shook his head. "A couple of days? Not long."

"Can you prove you were at the grocery store?"

"Sure, sure. I had a receipt and the little girl behind the register knows us there."

"Then?"

He studied my face for the longest time. Finally he said,

"Then I went home, turned on the TV, made myself dinner, and fell asleep in the den."

"You didn't talk to anyone that night? Maybe Maddy? Or see a neighbor?"

He shook his head.

"What was on TV?"

"How should I know? I fell asleep."

"What was the last thing you remember watching?"

Mitch's face looked completely blank. "The news."

"What time was that?"

"My memory's not so good anymore. I don't know what time it was."

"Well, was it closer to seven-thirty or eleven-thirty?"

"I don't know."

"What channel were you watching?"

Mitch and I were locked in a staring contest. Finally I blinked. Why was he making this so hard?

"Uncle Mitch, it makes everything a lot easier if you're completely honest."

You could have heard a pin drop. Then Mitch said, "Listen you little *pisher*, one thing you don't do is question my honesty. I was home. I fell asleep. I don't know what the hell was on the television because I never watch it anyway." This was all said in one breath. He gulped for air when he was finished. His scalp was now beet-red.

Mitch looked at Mark who in turn looked at Elly who was looking at me. Without taking her eyes off me she said, "Dad, cancel your one o'clock appointment."

Mitch took a deep breath, raked his fingers through what was left of his hair, and finally huffed to his feet. "Okay, okay," he muttered, as he left the room to make whatever arrangements he had in private.

When he was out of earshot, Mark turned to me and hissed, "What's wrong with you? You had to tell him what Hickey said?"

"Of course I did. The man needs to know the truth."

"Don't be ridiculous."

His contempt confused me. "Maybe you think ignorance is bliss, but the fact is most people prefer to be treated like adults, Markey." I deliberately used the nickname I knew he'd hated as a kid. "Now, you people can play whatever games you need to maintain family harmony, but I don't have time for that. Don't forget, it's *his* life on the line."

"*You* people?" Mark oozed sanctimony.

I was reminded of my call with Minnie the day before. *"These people are desperate, elsewise they wouldn't have called you—" "These people ... listen to yourself. These people are my family."*

"We happen to be family, Sydney. In case you didn't know it, that's why you're here." Mark's arrogance was beginning to bug me.

"Actually, Mark, you're wrong. I'm here because I choose to be. Because I don't like to see innocent old men go to jail for crimes they didn't commit. And just for the record, in case *you* don't know it, I haven't seen you in four years, and I haven't known you in at least ten, so please don't assume you can tell me why I do anything."

"Would you two please stop it?" Elly pressed her hands against the table and growled, "This is hard enough without the two of you going at each other."

"No one's going at anyone." The corners of Mark's mouth curled up when he said that. I had no doubt that my cousin's smugness worked well for him in the business arena, but when it came to winning friends and influencing family, it was most unappealing.

Mitch came back and I questioned him until just past two, when I excused myself to call both my office and Alfred Hickey. Kerry reported that Miguel would be just fine, though he had to watch for any symptoms of concussion. When I called Alfred Hickey, he was there and assured me he would be in his office all afternoon. I should feel free to just show up.

By the end of our question and answer session, I knew Mitch was holding back, but I didn't know what or why. Paul called during our meeting and told Elly that he would bring pertinent files home for me to see. I suggested that he messenger it to my office, to which he counter-suggested that I stop by his office that afternoon on my way home. That was when I took the phone from Elly.

"Paul, Sydney. You're in Manhattan?"

"Hello, Sydney. How are you? It's been such a long time." He sounded sincerely sincere.

"I'm good, Paul. But I need those files."

"I know you do, and I want you to have them, which is why I thought I'd bring them home tonight. That way you could get them this evening if you're there, or El could get them to you tomorrow." Though it had been awhile, I could just see Paul in my mind's eye. We used to call him Mr. Skeward because he is a skewed kind of guy whose clothing and glasses, neckties and handkerchiefs are always slightly crooked. Just looking at him can give you seasickness.

"Why don't you just have your secretary send them to my office via messenger?"

"Of course, a messenger—what a good idea. That was silly of me. All right, I'll have her send them off to you right away. You should have them by tonight." It was at this point he had to insert another nickel in the phone. "Sorry about that, but I'm at the courthouse. Could I say good-bye to Elly, please?"

"Sure. But Paul?"

"Yeah?"

"Do you have my address?"

"Oh for God's sake, silly me. I'm telling you if my head wasn't screwed on . . . I have a pen. Shoot."

After I got off the phone with Paul, Mitch agreed to let me check out his garage, but there was clearly something making him uneasy. Since Mark needed to get back to work and Elly had to pick up the kids, my guess was, more than anything, Mitch was uneasy at the prospect of being alone with me. I promised him it would take less than fifteen minutes because I had another meeting I had to get to. As soon as I got in my car, I could feel a knot starting to bunch up in my stomach. Either I was hungry or having trouble digesting the fact that I was helping my uncle out of a pickle he had created for himself, while at the same time trying to protect him from having to deal with me.

Having gotten a frightening picture from the family as to how quickly Paul hops to things, I decided that despite Paul's assurance that he'd be sending me the report, I wanted to meet with Alfred Hickey one-on-one and get his personal take on this case. Something was wrong, but I couldn't put my finger on it. Maybe, just maybe, Alfred could give me some solid answers.

Seven

I arrived at Mitch's before he did, so when I got there, it was just Aunt Maddy and me. As soon as she opened the door, she pulled me in a viselike hug. I didn't know which hurt more, my back, or how her kindness only seemed to emphasize Mitch's indifference.

"Oh, Sydney, dear, you look wonderful." Maddy held me at arm's length and gave me a little shake, which sent pain staggering down my back, but I couldn't pull away from the one person in my family who had taken the time to embrace me, to actually see me.

"So do you, Mad." I couldn't help but smile when I looked at her. Her unruly mop of silver hair tumbled over her glasses, into her eyes. She brushed it away with the back of a hand covered with rings and bracelets. Despite the rhinestone-studded workshirt and all that they had recently been through, she looked positively stunning; a *zaftik* tan woman whose face reflected the lines of a person who has lived her life well.

It had been years since I had stood at the threshold of their home. Nothing had changed and yet everything was completely different. It was like stepping back into a perfectly preserved past, but one into which I no longer fit.

"Come in, honey. Can I get you anything? Something to drink? Are you hungry?" She took my hand and led me to the back of the house. We went through the foyer and into the living room. I was flooded with memories as we made our way through the house. The formal living room looked as if it still was used only for special occasions; birthday parties, high holy days, sitting *Shiva*. Family pictures still cluttered the polished ebony piano as well as the wall across from the never-used fireplace. I always thought it odd that the biggest room in the house was essentially off limits, which had only enhanced its allure when we were kids. One time my brother David had staged a fantastic game of submarine in this room. When we kids became suspiciously quiet, our parents found that the living room had been transmogrified into the ocean, where we allies waited patiently for the enemy. We had overturned the two armchairs, the loveseat, and the sofa, and under each of those were us kids; my sister Nora and her friend Zoe were lying under the loveseat, David and Mark were under the sofa, Elly and I were tucked under an armchair, and my cousins' dog, Spike, a toy poodle, was sleeping under the other armchair. The moment we heard the enemy approach, we aimed our fully loaded weapons (water pistols given to us by Aunt Maddy's brother, Charlie), waited until we saw the whites of their eyes, and then let them have it—after all, it was democracy we were fighting for. I'll never forget Uncle Mitch, his shirt drenched, lifting Mark up by the seat of his pants, stuffing him under his arm, and disappearing into the other room. Our laughter had withered into stunned silence when we heard Mark scream behind a closed door. Little did we know, Mitch was slapping his hands together and Mark was screaming out, as directed, proud as peaches to be in on Daddy's joke. When the two of them came out laughing, the rest of us kids ignored Mark for the next twenty minutes. Considering what a jerk he had grown into, I wondered if maybe we should have ignored him for the next twenty years.

"What do you think of that?" Maddy asked, as we entered the kitchen, which smelled of onions and garlic. The counters were covered with dinner in preparation—carrots, onions, spices—but she nodded her mop of hair in the direction of the far wall, which was covered with washable wallpaper depicting happy dancing cooking utensils. Along this wall there was also a refrigerator covered with photographs and handmade cards from the grandkids, a yellow Princess wall phone, and a framed watercolor of a single asparagus spear, with no shadow and no character.

I didn't know what she was talking about, but I assumed it was the asparagus. I was searching for an appropriate compliment for her artwork when she said, "That's the refrigerator you gave us when you renovated. It still works, can you believe it?" She went to the oven, peeked inside, and played with the thermostat.

"Wow, that refrigerator was old in '81. I'm very impressed."

"Your mother only bought the best."

From where I was standing I could see into the addition, the family room. Every house has one, and they usually look somewhat the same: two tastefully appointed La-Z-Boy recliners in front of an entertainment center, a coffee table covered with newspapers, and an expensive but worn sofa off to the side of the room. So ordinary, and yet there was something about the room that touched me, something endearing and foreign about it at the same time.

"Mitch called," she said, as she took a stockpot off the stove and set it in the sink. "He said he had an errand to run before he'd be home." Maddy wiped her hands on a dishtowel and said, "So tell me, it's bad, isn't it?"

I unzipped my jacket. "Well, he's been indicted for arson and murder. I'd say that's bad." I unwrapped my scarf but left it hanging from around my neck. "However, all we have to do is prove he didn't do it." I offered a "no big deal" gesture and said, "Piece of cake."

"My foot." Maddy shook her head. "I told him to call

you when the police first suspected him, but he is so goddamned stubborn . . ." She stopped and looked stunned. "I
didn't mean it like that . . ."

"It's all right, Mad. I prefer honesty. As long as we're
being honest, let me ask you a question."

"Anything."

"What's your take on all this?"

She took a deep breath as she folded the dishcloth. When
she shook her head, her dangle earrings tinkled. "Mitch
didn't do it, I know that for sure. He would never do a
thing like that. He's got a big mouth and God knows he's
full of steam, but he would never hurt anyone."

I considered my conversation with Minnie the night before. I figured now wasn't the time to dredge up the past.

"And I hate to say it because he's my own flesh and
blood, but I don't know Jake anymore. Ever since Brenda
left him, he's been different. I mean, God knows, he and
Mitch have always had their problems, ever since they were
back in the Bronx, but this, I just don't understand."
Maddy, Jake, Mitch, and my mom had all grown up in the
Bronx together. "And . . . I don't understand how that weasel could say he *saw* Mitch and they believed him." She
shook her head.

"What do you mean?"

"At the fire." Her warm eyes scanned my face.

"I don't understand."

"The man who said he saw Mitch at the fire? Didn't he
tell you that?"

"No, no one did. Who's the man? Jake?" That I had
just come from close to two hours with Mitch and Elly and
Mark, and none of them had mentioned this point, made
my skin crawl.

"No, no, not Jake. Some liar. Bill something-or-other. A
real weasel of a guy. Mitch didn't tell you this?"

"No." If this had been any other case, with any other

client, I'd have been out the door. Why did these people seem hell-bent on withholding information from one another? First Elly and Mark hadn't told Mitch about either Hickey's findings or my participation. Now the collective was holding back facts from me.

After about fifteen minutes of questioning Maddy about the man who saw Mitch at the fire, I asked if she could show me the garage. I wanted to get to Hickey before four, and it was already nearing three-fifteen. Bayside wasn't far from Great Neck, but time depended on traffic. Besides, I was angry. Though Mitch was my uncle, he was still a client and I had to assume that I had been hired to do what I do best: get to the truth. That didn't include waiting for Mitch Gerber to pull strings and open doors for me.

The garage was attached to the house through a tiny mudroom, off the family room. Maddy led the way and I followed behind her.

"You sure you're not hungry?" she asked over her shoulder. "Maybe you could join us for dinner?"

"Thanks, Mad, but I need to get back to the city."

The mudroom door opened to the back end of the garage. In the far parking stall was a two-door black Jaguar. The space closest to the house was cleared and waiting for Mitch's silver Town Car. The space was filled with boxes, work tools, bicycles, shelves of canned goods, paper towels, car parts, sleds, and garden tools.

I was amazed that it was all so organized. If memory served, Uncle Mitch's garage was renowned as a contained junkyard.

"Wow. Look at this place. It looks like you even washed the floor." I remembered the day the concrete floor had been painted gray. I was seven, and it was a most memorable day; we kids got to leave our handprints in the paint. It was also, probably, the last time most people saw the floor in there.

As if on cue, the garage door opened and Mitch gave two quick taps on the horn as he eased his car into place. The honks reverberated off the walls. If nothing else was happening during this investigation, one thing was certain—the old hold my uncle had once had over me was dissipating quickly.

"Mark did it," Maddy said to me, as she waved to Mitch.

"Mark did?" I repeated, in awe of the order that surrounded me. Mark didn't seem like the type to interrupt his very busy schedule for someone else, especially cleaning for someone else.

"Mark did what?" Mitch asked, as he slammed his door.

"Cleaned the garage," Maddy explained from the doorway.

"Sure, Mark cleaned it." Mitch nodded his approval. "But you know Mark." He rubbed the back of his neck, totally unaware that I did not know Mark anymore. "A couple of weeks ago, he got fed up with the mess, and he spent a whole weekend cleaning. Even nails are grouped."

"What did it look like when the police were here?" I asked, as I walked the perimeter of the room.

"*Oi*, you don't want to know." Maddy flapped her hand as if to ward off a bad smell.

"No, I do. Believe me."

Mitch let out a derisive laugh. "The detective wants to know?"

"That's right. The detective wants to know. How bad was it?"

"Not so good," Mitch muttered, while Maddy said, "Very bad. In fact, it was so bad I had to leave my car with my mechanic when I went to Detroit."

"Because you couldn't park in here?"

"That's right. I'm telling you, it was a mess. You know what it's usually like in here. Well, one day I pulled my car out and everything just came tumbling down, like Fibber McGee and Molly's closet."

"So Mark cleaned this all out?" I asked.

"That's right," they said in unison.

"That would be, what, maybe four months after the fire, is that about right?" I asked.

Maddy nodded.

"So, how easy is it to get in here?" From what I could tell, the garage doors were both manual as well as electric, and the only other door seemed to be an internal one leading into the house.

"This is a secure house," Mitch boomed, defensively.

"I don't doubt that, but if you didn't put the crowbar from Jake's in here, that means someone else did. In order to do that, they would have to have access to your garage. That means they entered either through this door . . ." I gestured to the garage door behind his car, à la Vanna White, "or that door." I pointed to the doorway where Maddy was still standing.

"Or there." Maddy pointed to the wall across from her, where various household props were hanging. I saw no doorway.

"Mark put up plywood along that wall. But there was a door there before. You don't remember?" Mitch asked.

"No. Why did he put up the plywood?"

He shrugged. "He thought it was maybe where the *mamzer* who framed me came in and he worried that they might come back the same way. Mark believes that if there's order, there's calm." Mitch rubbed something off the hood of his car with his thumb.

Maddy nodded as she crossed her arms under her bosom. "Mitch's chaos has always made Mark nervous. Elly and I learned to live with it, but it's always rankled Mark. I think his OCD is a direct result of that."

"Mark has OCD?" I asked, not aware that he had an obsessive compulsive disorder.

"A little." Her head moved forward as her shoulders moved up. Her entire face frowned.

"What's a little?" Mitch dismissed her with a wave of his hand, and turned to me. "How do you have a *little* obsessive problem? That's like a *little* alcohol problem, right? She doesn't know anything. The boy's not OCDC or anything else, he just got fed up. You don't see him washing his hands a thousand times a day or checking to make sure he turned off the water; he just likes order, that's all. Besides, I've been on him for a long time to clean up this place."

"A long time? Try thirty years! And what's this *I don't know anything*? I know plenty, mister. Plenty," Maddy grumbled, as she went back into the house.

"So, there's a doorway behind that piece of plywood where someone probably got in here?" I asked.

"That's right," Mitch said to me, but it was clear that his head was back in the house with Maddy.

"Can I take a look at the doorway from outside?"

"Sure, I'll let you out here." He reached for the button to release the garage door.

"Do you know if he nailed the plywood in place?"

"I don't know," he said impatiently. "Look, I'll be right out," he said, as he went back into the garage, and, I suspected, back to Maddy.

It was only just past three-thirty, but it was already getting dark. I took the flashlight out of my pocket and stepped out into the driveway. It was noticeably warmer. I then went around to the side of the house and found that the door had only a simple lock and one that had obviously been tampered with in the past. I turned the knob; it was locked. I took out my little tool kit and in less than two minutes I had the door open and I was facing a plywood wall. I pushed at it and discovered he had only tacked it up. It wasn't exactly what I would call security.

"What did you do?" Mitch was standing at the corner of the house, peering over at me and the opened door. "Oh my God, he left that *open*? What's wrong with that boy? And she thinks he has a whatchamacallit disorder. I told her, he's just—" Mitch stopped short, and sniffed at the air. He looked both sheepish and suspicious as he pushed his chin up. "So, what?"

"Mark had locked it. I'm just good at getting into places," I said, shutting the door. The lock caught and I pulled at it so Mitch could see it was secure. I walked back to him and said, "He did a nice job for you."

Mitch raised a brow and pulled his head back a fraction of an inch. "What's that supposed to mean?" he asked.

"It means if he ever tires of his nice white collar job, he can probably get work as a contractor." I smiled up at Mitch, who was feeling more and more like an unpleasant stranger to me, than the man who'd introduced me to Dairy Queen. "When were you going to tell me someone placed you at the scene of the fire?" I asked.

His dark eyes, once so loving and warm, hardened as he looked down at me. "I didn't think it was important. It was a lie."

"Really? The grand jury obviously believed it."

"It was a lie," he repeated.

"And your fingerprints were on the crowbar simply because you 'moved the damned thing' off your car."

"That's right." When he scowled at me, the corners of his eyes pinched into a network of deeply etched lines.

"Lying to me—"

"I haven't lied to anyone," he yelled.

I kept talking over him. "Omitting something as serious as an eyewitness is as good as lying, and it only makes you look guilty. I can't help you if you tie my hands behind my back and blindfold me."

"If you think I'm guilty, Miss Sinda Smartypants, then I suggest you—"

"Uncle Mitch, my name is Sydney. You and I both know I've been called Sydney basically since I was born, and you know I changed it legally so . . ."

"Sydney is a man's name."

"That may be, but it's still my name. I call you *Uncle* Mitch, and you can call me Sydney. And my name has nothing to do with—"

"You should be ashamed. If your poor mother were alive . . ."

"If my mother were alive, she'd be ashamed of *you* this time, Mitch. Tell me, was she ashamed the last time you were arrested?"

In an instant he looked old and vulnerable and I felt like a bully.

Mitch's nostrils flared and he tried his best to look stern, a look which may have flattened me when I was a kid, but now I could see it was just air and posturing. I didn't mean to hurt him, just reacquaint him with the truth, but then, what is the truth? The seconds that passed between us were charged and exhausting.

"When did you learn to be such a hard ass?" His voice was muted and rough.

"Uncle Mitch, I want to help you, but you insist on either insulting me or withholding information—"

"I have *not* insulted you." He waved a dismissive hand at me, which I grabbed and held in front of his face.

"This," I gave his hand a shake, "is insulting. 'Smarty-pants' is insulting. Not letting me know in the first place that you were in this kind of trouble is insulting. Lying to me is insulting!" I thrust his hand back at his chest.

"What kind of detective gets insulted at name calling?

Sensitive people don't make it in your profession, Sinda, believe you me, I know what I'm talking about. As far as no one telling you about this in the first place, you don't read the paper?'' His voice was booming now as his anger worked into high gear. "You couldn't call *me* when you knew there was a problem, you need a special invitation?" Even in the waning light his face was crimson.

"I was out of town!" I may have sounded like an indignant adult, but I knew that the shell of me was simply covering an eight-year-old who only wanted to please Uncle Mitch. It felt as if I was in limbo, hovering between Sinda the very good little girl and Sydney the woman, as if they were two completely separate entities. I took a deep breath and said, "Uncle Mitch, if we're going to keep you out of jail, we have to work together." I eased the tension in my shoulders. "Just for the record, I don't think you're guilty. I also think we have to be completely honest with one another. So, I need to know . . . is there anything else you haven't told me?"

We studied one another for a good long minute and I knew, no matter what happened going forward, there was no going back.

"You should say good night to your aunt before you leave," was all he said.

I saw myself grabbing his arm, spinning him around, and screaming, "This has to stop. You can't have changed this much from the man I knew when I was a kid." But I didn't do anything. I just stood there as I watched him walk away, his gait slightly stooped with age, and his hands clenched into fists at his side. I wanted to grab him by the front of his shirt and shake sense into the old man. That's when I heard myself; grab, shake, scream . . . surefire ways to reveal the heart and be heard. It takes two to tango, and there was no question that I was just as much at fault as he was in our miserable little dance of sidestepping.

As I pulled out of their driveway, I had a fleeting recollection of dancing with Mitch at my brother David's bar mitzvah. Mitch was so handsome in his tuxedo, and I, as a cowgirl, felt terribly silly in my ruffled anklets and party dress. Mitch had come over to where I was hiding in the shadows, held out his hand, and asked, *"May I have this dance?"*

"I don't know how to dance."

"I'll show you."

"I look stupid."

"You look like a princess."

Pulling out on to Northern Boulevard, headed to Hickey's office, I realized it hurt to remember that by the end of that cha-cha, I felt like a princess.

Alfred Hickey's office was above a Chinese take-out restaurant in a downtown location that had, no doubt, been bustling before someone invented the mall. The building seemed to be all but abandoned. There was no intercom, no light to guide you up the dirty wooden staircase that led to the second floor, and no answer when I knocked.

Hickey had told me an hour earlier that he would be there all day, so I had to assume he had simply stepped out for a coffee or maybe some Chinese food. I tried the door. It was open. I went in.

The office was a single room that had seen better days. There was a thick layer of dust on all surfaces. Two large wastebaskets were overflowing with crumpled papers, newspapers, empty food containers, and paper coffee cups. His still-wet galoshes were several feet from one another, as if he had taken them off en route to his desk. His coat had been carelessly tossed on a hook on the wall and his scarf was falling out of a pocket onto the floor.

The furnishings, which were old, had probably been bought used. Most of the brass studs were missing from the cracked brown leather that covered the wooden chairs. The desk was an old mahogany thing lost under a sea of papers. But perhaps most striking of all was Alfred Hickey himself, dangling just inches above his desk, his feet looking almost delicate in their scuffed black oxfords.

He was a large man whose clothing was as worn and dirty as his surroundings. His head hung at the same angle as that of one who might have fallen asleep on the subway or bus after a long day at work. A patch of his belly peeked through a gap in his shirt where a button was missing, exposing coarse red hair. His hands hung open at his side and the front of his pants was stained with urine.

He was hanging by rope from one of three support beams that ran the width of the cathedraled room. The shadow his swaying figure cast along his desk and across the floor ended where I stood.

"Goddammit," I muttered, as I went to his desk. I decided to leave the old black rotary phone untouched and dialed 911 from my cell phone.

In the ten minutes it took for the police to arrive, I was able to reach several conclusions of my own. One, Alfred Quentin Hickey was not a suicide. There was a deep groove marked by bruising across his neck, but that line was lower than where the rope was suspending him. This would lead one to believe he had been strung up *after* he had been killed, which meant that whoever had killed him had to be pretty damned strong, since Hickey had to be close to 5'10" and over two hundred pounds.

In his paraphernalia of pictures, papers, and memorabilia, I was also able to conclude that Alfred had been a brave man in Vietnam; he was way behind in various bills, including rent at both home (the address of which I noted) and office; he liked Scotch; he had a thing for big-breasted women, and most of his work centered on domestic disputes, which meant divorce cases. There was something

wrong with the office, other than the dirt and the dead man
hanging in the middle of the room, but I couldn't put my
finger on it. Something was off, something was missing.

Rummaging quickly through the papers in his file cabinet, those scattered on his desk as well as in his swollen
briefcase (which was held together with bungee cord), I
wasn't able to find anything resembling Mitch's file, though
Alfred had told me when we'd spoken that he had the papers there for me.

The first two officers to arrive at the scene were respect-
ful, professional, and capable. One took my statement,
while the other secured the crime scene. I then spent the
next hour at the only table in the Chinese take-out restaurant that smelled like old mops and ammonia, answering
questions posed by Detective Nelson, a kind woman with
bad skin. During that time I received one call from Kerry,
telling me that George Davis had phoned. At about five-
thirty, my stomach started to protest loudly.

When Nelson asked why I was there, I explained that
Hickey had recently worked on a case that I was now investigating. Clearly I had nothing to hide, so they had no
reason to hold me. When I left them, I made a beeline to
the nearest Burger King.

As I dipped into the fries, it occurred to me that I hadn't
been at all fazed by Alfred Hickey's death. Normally I find
the end of a life difficult to witness, whether I knew the
deceased or not. The finality of death has always had a
profound effect on me, and yet there I was, an hour after
the grisly discovery, preparing to down a burger, fries, and
a Pepsi. I sat in the Burger King parking lot in Bayside and
wondered if perhaps I had been doing this detective thing
too long. Had I become jaded to the point where the violent
end of a man's life no longer touched me?

Two bites into the burger, I lost my appetite. I called
Leslie, who was home with Auggie, planning dinner, and

told her I'd be home by seven, at the latest. I figured as long as I was in the neighborhood, I'd stop in and pay an unexpected call on Jake, who lived just minutes away, in Bay Terrace. The last time I'd seen Jake was back in 1981, at my dad's funeral. All I could remember about him from that day was that he had come to the funeral alone, and made a pass at my then-partner, Caryn. I couldn't picture him. All I could see in my mind's eye was the man I knew as a kid: pencil-thin mustache, greasy black hair, and inordinately large ears. I remember thinking as a child that Jake was more like a cartoon than an adult.

Eight

The doorman at Jake's building looked down his long nose and for the second time asked what my name was. I repeated it clearly and motioned to the receiver in his hand.

"Would you like me to talk to him?" I asked.

He turned his back to me. I didn't know how to explain to this guy that people who live in Queens really have no cause to cop an attitude. Not than I'm a Manhattan snob, but Bay Terrace isn't exactly Fifth Avenue or Grosse Point.

He mumbled into the mouthpiece and turned back to me. "Apartment 22D." He exhausted himself with the effort and pointed me to a bank of elevators in the back of the building.

The attempt to make this 1960s building feel like the beach went beyond the simple use of beige and powder blue tiles to cover the floors and walls. An ambitious decorator had found maple furniture reminiscent of Florida with seashells lacquered onto the sides and legs of tables and settees.

Signs locating health club, pool, commissary, and hospitality rooms were framed between the elevators. I suffered through a rousing rendition of the Percy Faith Orchestra's go at "Downtown," piped into the elevator, and couldn't get it out of my head until I rang the bell to apartment 22D.

Jake swung open the door and practically yelled, "Sydney! *Bubeleh*, look at you, you *shaineh maidel*, you look great! What the hell are you doing here? Huh? Huh? My

God, I haven't seen you in ages, not since, what? Since you were a little *pisher* and would come to work with that piece of *dreck*. But my God, you've grown up, haven't you?'' Jake held the doorknob with his left hand, and the door frame with his right. He was about three inches shorter than me, which put him at about 5'5" and weighed maybe a hundred and twenty pounds. He still sported the pencil-thin mustache of his youth, only now it was enhanced with a Grecian 21-like product. His toupee looked perfectly flammable. "Look at you! The spitting image of your mother, God rest her soul. If I didn't know better, I'd swear you were her.''

He finally took a breath and I asked how he was.

"Good, good, all things considered. I got my health, so I can't complain. The rest . . ." He shrugged. "The rest is gravy, don't forget it, you hear me? Huh? Huh?'' He offered a conspiratorial wink with his wisdom, as if to say, *'No one else knows this, but . . .'*

"May I come in?" I asked, glancing behind him into what I could see of the apartment, which wasn't much.

"In? *Oi!*'' He slapped his hand against his forehead, which made his rug move a fraction of an inch back onto his head, elongating his brow. "What the hell's the matter with me? Of course, of course, come in. Come in.''

He didn't seem to notice that his phony hair was askew, so I didn't point it out.

I followed him into what he proudly called his "bachelor pad.'' I took up his offer for a Coca-Cola. I didn't want the drink so much as I needed time alone. It was as if I had been plucked out of the real world and deposited into *I Dream of Jeanie's* famous bottle. All squared corners were hidden behind ornate red screens and essentially the only thing resembling seats were enormous scarlet, emerald green, and yellow pillows threaded with gold designs. Low tables covered in brass knickknacks and ivory elephants were scattered throughout the room. Billowing velvet drapes covering normal high-rise windows gathered in folds on the floor and trailed four feet into the room. Ten-foot-long gilded mirrors hung on either side of the room, creating a frightening funhouse effect.

Jake Aronson lives here? was all I could think as I spied my thousand-and-one reflections in the mirror.

"Here you go." Jake thrust a can of soda at me and motioned to a group of pillows. "Sit. Sit. What do you think, huh? Some fancy digs I got here, huh? Huh?" His toupee was still off kilter. "It's all thanks to the woman I'm seeing, Lola. She's not much of a *balebosteh,* but she's a dream in every other way. I never could have done this on my own."

"Noooo," I said, as if he should perish such a thought.

"Oh yeah, I'm telling you, she's got all the taste."

"Well, you picked her, so that says something about you."

He puffed his small chest out with pride and hiked up the knees of his jogging pants to sit on a mound of pillows. "*Oi vai iz mir,* I'm getting old. As much as I love 'em, these pillows can be a real pain in the you-know-what." Once settled in, he asked, "So what brings you here?" He must have felt a breeze on his forehead, because he repositioned the toup as subtly as he possibly could, making it look as if he was scratching an itch rather than moving his hair.

"I'm investigating what happened at your factory."

"Is that so? And for whom?"

"Mitch." I watched Jake's face carefully. Aside from obvious dislike, he revealed nothing.

"Mitchell Eli Gerber is a fool, an old fool, who is finally getting what he deserves."

"You really think he torched your business?"

"The police think he did, a grand jury thought he did. What? I should think differently?"

"I suppose I'm asking what you think from your heart."

"Heart, from a detective? There's a switch." Jake took a sip from a glass he had had working before I'd gotten there, a clear liquid with two limes. He wiped his mustache with the tip of his index finger before finally answering. "Quite honestly, I absolutely think he did it. I think the *mieskeit* fell off the deep end and now he's trying to save his ass. Now, I never would have thought he had the *balls* to do it, but he's an angry man, a man I don't know anymore, so who knows? A very reliable witness places him at the scene of the fire, so what can I say?"

"Where were you the night of the fire?"

Jake studied me carefully, his eyes surprisingly intelligent for a man living in a Queens harem. "You know, *ziskeit*, I don't have to answer your questions." He lowered his chin (or lack of it), and looked at me beneath his lifted brows.

I hadn't been called a *ziskeit* since my grandmother died when I was twelve. I knew it was a term of endearment, but I couldn't remember what it meant.

"I know." It was hard not to look at his toupee, which was now listing to the left side of his head.

"I'm answering your questions because I have nothing to hide, I want you to understand that. Okay?"

"Okay."

"And because you look like your mother and I always had a thing for her, *not* that I didn't like your father, too, God rest his soul—now, there was a *mentsh.*" He picked up his glass and took a larger sip. "On the night in question, I was in the company of my lady friend, Lola."

"Do you mind if I take notes?" I asked, reaching into my bag for pad and pen.

"No. Please. Like I said, I have nothing to hide."

"Tell me about that night, Jake."

Jake explained that November second had been an amazingly cold day and that despite the fact that it was Saturday, they were working against a deadline, so they had been open all day. He closed the shop at around eight-thirty, drove home, showered, changed, picked up Lola—who is apparently Italian, with legs that don't quit—went to dinner at Stella Dora's restaurant in the Bronx, and then to a dance club, and finally back to her place at one in the morning, where, it should suffice to say, he had an excellent alibi. I didn't point out that his "excellent alibi" could easily be collusion between lovers, but I tucked it away in the back of my head.

"When did you hear about the fire?"

"A little after three in the morning."

"How?"

"My son, Danny, called me at Lola's. He was here when the authorities called, not long after it was under control."

"Danny was where? Here? In this apartment?"

"He was living here at the time. His apartment was being painted. He and I met at the factory—or what was left of it—maybe half an hour later."

Jake and I went through the details with a fine-toothed comb, in part because he was willing, and in part because I didn't want to have to go through this with him again. The pervasive stench of patchouli oil was making me nauseated.

When I asked why he'd opened Elite, despite the non-compete agreement, he squeezed out a sour smile. "Lemme tell you something, kid—that uncle of yours has been a bee in my ass my whole life, if you'll pardon the expression. He likes to think that *our* business, the business that was started by *my* father, was successful despite my presence. It was all due to *his* hard work. To hear him talk, you'd think that at best I was a daily obstacle he had to overcome.

Well, lemme tell you something you may not know—Jake
Aronson is every bit as much a rag man as that pompous
bastard. I started my business to prove that I am just as
good as him, if not better. And you see what happened."
Here his eyes sparkled with triumph. "He couldn't take the
competition, so he burned me out. Sad. It's very sad," he
said, but I could tell he didn't really think so.

"But the noncompete clause in your agreement . . . ?" I
asked again.

Again he shrugged. "As I understood it, he would have
had to prove that I had caused him *irreparable harm*." Jake
snorted a laugh. "The only thing that could kill that business after all these years is if the owner went crazy and
wound up in jail. And even *then*, if there was someone to
take over for him, chances are it would *still* do well. It's a
good, solid business."

"Who would take over for Mitch if he had to step
down?"

"For that, *ziskeit*, you have to ask Mitch."

"And what about your business? What happened to it?"

Jake studied me long and hard before looking away and
answering. "I told my clients that another contractor,
Moody Plevin, would be taking over all my orders. None
of them batted an eyelash, and you know why?"

I shook my head.

"Because no one wanted to take their business back to
that *chozzer alter kocker*! I'm sorry to say, but he's a worth-
less old glutton, that uncle of yours. Plevin's been in business a long time and is just as well known as Harriman's,
which *my* father built, not his, which he tends to forget."

I walked away from our little tête-à-tête with several
facts. I now knew that Danny had been staying with his
father when the fire broke out, though he actually had his
own apartment in Long Island City. Elite was Jake's own
business and God should spit on his grave if it was a sweat-

shop. "I know how to cut corners. Unlike Mr. I-Know-Better-Than-Everyone-Else, I don't need a sweatshop to make quality for less." His insurance company was none of my business, thank you very much, but it should suffice for me to know that they had been satisfied with the fact that Mitchell was responsible. With regard to the dead woman in his factory, he assumed it was the cleaning woman, with whom he kept flexible hours. "As long as my office was cleaned by Monday, I didn't care what she did." Did he know where her family was? Did he know that she was still in the morgue? Did he care? No. No. No. What was her name? Again he shrugged. "Maria something. Hey, come on. I paid her off the books. Cash. I didn't need her information." Not even a home number? "It went up in the fire. Look, what are you so concerned about? You didn't even know her." When I pointed out that she was someone's daughter or wife or friend, and they would probably want to know what had happened to her, Jake lifted his brows and tightened his mouth. "I got enough troubles of my own. I can't worry about every immigrant." No, of course not.

As far as he knew, the man who had identified Mitch was named Bill Mazzio, a guy who was in the neighborhood because he was visiting a girlfriend. "He's definitely a weirdo, but the fact is, he swears he saw Mitch leaving the building not long before the fire broke out, maybe one-thirty." Jake was unable to suppress his smugness.

By the time I left, it was dark, and rush hour was still going strong. I let my mind wander for the hour-long trip home.

When I got home the elevator was on the tenth floor, so I started toward the marble staircase. I love that staircase. The large apartment buildings along West End Avenue were basically built before the Depression in '29, which accounts for the ornate stonework as well as the use of marble and stained glass. It is amazing to think that this avenue of remarkable buildings was historically never considered *the* place to be until as recently as the 1980s. In 1949, my folks rented the same apartment I moved back into when my dad died in 1981. Rumors of co-oping are finally floating around the building, but we are probably the last bastion of rental structures in the neighborhood.

As soon as I opened the apartment door, I could smell the wonderful combination of rosemary and sage. Auggie practically knocked me over when she threw herself at me in greeting.

To my surprise, Miguel was having a glass of wine with Leslie in the kitchen. The kitchen is perhaps my favorite room in the apartment. Long ago I had taken down the wall dividing the dining room from the kitchen and turned them into one big room. When Leslie moved in two years ago, we decided that there had to be a sense of her in the space. Since she is a sought-after decorator, I had assumed she would want to do a complete overhaul, but this was not the case. The den went through a metamorphosis and the guest room now doubles as a storage space for her work when she needs it, but for the most part (aside from installing a built-in wine rack along one wall in the kitchen and replacing the old sofa in the dining area with a new one), the rest of the place has remained intact. Even a portrait that my ex, Caryn, had done of the two of us when we lived together still remains up in the living room. This is something I never would have predicted when Leslie moved in. Despite the fact that Caryn was living in Ireland when I met Leslie, and they'd never met, Leslie was jealous of her. When they finally did come face to face, they became best friends. Now, as it turns out, Caryn's work has gotten international recognition and works of hers grace museum walls.

"Hey, how did it go with your family?" Miguel asked, when I dumped my bag on the floor.

I cast a critical eye at his glass of wine. "Should you be having that, after today?"

"I'm fine, Sydney," he sighed.

"Famous last words." I pecked the top of Leslie's head with a kiss and went to get my own glass. "What smells so good?"

"Rosemary chicken and potatoes. You going to join us, Mickey?" Leslie is one of the few people who call Miguel *Mickey* as a general rule.

"Nah, but thanks. I got things I gotta do." His eyes came back to me. "So, how did it go with your family?" he asked again as I took my first sip of wine, a tasty Beaujolais.

"Okay, I guess, but you know that detective, Hickey?"

"Yeah."

I looked at Leslie and realized that the information about Hickey could wait until Miguel and I were alone in my office. There was no need to upset her.

"Actually, I have some papers in my office, why don't we talk in there?" I said, walking to the doorway that leads into the living room and the rest of the place.

"What? I can't listen to this?" Leslie rolled her eyes at Miguel as she got up from the table and went in the opposite direction, to the stove. "Really, Sydney, sometimes you have a warped image of who I am."

"Yes, dear." I took my wine into my office and knew that Miguel, who would feel the need to placate Leslie, would join me as soon as he could.

I was emotionally exhausted and couldn't stop thinking about my family, these people who knew a me that once was, or now, only partially exists. By necessity, we define each other by history and not current events. *Sydney is a man's name.*

History.

"Uncle Mitch, for twenty-three years you've loved me. It's still me, I'm the same person I was before I told you about Caryn." I had tried to sound casual, as if this really was no big deal.

His eyes took in the restaurant, the white linen, the table setting, everything but me. "I can't help it, Sinda, I think it's wrong."

"You think I'm sick," I said, knowing he would deny it and bring us back to a workable reality.

Instead, he swallowed and reached for his salad fork. I watched his Adam's apple bob slowly, as if he was choking. He dragged the tines of the fork along the tablecloth, making deep lines in the linen. His fingernail was white with a streak of red in the center, from the pressure he was exerting on the fork. "It's not that I don't love you . . ." His voice broke.

"But you can't accept me." I saw a waiter behind Mitch approaching with our salads.

"No. I can't. This would break your mother's heart."

"You think so? I like to think Mom would want me to be happy."

Neither of us ate dinner that night.

I heard a knock and looked up at Miguel, who was standing in front of my desk. "Yo, boss, where the heck are you?"

"Here." I released the tension in my shoulders and told him to have a seat.

"So, what gives?" he asked.

"So this Hickey? I talked to him at around two. He said he had the file on his desk, all ready for me. However, I got there at three-thirty, and guess what?"

"He wasn't there?"

"Well . . . part of him was."

Miguel paused. "Which part?"

"His body."

"So? What was missing?" he asked, as he sat at the cushioned window seat where he had a great view of West End Avenue.

"His soul, Miguel, his soul."

"So the man was . . . *dead*?" Miguel's eyes widened.

"Most definitely. And if it wasn't *murder*, I'll eat my shoes, but the real question is: was his murder related to *our* case, or one of his own? It looked like the bulk of his business was domestic relations."

"Divorces," Miguel said.

"That's right." Auggie pushed past my feet and curled up under my desk with a sigh.

"Oh man, some dude probably didn't like the pictures this guy took, and boom, *adiós amigo*."

"That's what it was!" I snapped my fingers.

"What?"

"I knew there was something missing from his office, but I couldn't figure out what it was. Now I know; I didn't see a camera there. For an investigator like that, a camera is his right hand."

"Was anything else missing? Shit, man." He twitched a fist in the air. "Why is it you always get the good stuff?"

"What's the good stuff? Seeing a dead man?" I was sitting at my desk and had to lean forward and look to the left to see him. I flattened my fingers over the base of my glass. "Is *that* what you think is the good stuff?" I asked again.

He took a deep breath, closed his eyes, and twitched his shoulders.

"Oh, it's very exciting. I mean, you haven't lived until you've seen the bloated body of a floater whose eyes and face are so distorted you can't tell what the hell it was, except that you have nightmares about it for weeks afterward. Or maggots feeding off a corpse, that's always cool.

Decapitation. Charred remains. Why, just the stench of death is an exhilarating experience.''

In the silence that followed, I knew I'd made my point.

"Tell me about your afternoon," I said, taking out my notepad and a pen.

"I met Mali," Miguel said timidly.

I turned slowly and studied his fine face. "You mean, Jake's manager?" I asked, and waited until he nodded slowly. "What do you mean, met him?"

"I mean, like I met him and talked to him." He cleared his throat and leaned back, out of my line of vision. "It happened real natural, you know? I mean, I know you always say I should just follow and not talk, but I tell you, Sydney, I got a face people trust. I think it's going to be real good for me in this line of work. You know?"

"Why don't you come over here where I can see you and tell me everything? For example, how did you introduce yourself to Mr. Mali?" I asked, feeling my blood begin to boil. The last thing I needed was an operative going out and acting like he was a licensed detective. It's not what you would call good for business, and Miguel knew it.

"His first name is Mali," he said, coming out into the open, completely unaware that I was ready to blow. "I told him I was looking for a friend."

"Where did you meet him?"

"Him and his girlfriend have an apartment in Brooklyn." This time he perched on the edge of the red Morris chair directly across from my desk. "I was downstairs, just looking up his name on the, um, you know, directory like thing, and this woman asks me in Spanish who I'm looking for. Well, I turn around and she is a total drop-dead knock-out, so naturally, I tell her who I'm looking for, cause it's not like I have anything to hide. Right?" He paused. I waited. "You're never gonna guess who she was," he prompted.

"Mali's girlfriend."

"Right! How did you know?"

"And you said?"

"I told her I was looking for Mali because he probably knew a friend of mine I was trying to find."

"A friend?"

"Yeah, you know the woman who was killed in the fire? I figured, no one knows who she is, maybe I could be looking for her."

I sighed.

"Hey, listen, I had no choice, I had to talk to this woman. She approached me. I was thinking fast and it worked. This woman knew all about the fire."

"I should hope so."

"Anyway, she's got a couple of bags of groceries, so I offer to help her upstairs. Mali's not home, she tells me, but she was expecting him any minute. Now this woman doesn't speak a word of English, so it's a good thing that *I* was the one who went to see them and not you, if you stop and think about it. Anyway, she seems very sympathetic. I mean, the woman's not only beautiful, but she's a very nice lady. Naturally, I accepted her offer when she asked if I wanted a cup of coffee. It would have been rude not to, right? Anyway, Mali came in before it was even brewed."

"I'm sure he was thrilled to see you."

"Oh boy, at first I think he thought I was the Immigration Department, because the guy looked like he was gonna shit bricks." Miguel seemed quite pleased with the reaction he had elicited. "I told him I was cool, that I was just looking for a friend." At this point, Miguel took out a piece of paper from his back pocket and unfolded it once, twice, four times. "I took notes, but I waited until I was out of there, because I didn't want him to think I was threatening, you know?''

I nodded. He was learning.

He read the notes like he was memorizing them and re-folded the page before saying, ''He says he doesn't know who was killed in the fire. But he said that the woman I described didn't fit no one there that he knew.''

''Anyone. Whom did you describe?''

''Dummy Doreen. She was the only one I could think of. Anyway, he said he didn't have contact with the clean-ing lady, and that's who everyone thought it was.''

''Anything else?''

''Well, I got the impression that he wasn't too keen on Jake, but he didn't say nothing like that. The girlfriend, however, had called Jake a *hijo de puta* before Mali got home. That's like a son-of-a-bitch,'' he explained unnec-essarily.

''Before I forget, do you know if Kerry got anything on the insurance?''

Miguel shrugged. ''No.'' He stretched out his legs and rested his glass on his stomach. A slight smile slowly stretched across his lovely face.

''What?'' I couldn't help but return his smile, in spite of myself.

''I'm telling you, chief, this guy knows something.''

''What does that mean?''

''It means this is the man who knew how that place worked and what shit was coming down.''

''Is that right? And how do you know that?''

''It's my instinct. Only one problem.''

''And that is?''

''He's not talking.''

''Why not?''

''Because people who work in sweatshops usually like

to keep pretty quiet about it, at least to outsiders. It's a nasty little thing concerning immigration.''

"Jake swears Elite wasn't a sweatshop.''

"You talked to him?''

"Yes.''

"Right, and Mr. Clinton didn't inhale. Go on, you believe that shit?''

"I'm not sure.''

"Well, apparently, from what the girlfriend said, no one was real fond of Jake. I think he owed everyone money, and it's not like they pay these people a lot.''

"She worked for him, too?''

"No, but she's a talker. She also started to talk about Jake's son, but that's when Mali came home.''

"What did she say?''

"Nothing, really. But I bet if I had some time with her, she'd tell me an awful lot.'' He finished his wine.

I held out one hand to Miguel and reached for my reading glasses with the other. "Let me take a look at those notes.''

"Porqué?" he asked, while reaching into his pocket.

"Consider it classroom work.'' I unfolded the fragile paper and tried to decipher his chicken-scratch Spanglish. "The first thing a good detective must learn is organizational skills. This is a mess.''

"Maybe, boss, but I got one hell of a filing system.'' He tapped his head with an index finger.

"Okay, then what I want you to do is type this up tonight and meet me in the office at seven-thirty tomorrow morning. We'll go over it then, along with my notes.''

"Seven-thirty?''

I hate whining. "Look.'' I handed him back his list. "Let's say for the sake of argument that Hickey was killed because of our case, and not a jealous husband, okay? As far as I'm concerned, that means we're in danger."

"Which means seven-thirty tomorrow morning." He stood up and put his empty glass on the desk.

After he left, I found that in the kitchen, the candles were lit, the table was set, and Samuel Barber's *Adagio for Strings* was playing quietly in the background. I followed Leslie around the kitchen and decided to see what she had up her sleeve. "Anything interesting at the renovation site?"

"No, but Fifth Avenue has been practically shut down with a water-main break." She handed me a basket of biscuits, which I took to the table.

"Really?" Though I had the radio on in the car, I'd been so lost in thought I hadn't heard a thing.

"Really. So you know what that means." She motioned for me to carry two plates over to her at the stove.

"What?"

"Dorothy will be staying with us until it's fixed." She piled the first plate with rosemary chicken, well-done roasted potatoes, parsnips, carrots, and peas.

"Your mother is staying with us?"

"Well, she couldn't stay with Marcia, could she?" Leslie asked, loading up the other plate.

"Why not? Your sister would love that. Dorothy could babysit." It's not that I don't like Dorothy—I do. She is a good woman who has accepted me as a part of Leslie's life, despite the way I first met them, which was painful at best (I proved that the man they thought had killed Leslie's dad was innocent, which wasn't nearly as agonizing as proving who *had* done it).

"Mom would go crazy with Marcia. Besides, her kids are at the bratty stage." Leslie reached out and took my hand. "Bottom line is, my love, I want my mom to stay with us, and that's all there is to it."

I nodded, knowing there are just some situations you can't win. This was one of them.

"Now, tell me about *your* day," Leslie said with a sly smile as she returned her attention to dinner.

And so I did, leaving out nothing.

Nine

"The insurance company is Abilene." Kerry was curled up blurry-eyed on one end of the sofa in my office, practically embracing her coffee and clipboard. "I have a call in to the woman who handled Jake Aronson's account, but she was out yesterday with a cold, so we have to be patient. As I understand it, they have investigators they work with on a steady basis. From what her secretary alluded to, though, my guess is as far as they're concerned, this baby *isn't* really closed yet." Kerry was conservatively decked out in jeans, a tattered tee shirt, a tight black V-neck sweater, and a bulky gray sweater over that. So much for office dress codes.

"Golly. And Jake said it was closed. I'm so surprised. Oh, by the way, did Paul Levin messenger me the report yesterday?" As I reached for my coffee, my back pinched. I knew there was an ugly bruise where I had landed the day before.

"Nope. I thought you were going to see him yesterday." She patted the seat beside her for Auggie to climb up, but fortunately, Auggie is better trained than Kerry, and knows she is not allowed on the furniture. Instead, she put her paws on Kerry's knees, cocked her head to the side, and leaned forward looking oh so cute, no doubt hoping for a bite of bagel.

"I didn't. He was in court all day."

"So you still don't know what's in the report?" She gave Auggie a taste of bagel.

Before I could answer, the door burst open and Miguel came racing in, full of excuses. "Oh man, am I sorry I'm late, but it's not my fault. *Seriously*." His eyes grew about eight times bigger when he addressed Kerry's snort of incredulity. "*You* take the A train and not get totally screwed," he said, referring to the Seventh Avenue subway. "We were almost at Forty-second Street and shit, man, it just stops."

"No, *you* stop," I said, losing patience. "It's already eight o'clock and I don't have time for bullshit. I don't want to have to repeat myself so little Miguel can be briefed."

"It's not bullshit," he mewled.

I turned to him and said as calmly as I could, "If I had told you that at seven-thirty this morning, and not a second later, you would be handed a check for five million dollars, I have a feeling you'd have been here on time. Bottom line, Miguel, is either you take this job seriously, or find something else. That's it," I said, sounding dangerously composed. "End of discussion. There's coffee outside, get yourself a cup and let's get started."

Miguel shook his head, tossed his jacket on a director's chair, and muttering just under his breath, took his misunderstood self into the other room.

"Okay." I turned my attention back to Kerry. "So I expect that by the end of the day we'll have something from the insurance company. Find out if Hickey is one of their investigators. Find out who's on this case, or who was. Did you read the paper this morning? Do you know if Hickey's death was mentioned?"

"Who's got time for newspapers? I'm reading Rosalind Russell's biography."

"Okay, so I need you to get as much on Hickey as you

can. Before I leave, I'll put a call in to Detective Nelson, she's the one who's investigating his death, but I want everything you can possibly find out about this guy—family, friends, clients, financial status, licenses, everything. Also, I want you to find out who actually owned Aronson Elite.'' I watched Miguel slink across the room and settle on the window seat facing the side street, rather than Broadway. ''I have to say Jake was amazingly sincere when I interviewed him, but right now I don't trust any of them.'' If I hadn't been feeling so anxious I would have told Kerry and Miguel about Jake's harem apartment, but right then, at that very moment, all I wanted was to be done with this case. Not even twenty-four hours into it, and I was ready to wrap it up. Maybe it was working so closely with family, but I didn't have a good feeling about this.

Kerry nodded as she took notes. ''Okay, so I have the insurance company, Albert Hickey—''

''Alfred. Alfred Quentin Hickey.'' I looked at Miguel and pointed to a bag on the corner of my desk. ''Bagels,'' I said, by way of a peace offering.

''Thanks.'' He reached for the bag.

''Insurance. Hickey. Ownership.'' She sighed. ''Anything else?''

''That should keep you busy most of the day.'' I pulled a legal pad out from a drawer.

''Most of the *week*,'' Miguel amended.

''It looks as though a lot of my time is going to be spent in Queens and Long Island,'' I said, sliding the pad of paper and a pen over to Miguel. ''I figure if the three of us know what's up with all aspects of the investigation, we can keep tabs on one another. Let's start from the top.'' Normally I would be sitting there going over details with Max, but St. Bart was a world away. Having worked with Kerry for so long, I knew I could trust her to deliver. Miguel was smart, but prone to act out of machismo rather than methodology.

I was feeling only somewhat alone when we started working.

I gave Miguel an overview of what Kerry and I had sorted through in his absence, as well as the list of things she would be undertaking from the office.

"Now, we know that on November second, at approximately two A.M., Aronson Elite was deliberately torched. The body of a woman was discovered in the wreckage, and an eyewitness places my uncle at the scene of the crime."

"No shit!" Miguel was taking this like it was his family instead of mine.

"What?" Slack-jawed, Kerry put her empty cup on the coffee table.

"The worrisome thing is that neither my cousins nor my uncle told me about this eyewitness."

"Who did?" Miguel asked with a mouthful of a cream cheese–slathered cinnamon-raisin bagel.

"My aunt. Then I got the actual name of the witness from Jake."

"Oh Christ, that blows." Kerry shook her head.

"It doesn't bode well, no." I paused as I leafed through the notes I had gathered from my coffee shop meeting with my cousins, to my interview with Jake.

"To continue, we know the woman died as a result of the fire. We know that Mitch had threatened Jake a week before the fire . . ."

"Do you think he did it?" Kerry asked.

"No," Miguel answered for me.

"It doesn't look good for him," I answered. "Even from my vantage point. First of all, there's the threat. Apparently a crowbar that was used at the fire to open the door was found in Mitch's garage, with his fingerprints on it. Now he insists that it was on the hood of his car Sunday morning, and that his fingerprints got on it when he moved it and tossed it in with the rest of the crap in his garage, but

I found it very disturbing that yesterday, when I went to Mitch's house, Mark had cleaned the garage to look spanking new. Understand, Mitch's garage has been in a state of utter chaos ever since I was . . .''

"Maybe he was cleaning up for his daddy," Miguel suggested, as he reached for another bagel.

"Sure he was, but unfortunately it leads one to ponder just what it was it he *needed* to clean. Perhaps Mark knows something we don't and doesn't want to share the information, which is starting to look like it's the norm with this family."

"*Your* family," Kerry reminded me, as she got up and took her coffee cup into the other room. "Keep talking, I can hear you. Anyone want a reheat?"

"No, thanks. Anyway, despite your gut feeling that Elite was illegal, Miguel, I'm not so sure that focusing on Jake's staff is the way to go with this. I hate to say it, but my instincts are telling me that my family is somehow at the bottom of all this. It may be wise for us to simply combine energies and follow up on them first."

"I disagree, boss." Miguel wiped his hands on his jeans and put his empty cup on the edge of my desk. "You figure as long as there's three of us, we can go in three different directions, right?"

"Go on . . .''

Kerry came back with a fresh coffee and walked to the windows looking out on Broadway. The day was cold and gray, the promise of snow biting the air.

"Here." Miguel pulled a manila folder out of his pea jacket pocket and tossed it on my desk. "So, most of what's in there I told you last night, but there was no question in my mind that this Mali didn't like Jake. Now, maybe I don't know that they didn't like him enough to go and burn his joint down, but we won't know until we check it out, right?"

"Right." It was a stretch, but I wanted to see where Miguel would go with this.

"I figure if I can get this guy Mali to open up, I can find out what went down there, you know?"

I leafed through Miguel's badly typed report and felt a sense of pride at how well he was adjusting to this line of work. From the way his report was written, one would have to conclude that Jake was running a sweatshop.

"You know anything about sweatshops?" I asked Miguel.

He shrugged. "Not much, but I'd like to learn."

I studied his young, handsome face. "Why?" I asked, masking how pleased I was with his curiosity.

He gently rubbed his knuckles against his goatee. "I don't like people who take advantage of other people. My grandma was an immigrant and she was taken advantage of when she first started out here. I don't think the world should work like that, you know what I mean? I mean, I know it does, and I'm not gonna be the one to stop it, but I can at least try when I have the chance, you understand?"

I did. It is that sense of decency that will make Miguel excel in this business. It's also the one thing that might just break him.

"Let me think about it." I studied the pad I had been using for notes. "In the meantime, our suspect list isn't very encouraging. Aside from Mitch, I don't see any real contenders. Except for maybe Mark—who has absolutely no motive as far as I can see, and then maybe Jake . . . but that's really stretching it."

"Where was Mark when this went down?" Miguel asked.

I read from my notes. "Says he was in Quogue, at a friend's house."

"Quogue?" Miguel asked.

"A beach area way out on Long Island," Kerry said

softly, sipping her coffee, apparently mesmerized by the street below.

"You believe him?" Miguel turned back to me.

"I don't believe anything right now. However, before we go racing in a million directions, we need to focus. Oh, there's also someone named Moody Plevin, a clothing contractor. After the fire, Jake arranged for all of his clients to be serviced by Moody."

"Were they business partners?" Kerry asked.

"That's what I want to know. Will you find out, please? One of the things Elly said the other day was that Jake didn't have money to fund opening a shop on his own. She felt certain that he had been subsidized somehow." The phone rang and I picked it up. "CSI, may I help you?"

"I doubt it, but maybe I can help you."

"Ah, Georgie. I've been waiting for you." I motioned to Kerry and Miguel that this would take a minute. Kerry headed back to her office and Miguel, with no place to call his own in our beautifully appointed professional space, took Auggie into Max's office.

"Got some news for you," he said with a sigh.

"Great." I flipped to a fresh page on the pad and prepared to take notes.

"You should know this makes me very uncomfortable." He paused and I could hear his even breathing on the other end of the line. Finally he exhaled loudly and said, "I am only doing this because you're a friend."

"I appreciate that, George. Really."

"You didn't hear any of this from me, got it?"

"I promise."

"First you should know, it *was* arson. Next, because of the homicide, it went straight to the police, so I don't have many details."

"Okay."

"But I'll give you what I can, because it's your uncle.

First of all, the perp used gasoline, which he poured by the front entrance. Whoever it was tried to make it look like an electrical fire by dousing an outlet. In other words, it wasn't the kind of impulsive thing where they just ran in, sprinkled the place, and bolted.''

"Professional?" I asked, wondering if someone had hired a pro to torch it.

"Who knows? If it is, they're not very good. The only thing I would infer from their trying to make it look electrical is that whoever did it gave it some thought beforehand.

"Now, the report says your uncle came out clean—for example, no singed hair or other physical evidence to suggest that he was there, which is good for him, but his prints were on this crowbar that was evidently used at the scene of the crime, which is bad.''

"Right."

"You knew that?"

"Yes. Go on."

He sighed. "I dunno, Sydney." Again he took another deep breath.

"The eyewitness?" I decided to make it easier for him.

"Yeah, how'd you know?"

"It's what I do. You have a name?"

"Yeah, a Billy Mazzio. I even have a number here." I knew from the tone of his voice that George thought Mitchell was guilty as hell and I wouldn't have a prayer of vindicating him. He was helping me out because he was a good man with a big heart and knew I had to learn things my own way.

"Nothing else. From here on in, it's a police matter." He gave me the name and numbers of the officers who handled the case, as well as Mazzio's number. I knew that Paul Levin, Elly's ineffectual lawyer husband, would have all this information, but who knew when the hell he would get around to sending it to me?

I thanked George for his help and promised him a dinner at the Lone Dove when Max and his bride returned.

After I hung up, I called out to Miguel. In the eight seconds that it took him to come back into my office, I already had Billy Mazzio's number in hand. "Listen, I'm going to Queens today. I want you to follow Mali." *Follow Mali*. It sounded like an Indian delicacy.

"Okay," he said, trying to mask his excitement, but his body was practically vibrating with anticipation. I knew exactly what he was feeling because it happens to me at the onset of every case, in that moment when you know you're off and running.

I stopped and made sure we had direct eye contact. "Let me repeat, you are to *follow Mali*. You do not make direct contact, do you understand?"

Miguel made a face as if to say, *What, are you crazy?*, but we both knew his track record included talking to the wrong people and making things difficult for Max and me.

"I am only doing this because I trust instincts and it's time we tested yours. If you're so hot on this sweatshop concept, then I'm behind you. Do you understand?"

"Yes." He started for the door.

"Before you go." I stopped him and ignored his obvious itch to be gone. "Do you know why you're following him?"

Miguel inhaled as if to answer, looked around the room, and finally exhaled. "Yeah," he lied.

"Really? Why?" It was the only way he was going to learn.

Big sigh for the really stupid question. He tweaked a piece of nothing off the arm of the sofa and said, "This way I'll know his schedule, who he hangs with, maybe get something on other people he has contact with." He looked up timidly and asked, "Right?"

I bobbed my head from side to side, attempting to be noncommittal. I figured the most important thing was that Miguel not just rush into his task—or this business, for that matter—without giving his actions, and his objectives, a great deal of thought. He *had* to understand that he needed an objective or he wouldn't be able to see anything; it would all become amorphous.

It would have been easy to give him the simple exercise of tailing someone, to see both what he could ascertain about his quarry, and whether he could avoid being detected himself, but as far as I'm concerned, that's just a matter of going through the motions. If he stopped to consider what it was he wanted to learn from Mali, his vision would be more acute.

"You have a pad and pencil?" was my response.

"Un-huh." He tugged it out of his pocket.

"Do you know where you're going?"

"He lives in Brooklyn. I'll start there." He paused, as if watching the words float between us. It was as if saying it out loud made visible the big gaping holes in his logic. This was because he hadn't thought it through; he was acting on impulse. Naturally, I had to point this out.

"You know he's there?"

"No," he murmured, less sure of himself.

"So, what? You're just going to wait for him downstairs until he shows up?" I nodded and turned my attention back to the phone. "Just remember, it's always best to walk into a situation with as much background information as you can get. Also, you should probably relieve your bladder before you go. Oh, and Miguel? Remember, if you do find him, just follow him. *No contact.* Know what it is you want from him."

With that, I put on my reading glasses and dialed Billy

Mazzio's number. Auggie followed Miguel to the front door and cried when he was gone.

The number I called yielded a standard message indicating that the number had been changed with no forwarding number. I called Paul Levin next.

When I told his secretary that I was calling from the Manhattan district attorney's office, I was put directly through to Paul.

"Hello Paul, it's Sydney," I greeted my cousin's husband with reserve.

"Sydney." He sounded as if he was checking his mental rolodex.

"Yes, Sydney. Remember, your cousin by marriage, the one who is still waiting for Hickey's report from you?" I paused, hoping he would fill in the gap. "*Hellloo*, are you there?"

"Yes, of course I am." He was evidently preoccupied.

"Paul, what's the problem? I'm just trying to get this simple report from you."

"There *is* no problem." It was like I was talking to a schizophrenic; one second he was preoccupied and the next he was convivial to the point of being jovial.

"Really? Then why haven't I gotten it?"

"You didn't get it?"

"No."

"I don't understand. I told my secretary to get it out to you yesterday."

"Paul. Did you know that Alfred Hickey was killed yesterday?"

There was a long pause on the other end of the line. "No, I didn't. How? How did you know?"

"I found him in his office. What I think is so odd, Paul, is that Hickey was expecting me. He was going to give me his files on Mitch to look through for my investigation. I got there not an hour after I'd talked to the man, and he was dead.''

"Oh, my God, that must have been horrible for you." He was able to turn commiseration into a whine.

"Paul, there were no files there regarding Mitch. Nothing.''

"So?"

"So that makes me suspicious. I talk to him an hour before I get there, and when I arrive, not only is the man dead, but the papers I've come for are missing. Don't you think that's odd?"

"Well, now that you mention it . . . but wait, you don't think *Mitch* killed him, do you?"

Either Paul Levin was the dumbest man in the world, or he was playing dumb. I couldn't even dignify his stupidity with a response.

"Why don't you and I meet later today, Paul? That way you can just give me Hickey's report."

"Okay, well—my schedule is tight today, but I'm sure we can meet. How does . . . three o'clock look to you?"

"That's fine."

We arranged to meet at a coffee bar in his midtown office building. As soon as we hung up, I remembered to ask him for Billy Mazzio's number, but when I called back I made the mistake of telling his secretary I was me and she left me hanging on hold for three minutes. I would get Mazzio's number later when I met Paul. In the meantime there were plenty of things I could be doing—for example, I wanted to check out Hickey's office.

I had Hickey's home address from snooping in his office the day before. Just as Miguel had a gut feeling about the sweatshop, I had a gut feeling that Hickey had somehow played a key role in this. As a matter of fact, if he didn't, I'd eat a plate of fungus.

Ten

Despite Kerry's protests, I took Auggie with me to Bayside. In less than half an hour, I was standing in front of Hickey's office, wondering if the excessive yellow police tape threading the frame was really necessary.

I decided it wasn't, but as an ex-cop, I could no more cross that crime scene line than I could fly a helicopter. Instead, Auggie and I left the darkened hallway and went downstairs where Auggie—ever the connoisseur—took her time inhaling fire hydrant perfume in front of the Chinese restaurant in Hickey's building. A man and woman approached on the relatively desolate street.

As they neared, I could see that they were the owners of the restaurant where I had been questioned for an hour by Detective Nelson the day before. Though we'd barely spoken to one another less than twenty-four hours earlier, our meeting now was almost a sigh of relief. Recognition of having shared such an ugly event brought with it a warm greeting, as if long-lost friends had been reunited. Smiles, nods, a painful grimace, and then an uncomfortable moment.

The man, ready to start his workday, unlocked the gate protecting their business and shoved it noisily up into its metal sheath. The woman, whose dark, permed hair was sticking out from under a felt hat, finally broke the awkwardness. "I'm Isabel. That's my husband, Ken." He turned and nodded solemnly in my direction, but didn't seem to look at me directly. He then turned his attention back to the front door, which resisted until it finally gave in to the force of his shoulder.

"I'm Sydney. That's Auggie." I pointed to my pal who was sitting there, with her head tipped to one side, as if awaiting the introduction.

Isabel crouched down to Auggie and with a wide smile revealing extraordinarily crooked teeth, said, "Oh my, she's beautiful." After Ken disappeared into the darkened space, she asked, "You want tea?"

I glanced at Auggie.

Isabel stood up and moved toward the door. "Bring her in. It's okay. No one will see."

I warned Auggie to be on her best behavior as we followed Isabel and waited by the table where I had answered Nelson's battery of questions the day before. The place still smelled like wet mops.

Auggie found a spot by the small radiator in the window, curled up with a sigh, rested her chin on her paws, and within minutes was sound asleep. Such a difficult life these dogs have.

The overhead fluorescents flickered until the room was bathed in a stark white shadowless light. Isabel came back, smiled at Auggie, and told me to "Have a seat. Tea will be ready in a minute or two."

Ten minutes later she and I were sitting at the wobbly gray Formica table with tea and almond cookies.

"You knew Alfie?" she asked, as she moved the cookie plate closer to me. "Nice guy. Gonna miss him."

I warmed my hands on the chipped handleless teacup and asked her if she knew him long.

"Oh yeah, long time." Without her hat, her hair frizzed out as if she *was* static electricity. Her flat lips seemed to flatten even more when she frowned. "We all been in this building long time. Fifteen, maybe sixteen years." She tightened the corners of her mouth, which dimpled her chin. "Alfie was our first customer. I never forget. He had two egg roll and a Coke. That's his two-dollar bill." She motioned to a greasy wall taped with various denominations of currency, as well as an enormous one-hundred-dollar-bill with the owner, Ken's face, in place of Franklin's.

"Do you know what happened to Mr. Hickey?" I asked bluntly.

Her face became a mask as she brought her left hand to her hair, in an attempt to tame it. "Police say he hung himself."

"You knew him. Did he seem like the kind of guy that would do that?" I asked, though half of my question was swallowed by the noise of woks banging in the kitchen.

"They also want to know who went up to see him." She ignored my question and stole an almost coy glance at me.

"Do you know who went up to see him?"

She thought about this carefully before saying, "You."

"Yes, but they know I was there. Did you see anyone go up there, say, after three?"

"You *know* Alfie," she said, only this time she had shifted emotionally. Her voice had softened, and I realized that this guarded woman needed to share her sense of loss with more than the man in the kitchen making all the noise.

"I'm beginning to." I studied her face as she stared coldly out at the empty street. "You were close?" I asked, discreetly leaving my inference unspoken.

There was an imperceptible flash in her eyes, but enough for me to catch it. If Mr. Hickey and Isabel weren't paramours, I'd give up this business. The tip of her tongue barely peeked out between her dry lips and ran the length of her mouth.

"My guess is, the police think he was murdered," I said in a normal tone, knowing that Mr. Husband was fifteen feet away and could at least hear our voices under the clanging and banging in the kitchen.

She brought the tea to her lips.

"I know he was," I continued. "Which means they'll be asking you a lot more questions, if only because you had daily contact with him."

"They started. Yesterday. After you left." The unhappy woman beside me seemed resigned that her life had been irrevocably changed. "Who are you?" she asked without guard and with the cool reserve only a lover could ask of an unknown entity.

"I'm a private investigator. Like Hickey."

She regarded me carefully. "You worked together?"

"I've reopened a case he closed a while ago. Did you know anything about his work?"

She pulled at the long sleeves of her white shirt and I could just envision them together: the burly auburn lumberjack of a man and the Asian woman with large hands toughened from years of kitchen work. She eyed me carefully.

"I'm a safe place to talk," I said softly, as I brought the cup to my mouth, never once breaking eye contact with her.

She was like a bird listening for the cat and the worm at the same time. "Four o'clock. We talk then."

"Where?"

"You know Washington Square Park?"

"In Manhattan?" I asked.

She nodded. "I have to go downtown today. I meet you there. By the arch."

"Can you make it four-thirty?" I asked, knowing that I had a three o'clock appointment with Paul Levin in Manhattan.

She barely nodded, but I caught it.

"I'll be there."

Just then, Ken came shuffling out from the kitchen mumbling something in Chinese that sounded more like sound effects than an actual language. Isabel pushed her chair back and said, "It's where it always is, Ken, under the sesame oil." She went behind the counter and disappeared behind the partition. Ken shuffled to the table and stood there staring down at Auggie.

"You friend Alfie?"

From his intonation, I didn't know if he was asking about Alfie, or if Alfie and I were friends. "Yes?"

His eyes were void of emotion.

"Too bad about him. Police ask lotta questions yesterday."

"Yes."

"You saw him?" He glanced briefly at me, without turning his head, and returned his gaze to Auggie.

"Yes."

"Messy."

"I beg your pardon?"

"He was a messy man. Always food on his shirt, like he miss his mouth." He wiped invisible *shmuts* off his chest.

After several seconds, he turned to me squarely and said, "You know, mostly people get what they ask for."

It was a point I might have easily debated, but I had a feeling Ken had said all he had to say, so I let it go.

As I drove over to Hickey's apartment in Flushing, I couldn't help but wonder if Ken knew about his wife's affair with Hickey, and if jealousy had played a part in Hickey's end.

I opened the car windows a crack and left Auggie snoozing soundly in the back seat. Hickey had chosen a safe enough neighborhood in which to hang his hat, and I felt comfortable leaving Auggie unattended in the locked car.

In a block of two-family structures, Hickey's three-story

brick apartment building stuck out like a sore thumb.

"You the police?" a tired woman in pink curlers and a soiled housedress asked from a doorway behind me as I stood in front of Hickey's door, assessing the situation.

I turned and said, "I'm an investigator. Did you know Mr. Hickey?"

She shrugged and several of her chins jiggled. "Who knows anybody?" She hadn't struck me right off as a philosopher. "I thought you guys got what you needed last night." She bent down and picked up the newspaper, which was probably why she had opened the door in the first place.

"These things take time."

"What's happening with his apartment?" she asked.

"I don't know. You should probably ask the super." Before I could ask anything more of her, she turned and closed the door between us, clearly uninterested in anything other than Mr. Hickey's apartment.

For a man who had made his living prying into others' lives, I was surprised that he had protected his hearth and home with a simple single lock. Then again, once I had let myself in, it was obvious that this was a man with nothing to hide, since he kept everything he owned either on the floor or on countertops, spilling from drawers or piled on the furniture. His one-bedroom pigsty was on the third floor in the back of the building, and it took me a minute to conclude that his home had not been ransacked, or upended by the police, but rather, this was how he had lived. It was a sobering sight and one which made me question whether the organizationally impaired Hickey had even known where the Gerber file *was* when I had called.

Earthly possessions plainly meant nothing to Alfred. The living room consisted of a futon sofa whose fourth leg was a pile of paperbacks, a lopsided card table surrounded with three metal chairs, a bookshelf made from planks of wood and cinderblocks, and a small black-and-white TV with a hanger antenna. The TV and a clock radio seemed to comprise his entertainment center. The shelves were not for books so much as another place to toss the debris of his life, including condom packets, a half-eaten peanut butter and jelly sandwich, *Sports Illustrated*, *Screw*, *Playboy*, newspapers, mail (only half of which was opened), and loose photographs. I glanced at the pictures and noticed one which was wedged between the shelf and the wall. It looked like his lover, Isabel, Ken's wife. I walked to the window to see it better. Sure enough, it was Isabel, naked and posed in an impossible position I had to assume was Hickey's idea. Either that, or Isabel was some mean masochist. It was an embarrassing photograph and I wondered if I ought to take it to return to her for our four-thirty meeting. That way she could destroy it as she saw fit. Then again, since I had no right to be in Hickey's apartment and could legally be charged with breaking and entering, maybe it should be left for the police to find, or whomever would be cleaning up his life. Then again, if what Broomhilda, across the hall, had said was true, the police had already been here. Decisions, decisions. I put the picture back on the shelf and decided to decide later.

The bedroom was frighteningly filthy and the stench from the adjoining bathroom was nearly overwhelming.

Hard as I looked, I found no camera and no papers even vaguely related to Uncle Mitch's case. However, if warranty papers I found were up to date, I knew that he had purchased two new Nikons within the last two months, a sweet little autofocus model for quick shots (which is worth its weight in gold for *any* investigator), and an expensive manual with a variety of lenses, including zoom, for distance peeping. From the cost of the two cameras and his homey furnishings, it didn't take a genius to figure out that Hickey's focus was his work.

I poked around in his closets and cabinets, where I found several science projects, but nothing of real interest. Checking the undersides of drawers exposed a few more photos of women—not Isabel—doing dreadful things to everyday household objects and animals. It was the back of his bedroom closet, however, that made my adrenaline surge. Hickey had taped a computer floppy disk to the wall behind an empty hanging shoe rack. I carefully peeled it off the wall, slipped it into my bag, and traced my steps back through the living room and into the kitchen.

For any normal person, the kitchen would have been ideal, with a pantry off to the side, two windows (one over the sink), a dishwasher, and enough room for a table and chairs. Unfortunately, this was Hickey's home and there were neither a table nor chairs, but rather two barstools, one stacked with two phonebooks and a cordless telephone. The other was an end table for two empty beer cans, a softball and a tape dispenser. I picked up the phone and hit the redial button. The seven dial tones sounded oddly like "Mary Had a Little Lamb," but before anyone picked up on the other end, I was interrupted.

Fear is an amazing emotion. When I looked up and saw the person standing in the kitchen doorway, it felt as if my heart had literally stopped, turned to lead, morphed into putty, and bounced off the insides of my chest cavity. And yet I tried to make it look as if I wasn't the least bit fazed. "I'll be right with you," I told the figure who, dressed in black from head to toe, looked as if he was a Navy Seal in training.

I half turned away from him, then swung back around and hurled the phone directly at his head. No big surprise, he ducked.

A good detective can think on his or her feet and act out of sheer instinct. Or fear. In my case, at that moment, it was fear which compelled me to grab a pot encrusted with moldy spaghetti off the window ledge. I held it just below shoulder level, only because my bruised back resisted further range of motion. I hadn't reached for my gun because I knew he would have been on me before I could even swing my bag around and off my shoulder.

But I was wrong. I would have had plenty of time.

I could only see Mr. Seal's eyes and lips, since he wore a stylish black ski mask. The rest of him was also sheathed in black: black army boots, black jeans, black gloves, black ski jacket. He—and he was clearly a he because his snug outfit covered what was definitely a male body—seemed to be enjoying this as he stood staring at me from the doorway.

"What do you want?" I asked, knowing perfectly well that people in black head condoms usually don't just offer information.

He shrugged.

"I'm a police officer," I lied. I figured if, for some reason this knucklehead was with the force, he would at least ease off and ask for ID.

Instead he shifted his pelvis slightly forward, cupped his right hand to resemble a C, and stroked at the air in front of his privates. Oh, those international symbols—where *would* we be without them?

Okay, so now I knew he wasn't with the police force.

Options. The window ledge from which I had taken the spaghetti pot led to a fire escape. It was a guess if the window would open or not, but given how well Hickey tended his home, I suspected not. The window above the sink was too small to even consider, which left the doorway, where the great communicator stood, his hand resting atop his groin.

It was an abbreviated stalemate, but it gave me enough time to bring my pulse down to the point where my hands weren't shaking.

He dropped his hand and stepped toward me. I didn't move back. I smiled. He crouched and extended his arms at his side like a wrestler stalking his opponent. In that position, he effectively blocked the doorway. I inched to my right, toward the center of the room, where I wouldn't feel so trapped.

But he was fast. He leaned forward and in a flash he tackled me and had me down, his arms clenching my waist with what had to be his entire body strength. I felt like a tube of paste. I hit the ground not only with my full weight, but his as well. His arms and my shoulder bag broke my fall, but only somewhat. Between landing on my back—for the second time in two days—and this jackass crashing on top of me, it felt as if someone had sucked the air out of my entire being. Just below my rib cage, my lungs were crying out in agony, but oddly enough, throughout the initial skirmish, I was able to hold onto that filthy pot.

Given our positions, there wasn't much mobility, but his head was tucked just to the side of my right breast. Pain or not (and I was in plenty of it), I took that pot and cracked him as hard as I could over the head. He squeezed harder, clearly trying to break my back. As he tightened his hold on my waist, he tried to hoist me up so he could position his knee between my legs and get a real firm hold of me.

I tried to snatch off his cap with my left hand, but he wasn't about to be unveiled. He released my waist, snapped his right hand out from under me, and in a nanosecond had my left arm pinned over my head. In doing this he flattened his body against mine and I discovered, not surprisingly, that he found his line of work very stimulating.

I don't like fighting, and quite honestly, I'm getting too damned old for it. That's why we had hired Miguel, but even Miguel wouldn't have been a match for this one. There was no way, given this position, I could win. By the same token, neither could he. He pushed his groin into me and gyrated, which naturally pissed me off. Having already seen this bastard flinch when I'd tried to remove his mask, I squeezed his head between my side and my arm, gathered a mouthful of the crown of his cap between my teeth, bit down, and released him from my grasp while at the same time jerking my head back. The cap inched up and he went ballistic.

He was up on his knees in an instant. With his right hand he secured the mask in place, while he yanked his left arm out from under me, making me roll slightly to my left. Without missing a beat, I flattened the pot across the left side of his head and caught him square on the temple. If sound was any indication, the son-of-a-bitch was hurting. At the same time, because he had moved off me a bit, I bucked the right side of my body until it was off the ground. It was like poetry in motion when I saw his arms shoot into the air as his body lurched off balance, off me.

I slammed him again with the pot as I rolled in the other direction and used my feet to fight. There is a method of self-defense called *model mugging*, where women are taught how to be more evenly matched in a fight with a man. On our feet we're ordinarily no match, physically; men are faster, stronger, have a longer reach, and are usually more instinctive about fighting. But if a woman uses the power behind her legs and feet, she can be amazingly effective.

I pummeled the Navy Seal, landing solid, hard kicks on his legs and side. I wasn't in a great position, but at least he was off me, and if nothing else, I was bruising the hell out of him. Despite my hard work, he was able to twist back around and grab hold of my foot. I kicked free from him and tried to quickly slither on my backside to the door. He fumbled for my legs again and fell onto my left foot and shin. We were like two mud wrestlers, unable to get our equilibrium. I reached for my bag, and while I continued to kick him everywhere I could, I was also trying to work the Walther out of my bag.

One second of distraction is all it takes. In the second that I took my eye off him to unlatch the strap of my bag, he was able to thrust himself forward just enough to meet my chin with a well-landed right.

I have a thing about men who hit women. It really makes me angry. And since I'm a woman who's been trained how to fight back, I wasn't about to let this worm get the better of me. My head moved with his punch, but I rammed my foot deep into his stomach. I knew that one would take him out of commission, if only for a second. It was just enough time for me to get to the doorway and up on my feet.

My friend, however, had recovered enough to have hoisted himself up, using the counter as a support. On this counter was a knife. A really big knife.

Just as a good detective can think on his or her feet and act out of sheer instinct, he must know when to cash in the chips and run like hell.

I was out of the kitchen and halfway to the front door when he caught up with me in the living room. Aside from being trapped in a dead man's apartment with a knife-wielding psycho, there were two other problems I had to face. First, the clasp to my shoulder bag was stuck. Second, and perhaps more important, the tea I had had with Isabel was making my bladder feel like an overinflated water balloon. This was not good.

I could feel him just inches behind me. I took a leap forward. At the same time I spun around, my shoulder bag clasped firmly with both hands, and using it like a mace, I caught both his knife-holding hand and his head. The element of surprise is an amazingly effective weapon. It can turn the most formidable opponent into a blithering idiot, if only for a moment, and often a moment is all you need.

The knife went flying behind him, as he lost his footing and slipped on an empty pizza carton. It's funny, the things you notice in the midst of life-changing events. For example, I can still remember the sound of my mother's last breath and the scent of jasmine oil worn by an Indian internist who had stopped in to see how she was. I remember the sweet voice of a little neighborhood boy singing ''I'm Forever Blowing Bubbles'' when I learned of my father's death. And in that very same way, I saw that several slices of pepperoni were stuck to the lid of the pizza box the nasty man had slipped on.

Again, there are times when one should face down his opponent, and times when it is better to let it go. Though I could see that he and I were similar in size, it was equally clear that he was a lot stronger, and since his objective was to hurt or perhaps kill me, and mine was simply to survive, I grabbed the doorknob and bolted down the stairs like a bat out of hell.

I paused on the second-floor landing, both to catch my breath and listen for his footsteps. By now I had managed to open my shoulder bag. I had the Walther firmly in my grasp, but I kept my hand in my bag, in case a neighbor came out.

In the natural order of things, this guy would have been hot on my heels, but he wasn't. Now that I had the gun in hand, I could return to the apartment and confront him again, this time with some sense of being in control. Then again, what was to say he didn't have a gun? Granted, he hadn't pulled one at the kitchen door, but then, he might well have thought I would be an easy target. This was a man who knew how to fight, who knew how to destroy with his bare hands. If I returned to the apartment, I ran the real risk of getting killed, or killing him, neither of which seemed particularly inviting.

At that moment I was hit with an illogical panic: Auggie. I didn't know if the intruder was simply there to rob the place knowing it was empty, or if he was connected to Hickey through his work and was looking for something between them, for example, one of his porn pictures. There was the third possibility that he had followed me there. If he had, he might know that Auggie was downstairs waiting in the Volvo. I flew down the last flight of stairs and bolted to my car.

Any concerns I had for Auggie's safety were quelled when I found her sleeping right where I'd left her. I decided it might be prudent to wait in the car and see if Mr. Navy Seal came out.

Forty-five minutes passed without any movement from Hickey's building. The only activity on the street was a grocery delivery to the house next door, and an elderly woman leaving Hickey's building with a canvas tote. I figured, if the guy was at Hickey's to steal his valuables, he would have been out of there in under two minutes. If he was looking for incriminating pictures of a wife or female companion, it might take longer. If he was looking for the disk I'd found, he might well still have been in the apartment.

The car was cold. I was in need of a bathroom, and Auggie, not understanding the fine art of surveillance, bounced around the car, urging me to play. I decided to call it quits and head back to the city the third time she landed on my bladder.

Before I pulled out of the parking space I tried to call the police. After all, it was my civic duty to report a crime in process. If Hickey's visitor was still up there, I knew the police would want to have a chat with him, but there was too much static on my cell phone to hear anything. Figures.

You go to all the trouble to ensure you will always be by a working phone, and bam, the Cosmic Joker gets you. At the rate I was going, I could hardly wait to see what the rest of the day had in store.

Eleven

I was anxious to find out what Hickey was hiding on that disk, but between my stiffness from the day before and my most recent scuffle with the man in black, more than anything, I needed to be good to myself. In the back of my mind I heard Max's voice nagging at me to report the confrontation at Hickey's to the police, but I decided a quick trip to Tina's Gym was the first order of business. Not only could I get a puppy-sitter for Auggie, and a workout, but I might be able to test the disk on a PC in case it wasn't formatted for a Mac, which is what I have. Parking, on the other hand, proved not so easy. I circled a three-block radius of the midtown block where she is located above a pizza parlor ten times before parking at the overpriced minilot a block away.

My friend Zuri, who is both a boxing coach and a computer whiz, was behind the counter when we arrived at the gym. Ever since Auggie became a part of my life, I've learned how to play second fiddle. Do my friends ever greet me first now? No. Now it's usually a high-pitched squealed greeting that sounds something like, ''OhAuggiepuppy-comeheresweetheartandgimmieakiss.'' Followed with, ''Sydney, how could you name her Auggie? It's an awful name.''

For the record, I did not name her Auggie, though I am not apologizing for the name; it suits her. Auggie was named by her first owner, a cartoonist whose life ended abruptly and without warning. The cartoonist's husband had no room in his life for a dog, one thing led to another, and though I resisted at first, I became alpha dog to the most amazing animal in the universe.

Both brilliant and beautiful, Auggie is "a real catch," as my Aunt Sophie would say. Half golden retriever and half Samoyed, she has enormous brown eyes, wonderfully floppy ears, black lips that curl up into a wondrous smile, and a big black nose. She is biscuit colored and resembles a Günd stuffed animal. She tells you when she needs to go out; she will go to the pantry if it is a treat she has a hankering for; she cocks her head from side to side as she listens attentively to all you say; and she has a wonderful fashion sense. When Leslie dresses in the morning she will ask Auggie, "How do I look?" If Auggie mumbles— which is guttural growling—and then hides under the bed, Leslie changes. If Auggie sighs and drops her head onto her paws, Leslie changes. I have suggested she quit asking Auggie, because clearly nothing is good enough for her.

"Auggie!" Zuri held out her hands for my furry friend.

In great excitement, Auggie raced over to Zuri, skidded around the counter, pounced up on her lap, and issued a series of high-pitched puppy yelps as she licked Zuri's face.

"Should I tell you where her mouth has been?" I asked.

Tina Levitt, the institution behind the institution, came out of her office as soon as she heard Auggie.

"Where is she?" Tina asked, wiping her glasses on her shirttail. Before she could get the glasses in place, Auggie was barreling toward her. Tina raised a knee and slightly turned her body. "I'm too goddamned old to risk breaking a bone because of this one." She then bent down to Auggie-level and offered the mature welcome, "Whatza-whats?" She repeated it several times over through clenched teeth and a broad smile.

"Girl, you *know* her mouth is a fat lot cleaner than

yours.'' Zuri stood and followed Auggie with her eyes.

"My mouth is just fine, thank you."

"Sure could have fooled me." Tina glanced up from rubbing Auggie's exposed belly.

"What's that supposed to mean?" I asked, shifting my weight from one foot to the other, knowing it was my bladder I was concerned about.

Tina and Zuri glanced at one another.

"What?" I repeated, only this time I didn't wait for a response. Instead, I excused myself to go to the ladies' room. It was there I caught a glimpse of myself in the mirror.

The lower left portion of my chin was already swollen, and the redness promised a bruise was soon to follow. Three strands of Hickey's old spaghetti had also apparently dislodged from the pot and clung to the top of my head. Very attractive.

Auggie was in Tina's office with the big boss herself, playing a rousing game of tugga-tugga with a jumprope. Tina had the handles in one hand and Auggie had the midsection of rope in her mouth. Tina, who was sitting on her desk chair, was being rolled around the room by a very determined puppy.

"You need some ice?" she asked.

"No, but I need your computer." I unfolded a card chair she had stacked next to a file cabinet and made myself comfy behind her desk.

"Don't break anything."

"I won't."

"What are you going to do?"

"I just want to look at a floppy."

"Maybe you should ask Zuri to do it . . ."

"I don't need Zuri . . ." I slipped on my reading glasses. "I just want to see if I can read this."

"Zuri!" Tina called out. "Come in here for a minute, will ya?"

Bingo. The computer accepted the floppy. I opened it up and saw there were fifteen GIF files listed, which meant that what we had here were pictures, not document files.

"What?" Zuri stood in the doorway. Even in sweats the woman looks great. She had recently shaved her head and the effect was startling. First of all, her skull is amazingly dent free. Add her long neck, high cheekbones, almond-shaped eyes, and skin as smooth as honey, and she resembles Grace Jones more than a boxing trainer.

"Nothing," I said as I opened the paint program from accessories so I could see what I had here.

"I don't want her to break anything," Tina stated from the far side of the room, where fickle Auggie had dumped her to go acourting Zuri.

Zuri came and stood behind me.

"I won't break anything." It was like negotiating with one's mother. Zuri and I waited for the file to open.

"Famous last words. That's all I need, you know."

"Teen, you're turning into a cantankerous old coot."

"Yeah, well, money doesn't grow on trees." Tina rubbed her khaki-clad thighs. "If you need a computer, you should get a real one and not that antiquated piece of garbage you have."

"Girl, you need a man, that's what I think," Zuri said to Tina, as she rested her hand on my shoulder.

Tina hooted. "I *had* a man."

"Uh huh, that was *how* many years ago?"

"Oh, for Christ's sake, a drink will do me a lot more good than a man at this point." Tina wheezed a laugh.

"Amen, sister." I squinted at the screen.

"That is disgusting," Zuri said, when the first picture became clear.

We both leaned forward and peered at the screen.

"What?" Tina asked, as she wiggled the rope at Auggie, who had discovered the wastebasket.

"Oooeee, that has to hurt." I grimaced at the picture and opened a new file.

"What?" Tina started toward us, using her feet to paddle forward on her chair.

"Too late," Zuri said, as she headed back to the reception desk. "Disgusting pornography, that's all. Not what you would expect from Sloane."

"Really?" Apparently Tina found the prospect of nudie pictures so irresistible, she got up and pushed her chair back to her desk.

"And you think you don't need a man," I said, as I moved the folding chair out of her way. I asked if she would watch Auggie while I did some stretching.

"Go, go." She waved me out, her eyes already focused on the computer screen.

"Let me know if you find anything interesting." I left her, changed into workout clothes, and spent the next hour trying to make right what felt terribly wrong.

Before I left I placed a call to Kerry. It was already almost noon and we hadn't been in contact all morning.

"Where the hell have you been?" She made me feel like a wayward daughter. "Your friggin' cell phone kept saying you were out of range."

"Is everything all right?"

"Everything is fine. Except that I'm starving."

"It's not even noon."

"Yeah, so?"

I could tell that she was ready for a fight, so I quickly shifted from boss to sympathetic friend. "You haven't had lunch?"

"Nooo, I'm swamped. Remember, I'm Cinderella left

behind to make things easy for everyone else while they
go to the ball.''

"Speaking of Cinderella, have you heard from Miguel?''
"No.''

"All right, listen, I'll be back within half an hour with
lunch. Anything I need to know?''

"No.''

"Good, I'll be there shortly.''

I put the disk, which Tina deemed disgusting, back into
my bag and headed back to the office.

Kerry was on the phone when I walked in with Auggie
and a couple of trendy vegetable sandwiches. Her eyes
grew wide with excitement. "It's Max!'' She pointed to
the receiver.

I dropped the sandwich bag on her desk and made a
beeline to my office. Max assured me that he and his new
bride, Marcy, who happens to be one of my favorite people
in the world, were having a perfect honeymoon.

Auggie went directly to her little basket of toys and
plucked out a fleecy camel complete with squeaker.

"Then why the heck are you calling us?'' I asked, more
loudly than was probably warranted, what with fiberoptics,
but hey, they were half a world away in St. Bart. It was
then that I noticed the rectangular package wrapped in
brown paper on my desk.

"Just checking. Making sure the business is surviving
without the glue that keeps it together.''

"It's not easy, Elmer, but we're trying our best.'' I proceeded to tell him about Uncle Mitch's case and all the
feelings it stirred up in me. Auggie pushed Mr. Camel
against my legs, prodding me to play with her. I took the
camel and tossed it across the room, where she chased it
and made a mighty pounce, trapping it beneath her big
paws.

"Why didn't you know about this in November?'' This

bothered Max almost as much as it did me. "Does Nora know?"

"I can't imagine she does. She would have called me." It disturbed me that I hadn't even considered my sister before. I scribbled a note to call her. "As far as *my* not knowing, apparently it was buried in the newspapers, but Minnie and I were both out of town that week. Elly said no one from the family called because they were embarrassed."

"That sounds like bullshit."

"I agree. But in all fairness, I think they were angry I hadn't called them. Mitch gave me the impression that he was hurt I never contacted him. But I didn't know."

"Did you tell him that?"

"Of course I did."

"Did he believe you?"

"Who knows? I can't read these people anymore." I read the return address on the package. It was from the law firm representing my dear dead friend Ned. I pulled scissors from the desk drawer.

"Well, that's definitely one of those things you need to be clear about."

"I will." I sighed.

"Essentially from what you've said, they have one piece of evidence—the crowbar with the fingerprints, right? That's no big deal . . ." Max said.

"Nooo," I hedged. "Don't forget, he has no alibi," I reminded him, as I snipped at the twine fastening the package.

"Right. Also, as you said, he's got excellent motive, opportunity, and access."

"Right. And an eyewitness places him at the scene."

"What?"

"Apparently this guy sat on the witness stand and swore he saw Mitch at the factory near the time it went up."

"Well, that's not good."

"By gumbo, I like the way you hit the nail on the head."

Auggie gave up on the camel and curled up under my desk with a big sigh.

"Why, thank you. So . . . the investigator who was hired to prove Mitch's innocence told the family they didn't have a prayer. Not liking his assessment, you're called in to have a look-see, and—poof—he's killed. You think his death is connected to Mitch?"

I paused. "Hard to tell. From what I've been able to gather, Hickey specialized in family matters. But it looks as if he did more with his camera than just catch spouses in the act." I told Max about the dirty pictures, Isabel, and her husband's cool reaction to Alfred's death.

"So, Mr. Hickey could have upset any number of people."

"Right."

"Including Uncle Mitch."

"Right. Or anyone in the Gerber clan."

"Well, it'll be interesting to see what you find out from your cousin Paul. How's Miguel working out with this? Is he helping?"

I gave Max a detailed account of our wunderkind's progress and ordered him to get back to the beach and Marcy. I neglected to tell him about my tryst at Hickey's.

After the call, I opened the package. Inside it was a tarnished but beautiful trumpet, the one that had belonged to Ned. I read the formal letter from the attorney and picked up the instrument. I don't play, but Ned had made magic with this thing. I slid the mouthpiece into place and wondered if, having been neglected for all these years, it would ever play again. I turned it around and looked into the bell. Much to my surprise, there was something in there. A piece of paper. It read:

Dear Syd Baby,

If you're holding this, then you've won the bet and I'm proud of you, my little chickadee. If someone else has it, a hex on you, buddy.

Syd, baby, remember what BB once said: "Don't be afraid of death so much as an inadequate life."

Well, darlin', chances are I'm having too much fun to miss you. Hope you can say the same.

Always,
The Tempo Maestro

The handwriting was tight and squished, slanted at an uncomfortable angle, just the way I remembered it. I could just picture Ned, crouched close to the paper, clutching the pen as if it might pop out of his grasp.

I missed my old friend.

"Kerry?" With his note in one hand and the trumpet in the other, I went to the outer office. She was already halfway through her sandwich. She looked up from her computer screen with a full mouth and raised her eyebrows in response.

I held up the note. "Remember Ned?"

She nodded and swallowed. "Oh wow, his trumpet. You finally got it. Hey, are you okay?"

"He left a note." I handed it to her.

She read it and asked, "Who's BB?"

I shrugged. "I don't know. Who?"

"I don't know. *You* don't know?"

"No."

"Well then, knowing Ned, this has got to be some sort of game-from-the-grave thing, don't you think?" She was up, out of her seat, wiping her hands on her jeans, and leading the way back into my office. "Give me your ad-

dress book,'' she said over her shoulder, as she went to my
desk and pulled out a printout of the address book on my
computer. ''B.B. I bet he quoted someone you both know
and you maybe fell out of touch with.''

''Why would he do that?'' I asked, carefully pulling off
the mouthpiece.

''Oh, come on, that would have been *just like* Ned. Heck,
look at how he continued your bet after he died. This is a
man with a scheme.''

''Was.'' I put the trumpet back in its worn blue velvet-
lined box.

''What about Robert Bendler?'' she asked, as I dropped
the mouthpiece back into a velvet jewel bag. ''Who's he?''

''Robbie's that chiropractor I introduced you to a couple
of years ago. Remember, the one who lives in Seattle?''

''Oh my God, how could I forget him? I slept with him.''

I turned and faced her. ''You did?'' The thought of Bob
and Kerry romantically linked was almost absurd. She was
Kerry, and he—well, he looked like (and had the personality to match), one of those rubber dolls you squeeze and
their eyes and tongue pop out.

Her right hand was covering her chest as if she was about
to pledge allegiance. ''I can't believe I forgot his name.
This officially makes me a slut, doesn't it?'' She looked up
from the address printout. ''I have finally slept with so
many men, I can't remember them anymore. Okay. Okay,
it's a sobering thought. My mother would be ashamed. You
got something on your lower lip.''

I touched my mouth and felt the bruised spot from the
Navy Seal. ''Look, you haven't been with anyone since
Patrick, right?'' I was referring to her artist boyfriend.

''Of course not.''

''In that case, I don't think you qualify for slut.'' I
reached for the printout. Maybe she had a point, maybe
Ned was trying to tell me something from the great beyond.

Right, and the next thing I knew, I'd be basing life plans on my horoscope.

"Really?" She seemed relieved.

"Really." I paused. "An old tramp, maybe, but not a slut."

"Oh well, hey, that makes me feel much better."

I reread the note. *Don't be afraid of death so much as an inadequate life*. "Maybe he was trying to tell me that he thought I was in danger of living an inadequate life," I mused. "You think I have an inadequate life?"

Kerry scratched the back of her neck and yawned. "What's inadequate, anyway?" She got up and stretched. "Look, he was just probably passing down some wisdom before he kicked the bucket, you know? I wouldn't even waste my time thinking about it."

"Really? This wouldn't bother you?"

"Of course it would bother me, it would make me totally paranoid. But you're not me. You're more like Xena, Warrior Princess. In the meantime, being the trusty but thorough sidekick, I have some stuff on Hickey. I'll be right back."

Being mere mortal and not a TV princess, I admit, the note disturbed me.

I reached for the phone to report what had happened at Hickey's to the police when Kerry came in. "So, I got some stuff on Hickey," she said, as she flopped on the sofa.

I hung up the phone. "Oh, good, that reminds me, I have to look at a disk I took from his place."

"Now?"

"No, I can't. It's formatted for a PC."

"So?"

"So, we have Macs here."

"So?"

"So the left hand can't see what the right hand's doing."

"I have a new Mac, Sydney."

"So?"

"So, depending on the file format, I maybe able to read your floppy."

"Really?"

"Really."

"Let's do that."

She heaved herself off the sofa and continued talking as we got situated at her desk. "Hickey, who turned forty-four last week, was born and raised in Jersey, went to Vietnam like a month out of high school, got all sorts of medals, and came back a hero, but no one cared. This is it?" she asked, taking the disk I held out to her.

"Yes."

"When he came back he joined the police force for a while, but it wasn't an easy time for him. First, he seemed to have a discipline problem. Second, evidence would sometimes disappear when he was involved in a case."

"Drugs?"

"Money and drugs. But no one could ever pin anything on him. When his father died in '79, he left the force and opened his own security company. Don't forget, the guy's only, what, twenty-eight at this point, a vet from a mind-altering war, and an ex-cop with a touchy background."

"What are you doing?" I asked, as she zipped through the keyboard commands as quickly as her story.

"These are all picture files, I'm going to open them in a paint program."

"Right. I did that on the PC at Tina's. These are pornography," I warned her.

"Cool." She folded her hands primly in her lap and waited. "He was married for two years, but that was when he was a cop. They divorced; he never remarried. He has been in business as a private investigator for the last fifteen years or so and he has a reputation—oh my God, how can she do that?" Kerry gaped at the screen.

As we went through the fifteen photos—each more disturbing than the last and several featuring Isabel Wang—I couldn't help but think of Tina, sitting at her desk, clicking through these images of women in submissive, abusive positions. I felt ashamed.

"Jesus Christ, this guy was a sicko," Kerry proclaimed, when the show was over.

"Could this have been what that guy was looking for?" I wondered out loud.

"What guy?"

I gave Kerry an abridged report of my morning adventures, including my encounter with Isabel and a toned-down version of my wrestling meet at Hickey's apartment. If I recounted the full-blown fight, I would only scare us both.

"I can't imagine anyone would attack you for a dozen filthy pictures."

"Not even if his wife was the one with the chimpanzee or the sumo wrestlers?" Just the thought of the photos made me sick, because they went way beyond pornography. It forced me to consider yet again what it really is that sets humans apart from the rest of the animal kingdom. Only the human mind could contrive such torture and humiliation *and* feel the need to record it on film. I was haunted by the faces of the women in the photographs and couldn't help but wonder if this was something they had done willingly, and if so . . . why? Why would Isabel Wang, for example, allow herself to have been photographed in such demeaning positions?

Ned's words filled my head, loud and clear: *Don't be afraid of death so much as an inadequate life.*

"Could this have anything to do with Mitch?" Kerry asked softly, as she handed me back the disk.

"No." I barely heard my own voice as I got up and started back to my office. "I have to believe that Mitch and this are two very separate issues. You know, Mitch may not approve of me, but he's a man with a great deal of integrity.''

Kerry nodded, but we had both seen those photographs and we both knew the world well enough to know that anything is possible.

"What are you going to do with it?'' she asked, referring to the disk. ''I mean, the last thing you want is for someone to find that here, right? That would be totally embarrassing.''

"You're right.'' I paused before entering my office and turned left. ''I'll put it in Max's desk.''

Twelve

Kerry agreed to take care of Auggie for the rest of the afternoon and bring her home at the end of the day, which freed me up to meet Cousin Paul, who was waiting for me at a tiny marble table covered with torts and tortes.

"Sydney!" He held out his arms but didn't budge from his seat. His eyeglasses moved up on his cheeks when he smiled, and he seemed genuinely glad to see me. "I hope you don't mind, but I took the liberty of getting you a nice piece of Linzer torte. I saw it was the last one on the plate and I remembered you like raspberries." His brown suit jacket strained against even the slightest movement. "Sit. Sorry about the mess." He shuffled the papers into one big pile and rammed them into his big brown briefcase. He was extraordinarily pale.

"I'm touched you remembered I like raspberries."

"Oh, yeah, well, who could forget the raspberry sauce you made for Elly's cheesecake that Thanksgiving?"

Clearly I could. It had been over ten years since I had shared Thanksgiving with my mother's side of the family. I nodded in a noncommittal way and took my seat. "You look like a busy man, Paul."

"*Oi*. Busy isn't the word." Having cleared the table of papers, he went on to rearrange the plates. I got the Linzer torte and he took the dregs of an espresso and what looked to be coconut cream pie. "You look good." He nodded, but it seemed impossible that he could see me through his smudged glasses. His lips were unusually red against his very light skin and I was reminded of the cartoon *Clutch Cargo* from my youth. In that animation, which I saw only at my paternal grandmother's house in Wisconsin, they had inserted real mouths in the cartoon heads, creating an effect that made watching the action of the show impossible for me because I was so mesmerized by the teeth and the lips. I looked away from his mouth and scanned the room for a waitress.

"Thanks. I feel good."

"Good. Good. Life is good?" He continued nodding.

"Yes, life is very good." I caught a waiter's eye. "Aside from this nasty bit of business with Mitch, I'd say life is good for all of us."

"*Oi,* Mitch." He bent his head sadly as he clicked his tongue against his teeth. I could see his scalp through his thinning pate of sandy brown hair.

"I'll have a coffee, please," I told the young waiter, who had absolutely the most enormous nostrils I had ever seen, no doubt enhanced from my vantage point.

"You?" He poked his nostrils in Paul's direction.

"Yeah, yeah, I'll have another ex-presso. Two twists." He held up two fingers in case the waiter didn't get it. The boy sniffed and went to get us our caffeine fixes.

"So . . . things are good." Paul checked his watch.

The thought of trying to make small talk with Paul was more than I could bear.

"Do you have the file?" I asked, getting right to the point.

"Oh right, yeah, sure. Sure. It's right here." He slammed a fist into his briefcase and started rummaging through the contained confusion.

"I forgot to ask you when we spoke earlier, but I also need Billy Mazzio's phone number and address, if you have it."

He took out a fistful of papers, examined them over the rim of his glasses, and shoved them back into the mess.

"Do you have Mazzio's number?" I asked, as I watched him extract a file folder from his case.

He glanced up at me. "Mazzio? Sure." He pushed his glasses back up on to the bridge of his nose.

The coffee was delivered and I tried not to peer up into the caverns of the waiter's nose. Instead, I added milk and sugar to my cup and wondered how a man like Paul could represent anyone in a court of law and hope to win. He was like a cloud of confusion.

"Ah, here we are." Paul scanned through the crumpled pages before shoving them into a folder and passing them over to me. "Elly told you that Alfred Hickey thought Dad was guilty, right?"

"Yes."

"As you'll see from his report, he concluded that the evidence against Dad was just too compelling, especially with the eyewitness."

"Do you think this Mazzio was telling the truth?"

"Unquestionably not. The man was lying through his teeth, any fool could see that."

"Any fool except the grand jury, the investigators, the DA's office, and . . ." I rustled the papers in front of me, ". . . it would seem, Hickey."

Paul pushed out his lower lip in distaste. "What I don't understand is, why would the kid lie about this? At first I thought, maybe he wants to get even with Mitch about something, but he doesn't even know Mitch. So then I ask myself, why would the kid be in that neighborhood at that hour, anyway? He lives in the East Village, so naturally I figured it had to do with drugs. That was one of the first things Alfred investigated. But," he motioned to the folder in my hand, "the kid was clean. He even volunteered for drug testing and a lie detector test."

"And he was in Corona at that hour because . . . ?"

Paul sneered. "He said he was in the neighborhood because he had been rehearsing with a woman in his acting class. He says he was walking to the subway and just as he passed Jake's place, he bumped into a man who was leaving. In a hurry."

"Mitch," I said.

He nodded.

"What about his rehearsal partner?"

Paul pointed limply to the folder in my hand. "Her name is Kirstin Johns. Both hers and Mazzio's numbers are in there." He sighed. "Unfortunately, it all gels. She says Mazzio was with her, until about one, one-thirty, she couldn't be exact. Apparently she's a *very reliable witness*. My ass. They're both lying through their teeth, but I'll be goddamned if I can figure why." He popped one lemon twist into his mouth and squeezed the other into his demitasse cup.

"Usually people lie because they're protecting someone, or getting paid."

"Yeah, well, maybe you'll figure out which it is. Hickey seemed to think that they were on the level. I *still* don't buy it. But then again, I hired him for his expertise." Unable to fit his fingers into the demitasse handle, he delicately lifted the cup between his thumb and middle finger.

"Why did you drag your feet with Mitch's suit against Jake?" I decided a question from out of left field might result in an honest answer.

Paul faced me straight on, but much to my surprise, he was able to disguise his feelings brilliantly. My clumsy, cordial cousin turned from putty to steel before my very eyes, a metamorphosis that was almost as disturbing as the fact that he had dragged his feet with Mitch's initial lawsuit.

"I'd say that's a nasty accusation," he growled, as well

as a man with a painfully nasal voice can growl.

I looked the picture of innocence.

"Just where do you get your information?"

"History." I neatly tapped the papers back into the Hickey folder and placed it in my lap. "Jake opened his business, knowing perfectly well that Mitch would sue him as soon as he opened the doors. Mitch finds out about it, comes to you, and nearly three months later, still doesn't have a court date?" I rested my arms on the small table and leaned forward. "I'd say that was dragging my heels, wouldn't you?"

"When did you get your degree in law?" He tightened his face, squinting and pursing his lips into an ugly smile. It only made him look like a nearsighted mole.

"Look, I am going to find out what happened at Jake's, which will mean a thorough investigation. Naturally, that will include you and whatever role you might have played here—"

"Are you suggesting . . ."

"Relax, Paul, I'm not suggesting anything. I'm informing. I'm telling you because as I see it, you and I are working together to gather the proof needed to vindicate an innocent man, who happens to be my uncle and your father-in-law. Now, as part of this investigation, I have to look at it from the very beginning, which means answering the first question, which is: why was this case not settled months earlier? Why had this thing not gone to court two months earlier? If nothing else, why hadn't Jake been slapped with an injunction of some sort at least to curtail his activity? Maybe I'm wrong, but the man had signed a noncompete agreement. I should think that that alone would be enough to close him down in a second."

Paul shook his head smugly. "Not quite, Sydney. It is illegal to prevent an individual from making a living. The law is very clear about that." He scooped up the last of the coconut cream pie and shoveled it into his mouth. "Also, contrary to what you may think as a layman, the system is not nearly as simplistic as TV makes it look. We are dealing with people's lives, and thus the system is a methodical process. All steps were made to prevent Jake from conducting business. The records will show that I did everything humanly and legally possible to hasten this case. If you feel the need to question that, I can only infer that you doubt my veracity. If that is the case, I don't see how you can then presume that we are 'working together.' "

Check.

I knew that if I wanted anything from Paul in the future, I had to concede at this point.

I held out a white flag. "I would never doubt your veracity, Paul. But if I'm going to do my job correctly, I have to question everything, even the things that seem most innocent. Surely you can appreciate that."

Paul polished off his espresso, placed the empty cup in its little saucer and wiped his lips with the heel of his hand. "Of course I appreciate that. You're a professional, which is why you just might be the one to pull Mitch out of this unfortunate mess." We were best friends again. "We all know how talented you are, Sydney."

I didn't know who "we" was or what sorts of talents "we" thought I possessed, but his tone of voice was fused with both intimacy and sarcasm. I had no doubt that Paul was sending me a message, but it went way over my head.

"So. How did you know Alfred Hickey?" I changed our direction.

"Al and I had worked together a few other times in the past. Very successfully, I might add. How did I meet him?" Paul mused. "Word of mouth. One attorney tells another, who tells another. Before you know it, you've built up a practice . . . isn't that how it works, detective?" He winked conspiratorially.

"Were you friendly?" I asked, as amiably as I possibly could.

"Friendly?" He sighed. "No. I wouldn't say that we were friendly. But wait, in qualifying that I'd have to say that we were friendly, but not friends. We never socialized, if that was what you really meant to ask." He smiled. I didn't tell him there was pie on his chin.

Though we had just made nice-nice, Paul was angry, and his anger alone revealed a great deal.

"That is what I meant, thank you." I took a sip of weak coffee. "Were you satisfied with how Hickey handled his last assignment for you?"

"Well, I certainly wasn't pleased with the outcome."

"No, I know that. But were you satisfied with the way he had conducted the investigation?"

Paul looked utterly blank.

"What?" I asked.

"Well, now that you mention it, I don't know *how* he conducted the investigation. I mean when he was finished, he handed me his report, along with an invoice." Paul gestured to my lap, where Hickey's report lay. "I disagreed with his determination. I talked to Elly, and then Mark, and then we all decided to call you. But I hadn't assumed to even question the way he went about investigating this for us."

"What about the rumors that Jake's place was a sweatshop?"

"Between you and me?" He glanced up at me over the rims of his glasses. "I think it's just that; rumors. I know what Elly and Mitch say, but I think they're letting their emotions overrule logic. Think about it, a man with Jake's reputation would never run the risk of doing business like that. It wouldn't make any sense."

"Why not?"

"You don't work your whole life to build a reputation

for being one of the most consistent estimable contractors in the business and toss it off. For what?''

''Profit?''

Paul pooh-poohed this notion. ''Jake doesn't need money. Between the settlement and his investments, the man is quite comfortable. From what I understand.''

''Then why start a new business at this stage in life?''

Paul gave me the same exact response Jake had, almost verbatim. ''To show Mitch up.''

''How close are you and Jake?''

''I like Jake. I always have,'' he said, defensively at first, but then, as if hearing himself, he softened. ''Don't forget, I married into this family. I understand the rivalries, but they're not necessarily mine. I mean, I may not always agree with the way my family sees things, you know what I mean?''

''Yes, I do.''

''Of course you do. You've been off Mitch's A-list for a long time now, haven't you?'' There was a snakelike quality to Paul I'd never noticed before, but then, we'd never had more than a passing conversation at family gatherings.

I smiled.

He smiled.

The pie was still on his chin.

''Speaking of which, how is your friend?''

From the oily way he'd asked, I could only assume that he meant Leslie; however, as the attorney had not qualified himself, I answered (with a sincerity befitting Pippi Long-stocking), that Max was doing just swell. ''He's married now,'' I added, and pushed away from the table before he could respond. ''Listen, as much as I'd like to stay and chat, I have a meeting in fifteen minutes. What do you say I call you tomorrow, to touch base?''

Paul looked confused. "But wait, the Linzer torte," he whined, as I motioned for the waiter.

"It looks great. You have it." I motioned for another espresso, with two twists, and was out on the street before Paul could remember I had Hickey's folder.

On the subway to Washington Square, I read what Hickey and Paul called a report; however "report" was an exaggeration, as it was slightly more than a page and a half outlining what Hickey said he did and found. There were names, dates, vague recollections of conversations, and Hickey's impression of each interviewee. The last paragraph summed it all up.

```
Hickey Investigations respectfuly sub-
mits that we have been unable to uncover
sufficient evidence to prove Mmitchell
Gerber's innocence. Bassed on an exhaus-
tive investigation (See exhibits A thru
H), it is mmy opinion that Mitchell Gerber
would be best served pleeading temporary
insanity.
```

Thirteen

Though I was ten minutes early, Isabel was already pacing anxiously under the arch at Washington Square as students, tourists, locals, and drug dealers went about their business and pleasure. She was wearing the same outfit as before, complete with felt hat, only now she had accessorized it with a plaid scarf. A large brown paper bag banged against her leg as she walked from one side of the arch to the other. It was hard to imagine that she was the same woman in the pornographic pictures I had seen earlier.

Despite the cold, the park was packed. A gaunt man in a lime green, lemon yellow, and strawberry red knit cap constraining what had to be snakes and snakes of dreadlocks strolled past me. He summed me up with glassy eyes and asked, "Yo, mama, you need something? Anything. Just ask for me, Lifesaver."

I wondered if I looked like I could use something. Ten paces away from Isabel, I called out. She turned, as if shocked with a cattle prod, and let out a sigh when she saw it was me.

"Are you okay?" I asked.

"The police came back today. After you left." Her eyes were bloodshot.

"You knew they would."

"They took Ken." Her eyes couldn't conceal her panic.

"The police took Ken in for questioning?" I made her stop pacing to answer me.

"Yes."

"Did they arrest him?"

"I don't know. I don't think so." A thin blue vein in her forehead looked ready to burst.

"It's going to be all right. Look, why don't we go someplace where we can talk? I'll buy you a drink."

She slapped her thigh, said something in guttural Chinese, and went to storm away. She got two steps before she turned around and said, "You Americans. Is that all you think about? Money, sex, and drugs? You all alike!"

She looked so innocent, clutching the shopping bag in front of her with both hands, but considering that I had seen pictures of her as a sexual contortionist, I figured this was a clear case of the pot calling the kettle black. I studied her haggard face, taut with anguish, and felt only compassion for her. "Come on," I said, gently taking her arm. A stiff wind snapped through the park, blowing garbage and old leaves into eddies. "I know a place nearby." She let me lead her out of the park, onto a side street, to a restaurant four steps below street level.

It was too early for the dinner crowd, so Francine at Mama Leah's was glad to give us a table for cocktails. The dark hole-in-the-wall of a restaurant was the perfect place for the kind of anonymity that Isabel needed. We slipped into a small wooden booth, lit only by a dim wall sconce and a red votive candle. I ordered a cappuccino and Isabel ordered a double Scotch neat, water on the side.

I waited while she slipped out of her scarf, coat, and sweater. The felt hat remained firmly in place.

"Do you have a lawyer?" I asked, after she had taken her first sip.

"Not criminal." What with her fingers and shoulders and face contorting with tension, her body was shrieking, but her voice remained surprisingly calm.

"That's okay. Now, I want you to tell me what happened."

By the time she had finished, she was halfway through her drink.

Essentially, the police had found out that Isabel and Alfie were friends. "Good friends," she explained, but didn't go into detail. "Then they came to ask us questions. Lunchtime is very busy for us. First they talk to me."

"Who talked to you?"

"Same woman as yesterday. Same woman who talked to you."

"Detective Nelson."

"Yes, that's right. She was nice, very nice, but the next thing I know, after they talk to Ken, she told me they have to take him with them." Isabel was ashen.

"Did they say why?"

She shook her head. "No. Only that they needed to ask more questions."

"What kind of questions did they ask you?"

"They didn't ask about Alfie."

"What do you mean?"

"They only ask questions about me and Ken. Like how long we been together. How we stay so young looking." Isabel squeezed out a sarcastic smile. "She very nice and tell me I don't look fifty."

"You're fifty?" I asked, totally floored. The woman looked a good ten years younger than I did, both in and out of clothes.

"Tai chi. It keeps you limber. And yoga."

"Ken does tai chi, too?"

"Yes. Ken also has black belt in karate. He teaches."

"Did Ken know that you and Alfie were lovers?" I asked, after Francine placed a complimentary plate of bruscetta on the table between Isabel and me. The blended aroma of piquant garlic and sweet basil was nearly intoxicating. My stomach let out a long, mournful growl.

Isabel winced, but she never took her eyes off mine. "How did you know?" she finally asked.

I gave a shrug, told her it was pretty obvious and asked again if Ken knew.

"I don't know. I think he suspect for a long time." She pushed her drink away from her. "But he knows now."

"Has he seen the photographs?" Elbows on the table, I rested my chin on my thumbs, trying to look casual, as if this were no big deal.

She hid her face behind her hands.

"Do you know if the police have found them?" I asked.

She uncovered her face and shook her head. "I don't know. Probably. Oh God, I just know they gonna show him the pictures. That's why they took him away, they gonna show him the pictures and blame me. They gonna think I killed Alfie."

"You killed Alfie?" I couldn't hide my surprise. "They won't think you killed Alfie. If anything, they suspect Ken, which is why they probably took him in for questioning. But without a shred of evidence, they won't be able to keep him."

I knew from what she had already told me that he had been taken into the precinct at about one o'clock. Detective Nelson had assured them that there was no need for Isabel to come to the stationhouse. She had further assured the frightened woman that Ken would be home in time for dinner. Ken insisted that he would be all right and that Isabel should finish the lunch shift. I didn't know if Ken had seen the photographs, but since jealousy is always a good motive for murder, I asked again.

Her body practically vibrated when she sighed. "I don't think so," she said uncertainly.

"Do you think Ken killed Alfie?"

She shook her head. "No." This time her eyes met mine

with absolute certainty. "Ken would never hurt another
person."

"Really? Not even if the man was fucking his wife?"
Crude, but effective.

She glared at me for several seconds and I could see the
debate whether to stay or leave raging in her eyes. In the
end she chose to stay. "No. Not even if a man was fucking
his wife. You and Alfie do same thing," she added, never
taking her eyes off mine.

Not wanting my calculated crudeness to be mistaken for
Hickey's style of trash, I felt the need to clarify what she
might have meant. "We're both private investigators, is
that what you mean?"

She nodded once, opened her bag, and pulled out a standard size ten envelope. I was surprised by its weight when
she handed it to me.

"Alfie gave this to me night before last. He told me,
'Anything happen to me, you give this to the lady detective.' He wouldn't tell me what he was doing, I think because he was afraid for me, but he said he checked on you
and you have good reputation, not like him." She paused
long enough to work her mouth into a bittersweet smile.
"He said if I don't get something from you, I should tell
police what I gave you."

I slid my index finger under the sealed flap and opened
the envelope. The reason for the heft of the envelope were
ten packets of crisp new hundred-dollar bills bound in the
neat, official paper wrap popular in banks. One hundred
hundred-dollar bills, which meant that I was sitting there,
in a public place, with ten thousand dollars. Fortunately I
hadn't pulled it out of its wrapping for the world to see,
not that Francine and three waiters were the world, but one
can never be too careful with lots of money.

Also in the envelope was a letter. I read it carefully, and

by the time I finished reading Hickey's note, I was in a foul mood.

Dear Ms. Slone,

If your reading this, that means I'm shooting pool with Pappy. It also means you are envolved in the bullshit. Now, I could make it real easy for you and just tell you who did mme and why, but I figure you like to solve things and if your anything like mme, you could use an extra buck. So here you go, your lucky day.aA client from the grave.

   Find out who 86ed me, and skim off ten Franklins from the inclosed pile. Give the rest to Izzy, she could use it.

   Two steps away
   Where it began
   Youll find the man
   Who mmet the man
   Another man will hold the key
   Of what befel poor Mmitch and me.
               Happy hunting, and thanks.

                    Yours in the afterlife,
                    Alfred Quentin Hickey

I read the note, annoyed at this idiot's idea of fun. My face must have revealed what I was thinking, because Isabel said, "Alfie can be real frustrating." She said this, however, with affection, and affection was the last thing I was feeling for good old Alf.

I slipped the note and bulging envelope past the plate of bruscetta to her side of the table.

As soon as she saw the wad of bills, her hand flew to her chest and she gasped. "Oh, my God," she exhaled. She looked carefully around the empty restaurant, and holding the envelope close to her chest, read Alfred's letter.

"Do you know what he's talking about?" I asked.

She shook her lowered head.

"Can you tell me anything about the case that he was working on? Or people you saw visit him during the day? Anything."

Isabel looked up. "Like I told the police lady, there isn't much traffic in our building and you can't always see if someone is going in the front door or past it."

"Are there other occupied offices in the building?" As I recalled, the building had felt pretty empty.

"No. The landlord wanted to renovate and charge a lot more money for rent, but Alfie had two more years on his lease and he was holding out. He wanted them to give him money and find a new place for him to relocate in the same area."

"What about the restaurant? Were you and Ken going to be evicted, too?"

"Our lease is up in August. I don't know what we're going to do."

"So you didn't see anyone going into the building that day?"

She shook her head.

"When was the last time you saw Alfie?"

"The last time I saw him was yesterday. He stopped in to get lunch, maybe about one o'clock."

"What did you talk about?"

"His lunch. The weather. The landlord." She paused and sighed. "Ken was there. We always tried to be cool when Ken was there." This was clearly not an easy confession, and I was having a hard time matching the docile woman sitting across from me with the one in the pictures.

"When was the last time you and Alfie had a chance to really talk?"

"The night before we spent some time together. That's when he give me this." She tightened her hold on the envelope. "Ken was teaching." She blushed and looked away. "But we didn't talk much. He not the kind of guy to talk business with me."

"Did you have the kind of relationship where he would open up to you, confide in you? Was he in good spirits when you last saw him, or was he tense? Did he mention anything about work? Perhaps someone was giving him trouble . . . anything."

Isabel reached for the Scotch glass again and clasped it tightly in her large hands. "You know, now you mention it, he got a call that night that disturbed him. I know it was a man, because I heard the voice when the answering machine picked up."

I couldn't remember seeing an answering machine in Hickey's apartment.

"Did you hear a name?"

"No. But Alfie raced to the phone when he heard the guy."

"Where was the machine?" I asked.

"In the bedroom."

"Did you hear any of their conversation?"

She took a sip of Scotch as she thought about it. Unable to contain myself any longer, I reached for a bruscetta. The warm bread had soaked in the juice of balsamic vinegar, olive oil, tomato, and garlic, and it was just sheer willpower that kept me from moaning in food ecstasy.

"I heard him say, 'You can't buy her, man,' and then he asked me to get him a beer. When I came back, he was angry. He told the guy to go screw himself, hung up, and when I asked if he was all right, he said that some people just don't like to play the game. I didn't know what he meant, but there were lots of times I didn't really understand him. He was deep. Very deep.''

Deep was not the first adjective that sprang to mind with Hickey, but I let it go.

''And you said that was the same night he gave you the envelope?'' I asked.

''Yes. Just before I left to go home, he opened my purse and put it inside.''

''And all he said was if anything happened to him you should give it to me?''

''That's right.'' She studied the dregs of her drink. ''Funny thing, I didn't even question him about it. I hear the way it must sound to you, but that's not the way it was with us. What we had was, I don't know, it was . . . different.''

And so Isabel Wang summed up her relationship with Alfred Quentin Hickey as precisely and succinctly as was humanly possible.

Fourteen

It was after six by the time I got back to the office, so it came as no surprise that Kerry had left for the day. What did surprise me, however, was that she had left Auggie behind with Miguel Leigh, who, while waiting for me to return, was entertaining himself by reading a text manual for homicide investigation.

He looked quite comfortable, stretched out, shoeless, on the sofa in my office. His left foot was covered with a bright red sock which had a hole exposing his baby toe. The blue sock covering his right foot was perfectly intact.

"Nice socks," I greeted my associate.

"Lividity," he said, jumping right into a pop quiz.

"Okay, I'll tell you, but you're skipping chapters and quite honestly, homicide is about point zero, zero, zero one percent of our business."

"Yes, but don't forget, Sydney, homicide is what brought us together." He rested the opened book on his flat stomach, keeping his place near the gory pictures of dead people.

"As I recall, it was theft that brought us together, a bungled theft, at that, and *you* would be well advised to keep that in mind forever and always."

"Aaaayyee, quit being an old lady."

"Thin ice. Very thin ice," I warned him playfully, as I dropped my bag with Hickey's file and Isabel's hefty envelope on the desk. I flopped down on my chair. "Lividity, also known as livor mortis, is postmortem discoloration due to the gravitation of blood. In other words, when you die, your heart stops pumping, so the blood will pool in the vessels where you lay and fix in certain areas of the body. Now, you tell me four key things you should have on hand when tailing a suspect.''

"Food. Water. Reading material. And a jug to piss in." He kicked himself up into a sitting position.

"Well, one out of four isn't bad. What's this?" I reached for a stack of folders Kerry had left for me. Each was clearly marked with the tasks of her various research, and one was dedicated to my phone messages for the day. I fished my reading glasses out of my bag and discovered that in the folder marked *Abilene Insurance* there were two neatly typed pages. The first clearly stated that Brenda Hillsborough, the investigator handling the case, had determined that Jake Aronson had had nothing to do with the fire that destroyed his business and was therefore entitled to the reimbursement due him on his policy. The first line of the second page stated that for all existing records, Jake Aronson was the sole owner of Aronson Elite. With the rest of the page, however, Kerry explained how contractors in the fashion industry are oftentimes funded by mob-owned trucking companies. The trucking companies provide start-up loans, will arrange a rental lease as well as leasing equipment, and will even provide operators (who in this case would be Jake), with orders from manufacturers. Kerry ended this page with a personal note:

No indication that Jake was funded. Moody Plevin's name never enters documentation until after the fire. Jake's client roster shows that he was working with many of the same clients he and Harriman's still shared. His bread and butter seemed to come from Unicon, a corporation which owns several large de-

partment store chains and manufactures its own clothing lines. Unicon, however, has a history of working with sweatshops and has been brought up on charges in the past. Plevin's has never been investigated for unethical business practices. I will follow through tomorrow with more research on Unicon.

Another folder labeled *Hickey Dossier* was considerably thicker. Among other things, Kerry had run a credit check on Alfred and a quick glance was all I needed to confirm that the money he had passed on to Isabel (who'd begged me to hold onto it for her for safekeeping), would probably never show up on a W2 form. Though Kerry had run through much of the information with me before, she included the paperwork of Hickey's records. On paper before me was documentation of his life educationally (high school graduate), militarily (honorable discharge, many medals for bravery), professionally (police force for several years before dipping into the evidence till and leaving without benefits), and personally (only child, divorcee, parents deceased). It didn't add much to the picture I had already painted of the man myself.

"Aren't you wondering why I'm here?" Miguel brought me back to him.

"The thought had entered my mind." I opened a folder marked *Messages*. "But then, I just assumed you missed me today. Either that, or you're trying to make up for being late this morning."

"Jeez you don't forget nothing." He sat up and slipped on his shoes.

"Anything. Yes, well that's rule number eighty-four in the detection business, 'Forget nothing.' See? You're learning all the time. Isn't that exciting?"

"It is." He stood up and stretched his lean body, making

himself look like Silly Putty. "You know what I did to-day?"

"Hung around Brooklyn and waited for Mr. Mali?" I leafed through the messages.

"Nope. I went to midtown."

He tickled my curiosity. "Really? Why?"

" 'Cause that's where my friend Tim works. He's a union man."

"Ah-ha."

"But he like works on the computers, you know what I mean?"

"Nearly." I had a sneaking suspicion that Miguel had used his head instead of his passionate instincts this time at bat. I took off my glasses and gave him my undivided attention.

"Well, you know when I left here this morning I was like in a hurry, you know, but I wasn't real sure where I was going. As soon as I got downstairs, I heard you talking about knowing the background and telling me to focus. So I started walking. Downtown." As he told his story he wandered around the office, checking the streets below, straightening knickknacks and books on shelves, but never really looking at me directly. "Because walking helps me focus, you know? So by the time I got to Lincoln Center, I had one thing figured out." Here he looked at me; my cue to ask what.

"What?"

"If this Jake was running a sweatshop, you know the people who know these things would know it." He nodded proudly as he crossed his arms over his chest.

"They sure would. Now, which people would that be?"

"The *Union* people," he said, as if he was talking to the rationally impaired.

"Help me out here . . ."

"I don't know anything about sweatshops, but we all

know it's illegal and there has to be someone monitoring these things, right? Well, there is. And *I* know the man who's doing it!''

"Your friend Tim."

"Bingo."

Bingo is not a word I would usually identify with my young New Yorikan associate, but it is a word I frequently use. It was odd hearing it come out of him, and I indulged in a split second of recognition that there was a bond being made between us.

"So instead of going on a wild goose chase to find Mali, you went to your friend at the Union and checked into Jake Aronson's business."

He looked oh so proud of himself, standing there, posing like Mr. Clean in the middle of my office.

I was *k'velen* myself, thrilled that he had taken the initiative to approach this step by step, but instead of back-patting, I asked, "What did you find?"

"There was a report on record that Aronson Elite had been flagged as a sweatshop contractor, but these things are hard to prove." He took the seat across from me. "First of all, it wasn't your run-of-the-mill sweatshop. He had some heavy-hitting clients, most notably Unicon, who owns the Faber and Langer department store chain. But think about it, he had a legitimate background, and was respected, even, so no one's going to question him too much. However, they were keeping an eye on him.

"See, a lot of ugly stuff goes down in this business. The workers are treated like subhumans because all that matters is money, and believe me, it's not like the owners of most of these shops are raking it in hand over fist, especially if organized crime is involved, which it is a lot of the time. If they're involved, those guys suck up an enormous percentage of the profit.

"Anyway, apart from physical abuse, sexual harassment,

subminimum wages—and we're talking worst-case scenario, a salary of like ten dollars for a fifty-five-hour work week—these places are not only pigsties, they're fire hazards. It's not unusual that the workers are screwed out of half the money owed them because who are they going to complain to? Most of them are illegal immigrants.''

"Ten dollars a week?" It wasn't possible to exist in Manhattan for ten dollars a week. Street people make more than ten bucks a week.

"Well, like I said, that's the worst-case scenario, but it happens. Usually they get like three dollars an hour, but like I said, even then they rarely get their wages (a) on time or (b) in full. It sucks.''

"Jake was running a shop like this?"

He paused and held up a finger. "Jake was, in all likelihood, running a sweatshop, but, a sweatshop . . .'' He lifted his bottom off the chair and pulled a piece of tattered paper out of his back pocket, from which he read. "A sweatshop is defined as: '*a business that regularly violates both wage or child labor and safety or health laws.*' In the scheme of ugly ways to do business, maybe Jake wasn't as bad as the worst of them, but he was doing something wrong. That's why I wanted to talk to Mali. But this time, like you said, I knew what I wanted from him, sort of. At least when I went to him this time I'd know what I was talking about. See, I figure we're not going to learn anything about Jake until someone who was in there talks, right?"

"So you went to Mali?"

"I know you told me not to talk to him, but I made an executive decision. I was jazzed after what I found out from Tim, but I didn't just race off looking for Mali. First, I went to some of the buildings Tim told me had sweatshops in 'em.''

"Where?"

"Between Fifth and Ninth Avenues, stretching from Thirty-fifth to Fortieth, there's a whole slew of them. These people hand out maps of these places."

"Who does?"

"These Union people." Out of his other back pocket Miguel produced another folded piece of paper and flipped it onto my desk. Indeed it was a photocopy of a map of that area with building numbers indicating where one could find what I assumed were sweatshops.

"So I walk this stretch, like I'm looking for work, but let's face it I don't look much like a man of the cloth, so to speak, but after awhile I realize you don't even have to pretend you're looking because some of these places are wide open. They keep the doors open and anyone can just look in and see what's up. So if you're just passing by it looks like nothing. Anyway, at about four o'clock I went to see Mali again."

"Was he there?"

"No. But his girlfriend with the big mouth was. First thing she tells me is that Mali doesn't want her talking to me no more."

"Anymore."

"Right. So I put on the charm and I ask her why. At first she's what you would call reluctant, but then I give her this real pathetic face and she falls for it." He barely stifled a smug smile and continued. "Remember, she thinks I'm looking for a dead friend. Anyway, she says she doesn't understand him, that he just didn't seem to like me. Then she kind of smiled at me like she was sorry and she goes to say good-bye and close the door.

"But I don't let her. Instead I ask her if she worked at Aronson's, too, and she says no, she has a steady job cleaning for a nice lady in Manhattan who speaks Spanish. I tell her that's great, and then I ask if maybe I look like someone Mali doesn't like. She says, no, she doesn't think that's it.

Then she gets real quiet for a minute, like she's debating whether to tell me something, and finally she says that Mali was hit real hard by the fire at Aronson's. She said he wasn't the same after the fire. Her guess is he's having a hard time with me because he has such a hard time with that. I nod, real sympathetic and make a sound like, 'oh, the poor guy, what a tough break,' but again she says I should go and she makes a move to close the door. I'm telling you, I was beginning to feel like one of them door-to-door salesmen.'' As Miguel continued, I was struck by how mature and confident he looked. "Lucky for me, just as I was leaving, Mali showed up.

"Now, the second he sees me, I know something's up. His whole expression changes, he turns totally pale, like he's gonna be sick, and he misses a step. I honestly thought at one point that he was going to bolt. But he didn't. Instead, he comes right up to me and suggests we talk downstairs. When we get there, he asks what I want. So this time I don't even give him a song and dance about my friend that I'm looking for. This time I ask him point-blank if Elite was a sweatshop.

"Now I had his attention. The guy looks at me like he's really weighing whether or not he's going to answer me, but he doesn't. He just mumbles something about not knowing anything about the woman in the place and how sorry he was that I couldn't find my friend, but that maybe I should talk to Jake, or the police, because they have the body. I look at him like, what are you, nuts?''

"It sounds like he was trying to be helpful."

"Not if I'm looking for an illegal immigrant. And that pissed me off because I know he's lying, so I grab his arm as he starts to leave and I say, '*I know what happened.*' ''

"You did? But you don't."

"Right!"

"What did he say?"

"Well, first it stopped him right in his tracks. Then he snaps his arm away from me. I reach back for him, but I miss. He gets to the top step of his building and I call out, '*If you think I won't tell, you're wrong*!' And that's when he froze. Just totally stopped, turned back to me, and asked, 'What do you want?' " Unable to contain his excitement, Miguel was now up on his feet. "I tell you, I'm dying here. I didn't know what the hell to tell him I wanted, so I just look up at him real seriously and said, 'You tell me.' " At this Miguel did a little jig. "*You tell me!* Am I Clint Eastwood, or what? The man looks like he's about to wet himself and I am *cooool,* I have never been cooler in my life. He's looking at me. I'm looking at him, and then, after what feels like a friggin' hour, he says, 'Where can I reach you?' "

As pissed as I was that Miguel had deliberately gone against his directive, I knew if I had been in his position, I'd have done the same thing. And there was no question about it, his hunch had paid off. This was hot, and so far, I had to admit, he had handled it beautifully.

Miguel had told Mali that he would meet him at a Latino nightclub on Friday at midnight. Since it was now Wednesday, that gave us two days to find out just what it was Miguel was supposed to know. The first pieces of the puzzles were beginning to fit into place and the feeling was electrifying.

Miguel and I spent the next hour and a half going over every detail we had gathered. The white board was covered with information detailing the timing of things—who was where when, the exhibits A through H, which Hickey had appended in his report to Paul (this included his interviews with Danny Aronson, Jake Aronson, Billy Mazzio, Billy's acting partner, Kirstin Johns, Mali Cajina, and Mitchell Gerber, photos from the fire site, and his assessment on the evidence gathered by the authorities). All in all, it looked as if Hickey hadn't put much time or energy into the case, despite his having collected $5,000 in fees. Seeing all the facts up on the board got us both stirred up and we had hypotheses flying all over the room. One thing was startling clear, though: we had no firm alibi as to where Mitch was at the time of the crime, which was crucial.

"Maybe he was home, like he said." Miguel offered him the benefit of the doubt.

"No, I don't buy it."

"Why? We already agreed that the eyewitness was lying."

"We *assume* Mazzio is lying, but we haven't even met him. We may well believe him after we've talked to him." I saw the corner of Isabel's envelope poking out of my bag. "Oh, but wait, I completely forgot about *this*. Listen." As I extracted Hickey's note, I explained to Miguel what had happened during my meeting with Isabel. When he was updated, I read, "Two steps away, where it began, there was a man who met a man. Another man will hold the key of what befell poor Mitch and me. Happy hunting, and thanks. Yours in the afterlife, Alfred Quentin Hickey."

"What the hell's that?" Miguel reached for the letter, read it to himself before copying it up on the board.

" 'Where it began' has to mean the factory, right?" Miguel paced with a blue marker in hand.

"Or could it be Harriman's, the shop that Mitch and Jake co-owned? That could be the place where it all really began. But what I'm thinking is that there are definitely three men involved here, right? You find the man who met the man. What do you think, Mazzio and Mitch?"

Miguel erased more and more of our previous notes on the board as we dissected the riddle, trying to incorporate all configurations of known players. We were so involved in what we were doing that we were both startled when the phone rang.

"CSI, may I help you?" I answered.

"Do you have any idea what time it is?" Leslie asked.

"Umm," I glanced at my watch and was amazed to see that eight o'clock had come and gone. "Holy cow, look at that. Time just flies when you enjoy your work." I looked over at Auggie, who was lying by the windows, facing the avenue. She shot me a sad-sack look of the long-neglected puppy, which made me feel about a centimeter tall. I was starving my dog, and no doubt contributing to a future bladder infection.

"Okay, listen, Dot and I are going to the movies . . ." Leslie continued.

"Oh honey, I forgot your mom was coming."

"That's okay. I just want to know if you want to go to the movies with us?"

"What are you going to see?"

"A tearjerker. Mom wants to cry."

"Isn't that nice, well, you know what the lady said, '*Laughing and crying you know it's the same release.*' "

"What lady?"

"Joni. Mitchell? Joni Mitchell? *Big Yellow Taxi? Woodstock?*" The ten-year age difference between Leslie and me doesn't often rear its obvious head, but when it comes to music, she and I are in two completely different realms. Disco accompanied her childhood, whereas I got the benefit of Hendrix, Joplin, Taylor, Nyro, King, Morrison, Mama Cass, and even little depressed Janis Ian. Leslie asked again if I wanted to join them.

"No, thank you."

"Okay. There are leftovers in the fridge for you."

"What?"

"Meatloaf."

"Dot's meatloaf?"

"Yes."

"Ooh, thank you."

"I can assume you have fed Auggie?"

"Un-huh," I answered vaguely, figuring she could assume anything she liked.

"Did you find out who started that fire yet?"

"Nope."

"You will."

"Yep."

"I love you."

"You too. Have fun crying tonight."

"So what do we do next?" Miguel asked, as soon as he saw the call was over.

"First I have to feed my dog." I walked over, picked her up, and cuddled her. "Then we need to interview everyone involved, which means Billy Mazzio, Kirstin Johns, Danny Aronson, everyone. We need to check and double-check alibis, including cousin Mark's claim that he was in Long Island. I am determined to find out where Mitch was the night of the fire. I want to get as much information on Mali Cajina as humanly possible. Now my guess is Kerry should see how much she can get on Mali from here and you should verify all alibis, which shouldn't take all that long." I picked up Hickey's report and tossed it to him. "Here. Everyone's alibi is listed. You know, another thing that's been bugging me is that yesterday, when I was scheduled to meet with Mitch and my cousins, he had made another appointment."

"What do you mean?"

"I mean Mitch knew we were going to be working together and yet he had made plans to meet someone at one o'clock."

"Who?"

"I don't know, and oddly enough no one called him on it. All I know is that it was in the city, but I don't know where."

"So, what are you saying?"

"Nothing," I muttered, waving off the feeling in the pit of my stomach as hunger.

"You know, maybe he just didn't want to spend too much time with you. From what you said, you make him uncomfortable."

"Yeah, maybe you're right. What do you say we call it a day and start tomorrow at nine, okay?"

"Okay."

I took Auggie to Riverside Park on the way home, where she played the puppy version of tag with a beagle named Barney and a black lab named Coochie. I talked with the dog owners, trying to fend off the feeling in my stomach that I knew wasn't hunger at all. Something was gnawing away at me and I wasn't sure if it had to do with Uncle Mitch, Hickey and Isabel, or the general sense of foreboding I felt concerning Miguel's scheduled meeting with Mali.

After dinner I called the number for Billy Mazzio that I had gotten from Paul. It was different from the one George had given me earlier, and as it turns out, it was the correct one. He answered on the third ring.

"Speak." A television was blasting in the background.

"Billy?" I strained to hear against the noise on his end of the line.

"Yeah."

"Billy, my name is Sydney Sloane and I'm investigating the fire at Aronson Elite. From what I have heard, apparently you are the man to talk to."

"Sloane. Name doesn't ring a bell. Oh Jesus, look at that!" he called out to someone he was probably watching TV with.

"There's no reason it should. I'm relatively new to things. I was wondering if we could meet."

"Oh shit! Get up, you asshole! *Get up*!" I could hear cheers and hoots from his television as clearly as if it were my own. "Oh fuck. Fuck, you fucking asshole maggot scumbag wimp." The cheering and catcalls were severed. I heard Mazzio sigh.

"When can we meet?" I asked, in a far more civilized tone.

"What? Now?" He sighed again, probably making certain I understood his frustration.

"Whenever it's convenient for you. Tonight. Tomorrow. We need to talk."

"Tonight's not good."

"Tomorrow, then?"

"Yeah, lemme think. I have . . ." He trailed off as he mumbled to himself the various commitments he was obliged to the next day. Finally he said, "I can fit you in at ten A.M."

"Okay. Where?"

"Sado's. You know it? Over in Alphabet City?"

Sado's is a trend-setting eatery for the sado-masochist crowd in the Lower East Side. "Sure. Ten o'clock?"

"That's right," he sang. "Just ask for Billy."

"I'll be there."

Without another word he hung up.

I left a message for Kirstin Johns asking her to call my office the next day and then I called Danny Aronson, whose machine played its message and beeped, but the beep just kept going and going and going. I made a note to call him in the morning.

Needing to get my mind off work, I tried to read, but my attention keep wavering. Television had nothing to offer, and before I knew it I was sitting on the sofa with two photo albums; one my mother had compiled, and one I had put together shortly after her death, when I was nineteen.

Her album cover was thick panels of leather and the black pages backing the black-and-white photos were captioned in Mom's careful, white-inked script. On these pages, the histories of the Sloanes and the Gerbers were recorded in pictures. Sepia-toned photos of people I never knew or barely recognized gave way to black-and-white snapshots that covered my parents' courtship. I hadn't noticed it before, but in each and every photo of the two of them, there was physical contact between them. From the earliest stages in their dating, to the pictures I had slipped into the plastic sheaths of my album, they were touching one another; a hand on a shoulder, fingers interlaced, knees touching. Their love as palpable on the page as it was in life.

And for some inexplicable reason, this made me cry.

Fifteen

"Sydney, dear, it's time to get up." I had forgotten the tenderness of my mother's touch and how some mornings I'd pretend to still be asleep until she'd sit beside me and push my hair off my forehead with her fingertips.

"Sydney." I awoke to a gentle voice and the scent of lavender. Leslie's mom, Dorothy, was standing over me as I lay on the sofa. "Sydney, dear, it's time to get up."

Behind Dorothy, Leslie was holding Auggie and I felt a little like Judy Garland in the *Wizard of Oz . . . Oh Auntie Em, it was the strangest thing . . .*

"You missed a good movie, Syd." Inasmuch as Leslie's eye make-up was long gone, I came to the conclusion that mother and daughter had found the tearjerker for which they were looking.

"Those Italians do it to me every time. Are you okay?" Dorothy pressed the back of her fingers against my cheek, which made me feel vulnerable. I sat up and moved the photo albums off my chest and onto the floor.

"I'm fine, thanks. What movie did you see?"

Over tea, Leslie and Dorothy told me the entire movie plot, detailing the life of a postman in a small coastal village. Like witnesses at an accident, they disagreed on any number of storyline points, but both had been swept away with the final third of the film. Leslie rested her feet on my lap while mother and daughter disagreed with one another good-naturedly.

Early the next morning, after tossing the ball for Auggie in Riverside Park, and before Leslie and Dorothy had cracked an eyelid, I took off for an early swim at the local trendy gym.

I box (which is the most thorough calisthenic workout), I practice yoga to keep myself limber, I have taught model mugging, and I have been known to play a mean game of racquetball, but swimming is far and away the most Zen of all the disciplines I know. Within the last few years the gentle solo sport has really grown on me. The act of working out by propelling my body back and forth in a pool filled with ostensibly clean, cool water appeals to all my senses. Admittedly, as a New Yorker who craves big empty spaces, I do not particularly enjoy it when every lane is filled with swimmers, but on a cold, early morning in February, it can't be beat.

After working out, I picked up an egg on a roll with bacon and cheese from a wonderfully greasy deli just a few steps from the office. As much as I believe in proper diet and putting really healthy things into my-temple-my-body, the fact is, life is meant to be lived, which means one must partake in comfort food every now and then. It is no secret that fat and grease are essential ingredients for comfort food, to wit, a warm roll with cheese is a whole lot more comforting than granola with yogurt. Why? Because cheese is something that can really wrap itself around you and embrace you, whereas what does granola do? It's like a high colonic's best friend. With that in mind I got myself an extra large coffee. Heaven.

As soon as I got into the office, I tossed the morning paper, my shoulder bag, and breakfast onto my desk. I had just unwrapped my cholesterol-on-a-roll when the phone rang.

"CSI, may I help you?"

"Sinda?" I was surprised to hear Mitch's voice.

"I'm sorry, there's no one here by that name, but this is Sydney. Perhaps I can help you."

"Very funny," he said without humor.

"Uncle Mitch, is that you? Good morning. How are you?"

"I'm not so good. What, I have to hear from Paul that this Hickey character is dead? You don't talk to me?"

Whether it was wishful thinking or not, there was no question in my mind that this was Mitch's way of extending a white flag. Normally, I prefer the direct approach, but that's the thing about a truce: it demands compromise. "I've been a little busy, Uncle Mitch."

I took a bite of breakfast, holding the receiver well above my head so he wouldn't hear me eating. My chin still hurt where I had been punched the day before, but at least there was no outward sign that I had been in a scuffle. Oh vanity, thy name is *moi*.

"Your aunt wants you to come to dinner tonight." He paused. "We both want you to come to dinner tonight."

I swallowed and brought the receiver to my mouth. "You know, I think you and I need to maybe talk first."

"What talk? We'll talk tonight. Be here at six-thirty. Sharp." He hung up before I could tell him no.

"*Oi*," I grumbled when I dropped the receiver in place. I turned on the computer, finished breakfast, and checked to make sure Isabel's envelope was still in the locked file cabinet where I had left it the night before.

It was nearing eight by the time I'd finished my coffee and had a cursory glance at the paper. I checked the list of things to do which Miguel and I had compiled the night before.

Call: Kirstin Johns
        Danny Aronson

Meet: 10AM : Billy Mazzio @ Sado's Café

Kerry: Compile roster of Aronson employees. In-
         depth check on Mali Cajina. Get list of
         names of people closest to Mitch at Har-
         riman's.

Miguel: Alibi check on all selected parties involved,
         including: Mitch, Jake, Danny, Mark, and
         Elly. (Except Mazzio & Johns, whom I
         would cover)

I picked up the phone and dialed Danny's number. The
answering machine kicked in again, as it had the night before, only this time the beep was abbreviated and I was
able to leave a message. "Hey Danny, it's Sydney Sloane.
I don't know if your dad told you, but I'm investigating
the fire and I was hoping we could meet sometime today."
I left him my office number and called Kirstin Johns.

"Hullo?" a sleepy voice answered on the first ring.

"Hello, may I speak with Kirstin Johns?"

"Who is it?" As the female voice on the other end of
the line became more awake, her tone turned more sultry
than sleepy.

"My name is Sydney Sloane. I'm a private investigator."

Sigh. "You haven't called at a real good time."

"Gee, that's too bad, because I have a check here for
Ms. Johns." Okay, so I was lying, but I had a hunch that
without sweetening the ante, this young woman was going
to blow me off like a feather on the wind. The sad but
funny thing about people is that most of them will listen
when the prospect of money looms before them. The
woman left me no choice but to be fleetingly dishonest.

"A check?"

"Yes, indeed." I scribbled a checkmark on the pad in front of me.

"What for? For how much?"

"Is this Ms. Johns I am speaking to?"

"Yes." I knew by the edge to her voice that I had hooked her. Now it was just a matter of reeling her in without breaking the line.

"I am calling with regard to an inheritance, but perhaps I should call back at a better time?"

"Who are you?" she asked distrustfully.

"I work for the law firm of Lubendeck, Deckenmeil, Meilmike, and Covendeck." I made it a point to run my words together.

"Huh?"

"Perhaps I should call back tomorrow," I suggested, cradling the phone between my ear and shoulder. I wrapped an *S* around the checkmark so it looked like a dollar sign.

"Wait a minute, wait a minute." She had gone from morning sultry to nasal irritant in one easy swoop.

I slipped Ned's note off the desk and read. *Don't be afraid of death so much as an inadequate life.* BB. Who the heck was BB?

"Yes?" I prompted Kirstin while I studied Ned's handwriting. Who was I going to give his trumpet to? It had to be someone special, someone who would understand the real value behind it.

"Who died?" She cut right to the point.

"We represent the estate of . . . Ned Madison." This fine name was inspired from a photo of Madison Square Garden on the cover of the *New York Times*.

"Who?"

"Mr. Ned Madison? Unfortunately Mr. Madison met with an accident several months ago and his estate is only now being settled—oh, I am so sorry, did you not know about his passing? My, my what a horrible way to be told,

I do most sincerely apologize.'' I took a quick breath and continued at the same rapid pace, hopeful that she wouldn't be so gauche as to ask who was Mr. Madison when he left her money at his passing.

''But why?''

''Why am I sorry? Well, to be perfectly frank with you, Ms. Johns, this isn't the first time that Lubendeck, Deckenmeil, Meilmike, and Covendeck has had me break the news to unsuspecting inheritors. It places me in a very bad position, don't you think?''

There was a long pause on the other end of the line.

Undoubtedly, Kirstin would be pissed when she realized there was no inheritance; however, I was certain that if she knew I was investigating the Gerber case, she would have blown me off. I figured if I paid her off for information—especially when the money came from Hickey's payment to unearth the truth—it would be as good as an inheritance.

We agreed to meet at her apartment in Corona at five, which meant that I would be in the vicinity of Mitch and Maddy, and therefore, dinner at six-thirty was suddenly doable. I placed a quick call home and asked Leslie if she had any interest in meeting my maternal side of the family, an event which oddly had not arisen in the three years we had been together. She did.

Next was a call to Maddy and Mitch to make sure that it was okay with them that I brought Leslie along, after all, she was part of the package now. Maddy answered and told me that Mitch had left for the office at around four that morning, but had told her I was coming for dinner. It infuriated me that he had told her I would be doing something before he'd even asked, but this wasn't an issue to take up with Maddy. Instead I asked her if I could bring Leslie. ''I'd like you to meet her, Mad.''

''I can't wait. Anything she doesn't eat?''

''Liver.''

"Smart woman. We'll see you at six-thirty."

"Okay."

I called Leslie back. Since she had a client until four-thirty, and I had an appointment in Corona at five with Johns, we decided it would be best if she took the five-thirty train to Great Neck, and I would meet her there at six.

Miguel arrived on the dot of nine, very focused and carrying a knapsack, something he never does. He placed the bag on my desk and slowly extracted his carefully selected tools of the trade for his day of alibi hunting.

The first thing he pulled out of his bag of tricks was a four-inch-long cellular phone. "Thisss belongs to my mother, but her old boyfriend gave it to her—remember Jules, with the eczema?—anyway she doesn't use it and she can't stand him now, so she said I could have it. Only problem is, no one knows the number, so you can't reach me, but I can make calls with it and keep in touch with you."

Next he pulled out a composition book and a pencil case filled with pencils, pens, and a sharpener. I asked if he felt like he was back-to-school shopping when he bought his supplies. He graced me with a cool smile and held up a smaller notepad. "In case that book is too big." He tossed the pad of paper onto his growing stack of goodies. He next removed a small leather case, from which he pulled a nifty set of binoculars. After that there were three pairs of sunglasses (fabulous looks from RayBan and Revo and a three-dollar pair from a street vendor) and two baseball caps, one for a Boston Brewery and the other with a long black braid attached to the back. "In case I have to look like someone I'm not," he explained. The final items were a disposable camera and a Swiss Army knife.

He perched himself on the chair across from me and seemed infused with the heightened excitement that the unknown of any "first" brings. I felt like he was preparing for overnight camp, rather than a day of good old-fashioned detecting.

"Good God, what else have you got in there?" I asked, as I reached for his knapsack as a joke, really, to see what else was hidden in there. Miguel jumped up in a panic and shot his hand out for the bag before I could get it, but he was too late. I held the bag and could feel a weight pulling it down.

"What's in here?"

"Nothing." His handsome face grew dark as he held out his hand for the bag. "Give it to me."

We studied one another a good long while. Despite my professional snoop status, I am a firm believer in maintaining and respecting boundaries. I put the bag back on the desk and watched as he swiped it up into the safety of his embrace.

In jest I said, "If there's a gun in that bag, Miguel, and you don't give it to me, you're fired."

He exhaled a cross between a cough and a sneer, and I knew I had hit a button.

"There's a gun in there?" I was stunned. When he didn't answer, I knew there was. "You're not licensed to carry a firearm, and you represent CSI. May I please have the gun?"

Miguel's face fell, but he reached into the green bag and pulled out the one item he had forgotten to show me, a .22-caliber Derringer that seemed to weigh less than a pound. It looked as if it had never been handled before.

"Where did you get this?"

He twitched a shrug as he started to pack his bag with the glasses and assorted paraphernalia.

"Where did you get this?" I asked more firmly.

"Guns is easy to get, Sydney." He glared at me in defiance.

"*Are* easy. Miguel, sit down for a minute."

He complied, dropping his bag on the floor beside him.

"The way I see it, Mickey, something has gone very wrong in our society, and it all boils down to glamorizing violence . . ."

"You carry a gun," he interrupted with—if I do say so myself—a very good point.

"That's not the point," I said, placing his .22 on my desk. "I've been trained in firearms, and I'm licensed. I don't like guns, but I have a healthy respect for them because I know how and when to use them. If you want a gun I suggest you go through the system and get it legally, but, before you do that, think long and hard as to why you want one, what you want to do with it, and how you're going to ensure that none of your forty-eight nieces and nephews will get ahold of it and *accidentally* blow one another's brains out.

"And contrary to what you may be thinking, I am not doing this to stifle you, but because I care about you. You have to trust Max and me. We can teach you the profession, but we can't teach you how to be professional; that's up to you. This . . . ," I picked up the gun, ". . . is not professional. Your choosing to buy a piece of shit like this off the street does nothing to inspire confidence in you, especially because you know better."

"I didn't buy it off the street." It was his only defense.

"Where did you get it?"

Miguel paused and then graced me with a magnificent slow smile. "No way, boss. I may have been stupid buying it, and stupider for letting you find out I had it, but I ain't about to tell you where I got it. Plain and simple. So, what are you gonna do, fire me?"

"No way. Look, you're going to be an excellent detective and I want you on my side." It was nine-thirty and I had a ten o'clock meeting with Billy Mazzio way downtown. I took Miguel's .22 and was about to put it in the locked file cabinet along with Isabel's money when I asked, "What do you say I give this back when you have a license for it?"

He took a deep breath, looked down, and finally nodded.

"Thank you. In the meantime, why don't you get started tracking down the alibis. Start with this." I tossed Hickey's file on the desk in front of him. "I'm meeting Mazzio at ten, and later today I have an appointment with Kirstin Johns. I still haven't gotten ahold of Danny, but I think you had better leave him to me, seeing as I babysat for him once when he was little. Maybe it'll have some sway. Okay, I'm out of here. Do me a favor and wait until Kerry gets in before you leave, okay?"

He shuffled his feet and murmured an okay.

I stopped at the door and turned back to him. "Mickey? Are we all right?"

He gave this some thought before finally shrugging and saying, "Yeah, I guess so."

"Good man. See you later."

I like subways because they're fast and usually efficient, and I can catch up on my reading. However, I was so engrossed in *The Risk Pool*, by Richard Russo, I nearly missed my stop.

I reached Sado's with five minutes to spare. An emaciated woman wearing black lipstick and a spiked leather collar showed me to "Billy's booth," which was at the back of the room. The café was surprisingly light and airy, what one would expect more from an ice cream parlor than a sado-masochist bistro.

I took my seat at the booth facing the restaurant and soaked in the ambience. Upon closer inspection it was clear that this was, in fact, not a family restaurant. Two trapezes hung from the maize-colored ceiling and magnificent leather bullwhips and intricate harnesses of all shapes and sizes spruced up what at first glance seemed like ordinary décor. The tables and chairs looked simple enough until I realized that each and every stick of furniture had been handmade. For example, one table had a plain Formica top, but the four legs were each different; one metal leg looked like the end of a rifle, another like a prosthesis, one was a female mannequin leg on pointe, and the fourth was a sawed-off broom. What relation these items had to sado-masochism was beyond me, but together they provided a subtly disconcerting atmosphere.

"Billy's booth." I didn't know what to expect from the man whom, I was assuming, was *the man who met the man* in Hickey's riddle. Most of the clientele looked like average folk: clean cut, khaki-wearing, sightseeing visitors to our fair city.

The front door opened and in walked the man I knew was Billy Mazzio. He cocked a finger at the hostess and walked toward me as if he was cowpoke John Wayne and I was Maureen O'Hara, sure to fall under his spell.

Not a chance, Bub. Not a chance.

Sixteen

Billy Mazzio wore hiking boots, jeans, a ski jacket (complete with lift tickets dangling from the zipper), a green cashmere sweater, and dark glasses. He took off the jacket but kept the glasses on.

"Sydney Sloane, I presume?" He slid into the seat across from me and snapped his fingers. In less than fifteen seconds the waitress, who had biceps like Bruce Willis, placed a coffee and an orange juice in front of Mazzio. He glanced at his watch and murmured, "Good, Ginger, very good."

Ginger then took my order for coffee and gruffly asked if I wanted it with whipped cream. I said milk would be fine and turned my attention back to Mazzio. He didn't look like a man who would take a place like this seriously, but then again, what did I expect? Was I really naïve enough to think that people who are into S&M would *look* like they were into S&M?

Well, yeah, sort of.

"Did you have trouble finding the place?" Billy asked, pushing back his streaked wavy hair. His dark glasses remained firmly in place as he sipped his orange juice.

"No. Thanks for taking the time to see me."

He waved off the thanks with the back of his hand. "Are you hungry? The food here is really quite excellent."

"No, I'm fine, thanks, but you go right ahead."

Before he could respond, Ginger arrived with my coffee

and a plate of cinnamon French toast with fruit compote, a dish of warmed applesauce, and a side of thick bacon.

"I will." Billy slathered the applesauce on top of the French toast with his knife and proceeded to work his way through breakfast.

"I'm investigating the fire at Aronson Elite," I said, to get things started.

"So you said. What do you want to know?" His sunglasses reflected his breakfast and me, but made it impossible to see his eyes.

"I was hoping you could tell me what happened the night of the fire."

"Isn't it a matter of public record now?" As he bent over his plate, his bleached hair fell into his eyes. He tucked the errant hair behind his ear with the end of his fork.

"Well, yes, but you know, there's nothing like the horse's mouth."

"Is that right?" With his attention back on his breakfast, he looked up over the top of his glasses and I saw what I thought was a black eye.

"That's right. As I understand it, you were coming from a rehearsal at a friend's apartment?"

"That's right." For the first time Mazzio smiled. It was a smile worthy of a toothpaste commercial.

"Isn't that a little late for rehearsing?"

"I suppose it all depends on the schedule you keep. Some people are morning people, others prefer nighttime. Then there are those of us who can slip gracefully between the two, finding ourselves equally comfortable with daybreak or the dead of night."

"Was your relationship with Ms. Johns merely professional?"

"I don't see how that matters." He folded a slice of bacon into his mouth and chewed slowly. "Women like me," he said with an arched brow and a shy smile.

"I'm a little confused here, Mr. Mazzio. Are you saying that you and Ms. Johns had *more* than a professional relationship and that's why you were in the neighborhood so late, or are you saying yours was strictly a professional relationship and you just happened to be there?" I just didn't like him.

"What difference does it make?" When his smile was tight and forced, a dimple appeared in his right cheek. It was a charming look, but a forced smile would lead one to believe the man was uncomfortable. Discomfort *could* mean he had something to hide. A dimple is just the sort of thing that comes in handy for a gal like me in a situation like this.

"Well, assuming you're telling the truth about having seen Mitch Gerber in Corona the night of the fire, it wouldn't make a difference. But let's pretend for a moment that you're *not* telling the truth . . ."

"Why make a negative assumption?"

"Because I believe Mr. Gerber is innocent." Now it was *my* turn to flash a winning smile.

"Well, if you believe the man's innocent, that means you think I'm lying." The grin was gone.

"It would seem that way."

"You think I'm lying?" This seemed to stun him. He even put his fork down and wiped his mouth with his napkin.

"Well, I haven't yet drawn a conclusion . . . not enough data. That's why I wanted to talk to you and learn as much as I can."

I could only assume that he was staring at me from behind his Foster Grants, but he said nothing, so I continued.

"Now you ask what difference would it make if you and Kirstin were lovers. The answer is, it could make a big difference. The fact is, if you and Kirstin are simply classmates rehearsing a scene together, the likelihood is in your favor that she would have no need to lie on your behalf, especially in court, because, as I'm sure you know, perjury is punishable by law.

"Let us assume, however, that you and Ms. Johns are lovers. Now, for some bizarre reason, you decide to lie to the police about having seen Mitchell Gerber at the scene of the crime. I don't know why you would do that, but hypothetically speaking, let's say that's what you did. Now, let us further speculate that in reality you were . . . well, why not here? In this very restaurant, when you said you were in Corona. Yet when the police question you, you swear you were in Queens. I'd think you'd need some sort of proof. A lover might lie for you, even in a court of law. But you know, I just can't figure out why you would lie about having seen Mitch there, unless, of course, you had something to do with the actual fire. Hmm, now *there's* a thought." I looked him straight in what would have been his eyes, but were glasses reflecting only my own image and a figure, in the distance, behind me.

The dimple accompanied a huffed, singular laugh.

"Billy, *Bubeleh!*" The female voice came from behind me. Billy looked up, relieved with the reprieve.

"Yo Stace, how are you doin', babe?"

Stace was standing next to our table, her pale, scarred arms outstretched for an embrace. Every single item of clothing the woman was wearing had holes in it; even her Doc Martens had a tear along the toe. When Billy went to hug her, he took off his glasses and revealed a shiner that couldn't have been more than twenty-four hours old. Realizing what he'd done, he quickly replaced the glasses and Stace, who seemed more concerned with Stace than anything else, either didn't seem to notice his big ugly bruise, or found such marks to be old hat.

While Billy gossiped, the waitress came, took his dishes, and returned with a fresh cup of coffee.

When Stace left, Mazzio returned to the matter at hand. "Where were we? Oh yeah, that's right, you think I started the fire at that factory in Queens. Now, why would I do that?" He had regained his composure during his chat with Stace and seemed genuinely amused by my suggestion.

"Money?"

He shook his head. "I'm comfy."

"Revenge?"

He laughed, no dimple. "Against who? Look, I understand you have an obligation to prove your client's innocence, but the fact is, I was at Kirstin's apartment, rehearsing. And though I will admit that she and I *have* had great sex together, we're not what you would call 'lovers.' " He scratched the air with the middle and index fingers of both hands to denote his quote marks. "I left sometime around one-thirty, and on my way to the subway, I bumped into a man who was hurrying out of a building, a building I later learned had gone up in smoke."

"How did you hear about it?"

"The newspaper."

"The next day?"

"No, a couple days later. I don't always read the paper. I was . . . here, as a matter of fact . . . and someone gave me an old paper. That's when I saw it."

"How old was the paper?"

"Couple of days."

"So you approached the police?"

"That's right. I felt it was my civic duty, you know. I'm a very good citizen."

"Do you know Jake Aronson?"

"No. I mean, I know who he *is*, but I don't *know* him."

"And his son?"

"What's his name, George? Nah. Like I said, I know *of* them because of the case, but we had never met—at least, not before the grand jury did their thing."

"Can you tell me how you bumped into Mr. Gerber?"

"Smack, bang, man." He slapped his hands together and watched for my reaction. When I offered none, he continued. "Like, I had to reach out for him, I thought he was going down. Let's see, it was cold and I was kind of in a rush, so I wasn't looking up, you know, because I was kind of braced against the wind. Anyway, the next thing I know—boom—I ran right into someone. Instinctively I reached out for him, he stepped back, I looked up, and there we were, face to face."

"Can you describe him to me?"

"Sure. He looked exactly like Mitch Gerber." A flash of dimple. "I picked him out of a police line-up, which should be proof enough. Look, I understand why you don't trust me, after all, you're being paid to prove he's innocent, but hey, I saw what I saw."

"What was he wearing?"

"Who? Gerber?"

"Yes."

He twitched his head and shrugged. "I don't know. An overcoat . . ."

"What color?"

He paused and I could see his shoulders ease down. He sipped the coffee and said smugly, "Gray."

"Scarf? Hat? Was he wearing glasses?"

"Let's see, if I recall correctly, he had on a black sweater, black slacks, no hat, and black gloves. No glasses." He snapped his fingers for more coffee. Ginger filled his cup and backed away from the table.

"What happened to your eye?" I asked, motioning to his face with my chin.

He rubbed his unshaven jaw and sniffed. "A blind date."

"Did you know Alfred Hickey is dead?"

The rubbing stopped for an instant, then continued. "Was he the, what, the other detective?"

"That's right."

"I'm sorry to hear that. Was he a friend of yours?"

"No. He was murdered."

"Wow."

"Strangled."

"Wow." He started nibbling on a cuticle.

"I thought that might be of interest to you."

"Me? Why me?"

"Oh, I don't know. Maybe because his death was related to this case."

He said nothing.

"Also, he left a note."

"What kind of note?"

I smiled and shook my head. "A riddle, actually. There was something in it that made me feel I should . . . be concerned for you."

"Me? I didn't even know the guy."

I willed myself to see past his tinted glasses, but it was impossible. Instead I turned my attention to the dregs in the bottom of my coffee cup.

"If he left a note; that means it was probably a suicide," Mazzio reasoned.

"No, that's not it. He wrote the note as a sort of insurance policy, actually. Obviously he knew there was a possibility that someone would want to see him dead and he wanted to make certain they'd be caught."

"So he gave you a name? What? He gave you *my* name?"

I watched Mazzio as he worked nearly convincingly to maintain his composure. "I didn't say that," I said most innocently. "You know, I think Hickey would have liked this place."

"Oh yeah?" As Mazzio hunched over his coffee, his shoulders grew more rounded.

"Yes."

"I thought you didn't know the guy."

"I said we weren't friends."

"So, I don't get it. I don't understand why you think I would give a shit about this guy or why you're concerned for me. What's that about?"

"You tell *me*, Billy. Knowing that Hickey was murdered, is there any reason you should be concerned for your own well-being?"

He said nothing. There was no dimple, no hint of bravado, no bullshit; just a man sitting there with his thoughts. I do believe I'd hit a nerve.

I pulled a card out of my wallet and slid it across the table. "If you ever feel like talking, you can reach me at that number." I stood up, which seemed to stir him from his reverie.

"Leaving so soon?" There was a hint of flirtatious suggestion in his voice, but his face, what I could see of it, was flat and cold.

"I have work to do."

"Ah, work." He dismissed the very thought of it away with a backward wave of his hands. "Life is too short to live under the constant pressure of work, don't you think?"

"Yes."

"Everyone always seems to be scrambling in a panic to make a buck, to make sure that there will be something there for their old age. Security." He said the word with utter contempt.

"And what do you suggest?"

"Play." An eyebrow shot up from behind his glasses and the dimple returned. "No time like the present. You know, I have a feeling you and I could have a lot of fun together."

"Gee, I don't know. I figure life is hard enough without having to play games of dominance and submission or to inflict pain and humiliation on other people. Tell me, do you like to hurt people, Billy?''

His smile was slow and calculated. "Sometimes."

"And how often do you submit to the will of others?'' It was as if we were physically at polar opposites; as his smile faded, mine grew, and as he seemed to withdraw, I felt somehow bigger.

I left the café wondering if the satisfaction I had felt having one-upped Billy wasn't just a bit sadistic. Back out on the street it felt as if I had just exited the "outer limits" and was back into reality. The air was crisp, the streets were filled with traffic, and garbage collectors banged metal waste cans against the backs of their trucks while sleeping babies in strollers were rolled, undisturbed, past the din.

As I headed toward the subway, I couldn't get Isabel Wang out of my mind. Why would a woman subject herself to the humiliation that Hickey had asked of her? Had she liked it? Did she believe that she deserved to be recorded for posterity in positions both degrading and painful? And then Billy Mazzio slipped into my thoughts, nudging Isabel to the side. He was lying about having seen Mitch, of that I was certain; but why? I could only hope that the thought of winding up like Hickey had planted a seed that would shake him up enough to do something stupid, something that would tip his hand.

Mazzio. He didn't look like he'd be into harnesses and whips, but there you go—you can never tell about these things.

I took my seat on the L train and looked up from my book. Across from me an elderly couple sat holding hands. He wore a handlebar mustache and sat proudly beside his wife, who had an almost infectious comportment of seren-ity. And as I looked at them, I couldn't help but wonder how she'd have looked as a leather dominatrix and he with a collar around his fine, long neck.

I shook my head. Between my imagination and the nature of this business, there was no question that I was going to have to retire early. I could just see Miguel stepping into my shoes . . . spike heels and all.

I smiled pleasantly at the couple, who both smiled pleasantly back, and I thought: red.

The old dame would have looked smashing in a red tooled breastplate.

Seventeen

I decided to stop off at the office, check in with Kerry, get the car, and head out to Harriman's in Long Island City for a talk with Uncle Mitch and his merry band of manufacturers.

Kerry was on the phone when I arrived, but as soon as I opened the door, her eyes darted to her left. I turned and saw Isabel Wang sitting there, her head bowed, her shoulders sagging.

"Isabel," I greeted her gently. Detective intuition told me that the shit had hit the fan at the Wang home. Not only did Isabel look like the personification of misery, but she was in my office just before noon on a weekday rather than at the restaurant. She looked completely drained. I saw she was clutching the now-crumpled business card I had given her the night before. "Come in and we'll talk." I held out my hand, guiding her into my office, and shared a look with Kerry that said I was not to be disturbed.

"What happened?" I asked her back, as she stood at the windows looking out.

"Ken knows." She shoved her hands into the pockets of her winter coat.

"About you and Hickey?"

There was a long pause before she nodded and wrapped her arms around her shoulders, making it look, from behind, as if someone was hugging her. I remembered grammar school and how all the kids simulated passion by embracing themselves in such a way, making kissing noises.

"Isabel, come over here and sit down." The director's chair across from my desk seemed to swallow her. "Tell me what happened."

"Ken got home about eight o'clock last night. I don't think he saw pictures, but the police gave him a hard time. He said the police know he didn't do it, so they can't keep him." She told this all to the wedding band on her left hand, which she twisted around and around her finger. "He told me to get out. He said I no good." Her voice was so soft, it was as if a ghost had spoken. Here she looked me in the eyes. "You know, I been thinking a lot about me and Alfie, why I do what I did, and you know what I think?"

I shook my head.

"I think Alfie and me were okay." She slipped the wedding band off and fingered it. "I know what we did to Ken was not good, but Alfie and me, we really love each other. With Ken, I never know if he loved me. Never. I know he love his business. I know he love his mother. I know he love basketball. But I never know if he loved me. Alfie, I know. Alfie love sex, beer, and me.

"And as bad as it seems, what I did to Ken? We made a good team, Alfie and me. Plenty of times I tell him, 'Let's run away, just disappear,' but he always say no, that Ken need me." She almost smiled. "I knew it wasn't about Ken. I knew Alfie could never settle down, but he knew I knew, you know? It was like a game we played.

"But Ken's right. I disgraced him, and my family, so maybe it's best I go, you know? I mean, it's one thing he know for sure now that Alfie was my lover, but if he ever see those pictures—" Her eyes grew wide and she looked directly at me. Much to my surprise, she started giggling.

The giggles turned into laughter. A deep, unstoppable belly laugh.

I had no idea how to respond. It's difficult to watch someone having a laugh like that and not join in, but I knew the laughter had to be in lieu of tears. I also knew that with my luck, I'd start laughing with her and she'd burst into tears.

I glanced at my watch. It was eleven forty-five, which meant Auggie was with Leslie's mom, Dorothy, and the girls, playing bridge, which meant tea sandwiches, which meant evening puppy flatulence, not a pleasant thing.

I waited. As I'd suspected, her laughter finally turned to tears. I offered her a tissue. When she was finished, I asked, "Tell me, what do you want?"

"I don't know," she sighed.

"You must have friends you can turn to."

She smiled sadly. "No. Not about this."

"If they're your friends, they'll support you."

"You saw the pictures." She rubbed the wedding band between her fingers. "The people I know wouldn't understand. I was thinking, maybe you can help me?"

"How?"

"Maybe you could put me up?"

Oh yes, I could imagine it now. *Leslie, dear, we're going to have a charming woman as a house guest for a couple of weeks who can do remarkable things with ordinary household objects.*

"I have family staying with me." I tried to look apologetic.

"I understand. The last thing you need is to get involved with someone like me. Look, you give me my money and I'll just go."

"What do you mean, someone like you?"

She shrugged. "Look, I know what people think. People think Alfie and I were sick because of what we did. Hey, sometimes *I* think we were sick. I always keep it to myself because I was ashamed, not only because I was with Alfie, but because of what we do together . . . and how much I like it. Last night, you make me feel like I'm okay. After I left the restaurant, I start thinking, hey, Alfie and me didn't hurt anyone, except maybe Ken, and I'm sorry about that, but we loved each other.'' She looked away from me and I saw a woman who had just wanted to feel loved. For whatever Hickey was about, he had provided *that* for her . . . just as Leslie provided it for me.

It's unnerving, being a hypocrite. I had, albeit in the privacy of my own mind, passed the same judgment over this woman as my uncle had passed judgment over me all these years. I shifted uncomfortably in my chair.

"Look, running away doesn't solve anything. Now, I may not be able to put you up, but there are places you can go, and I have a feeling that if you give them half a chance, your friends might surprise you.''

I didn't have the kind of time Isabel required, so I set her up in Max's office and told her Kerry would help her get squared away.

Kerry, who is used to jumping in and helping above and beyond the call of duty with everything from finding lost pets to bandaging bruised parts, had recognized Isabel from the pictures the day before and had a feeling as soon as she saw her come into the office that the two of them would somehow be connected.

I quickly went over my schedule with Kerry before racing out. "First I'm going to Harriman's, which is Mitch's company, then at five o'clock I have a meeting with Kirstin Johns, and at six I'm meeting Leslie in Great Neck, where we'll dine with Mitch and Maddy. I have numbers here for everywhere I'll be, in case you need to contact me and the cell phone is on the fritz again. If there's any time between Mitch's and Kirstin's, I may try and track down Danny.''

"Danny Aronson?" she asked, checking through papers attached to her clipboard.

"Yes, why? Did he call?"

"He did. Nice guy." She handed me a message slip that had his name and daytime number. "He said he was sorry he missed you, but he's been out of town. He also said that he spoke to his dad, he understands what you're doing, and he'll help you in any way he can. Is he single?"

"I think so. But you're not."

She clicked her tongue against the roof of her mouth. "Not for *me*, but Lara is always looking for a good man. Maybe this Danny is Mr. Right."

"You never know. Let me meet him and scope it out for her."

"Excellent." She placed three messages on my desk, explaining each. "Minnie wants to talk to you. Says she's disturbed about a message she received from your dad."

Minnie, who communes with the deceased on a regular basis, has often mentioned information she has gleaned from my dad since his passing. Some of it—all right, most of it—has even been accurate. "You'd think she'd let the poor man rest, wouldn't you?"

"She could only have a dialogue with him if he was open to it."

"Next." I wasn't about to engage in a debate about spiritual things that go bump in the night.

She handed me another message. "Mullshire House wants to know who's stealing food and booze." The large New Jersey inn, run by a very nice compulsive, has been a client for several years.

"Can you handle that?" I asked, knowing that this was a routine assignment.

"Contract is on your desk, ready to be signed, and I've already put a call out to Pierson, to see if he's free to do undercover."

"Great." I glanced at the contract and signed on the dotted line.

"Gil Jackson called and wants you to set aside March eighteenth. It's his and Jane's anniversary."

Gil and Jane started out as friends of my parents when I was maybe seven, and have remained family ever since.

"Have you been able to get anything on this Mali Cajina?" I asked.

"Not yet. This one's going to be a slow process, if only because the guy's illegal. I will get you something by the end of the day, though. Girl Scout's honor." She tapped three fingers to her temple and kissed the air. She looked more like a cartoon character than a Girl Scout in her black cowl-necked sweater, purple-and-black dotted jumper with matching striped tights, and army boots.

"Did Miguel tell you anything about his meeting with this Mali character?"

She shook her head.

"Well, when they met yesterday, Miguel lied to Mali and told him that he knows what happened."

"What does he mean, at the fire?"

"Yes. And apparently this bit of information hit a nerve."

"Really?" A hint of a smile tugged at the corner of her mouth.

"Um-hm. When Mickey said he knew what happened, Mali turned around and asked what he wanted—"

"Like what? Like a payoff?"

I shrugged. "Who knows? But when *he* said *that*, Miguel threw the ball right back in his court and said, 'You tell me.' "

Kerry was delighted. "No! I love this."

"My guess is Miguel stumped him when he said that, because the next thing Mali said was, 'Where can I reach you?' Now, deductive reasoning would conclude that Mali is working for someone and has to get his marching orders from higher up.''

''Ah-ha. But from whom?''

''Well, now, therein lies the key that I do believe will solve this case.''

''So, you're getting closer.''

''Oh baby, piece of cake. Now all we have to do is find out who did it, why they did it, who the dead girl was, and how on earth Mitch got so deeply involved in this without having some connection to it.''

''Chin up.'' Kerry stood. ''Should I confirm Gil on the eighteenth?''

''No, just help get Isabel situated, okay? If she wants her money now, the envelope is in there.'' I pointed to the locked file. ''I recommend against it, but it's her money.''

An hour later I was in Long Island City.

Harriman's was a lot smaller than I had remembered. As soon as I walked in I expected to be greeted by Harriet Bushman, a round woman who wore thick glasses and gray dresses, but of course, Harriet was probably long gone by now. When I was a kid, Harriet would pretend that I was an important designer, and she would bring me specs to work, which were actually coloring books of cut-out dolls that she kept on hand for me. We would discuss color themes, the serious business of altering, accessories, and what hair colors would best suit the clothing. Always ahead of my time, I thought purple was a fine color for hair.

''Can I help you?'' a bored young woman with nasal congestion asked, when I paused in front of her metal desk.

''Yes, I'm looking for Mitch.''

She stared at me for the longest time before asking, as if this were a grievous hardship, ''Did you have an appointment?'' It looked like there was a huge red hickey on the left side of her neck.

''No.'' I smiled sheepishly.

She pushed her glasses onto the bridge of her nose and her whole face seemed to reflect acute physical pain. I waited to see if she was going to keel over.

"He's not here." With that she returned to the work on her desk. She had all the social grace of a stone.

"Do you know when he'll be back?" I continued pleasantly, all the while absorbing the changes the place had undergone since Harriet and I had worked as a team.

"Nope." She white-knuckled her pen, but didn't look up.

I placed one of my business cards on her paperwork and said, "I'm Mitch's niece."

She picked up the card and studied it. "I'll tell him you were here." She flipped the card into the out box.

"Does Carmine still work here?" I asked, believing it was plausible that Mitch's foreman from long ago would still be working.

"Who?" Clearly I was not making her day any easier.

"Carmine De La Garza?" I could tell from her blank expression that she was clueless. "He used to be the foreman here."

"Well, he's not now." She looked up and pushed her shoulder-length brown hair behind her ear, again revealing the red mark on her neck. Given where the mark was and her winning personality, I took a leap of faith.

"Do you play the violin?" I asked, as if this was the greatest coincidence in the world.

She studied me cautiously, but her face was softening. "Viola."

With my own neck exposed, I couldn't very well lie and say I did, too, so I did the next best thing. "I used to play the violin. God am I sorry I gave it up, but you know, one thing led to another, which led to another. The next thing I knew, I hadn't played in . . . forever." (At least that much was true.)

She nodded enthusiastically, and I saw that when she smiled she was actually quite pretty. ''I know exactly what you mean. I *took* this job because I didn't want anything to interfere with my music. You know, like the last thing I needed was a job where I had to work late and miss playing. So maybe there's not the growth here that my mom would like to see for me, but the fact is, they're nice people and it's steady work.'' Apparently Ms. Monosyllable was actually a regular chatterbox.

Her name was Janice and she'd been with Mitch for two years. She actually knew who Carmine was, but he was no longer at Harriman's. He'd retired when she first started. The only people left from the old days were Pete, who kept the machinery running smoothly, and Nomi, a maestro with a needle. When I asked where I could find them, she pointed me back outside and into another building. Expansion.

As it turned out, Harriman's expansion was the building across the street that had once been a costumer's warehouse. One time Mitch and a very strange lady who worked in the place took me for a tour through the theatrical wonderland of costumes used for Broadway shows, regional theater, and Halloween. I remember I had gotten lost in there and panicked when I couldn't find Mitch and suddenly heard the Alice in Wonderland costumes moaning. Scared the hell out of me.

Nomi was at one of the first machines when I walked in. Despite her gnarled hands, she was working the machine as if it were an extension of herself. I stood off to the side watching her, and I remembered a rainy day when I was seven and had come to work with Uncle Mitch. I had just had the mumps, and Nomi had made me a doll from unused scraps of cloth, buttons and newspaper. I had loved that doll. I had called her Mrs. Bobbins, and Carmine had drawn square glasses around her eyes that had looked just like Nomi's.

"Nomi?" I called above the din, as I approached her table.

She had been watching me out of the corner of her eye. Without looking up, she studied me under a single arched brow. "I know you." Difficult though it was to hear above the sewing machines, it was clear that her voice was still like a growl. Her tangerine lipstick shone in the overhead light and detracted from her crooked teeth.

"Sinda. Sinda Sloane," I said, using the name she'd know me by, since Uncle Mitch always introduced me as Sinda. I couldn't help but smile.

Her lips popped into an O and then spread into a wide grin. Her eyes, already magnified behind enormous glasses, grew even bigger as she jumped off her stool and opened her arms. I bent down and hugged her.

"Oh, my God! Look at you! When the hell did you get so *tall*?" She let go of the embrace, but held on to my arm. "Hey, Dennis!" she called to a man walking the aisles. "I'm going to take a coffee break. This is Mitch's niece." Without waiting for a response, she led me by the arm out the door, down a corridor, and into the lunchroom. I bought us each a coffee and joined her in the smoking section, where she was already halfway through a Marlboro.

"When the hell did you get so tall?" she asked again, as I neared the table.

"My thirty-fifth birthday. It was very odd. I woke up, and just like that," I snapped my fingers, "I shot up from four-eight to five-eight."

"I see you're still a snothead." She blew a thick cloud of smoke out of her nose and reached for three packets of half and half. "So, where the hell have you been?" It was as if we'd picked up where we had left off, only now she didn't have to watch her language.

I gave her an abbreviated update on the life and times of Sydney Sloane, making sure to mention that I was now an investigator hired for Uncle Mitch. In turn, I learned that her sister and mother had passed away within the year, and that she was lonely, but dealing with it, because now that her sister was gone, she could have cats. As soon as I could, I brought the conversation around to Mitch.

"So what do you think, Nomi? You've been here almost as long as Mitch and Jake. What's your gut reaction?"

She covered her mouth with her hand and scraped a tangerine-colored thumbnail between her two front teeth. She seemed lost in thought, as if she hadn't heard me, but she had. She dropped her hand away from her mouth, took a deep breath, and reached in her sweater pocket for another cigarette, the fourth in fifteen minutes, but who was counting?

"Between you and me?"

"Absolutely."

"Let's face it, I've known them both a long time, and for the most part, I like them, despite the fact that Mitch can be a cheap asshole and Jake will try and screw anything in a skirt. But do I think Mitch set Jake's place on fire?" Her eyes were like two big question marks. She slowly lowered her lids, pushed the corners of her mouth into a deeply etched frown, and shook her head deliberately back and forth. "No way. Mitch may hate Jake, there's no question about that, but he has too much self-respect for that kind of nonsense."

"Apparently he threatened Jake at a bar mitzvah, just a week before the fire."

"Oh, for God's sake." The cigarette dangled from her lips as she squinted the smoke out of her eyes and talked. Her hands were busy emptying the tiny metal ashtray into her mostly empty paper coffee cup. "Those two were always threatening one another." Her lower lip stuck to the filter as she went to pull the cigarette away from her mouth. "Shit. Anyway, there wasn't a day that went by when the two of them weren't going at one another. I'm telling you, I'm so sure Mitch didn't do it that I'll wager you ten thousand bucks." She pressed a fingertip to her lip and repeated, "Ten thousand dollars, and I am not kidding." She examined her finger.

"There was a witness."

"A liar."

"How can you be so sure?" I asked.

"I just know things."

"What kind of things?"

"Things." Nomi dropped the cigarette onto the other quarter pack that was floating in the cup. She picked up the cup and shook it, and the ember finally hissed for a second and died. Across the lunchroom, three women broke into raucous laughter. Nomi wiped her chest free of stray ashes and said, "Look, I have to get back to work."

Reflexively I reached out and grabbed her hand. It was smaller and rougher than it looked. "Nomi, I need help."

She paused and then eased her hand away from mine. "You're a nice girl, Sinda, but I can't help you."

"You know something."

"I know nothing . . ." She wasn't able to look me in the eye.

"Nothing you'd be willing to bet ten thousand dollars on? What if I took you up on that bet?"

"Ha!"

"You started it, Nomi. Ten thousand dollars." Mind you, I'm not rich, but the money I received from my parents' estates has been invested well. If I had to, I could scrape up the dough and write it off as a business expense. "Think of it—Mitch spending the rest of his life behind bars for a crime he didn't commit, when all along you had information that could vindicate him."

Nomi eyed the room uncomfortably. She sniffed. "It's not my business."

"Of course it's your business. You've known this man for over thirty years. Friendship and loyalty aside, are you ready to retire? Because if Mitch isn't here to run the place, Harriman's will have to close. Either that, or it'll be sold, and at what, fifty-something, I hate to say it, but you'll be expendable."

"Sixty-two," she told the pack of Marlboro. "And no, I can't afford to retire. Not just yet. But loyalty?" Her gaze was like iron as she seemed to look past my eyes and into my psyche. I didn't look away. "Loyalty can sometimes create problems."

There are times when it is best to let people draw their own conclusions.

I waited.

Nomi pulled another smoke from the pack and tapped the filtered end against the tabletop. She didn't light it.

Chairs at the far end of the room scraped against the floor as the trio of women prepared to leave.

Thirty years of loyalty . . . it was my guess that this loyalty was connected to Mitch and not Jake, because Nomi insisted that it hadn't been Mitch at the fire and was willing to bet money that Billy Mazzio was lying. I pretended not to watch her as she struggled with the decision of whether or not to share her information with me. Finally she put the cigarette between her lips, struck a match three times against a well-worn flint, lit the tobacco, crossed her arms under her chest, and blew smoke into the air like a geyser.

"I don't want you to get the wrong impression." She scraped a fingernail against the corner of her mouth. "I'm only telling you what I'm going to tell you because maybe it will help Mitch, but you have to understand . . ." She shook her head somberly. "I am placing myself in a very bad situation here. Very bad." She searched my face as if she might be looking for an out, but it wasn't there. Instead, I assured her that she was doing the right thing, and she could trust me to honor her confidence.

I took few notes during the next twenty minutes. I asked few questions. When the foreman, Dennis, came in looking for Nomi, after one glance at the two of us, he backed out of the room without saying a word.

I was exhausted when I walked Nomi back down the corridor to the din of the sewing room and the safety of her machine. At that very moment, I'd have done anything for a monotonous task. Instead, I stood outside in the cold, smelling like Nomi's smoke. I held my breath to ward off the feelings that were circling around me like a vulture over a corpse. I am a firm believer that there are moments in our lives when it is better not to feel, to become hardened, if only for a moment, against the very harsh reality that people are only human and that humans are often pathetic.

I was surrounded by warehouses, dirty pavement, gray sky, noise, and pollution. I could have interviewed Pete, the old janitor, or a handful of employees, but I saw the neon glow of a coffee shop hanging half a block away and decided the only thing that would take away all the blues was a tuna melt with fries. Burnt.

Eighteen

Benny's Coffee Shop was a dive that, given the aging photos on the walls, had been there since the early forties. Half a dozen regulars crowded the counter, and I took a seat at a booth by the window. I ordered my tuna melt on rye with burnt fries and a ginger ale and slipped *The Risk Pool* out of my bag.

I tried to lose myself in the book, but it was impossible; I kept returning to what Nomi had told me. "Hearsay," she'd kept repeating, but her hearsay had included names and places. If she was right, I now knew Mitch's alibi for the night of the fire, and it had nothing to do with falling asleep in front of the TV. Nope. It had everything to do with a woman in Brooklyn, cheating, and hypocrisy. Oddly, it all made sense, and it made me feel hollow inside.

As I ate, I thought about the people I had met during the last forty-eight hours. Sex, deception, and control seemed to be a common thread, which led me to conclude that if they wanted, any of them could play effective roles within the political, religious, judicial, or entertainment arenas.

Hickey loved Isabel, but in his work and his personal life, he was obviously absorbed with sex, control, and deception. And while Isabel hadn't deceived Hickey, the relationship had lasted a long time, which meant that she probably wielded a great deal of control over Hickey, no doubt using sex as her tool of domination.

Jake had deceived Mitch.

Billy had deceived a grand jury, and Mitch had . . .

"Something else?" the waitress asked, as she stacked my empty lunch plates in her hand.

"How's your coffee?" I asked.

She glanced back at the big metal coffeemaker and said, "Twenty minutes old. Try it, if you hate it I'll make you a fresh pot. Anything else?"

I eyed the banana cream pie in the revolving refrigerator display case, a handy little gadget no coffee shop is complete without.

"Nnnaaa." I pulled my gaze away, knowing dinner was at Maddy's, and like any self-respecting Jewish cook, she always made enough for an army.

The slender waitress shifted her weight and seemed to lean on one hip. "The banana or the Boston?" she asked, nudging her chin in the direction of the dessert case.

"Surprise me." I opened *The Risk Pool* again and was through three chapters, two coffees, and a heavenly slice of Boston cream pie before I looked at my watch. It was three o'clock, and I didn't feel the least bit guilty that I had just taken over an hour for lunch.

Knowing that a cell phone in this particular establishment would make me suspect, I dropped some change into the antiquated rotary pay phone and dialed Danny Aronson's work number. He was out for lunch. Kerry, however, was in and informed me that Isabel was already registered at a women's residence in midtown, she had gone home to gather her belongings before Ken returned, and Kerry had arranged for her a job interview the next morning in a health food restaurant in Soho. "I also got her an appointment with a therapist." She paused. "And a photographer." Another pause. "Just kidding. About the photographer, that is."

"Ha. Ha," I said flatly. There was still no word from Miguel and what she had been able to learn about Mali

Cajina had been minimal—just the basics that could wait until she had more to offer.

"Okay, well, I have a five o'clock appointment with Kirstin in Corona. As long as I've got time, I figure I'll stop by Hickey's office again and see what I can see."

"Isn't Bayside past Corona?"

"Yeah, but it's not too bad. Besides, I have the time right now."

"Okay, well, I'll have something on Cajina for you by tomorrow morning."

I was at Hickey's office thirty minutes later. I entered the office building from the left, rather than the right, in order to circumvent Wang's Take-Out. The police tape that had covered Hickey's office door was gone, save for a few threads dangling loosely on the frame. I tried the doorknob and wasn't surprised to find it locked. Like his home, however, it was as easy to open as a high school locker.

The room felt picked over, though by all outward appearances it hadn't changed much since I'd last been there. Granted, Hickey's body had been removed and the crime unit team had dusted the place for fingerprints, but other than that, his office seemed to be in the same disorder in which Hickey had left it. There was a faint smell of garbage in the closed room.

Given that it was getting dark early, and I didn't exactly want to call attention to myself, I pulled down the shades before I turned on the desk lamp and the answering machine. Someone had removed the tape from the machine, probably the police, so I focused my attention on rummaging through Hickey's business life on paper. It was a mess. The only thing remotely connected to Uncle Mitch's case was Paul's name and number on a scrap of paper in a drawer that seemed to be reserved for loose numbers. Other than that there were no files, no records, nothing to even suggest that he had been connected with the investigation . . . which as far as I was concerned was pretty danged fishy.

I sat on the visitor's chair and pulled out my notebook. I turned to the page where I had transcribed Hickey's note:

> *Two steps away where it began, there was a man who met a man. Another man will hold the key of what befell poor Mitch and me. Happy hunting, and thanks. Yours in the afterlife, Alfred Quentin Hickey.*

I sighed. The man who met a man. It was impossible for me to think of that as anyone other than Billy Mazzio and Mitch, but what if there were two completely *different* men he had been referring to? I considered all of the men connected even remotely with the case—Mitch, Mark, Jake, Danny, Mazzio, and Mali. There might have easily been others, employees of either camp or family members . . . I added Paul to my list; that made seven.

On the same page of the notepad where I was listing the band of merry men, I glanced at a name Nomi had supplied. Lady Macbeth had once said, "If it were done when 'tis done, then 'twere well it were done quickly." She, of course, was trying to push her husband to snuff out old Duncan, whereas all I had to do was pick up the phone and call Brighton Beach and yet the two acts seemed to be of the same magnitude.

To call or not to call . . . that was the question. I shook my head, trying to get the old bard out of there so I could get on with business. There were no phone books in the office, which I took to be an omen to wait on the call to Brooklyn.

I turned off the office light, pulled open the shades, and left the chaos that had constituted his life. The roads were surprisingly clear, and I made it to Kirstin's apartment in no time at all.

She had a ground-floor apartment in the back of a six-story brick box. I buzzed twice and wasn't altogether surprised when she didn't answer. I'd had a hunch that she was going to blow me off, despite the promise of an inheritance. It was four-fifty . . . I had to meet Leslie's train at six, which meant I had to be out of Corona by five-thirty, allowing for rush hour traffic, which would probably be awful and make me late anyway.

I was turning to leave when the door buzzed and a muffled voice said what sounded like, ''Come on in, I'm on the phone.''

She had left her door ajar. I am, if nothing else, cautious. I pulled the Walther out of my bag before stepping over the threshold of the door. Paranoid, perhaps, but in a situation like this, I always prefer it if the hostess opens the door personally. Something didn't feel right.

As I entered the apartment, I stepped into a small, dark living room furnished in early American student. From its perch on a strip of plywood held up with four red bricks, a stereo was playing a Donna Lewis tune about love. The place was thrown together with eclectic furnishings including a lava lamp, a futon sofa, two beanbag chairs, and a packing crate which doubled as a coffee table and was covered with books, soda cans, and several issues of *New Woman* magazine. Tacked on to the water-damaged walls were several nostalgia movie posters.

''Kirstin?'' I asked, listening for something past the music. To my left was a doorway which looked as if it led to the kitchen, and straight ahead was a door which I assumed led to the bedroom. To my right, in the shadows, was an enormous thronelike chair covered with purple velveteen.

Kirstin was sitting on the chair. Her head was listing onto her right shoulder, her arms were opened, palms up, resting on the arms of the chair, her feet were dangling a good two inches off the floor because of the height of the seat, and her eyes were open, as if she was surprised. She was motionless and I knew, as sure as I was standing there, that she was dead, and we weren't alone. Despite all the hooey that detectives' nerves are made of steel—whether they're men or women—the fact is, at that moment my heart was in my throat. And as much as I might have liked to have lost control and gone screaming into the hallway, I wanted to live, which meant total control.

I had enough sense to realize that whoever was there with me wasn't about to let me make it to the front door, so chances were they were behind me at that very moment. I swung around, leading with the Walther. Nothing. My shoulder bag felt like a ton of bricks. I backed up closer to Kirstin, which admittedly put me in a corner, but at least I would know the only thing behind me was dead, and therefore unlikely to do me much harm.

The lyrics coming from the stereo were melodically telling the listener to not look back because now it was time to live. What a swell idea. I inched back, trying to will myself to see and feel 360 degrees around me. I kept my breathing calm, all my senses on high. The briefest glance at Kirstin assured me that she was very dead, and, like Hickey, she'd been strangled; the end of the rope still hung around her neck as if it were part of a necklace adornment. I paused less than a foot away from her throne, where I could see her out of the corner of my right eye. I heard a movement in the other room, as if someone had bumped into a piece of furniture and it had scraped against the floor. At that precise moment, however, I caught a flash of motion out of the corner of my left eye. I swung around but I was too late; looming before me was a figure dressed in black. Before any images could register, before I could pull the trigger or duck or scream, I was thrown into blackness when he slipped a hood over my head. As he did this, he slammed a knee into my side, just at kidney level. The intense pain was followed with a blow to my forehead with a solid object that hit me with such force, my head snapped back and my legs went out from under me. Before I even hit the floor I felt myself being jerked up by my jacket collar. The back of a gloved hand caught me just under my left ear and followed through. Despite the cloth hood covering the upper portion of my face, it felt as if they had ripped through my nose and eyelid. I was aware that my torso was in a viselike grip, having the air squeezed out of my diaphragm, but unable to see and in a fog of pain, I couldn't figure out how this was happening.

I struggled to twist myself free, but my effort made me feel futile, like a fish out of water. I frantically moved my fingers, certain that if indeed I was still holding the Walther, it would have gone off by now, but the only sounds I could clearly decipher were my own breathing and laughter.

My head was now being pinched between two soft paddles, and it moved in slow motion until it met the wooden floor. Again. And again. And again. I tried to reach for the hood, tried to see who was at the other end of this torture, but it was impossible. My head felt as if it had cracked in half.

And then it stopped. I was still alive. I could feel that every single inch of my body was bruised, but at least I could feel.

I slowly tried to roll over on to my side in an attempt to sit up, but the pain was too intense. I rolled onto my elbow and paused, listening. I wasn't alone. I slowly eased the hood off my head. My left eye seemed to be swollen shut, but I still had vision with my right eye and the first thing I saw was blood. Lots of it. All mine.

"Feeling under the weather?" a voice whispered, near enough to my ear that I could feel the speaker's voice on my cheek. "I'm going to make you all better now."

I tried to move away from his breath. A hand moved in

front of my face holding an object I couldn't quite make out. The arm pulled away so I could focus on the object: a syringe. The gloved hand squirted liquid into the air. I must have tried to roll away from him, but the next thing I knew, he had shoved the arm of my jacket up, and the needle was piercing my flesh. I squinted, trying to see him actually depress the plunger, but moving my head the slightest degree sent shocks of pain shooting down my spine and ricocheting inside my head.

Within moments my body grew numb. My head fell back and I was resting against something, probably his arm. I opened my eyes and willed myself to see. It was the Navy Seal from Hickey's apartment. Hidden behind his face mask, he blew me a kiss. "Sleep well, princess."

I opened my mouth to say something, but the words wouldn't come. He moved his arm and let me hit the floor, a dead weight. I felt nothing. The only sensation I was aware of was a deep, unquenchable thirst.

And then oblivion.

Nineteen

It was stone still, it was pitch black, the air was sour and my mouth was dry. When I moved, the springs fastening the cot upon which I lay bobbed and let out a screech that sent sound waves ripping through my brain. The mattress smelled like mildew and was so thin, I could feel the metal coils holding it up imprinting on my skin. I took a deep breath and lay perfectly still, trying to let my eyes adjust to the darkness. I also did a body check.

It wasn't as bad as I'd feared. I tried a yoga exercise called The Lion, in which I pushed my mouth into an O, widened it, and stretched the lips back into a full grimace. My face was caked with what I knew had to be blood; I remembered there had been lots of blood. I couldn't tell if my headache was drug induced or the result of having been used as a drumstick, but the searing pain seemed to center in the very back of my skull.

My fingers were swollen and numb, but they still worked. My left wrist was probably sprained. I was able to raise my arms off the bed, but it wasn't what you would call a pain-free movement. It was dark, amazingly dark. I hurt from head to toe, but as far as I could tell, there were no dislocations or broken bones. It was my head that had taken the worst of it.

My eyes had adjusted to the darkness as much as they were going to. I could see just as much with my eyes closed as open.

Christ. Total blackness. Not a shred of light. History books and newspapers are filled with these kinds of horror stories because lunatics have been burying people alive since the beginning of time. But why on earth would someone want to bury me? It didn't make any sense. And on a cot?

I cautioned myself not to panic.

If I focused, if I got my bearings, I could handle this, I could take it one step at a time. *Breathe.*

I tried to take a deep breath as I inched my hands out to my side. I was definitely on a cot, which was just slightly wider than I was, and pushed smack against a wall on my right. There was no bedding—no sheets, no blanket. I moved my hand up and found that the wall was warm, which I needed to assume meant there were water pipes behind it, and not dirt. With my left hand I felt that just two inches past the edge of the cot was another wall. Too close. Way too close. I forgot to breathe for several seconds while I eased onto my side and pushed myself past the pain, up onto my knees, and felt frantically for the boundaries of my confinement.

The wall on my left was a door. Hallelujah. Double doors, to be precise, which was good, because it meant I wasn't buried underground.

I stood up on the cot and braced myself against the warm wall.

What did he plan on doing with me? Would he be coming back, or was this to be my sarcophagus? Who the hell *was* he, and what had triggered this killing spree?

The double doors might as well have been a wall. The knobs had been removed, and when I pressed my back and hands against the wall behind me and used my bare feet to push against the door, nothing budged, not even in the slightest.

Jake. This was all connected to the fire at Jake's. Maybe

Jake was at the bottom of all of this. Mr. Big.

No light came through what would be the normal cracks with doors on hinges, and there were definitely hinges.

No, Jake might have had something to do with the fire, I wouldn't put that past him, but he just didn't seem like he could be the brains of any operation. Besides, he would never go for something like this, whatever the hell this was.

I ran my hand along my neck. I was clammy, I was hot, I was so very, very parched. The absolute silence was deafening. White noise filled my head.

My watch had been removed, along with my shoes, socks, and jacket. My pockets had been emptied and the thought of that son of a bitch touching me, rummaging through my pockets, made me angry, so angry I wanted to kill him, but given that I was sealed in what was essentially a box, all I could do was cry. Crying, however, was a luxury I just didn't have time for. A box. A prison cell. No, a cell would be better—at least you could see, you could breathe. I couldn't think about that now, it would only make me crazy.

I sank down onto the cot and rested my back against the wall. It was impossible to tell how long I had been there, but I knew one thing for certain: I had to get out of there. Maybe the door felt like a wall because I had been sealed into it, maybe this madman had built a wall on the other side, like Montresor in Edgar Allan Poe's "The Cask of Amontillado." No, no, this was definitely not a productive way to spend my time.

I pulled my legs into a lotus position. *Think. Think, damn it.* If I at least understood what the hell was going on, I would have a shot at dealing with this mental case and getting out of there.

The man who met the man.

Mazzio. Could Mazzio be the sadist behind the mask? I hadn't connected the two when I met him at Sado's, but that didn't mean he couldn't have been the man I had run into at Hickey's apartment. But why? Why would Mazzio lie about seeing Mitch and then kill Hickey, Kirstin, and maybe me? This didn't make sense. How was it possible that it was so completely dark? *Could* he have sealed me into the wall? No. No, don't go there. If he didn't need me he would have killed me already. He had something he needed me for, something which was acting as my life insurance policy. Mazzio, think about Mazzio. He didn't strike me as being a killer. A lazy, middle class boy who wanted to play at being a bad boy and had learned to live off of others, maybe, but not a cold-blooded killer. No. Mazzio couldn't be the Mask. The Mask was evil. The Mask was going to kill again, and if I kept my wits about me, it might not be me.

There was something, a noise just beyond the door. I shifted around and pressed my ear to the cold wood. Nothing. All I could hear was my own labored breathing, and the gentle squeaking of the bed springs.

"You can hear vibrations, you just hafta listen." I was five and my sister's best friend, Zoe, was teaching me the ropes of being a very good Indian scout, ultimately the best Indian scout in the whole damned building. Zoe pressed her ear to the wooden floor in my parents' closet and assured me that the cowboys were far away, a whole floor away. I eased past the robes to the closet door, which I opened as slowly as I could, knowing there was a nasty squeak when it hit a certain mark, but it was a set-up. Zoe was a turncoat. "Never trust anyone," she told me, as I was led off to be tried by the local cavalry commander, who was also my brother, David. Conviction was certain.

I blinked. Eyes opened. Eyes closed. It was all the same. I shut my eyes, because the darkness was easier to handle that way, and settled against the wall at the head of the cot. The more I thought about it, the more I was convinced that all of the recent events were connected. The fire. Framing Mitch. Hanging Hickey. Strangling Kirstin. I did not want to be added to the list.

I stood up and started feeling the walls. I might have been stuck in this space, but I was going to do whatever I could to get out of there. Who knew what was in here? Maybe there was a latch, apart from the frame, that would open the door. Right, and maybe James Bond would be levitating through the floor any minute now.

Mazzio lied about seeing Mitch. Why? Money was the only thing that made sense. An out-of-work actor . . . someone had hired him to play the role of his life, but for how much, and for how long? Would Mazzio be the next one to die?

Or would it be me?

Oh God, I was thirsty. It felt as if I had gargled with sawdust, talcum powder, and sand. It was impossible not to think about it, and yet the more I thought about it, the worse it got. I braced my back and hands against the warm wall and wedged my feet against what was ostensibly the door. This was how I very slowly inched my way up the walls toward the ceiling. Who knew? Maybe there was an attic entrance.

Kirstin. She had probably gotten caught up in this through sheer happenstance. She was friends with Mazzio, maybe even lovers. Acting partners. Actors. People trained to lie convincingly. God, could she have been *acting* dead? But that didn't make sense; she was waiting for someone she thought was bringing her money. Unless, of course, she had spoken to Mazzio, who'd told her who I was. I paused, feeling a wave of nausea and the cold sweats come over me. How could I have been so stupid? I waited for the nausea to pass, willing my body to become one with the wall.

Go back, go back. If Mazzio lied for money, what compelled Kirstin to get up before a grand jury and lie? Had she been paid, too? Or was it the challenge of persuading a jury of twenty-three people that she was sincere?

Having had two years of training in the theatrical arts myself, I knew plenty of people who would have loved to have taken on a dare like that. Then again, maybe she'd acted out of love for Mazzio, or even fear. If they shared a sado-masochistic relationship, an area in which I am not at all well versed, he might have had a control over her which was more powerful than money, art, or even love.

Cousin Mark. Now, why did *his* name pop into my head? Could Mark be the Mask? I shook my head, which made me feel as if my skull would split in half.

Yes. There was a shelf just above me. I would have to turn around in order to face it, unless it was just resting on supports, which is often the case. With everything I possessed, I expanded myself and thrust my back and feet against their respective surfaces, which freed up my arms. With my right hand I gently tried to lift the shelf off its perch. It moved. Pain coursed through my body like it was on a joyride.

It occurred to me that I didn't like Mark. Sometime between the age of fifteen and forty, he had turned into a nasty jackass. But just because I didn't like my cousin was no reason to ascribe killerlike qualities to him. Mark was too self-absorbed to kill anyone. But did he have the kind of personality that would allow him to frame his father? And why would he do it? To get rid of him? But Mark wasn't even interested in the *shmatte* business. He was involved in investments, finding money here to invest there, to buy this business and then sell it overnight at a phenomenal profit; he was a very important man.

With my left hand, I tilted the other end of the shelf. Something rolled to the right.

Mark was also far too important to be cleaning his parents' garage after over thirty years of *shmuts*. Why did he clean that place, and why now? Why not hire someone to do it? And now that I thought of it, what kinds of businesses was he buying and selling, anyway?

The rolling object sounded hard, like it could be some sort of metal or wood. Whatever it was, I wanted it. My stomach was weakening. But if I could dislodge the shelf, that would give me . . . a piece of wood, and whatever was rolling on it.

What on earth was I doing?

My face was damp with sweat, which I gratefully wiped with my hand and brought to my mouth. Salty. At least it was wet.

The blackness was playing tricks on me. I squeezed my eyelids shut and opened them again, but she was still there. My mother was floating right there in front of me. Without ever opening her mouth, she said, "Life's too short, Sydney, be kind."

"Kind? To who? Mark? Like it or not, Ma, he turned into a *putz*." Feeling like Heidi, mountaineer girl, I inched my way to the left, so I could get a better angle on the shelf. "Things have changed since you were here, Mom. Just take a look at your brother. He turned out to be a real piece of work. Talk about hypocritical and self-involved." I lost my balance and slipped maybe an inch or two, causing considerable pain to the back of my head and my elbows, which I had instinctively thrown back to stop my descent.

"That was not helpful," I chided my mother, though she had vanished and was replaced with teeny, tiny dancing specks of white. It was as if I was actually able to see the air. I was far enough to the left now to feel the corner. I reached up, pushed at the shelf and heard the hard object— which was clearly not round—roll to the front right of the

shelf and tumble off. The barely audible *thup* it made assured me that it had fallen onto the mattress. Excellent.
Now for the shelf.

"Don't be afraid of death so much as an inadequate
life." Mother was back, stealing Ned's words.

"Ma, can you ask Ned who said that? It's really been
bugging me." I pushed the shelf, but it just fell back into
place. I needed to get higher.

"Bertolt." She seemed comfortable in her corner of the
closet. As I snuck a good look at her, I had to admit she
looked wonderful. Calm. Peaceful. As pretty as she ever
was before she took ill. "Brecht," she further edified.
"Bertolt Brecht."

"BB, of course."

Mom continued, "Brecht was a playwright."

"I know, but do you think Ned . . ." I paused. If my
mother was there with me, didn't that mean that a doorway
had opened between us, and I was that much closer to joining her and Dad and everyone else in the Land of Way-
beyond?

I was in a good position now with this shelf and I didn't
know how much longer I could keep myself up there.
"Okay, Mom, move. I don't want to hurt you."

"Geometrics would suggest that were you to push from
the center of the plank, rather than the corner, you would
be less likely to get stuck."

I smiled. I actually smiled. Geometrics . . . now I *knew* it
wasn't my mother. But she *did* have a point, so I took a
deep breath and did my Spider Woman crawl back to the
right.

I was actually feeling so confident I'd get out of this
mess, I promised myself that when I made it through this
alive, I'd give up the detective business and try something
more civilized, something like investment banking or running guns.

"Leslie would like that." Mom had moved to my left.

"Yes, she would. Do you know her?"

Mom smiled faintly and gracefully nodded once.

"And?"

"She loves you. She respects you. She worries about you. She laughs at your jokes. What more could I want for you?"

"Normalcy. Societal acceptance. Children."

"I would rather you lived a life that made you comfortable."

"Careful, now." Using both hands, I pushed the back of the shelf up and listened as it slid off its perch against the wall and landed with a crash. The noise nearly made my head implode, but it was still music to my ears.

I inched my way down the wall and with great relief sat on the bed. I was exhausted. My head was pounding. My body was shaking. I leaned forward and felt for the thing that had fallen from the shelf. It was cold. It was metal, rough, had a dense weight to it. One end was hollow enough for me to insert the tip of my index finger, whereas the other end was narrower and plugged.

A cable connector? A kitchen gadget? A nozzle? A car part? I didn't know, but it was a good weight, it was mine, and I was going to find a use for it.

I unwrapped my legs and stiffly stretched them out in front of me, but there was no time to rest. If I paused, I might consider the possibility that I really had been sealed into a wall, and I would lose my mind. I shifted my focus, instead, to the wooden shelf. How could I use this?

I put the metal thingie in my back pocket and kneeled on the cot again. I envisioned a big, ice-cold glass of milk and drank it down in no time flat. This, of course, needed an almost room temperature water chaser.

The shelf was heavier than I had expected, which I didn't mind, but it was totally unwieldy, which I did mind, because what with the milk and water, bladder control would soon be an issue. I struggled to stand it upright.

How on earth could Elly possibly be content living in the shadows of all these inflated male egos? Mark, and Mitch, and Paul! Of all people for her to have settled down with.

The shelf stood vertically until I brought it to rest on the cot, then it wouldn't fit.

How do you sleep with a man who wears his suits half a size too small? I figure men are difficult enough, but if you're going to live with one, he might as well have some charm or sex appeal or energy, or at least clothes that fit. Paul, however, had none of those. Paul also made it clear that despite what Mitch and Elly thought, he was on Jake's side. No, it wasn't that he was on his side, it was that he was fond of Jake. So what's not to be fond of, a little man in a bad toupee? A little weasel who doesn't care if the woman who dies in his factory is identified or gets a decent burial.

Shit. The shelf stuck at a forty-five-degree angle, covering the door. Damn. Damn. Damn.

Jake, Paul, Mitch, a bunch of knucklehead losers, and yet here I was, trapped in a closet by a lunatic, and each of them was probably at home at that very minute having dinner. Was Mitch giving Leslie the third degree? Was Leslie worried sick? Or had dinner already passed and were they sleeping? God . . . could it have been breakfast time? I had to believe that more than an hour had passed since I was attacked, but who knew?

Damn Mitch. Just the thought of what Nomi had told me made my blood boil. Mitch was guilty, all right, but not of arson.

I took the metal thingie out of my back pocket and started tapping on the wall. Three quick taps, three paced taps, and then three quick taps again. This was a building.

There had to be people here. Someone would hear me. Someone would surely understand three dashes, three dots. Someone was out there who could help.

Tap. Tap. Tap. Tap, Tap, Tap.

The darkness crowded in on me again.

Tap. Tap. Tap. Tap, Tap, Tap.

Someone had to help.

Tap. Tap. Tap. Tap, Tap, Tap.

''Mom?'' I murmured, as I felt my cheeks grow wet.

Twenty

It felt like hours, but it could have been minutes. I don't even know if I dozed. I heard a faint, distant sound. Movement. It was getting louder. Something was happening.

Zoe's voice came urging from the shadows of long ago, "Listen to the vibrations." It sounded like something heavy was being pushed across the floor. Very heavy. *Scrape.* Stop. *Scrape.* Stop. Whatever it was they were moving, they had to walk it one side at a time. I found my heart racing. I was going to get out of here. I was going to be set free. I remained perfectly still, my hands clenched into tight fists.

There was a voice on the other side of the door now. No, two voices. Light eked through the crack in the double doors. Subtle as it was, I found myself squinting against the pain. The back of my head was still pounding.

A moment of silence on the other side of the door put me into a low-grade panic. Had they left? Were they waiting for me to open the door? Light was still coming through. Maybe something had frightened them and they had gone and left the door unlatched so I could leave without seeing them. Not likely. I didn't move. I waited. I knew the Mask wasn't the type who would leave something as enticing as a vulnerable victim. I didn't breathe. I didn't blink. I didn't think.

And then it happened: the door opened. The effect was more than jarring. It felt as if someone had gouged red-hot pokers into my eyes. I turned my face away from the light and shielded my eyes with my forearm.

When I was able to squint through the glare, I straightened my back and used my hand as a visor. My host was standing there, his face still hidden behind his mask. How like a coward. He said nothing. He was leaning on the fallen shelf, which I saw now was white and very much in need of a fresh coat of paint.

I didn't trust myself to speak. My mouth was parched, my throat felt as if it was closed, and I was afraid that the sound of my own voice would only support my defenseless state. My release from this prison was proof of forward motion. Whatever it was that the Mask needed me for was going to make itself apparent sooner rather than later.

"A decorator, huh? Just like your girlfriend," he whispered, removing the wooden slat. "Very nice. Get up."

I squinted around my cell and saw that it was, as I thought, a six-by-three-foot closet. The room behind the Mask was an empty twelve-foot-square box with only one piece of furniture, a Victorian-styled dresser complete with claw feet and a frame to hold a vanity mirror, but no mirror. A shade covered the only window and a single halogen floor lamp illuminated the room. The ceilings were higher than I had thought.

The Mask reached out, grabbed my upper arm in a vise-like grip and hurried me along. My knees rejected the jerky movement and bucked under me. Instinctively I reached out to brace myself, but he must have thought I was going at him. He snapped my other wrist in his hand and clamped it between his amazingly strong thumb and middle fingers.

"I tripped." The sound of my own voice came as a surprise. It was gruff and hoarse, like a tough dame doing life behind bars with Susan Hayward.

He released my wrist but led me by the arm to the bathroom, a room that had obviously been prepared for me. Aside from the normal facilities, there was soap, a towel, and toilet paper; that was it. No mirror. No cabinets. No window. No radiator cap. No toothpaste or brush. No nothing.

"Three minutes and I come in and get you," he whispered, and I wondered if his was a voice I would recognize if given half a chance. He left the door ajar, but I could see he had no interest in my bathroom routine.

Three minutes later, I was somewhat revived. I was watered, I was as clean as I was going to get, and I was able to see that the thing I had found in the closet was a hose nozzle. Go figure, another one of life's paradoxes. Knowing that it would be impossible for me to hide the nozzle on my person for long, I decided the most prudent thing would be to hide it in the water tank, which I did.

The Mask was leaning against the only door to the room, looking more like a casual kind of guy than a psychotic killer. I mirrored him as best as I could, leaning against the bathroom doorway.

His smile was slow, but still visible in the clownlike mouth hole cut out from his disguise. "Hungry?" he murmured, disguising his voice behind a continued whisper.

"I'm sorry, I didn't hear you." I touched a finger to the back of my right ear.

He didn't do anything for the longest time; he just stood there, frozen in his casual guy position. When he finally pushed off from the wall, he turned right around, opened the door, and left me standing there. I wandered into the room and saw my sleeping quarters from a distance. To the side of it there was a whitewashed plywood board, the size of the double doors, that had probably been wedged between the vanity and the closet, which is why it was so dark in there. The cot was a solid, Army green metal frame. The shapeless gray-and-white-striped mattress was covered with brown stains. And then I saw it. Dead center, on the frame, facing out. Just where we'd put it.

My heart caught in my throat as I fought the nausea that was overwhelming me.

I knelt before the bed and bent down to be at eye level with the frame. There it was, just as my grandmother had printed it more than thirty-five years earlier. "5/25/57 Nana & Syd." This cot was forty years old and I had been the grandchild to inaugurate it with my first solo sleepover at Nana's.

"This is *my* bed, right, Nana?"

"That's right, sweetheart."

"Nora's gonna think it's hers," I said, knowing perfectly well that my big sister would call dibs on it the second she saw it, and I'd get stuck on the couch when we both stayed over.

"You want to share with your sister, don't you?"

I didn't.

"How about this?" Nana said, taking out a laundry marker. She knelt by the side of the bed and wrote the date and our names. "See? Proof that this was a special night for us both. But you must always be willing to share, don't forget that."

The door opened behind me.

I heard paper crumple. I turned and sat cross-legged on the floor in front of the cot. The Mask was holding two fast food bags.

"You can take off your mask now. I know who you are."

He paused. How could he think I wouldn't see Nana's inscription? No, he knew I'd see it, he wanted to get caught. But why?

He sniffed as he walked to the center of the room, where he gracefully slid into a seated position, maybe six feet away from me. "Dinner?" he asked, as he opened the two bags and spilled out the contents, including fries, burgers, soda, and even a chicken sandwich. How very thoughtful.

Never one to cut off my nose to spite my face, I knew I needed sustenance. I moved closer and reached for a large soda. There was every likelihood that this food was laced, but it was a chance I was willing to take. Despite the pain I was in, I was hungry.

He took off a glove, plucked a French fry from the bag, and popped it into his mouth.

I unwrapped a cheeseburger and took a very small bite.

"What time is it?" I asked, glancing at his hands. His right hand was still gloved.

"Does it matter?" He devoured half a double cheeseburger in one bite.

"Idle curiosity."

"Trust me, it doesn't matter. Time is something you don't have to worry about anymore."

"Really? Why's that?" The food was staying down. "Is this my last meal?"

He sighed and shook his head. "Oh no, I have much bigger plans for you than death."

The way he said it sent a chill down my spine. "Do tell." I sounded blasé enough to be believable, as far as I was concerned.

He crushed the finished burger container and reached for another. "Who am I, Sydney?" He was no longer whispering, and his vaguely familiar voice had an unusually menacing quality that cried out, *"This guy is a sicko."* He didn't sound like Mark, but who else could it be? Who else would have Nana's cot? Then again, why would Mark be doing this? And when did he learn martial arts?

"Look, you're going to have to take your mask off at

some point, so it might as well be now. Then you and I can talk face to face . . . as family should.''

"And family means so much, doesn't it?'' he said caustically.

I shrugged. Between the sugar and the caffeine, the soda was having a restorative effect on me. I ate little and took only small sips of the cola.

"All right. Seeing as how it won't make any difference at this point . . .'' He tucked his gloved fingers under his chin and started to pull up on the ski mask, but then he stopped, as if reconsidering. I held my breath, knowing perfectly well who was on the other side of that disguise. But what would I say when it was confirmed? He followed through and raised the curtain off his face.

I stared at him.

"Don't recognize me, do you?''

In truth, I didn't. I was so expecting Mark, that seeing this stranger before me had to have registered as a complete surprise.

"Yeah, well, so much for the importance of family unity and all that bullshit.'' He dropped the cap and resumed eating as if he had a grudge against the food.

"Danny?'' I never would have recognized him, but it was the voice on his answering machine. I hadn't seen Jake's son since I was thirteen and looked after him at a family gathering. Danny had been about three then, and was a nice kid, as I recalled. I quickly scanned the recesses of my brain to see what I knew about him. He worked as a computer programmer at a hospital. Elly never liked him, even as a kid; she said he was nasty. He started getting into trouble when he was about eleven, right after his mother left Jake and Danny, to move to Sante Fe with a young lover. After that, Jake had a hard time controlling him. From what Elly had said the other day, Danny had pulled a knife on Mitch, which sounded like the beginning of the end between Mitch and Jake. When I asked her why he had pulled the knife, she had shrugged and casually said, "Who knows why Danny does anything?"

"I'm flattered you remembered me, Sydney." He pushed a piece of lettuce into his mouth with his thumb.

"Danny, what are you doing?"

He pushed his dark eyebrows up, causing his handsome face to look like a baffled four-year-old's. He didn't look anything like Jake, so I had to assume he resembled his mother, Barbara, whom I wouldn't know if I fell over her. Several days' worth of stubble had covered his squared chin, which actually enhanced his good looks.

"I'm eating?"

"*What* are you doing?" I repeated. Now that I knew who it was, I felt less threatened. Christ, I'd babysat for this kid . . . he wouldn't hurt me. "*What are you, crazy?*" a loud voice inside my head screamed out. "*He has hurt you! The man is nuts.*" Logic is always a good thing to keep handy. Though I had never been held hostage before, I knew enough about it to realize that all too often the victims feel a kind of kinship with their captors. In my case it made sense that I'd be inclined to want to trust him because we were, though very distantly, related.

"This is your bon voyage party." He waggled three fries in my direction. "You really should eat up."

"Where am I going?" I asked, as I brought the sweaty soda cup to my mouth.

Danny's smile was a chilling thing. "East."

At least it wasn't south. "How far east?"

"Very far. I am surprised with you, I must say."

"Why is that?"

"You have much more stamina than I'd have given you credit for, especially considering what the family says about you." The look he shot me was a challenge. Danny Aronson was toying with me the way my puppy Auggie plays with flies. The big difference, however, is that Auggie is an innocent.

"Yep, very far east," he pressed on. Now that he had started talking, I realized that he possessed the schoolyard bully mentality that could propel him forward on his own steam. He glanced at his watch and nodded. "As a matter of fact, in about twelve hours or so, why, you'll have a whole new life."

"Really? Doing what?"

He laughed and I had to wonder if Jake knew what a mental case his son was. How do you hide something like this?

"Something you've probably never done before, come to think of it."

I don't normally like guessing games, but this one had a certain draw for me. I knew the longer I kept Danny talking, the better chance I had at either winning him over— which was unlikely, I know—or staying out of the closet. "Look, obviously you have a plan for me here, which I have a feeling I'm not going to like much, but before we go there . . ." I saw he was enjoying this. "Maybe you could tell me what happened at your Dad's factory."

Danny scratched at his lower lip and nodded contemplatively. "There was a fire." He looked over at me, the picture of innocence. "Your uncle started a fire that resulted in family chaos." He dotted his sentence with a nod of his head.

"Why did you set fire to your dad's place?" I asked bluntly.

He flattened his right hand over his heart as he reached for a container of fries. "But I didn't, Sydney. I'm really surprised. I'd have thought you had it all figured out by now."

"Sorry to disappoint you, Danny. But I didn't know anything. See?" I held my empty palms up. "This was all for nothing."

"No, no, not for nothing. My whole life has changed, Sydney, and in a way, I have you to thank. You see, if you hadn't gotten involved in all this, chances are Mitch would have gone to jail—for a very limited stretch of time, granted, but it would have been jail—and I would never have known what *real* power feels like. It's intoxicating, you know."

I shrugged. "It's okay."

His laughter reverberated off the walls. "A sense of humor! I like that. Too bad we never got to know one another. I think I'd have liked you." He crushed an empty fries container and tossed it over his shoulder, across the room.

"It's never too late, Danny."

"Oh, but it is. You see, you're going away, and with what little time you have left here, well, I've just got dozens of things to do, I couldn't possibly socialize." The edge crept in again and I could practically smell trouble. "You want this?" He picked up the chicken sandwich and bounced it in his hand.

I declined, having barely touched my cheeseburger. "Where are we going in the Far East?"

He sighed and examined his third sandwich. "Just you, I'm afraid. You see, as much as I wish I could get away and see the world, it's just too difficult, what with work and family obligations." He took a bite of the sandwich and studied me as he chewed. "I didn't start the fire. I know who did, but that's irrelevant at this point, don't you think?"

"Irrelevant? No. The fire is obviously why you killed Hickey and Kirstin, so how could it be irrelevant?"

"Because *who did it* is of no consequence. The important thing is that it was done. The fire created an occasion wherein Mitchell Gerber could finally get what was coming to him." His lips stretched into a tight smile as he reached for his soda. He slowly squeezed his chicken sandwich between tensing fingers.

"I don't understand."

"Mitch is not a nice man." It was a flat statement of truth for Danny. He eased up on the chicken and took a long draw of soda. I flashed on Kerry's asking if Danny could be Mr. Right for her best friend, Lara. Sad thing is, knowing Lara, she'd fall for him in a second. Then again, Lara has always struck me as the sort of woman who would propose to an inmate on death row, a phenomenon I have never been able to comprehend. *"Sure Johnny killed eight women, but he's a good man at heart. And he loves me. I know he does."*

"Tell me about it," I said conspiratorially. I needed a place for us to connect. If Danny and I were allies in our dislike of Mitch, he might be less inclined to hurt me, or send me off to the Far East.

"Mitch *thinks* he's a good man, which insults the intelligence of everyone around him. It also makes him dangerous. Do you have any idea how that man afflicted our lives when I was a kid?" He rested his elbow on his knee, as if weighing his cutlet.

"No. How?"

Danny was fighting some battle inside him I wasn't exactly privy to, but his face revealed his suffering and I found myself hurting for the little boy who was just as much a victim of his past as I was of his present.

"He treated my dad like he was garbage, always putting him down . . . even in front of me and my mom! You don't do that to a man. Why do you think my mother left?" I had to assume this was a rhetorical question, because otherwise, a good guess could have been that Jake was a womanizing jerk who was known to drink too much and throw a punch every now and then. "Because of Mitch. She was myopic, she couldn't see past Mitch's constant onslaught of digs and petty badgering. It didn't just stop with work, no. Mitch had something to say about every single fucking aspect of my father's life—the way he dressed, his friends, the way he was raising me, the books he read, the food he ate, and later on, the women he dated . . . nothing, nothing was fucking right as far as Mitch was concerned. And he always had to comment. *Always.* These snide little jabs. If you confronted him on it, he'd say, 'What you can't take a little constructive criticism?' or, 'For God's sake, I'm only kidding, where's your humor?' And it didn't stop with my father. Mitch was just as hard on me, but do you think he ever badgered his own kids like that? Never! No, but he always had something to say about me—that I was a good-for-nothing, or lazy, or headed for jail. He couldn't believe it when I got a job programming. I really think he's annoyed that I'm making good. I've wanted to hurt that bloated old windbag ever since I can remember.'' He examined the sandwich as if he'd forgotten he had it. Then he took an unenthusiastic bite.

"So now you've found your way to hurt him."

"That's right. You see, this way Mitch is publicly humiliated, convicted of arson because he was jealous, of *who*? My father, that's who."

"So, Hickey learned the truth and was blackmailing you?"

He shrugged as if this was the least important thing in the world. "It was just a matter of time. He was a lazy, greedy man. With a rotten sense of humor." Danny's appetite was returning. He reached for a second bag of fries. "He was, however, the first person I ever killed, and I have to say, there will always be a warm spot in my heart for him, given that."

I nibbled at the burger and recrossed my legs, which were beginning to tire. I wasn't sure why he killed Kirstin, but I had a hunch she wasn't the right thing to bring up then and there. Danny had opened a connection between us. Now it was up to me to make it work to my advantage. He was wound tight, too tight to reason with for long.

"I had no idea you felt that way about Mitch." I nodded approvingly and asked the cosmos to forgive me if I betrayed my loyalty to my uncle. As mad as I was at Mitch, I somehow didn't think he'd mind. "Revenge can feel pretty sweet."

"Yeah, it can."

"I haven't had much to do with the family."

"That's because you don't fit in nicely."

"How do you know?"

"Paul and I talk about the Gerbers all the time. He tells me everything. I've been keeping tabs on you for years, through Paul. He likes you. He's the only decent thing about them. Figures he'd be *married* into it." He shook his head sadly.

"Like Maddy," I encouraged him.

"Exactly. She's a good woman. And she's *Dad's* side of the family."

"I was supposed to meet Maddy for dinner. She'll be worried about me."

"Yes, well, I can guarantee you that they're all worried about you, Sydney, but there's nothing I can do about that now. The ball is in motion!" His manic side was surfacing.

"Danny. Let me go. No one will know, I promise."

He stared at me; the longer he stared, the more intense his gaze became, as if something was building up inside of him that would implode at any second. Then, like a frog spitting out his tongue to catch a fly, Danny had my ankle in his grasp. He slowly applied pressure.

"Have you ever killed anyone, Sydney?"

I had, but it had been self-defense, and it wasn't something I was proud of. I didn't say anything, but I held his gaze.

"When I felt Hickey's life end . . ." He squeezed my ankle harder and looked down at it, as if it were a mesmerizing foreign object. "It was amazing. When I felt his life stop, my whole life changed." He smiled as if in a trance and looked back up at me. "That kind of control, the life-and-death control over another person, that can really turn a guy on, did you know that?"

Danny was beyond crazy, and the frightening thing was, he was the kind of guy who could fit into society perfectly well. I could just hear his neighbors and friends voicing their utter amazement that this nice, handsome, well-spoken guy was a cold-blooded killer.

"You see? It was because of you asking questions that Hickey got gluttonous. And if I hadn't had to kill Alfred, I never would have understood that there is something in this world that *I* can excel at, something I can not only do well, but enjoy at the same time. I think it must be akin to being a professional athlete. I like feeling life seep out of another person, I like the control and the way they look when they are experiencing pure terror. And to think I owe this new insight to *you*, which is why I am not going to kill you, oh pretty lady. Unless, of course, I *have* to." Everything about his demeanor screamed "*insane.*"

He tightened his hold of my ankle and pulled me toward him. "Ready for your after-dinner treat?" Just looking at his eyes, I could tell he was gone.

I slapped a palm on the floor beside me to try and resist his pull. "No. Look, I haven't finished dinner."

"Too bad." His laugh was manic as he suddenly grabbed both my legs and pulled me under him. "Too bad," he sang through clenched teeth as he reached for my hands.

I threw the soda in his face, but this didn't stop him. He didn't even flinch. His hands were like iron vises and his mind had clicked into automatic. I flailed, I kicked, I tried

to bite and reason, but nothing penetrated. He was strad-
dling me, having pinioned my hands between his and my
thighs. He was clearly relishing his new found control.

"Now I want you to know that at first, your new life
may seem different, maybe even a little seedy." He
sounded as if he were preparing me for the first day of
school. He bit his lower lip and smiled. "But your new
owner is a very nice man." He squeezed his thighs as he
reached into his inside jacket pocket with his left hand.
"And I am sure you will be very glad to know, you fetched
quite a nice penny, for which I am again grateful to you.
You!" His right hand shot out and pinched my cheek. "You
are my new diva, my brain queen, did you know that? I
will forever and always be indebted to you because without
you, I am but a mere shell of a man."

"Danny, don't do this."

"Ah, but I must." He tapped my cheek and returned his
attention to his jacket pocket. "And you just may like it,
Sydney. I understand life can be very lucrative overseas.
Besides, your new benefactor is a man noted for treating
his friends very well. I had the distinct pleasure of making
his acquaintance when his mother was hospitalized at the
fine facility where I work. He and I got to talking one day
in the cafeteria, and, well, it's amazing how some people
you just click with. He was concerned about skyrocketing
hospital costs, and since I do have unrestricted access to
the computer system, well, one thing led to another. Funny,
I've made a lot of friends at the hospital because of the
way I can change numbers. I tweak someone's hours, and
they do me a solid in return."

He pulled another syringe from his pocket. "Now, I don't
want you to be afraid, so I will explain that the first shot
I gave you was a very nice, mellow dose of 'ludes, which
I am, admittedly, surprised to see how well you handled,
so . . . I am now going to use something a little stronger

and just increase the dosage." He extracted a small bottle from another pocket. "Ah, ah, ahh," he cautioned me as I bucked and twisted to get free from under him. "I can assure you that taken in moderation, *this* is a very nice high. Done it myself a few times."

It took everything inside me, but I brought my legs up and was able to unseat him enough to free my hands. At once I reached for the syringe. I was damned if he was going to put more garbage inside me. But I was weakened from before, and he was a very strong, focused man. He slammed a fist into my jaw which stunned me into momentary stillness, but it didn't last long because I was equally determined; I wanted out of there. When he reached for the needle, I tried to crawl away, but it was impossible. He pulled me back with his left hand, caught me in a scissors hold between his legs, and readied the needle.

His voice was frighteningly calm. "This is no way to thank me for sparing your life, Sydney. No way at all. But I like you, so let me tell you that in a few hours you and I are going to take a little ride to meet . . . Jack, we'll call him Jack, huh?" He squeezed his legs together, making me feel as if my insides would explode. While he did that, he shoved the sleeve of my shirt up and injected the drug into my muscle. *What drugs inject into the muscle?* I fought to remember, as if knowing would make any difference to my reaction. Several seconds later he released his hold of my waist. "Feels good, don't it?" he cooed. I was floating, struggling to get back to order and sharper senses, but it was no use. I felt my limbs relax and then my flesh. "See? It's not so bad, Sydney. Drugs and sex, what a fabulous life. God knows it beats the alternative."

I felt my mouth moving and saw him bend closer to me, listen, and then back off laughing.

"Why?" he guffawed. "*Why*? I'll tell you *why*. Because nothing will get in the way of my seeing Mitchell Gerber publicly humiliated. Mr. Holier-Than-Thou is gonna look like scum to his clients and friends. He already does, and I am not going to take that away from my father.'' He continued ranting, but he soon looked like a television performer on mute. I was there, but I was floating further and further away to a soft, calm, luscious place where there was absolutely no pain at all. Not . . . one . . . bit.

Twenty-one

I don't get the whole allure of drugs. They make me anxious, knock me out, leave me with powerful headaches, and make me feel as if the interior and exterior parts of my body are working on completely different planes. I cannot imagine volunteering to feel like this.

When I awoke, I was woozy and disoriented. It felt as if the top of my head was completely numb. However, below the surface, under the skull, the entire back portion of my head felt as if someone was threading large, rusty nails through my brain. It took me several minutes to understand where I was, that I was back on the cot, but that the closet doors were open. With my legs feeling like rubber, I groped my way to the bathroom and turned on the light. If the way I felt was any indication of how I looked, I figured chances were pretty good that my new *benefactor,* what was his name? . . . it didn't matter . . . would ask for either a refund or another model.

Selling people? Selling me? How was it possible? The thought was staggering, yet I knew this existed. It's not as if I'm not savvy to the *mishegoss* in the world, but being inextricably caught in its vortex was mind-boggling. Danny Aronson had sold me into prostitution. How was it possible that he had access to this kind of corruption? That alone was inconceivable, but that he truly believed he was doing me a favor added an element to this whole thing that shifted it from the merely frightening to the grotesque.

As I tried to revive myself, I wondered if Danny was born crazy, or was this an illness that grew with time. Were his parents at fault? Did they love him enough? Too much? Is homicidal behavior genetic or environmental? It was disturbing to think that people ask these very same questions regarding homosexuality, as if the two things could be thrown into the same pot, and yet they are, all the time.

I didn't know what time it was, but I knew I had to have been out for at least a few hours. Bigger dose . . . did he say that, or was I dreaming? Either way, I had been out. If I worked it backward I might be able to place myself, at least in time. Assuming I'd been sleeping for six hours, and before that I had been out for—what, three hours, or maybe it was only an hour, but then again, it felt like twelve hours, or even longer . . . but could I really have slept for that long? No, wait. Focus. If I only had a watch. Okay, I had arrived at Kirstin's at five. That I know, that I remember. Add three is eight, then an hour with Danny, plus six—but wait, how long was I locked in the closet before, when I was awake? It could have been an hour or it could have been ten—hell, for all I knew, it could have been fifteen minutes. Time was completely distorted, to the point where I don't even know how long I spent trying to figure out how long I had been there; it could have been a matter of seconds or hours, but then, could it really take hours to walk around a single room?

Nothing had changed much during my sleep. I repeatedly lifted the window shade and saw each time that the window had been riveted over with an implacable metal sheet. The halogen lamp was missing . . . just as well. The only light came from the overhead fixture in the bathroom. Garbage from dinner lay where it had been left. One look at my uneaten burger was enough to make my stomach pitch. The door was locked. Big surprise. There was nothing in the dresser drawers.

I had to get out of here. I heard a door close in the other room and light snapped through the cracks of the door. I made a beeline to the bathroom, turned off the light, and carefully lowered myself onto Nana's cot.

The door opened, and through the slit of eyelids, I could see Danny approach, another needle in hand. Faces floated before me; *Bad Seed,* Patty McCormick, playing the piano, a young Malcolm McDowell dancing in *A Clockwork Orange*, Bette Davis, ax in hand in *Hush Hush, Sweet Charlotte*.

I pretended to be asleep. I figured if I seemed to be out cold, he wouldn't inject me again. He wouldn't have a need.

He lifted my hand and dropped it. I was a perfect dead weight. He pushed at my shoulder as if to awaken me. I smacked my lips and curled up tighter onto my side. He whispered, "That's right, Sydney. In no time you'll be far, far away from it all."

There were several seconds of silence. I knew he was still by my side, but he wasn't moving; he was barely breathing. Then I felt it. He slipped his left hand around my arm, applied a gentle pressure, and inserted the needle. I tried to jerk away from him as soon as I felt the prick of the needle, but it was no use.

"Wake up. Up. Up. Up. Up. Up."

I tried to swat the fly away, but it kept landing on my cheeks. First one, then the other, back and forth. Big fly. Biting. Stinging. Pushing my face to the left, to the right.

"Wake up, Sydney. First day of school. There's a girl." The voice was distant, like at the end of a tunnel. Not Mom, no, not her.

My chin was resting on my chest. Every time I went to bat the fly away, I missed. My hand came to rest on my face and I felt wetness. Drool. I wiped it away with the back of my hand.

"Good girl. Now we're going to get you up. Ready?"

I opened my eyes, first one, then the other. It was impossible to focus. As soon as I opened my eyes, the pain started up again in the back of my head, distant, but steady. I reached out, flapping my hand lazily in the air. Someone took it.

"We're gonna make you nice and pretty to meet Mr. Jack." The chipper voice that was too close and too loud had to be attached to the force that was tugging me up off my bed against my will. I tried to snatch my arm away from his grasp, but it was as if I had no form, like I was ooze.

I was being held up, someone was behind me, holding me up. His arms were looped under my arms and my breasts, pushing up at a painful angle. I tried to disengage from his hold, but each time I moved, he only pressed harder, as if his arms were clamps that could rip my arms right out of the sockets. My body was tingling. I was moving across the floor, miles away, many, many miles away, effortlessly, yet each step tingled. I was a ghost, a shadow filled with pinpricks of what, pain? No, not pain. It was as if thousands of needles were prickling away at my flesh. There was a nasty fog, I could barely see, but I could feel the tips of my toes ripple across the floor.

A marionette. "I've got no strings to hold me down," I sang. Or did I? Was the sound merely manufactured in my head? ". . . To make me fret, or make me frown . . ."

No, no, it was an earthquake, and it was hurting my head. Where was I? There was a city rolling past, a blur of red and gray and black and white, but which city was it? Pretty. Wait, wait a minute, how did I get there? The streets were wet. I was cold, very cold. My feet felt like ice. I squinted out through the window, looking for something familiar,

something to connect to, something to jog my memory . . .
how did I get here? The window was cold to the touch. My
hand looked like a foreign object. I moved the fingers. They
were mine, all right. It was a pretty hand. Where was my
ring? Did I have a ring? Didn't I have a sapphire ring Leslie
had given me? Leslie, right? Leslie *what?* Washburn. My
Leslie, where was she? We were crossing a bridge. We?
Who was *we?* I turned my head to the left. There was a
driver in the front seat (I could only see the back of his
head), and a man to my left. His touch was gentle and
reassuring. He looked familiar, but I couldn't place him.
"Where are we going?" I thought I asked it aloud, but I
couldn't remember if he answered me. He smiled and patted my arm. What a nice guy. Oh, but God, I was so tired.
So very tired. I just needed some sleep and then I'd feel
better. Then I'd be myself, whoever that was.

An arm was bracing me as we climbed a mountain of
stairs. My body was moving, but there was no connection
between my head and my movements. The air was vibrating, boom, boom, boom. The floors, walls, people crowded
around were all vibrating with the pulse of the beat. At the
top of the stairs was a huge black room, packed tight with
gyrating bodies. I inhaled the blanket of smoke and limply
let myself be pulled through the wall of bodies to a seat.
A bar. My new friend helped me up onto a stool, and standing almost in front of me, leaning on the bar, yelled into
my ear, "What do you drink?"

My mouth was dry. I squinted at the row of people, hundreds of people, all their mouths moving at once, but I
couldn't make out any discernible sound. Then a woman
screamed beside me, practically scaring me off my stool. I
turned and saw that her red lips were wide open, exposing
her white teeth and pink tongue. Her false lashes looked
like little bugs over her eyes.

"Did you hear what she said?" She pointed to the back-

side of another woman as she played with the ends of a
red scarf tied around her neck. "Oh girl, I tell you, they
let anyone in here now with this new management, it ain't
what it was, you know what I mean?" She turned and said
to someone behind her, "Is that for me? You are so nice!"
She pulled the empty stool closer to me and my friend.
"You see that? There are gentlemen left in this world. My
feet are killin' me, you know what I mean? I mean, I don't
mean to be rude, but I was gonna scream if I didn't sit
down, not that anyone here would notice. It's all cause this
man sold me my shoes, half a size too small, can you believe that?" She didn't seem to need air.

"How about Scotch?" my friend suggested as he lit a
cigarette. If I could only remember his name.

I hate Scotch. But I couldn't remember what I like. Rum?
Wine? I reached for his cigarette and slipped it between my
fingers. Finally I murmured, "gin," but he didn't hear me.
A short glass of brown liquid and ice was set before me.
It stank like medicine and made me feel nauseated. I
brought the cigarette to my lips and took a deep drag.

I was thirteen. Jackie Jane Henderson was fifteen and
had just moved into an apartment on the fifth floor of our
building. Her mother had moved them there from Darien,
Connecticut, after having divorced her husband, Jackie's
father, who looked like Phil Silvers. Jackie also resembled
Phil Silvers. Maybe that's why she was such a tough kid
and wore white lipstick and smoked Winstons. She was the
one who'd showed me how to smoke.

The cigarette in hand tasted exactly like that first one
with Jackie in the bicycle room in the basement.

The man behind the bar slapped down a taller glass next
to the rocks glass, this one filled with a clear liquid.

"Water!" he shouted to me, and winked.

I tried to wink back. Unfortunately, I didn't have much
control of my muscles, and both eyelids fought for function.

I was becoming aware enough to know that I hadn't winked, nor had I blinked. Whatever it was I had done wasn't what I had intended.

I reached for the water. The cigarette had left a nasty film inside my mouth. Halfway through the movement, however, I forgot what I was doing and leaned my elbows onto the counter. I went to rest my head on my arms, but something pulled me back.

"Nah, ah, ah," a warning voice sputtered all too close, making it sound as if he was actually inside my head. The back of my head was being yanked, and I was pulled back up into a sitting position. "Remember, you want to make Jack happy."

Jack? Who was Jack? Why did I want to make him happy? Leslie. There was a Leslie. But Jack? Jack? The only Jack I could think of was Jack Tessler, a potter in Hell's Kitchen, a good one, too, but why would I want to make him happy? How?

Come on, girl, come back. I took another drag off the cigarette. It was like licking the bottom of an old ashtray, but it was helping me to focus. I studied my hand holding the cigarette, the ashes at the end of the smoke. My name was Sydney, Sydney Sloane. Okay, good. Now, where the hell *was* I?

I surveyed the room as far as my head would allow without considerable pain. Clearly it was a club, but where? How did I get here? I looked down and saw that my legs were bare. I was wearing a cheap red miniskirt that was hiked up as far as it could go without revealing all my secrets. How did that happen? At the end of my legs, I saw that someone had shod me in red spiked heels. No wonder I couldn't walk. The top half of my body was covered with a short, quarter-length-sleeved, thin quilted jacket. No wonder I was cold.

I held the cigarette like a pencil and looked for a place

to put it out. The grotesque woman to my right with the false lashes must have seen me reaching for the ashtray and pushed it closer to me.

I mumbled a thanks and looked her over. She wasn't so bad, really. Younger than I had initially thought, and actually quite pretty. Her smile was like this little ray of hope. *Hope.* I went to run my fingers through my hair, but it hurt. My friend took my hand in his and wrapped it around the glass on the bar.

No, no, no, no, no, something was wrong here—but *what*? I grunted a laugh. Maybe the lady next to me could help. Right, maybe if I knew what was wrong I could tell her, but I didn't know what was wrong. Well, for starters, maybe she could help me find out the guy's name I was with . . . that would be good.

As I sat there considering how to broach this, I flashed on the image of a girl, sitting on a throne, a look of utter surprise etched on her face. Chris. Chris who? Who was she? Who was she? Who was she? Oh my God, Johns! *She was Kirstin Johns.* Kirstin Johns was dead. Oh yes, yes, that was it.

My date pressed my fingers around the glass again, but I don't like Scotch, I don't even like the smell of it. I am Sydney, and I don't drink Scotch, and this date was . . . Bob, no, no, not Bob, *Danny.* Danny Aronson. Jack was just the man who had bought me. *Bought me!* Christ, I had to get out of there. Okay, so maybe I had the advantage of being in a public place now, but there was still no way I could fight Danny off on my own. Hell, I couldn't even lift a water glass, which I had tried to do several times because I was so thirsty.

I remembered a case from when I was a cop. A young woman's parents were trying to get her back from the man she'd eloped with. They'd hired a private investigator team who'd drugged her for transport across state lines. When authorities at the airport had questioned her condition, the detectives escorting her had produced exquisitely forged papers, proving that they were officials at a well-known psychiatric institution, and explained that the woman was a danger, to both herself and others. The detectives were actually assisted by the authorities when the woman became agitated and screamed that she was being kidnapped, which, in fact, she was.

Don't let him know. My thinking grew more lucid. I slumped against the back of the stool and scanned the room as best as I could.

This place was a Happyland disaster waiting to happen. There were no windows, just black walls. Apart from the door at the top of the stairs, where we had entered, there seemed to be only one other exit, behind the bar. Half a dozen disco balls spun slowly from the high black ceiling as strobe lights pulsed in time to the music, flinging little diamonds of light around the space. Black lights lined the wall behind the bar.

Our Lady of the Lashes seemed to have taken a shine to Danny. She pulled a gold leatherette case out of her wishful cleavage, snapped it open, and removed from the case a thin cigarette. She slowly, suggestively parted her lips and asked Danny for a light.

Ever the gentleman, he complied.

So much for possible allies. Right, she also looked like the type who would marry this idiot in jail.

I reached for another cigarette. A cigarette could make a good weapon. How well would Danny be able to see if he had the burnt end of a cigarette crushed in his eye? I made a mental list of everything within reaching distance that I could use against Danny and his benevolent buddy, Jack, who bought women like they were retail items. There was the Scotch; thrown in the right place that could sting and hamper vision. The glassware. The spiked heels that were a size and a half too small for my feet. The filled ashtrays. Okay, so maybe I was pushing it, but at least I was thinking . . . *I was back.* And I was not going to let this son of a bitch take me without one hell of a fight. I kept my head bowed as I rolled the unlit cigarette between my fingers.

As the drugs started to wear off, I could feel parts of my body I had no idea had been bruised, which included just about every inch of me from my collarbone to my ankles.

Danny moved the Scotch in front of me. "I'm telling you, drink something. It'll make you feel better."

"Gimme a light," I slurred, as I held the cigarette up to my mouth. He obliged and then I raised a listless hand, wrapped my fingers around the cold glass, and brought it to my mouth. Goose-pimples covered my forearm. I touched the rim of the glass to my lips and wiped it off with the back of my other hand as soon as the glass hit the bar. Just picking up the glass was a monumental effort. I couldn't imagine what stopping Danny would require.

"Ah, hello, my friend, here we are." Danny's forced, almost manic greeting informed me that another man had joined us. Jack, no doubt. "Can I buy you a drink?" Danny turned to the bartender and ordered a rum with a splash of water. He then slapped my thigh and said, "Sydney, I want you to meet someone."

I straightened my back the best I could and turned to meet Jack, a greasy short man in a shiny blue suit. Jack reached for my hand, but I pulled away. Undaunted, he moved his mouth millimeters away from my ear, set his hand on the small of my back, and pinched me with tal-onlike nails. "You be nice to me. I be nice to you." He smelled like sour pork. I turned my gaze back to the bar and pretended not to hear.

Danny handed Jack his drink, smiled, and said, "Hey, hey, here we go. I want you to meet my associate." Danny

held out his hand in introduction. Jack turned and nodded
to the third person to join us.

"What do you want, man, a beer?" Danny asked his
associate, as he leaned back against the bar and scanned
the room. I knew from the noise and the heat that the place
was packed.

Lady Lashes was staring at me. Intently. The way she
made her eyes bigger reminded me of Gloria Swanson in
Sunset Boulevard. Great, a million people at the bar, and I
get stuck next to a mental case with caterpillars for eye-
lashes. The music was blasting. The bar was now three and
four deep.

Trapped in a sea of bad smells, bad tastes, and deafening
noise, I knew if I didn't do something soon, life as I had
known it would be a thing of the past. No one was here to
help me extricate myself from Danny and his barnyard
buddy Jack.

I turned to get a glimpse of Danny's associate behind
me, but the physical action hurt too much to follow through
with. It was then that I understood I felt a panic which
could come only with clarity. I had to do something deci-
sive and brilliant within the next minute or I would never
see Leslie or Auggie again.

Jack leaned against me as he and Danny toasted the future. He also looped his free arm around my back, tightened
his hold, and before I knew what hit me, was biting my
right breast. Or I should say, trying to. First he had to get
past my arm, which I instinctively jerked out as soon as I
felt him nearing me. There was also the matter of my lit
cigarette. I could have extinguished it on Jack's bowed
head, but it meant possibly burning myself and wasting my
one good weapon on this smelly little man in a unsightly
suit. Instead, as I leaned away from him, I thrust out my
arm and caught Danny (who was reaching to catch Jack)
on the cheek with the lit end of the smoke.

At this point things started to move as if I was caught in a vortex, alternating slow motion and double time. Danny stopped reaching for Jack and caught my arm before I could snap it back. Out of the corner of my eye, I saw Jack stumble backward. Danny was facing me. He grabbed my right hand with his right, which meant that he'd either have to cross over himself to get me firmly in both hands, or pull me off the stool. I yanked away from him as hard and fast as I could, with every intention of throwing myself into whoever was standing next to me, but Danny didn't let go and it felt like my shoulder dislocated. With my body shot, I had no choice; I decided to scream. Though I ran the risk of my sound getting lost in the din of the club, I was not about to enter into his little agreement quietly.

Before the word ''help'' was even fully out of me, a fist shot past the line of my peripheral vision and caught Danny square in the neck. With this, Danny released my arm. Rather than following my plan A, which was to throw myself at the body beside me, I found myself on Danny like a wild woman deceived. With my arms flailing the best they could, I scratched at Danny's face until I was literally yanked off my stool.

Whoever had me was bigger than Jack. I figured it was Danny's other friend, the one I'd not seen. I kicked and twisted, screamed and clawed, but he had me in a firm hold. At least I knew that my kicks were well placed between Danny and whoever was holding me. I felt myself being turned away from Danny in a clockwise motion. I was stunned when I saw Lady Lashes riding Jack. Behind them, a slender, frightened man with almond-shaped eyes was backing away from the free-for-all.

Jack was screaming profanities, twisting and bucking, trying to get Lady Lashes off him, but she was holding on for dear life. ''You go, girl!'' someone to my right yelled out to her and hooted in support, all apparently an evening's entertainment. Too close for me to see clearly was a man who had Danny bent backward over the bar, but before I could witness any more than that, the man holding me whisked me out of the center of action.

From my vantage point it looked as if there was going to be a stampede. Everyone was screaming and shoving at what looked like the start of a free-for-all. With every ounce of energy I possessed, I kicked and kicked and kicked at the mountain who was still holding me a good foot off the floor.

Finally he gave me one good shake, and with the pain from my shoulder, my head, and my psyche, I just stopped kicking, stopped fighting. Whoever he was, he gently lowered me to my feet, turned me around, and yelled over and over again, "It's okay. It's okay." He pulled me into a bear hug of an embrace, shielding me from the chaos that surrounded us. I couldn't see who it was because my head was buried in his shoulder, but it was a man, and he was as gentle as he was big. He supported me as he back-ended us near the exit behind the bar, where he released his hold and held me out at arm's length to get a look at me.

I've known Gil Jackson forever. He's family; he's one hell of a cop. And he pulled me into a relieved embrace.

"Jesus Christ! Do you have any idea how worried we've all been?" He sounded harsh, but his hound-dog face was all love.

I allowed myself to fall against my old friend and shut out the world behind me. If I had turned around, I'd have seen that the bartender, who had winked at me, had Danny by the back of the collar on one side of the bar while Max, tanned from his truncated honeymoon, took one last shot at Danny, a man he wanted to kill. I would also have seen that Lady Lashes had Jack in a chokehold, and the man with the almond-shaped eyes was crying as a plainclothed police officer read him his rights.

But I didn't turn around. Instead, I buried my face in Gil's chest and cried like I hadn't cried in years. I didn't remember the stretcher arriving or being strapped into it. I didn't remember that Kerry and Leslie and Max's bride, Marcy, were standing on the wet pavement, a trio of friends holding hands, waiting for it to be over. I didn't remember Miguel, Our Lady of the Lashes, taking off his wig and telling me I was safe now.

But I was. At least for the time being. At least from Danny.

Twenty-two

"You *like* Jell-O." Minnie dismissed my complaints as she fluffed up as much comforter on my bed as she could, considering Auggie was sprawled out next to me, flattening half the bed cover. Sunlight was pouring into my bedroom, and despite some minor aches and pains and occasional moments of serious emotional distress (which Dr. Harris had told me could last for a while), I was feeling safe, whole, and loved. It didn't hurt that Auggie had been snuggled contentedly at my side since my return the day before.

"There is something intrinsically wrong with *green* Jell-O." I took a deep breath and felt my chest and throat constrict, no doubt an aftereffect of the cigarettes. My mouth still tasted like I'd eaten an ashtray, which was actually good, because it squelched any cravings I might have been having for an old nasty habit. "Besides, Min, if I wanted hospital food, I would have stayed there."

"Oh you're a big baby." She took the untouched yet well-sniffed bowl of green gluten, sat at the end of my bed, and tried a mouthful. "*De*-licious. You don't know what you're missing."

"Hey, hey, how's the patient?" Max and Marcy walked in behind an enormous bouquet of flowers. Leslie lingered in the doorway behind them, her arms crossed over her chest and her mouth set in a way that told me loud and clear that she was "concerned," which in all honesty, I could understand this time. Traditionally, Leslie has had a hard time with my being a detective. She is convinced that mine is a dangerous job and that I take unnecessary risks. Normally, I pooh-pooh all this as being overly protective; however, this time, even *I* had to stop and wonder what I was doing and why.

"I'm just fine," I said, more for Leslie's benefit than Max's. "But you two are supposed to be on your honeymoon." I kissed Max and asked Marcy, "How does it feel to be married to this guy?"

"I think I'll get used to it." Wonderful laugh lines emerge around her eyes when she smiles.

"Good thing, too," Minnie chimed in. "Because you know, I was just waiting for him to propose to me."

"Had I only known." Max took the bowl of Jell-O from Minnie.

Leslie took the flowers and disappeared into the hallway.

"You gave us quite a scare." Marcy planted a kiss on my forehead.

"I am very glad to be home." I cleared my throat.

"This is disgusting," Max said, his mouth full of green Jell-O.

"Ooo, I *love* Jell-O." Marcy took the bowl from Max.

"You sure it's not mold?" He swallowed. "So . . . do any good drugs lately?" When Auggie refused to budge from my side, Max bent down and rubbed her ears.

"I'm feeling almost perfect again," I said.

"Oh, to feel perfect, now there's something to aspire to." Marcy settled on the club chair across the room and asked Minnie if she wanted some Jell-O.

"No, thanks." Min shot a glance at me as she slid off the bed. "Not because it isn't delicious, because it is, but because I have things to do."

"Like what?" Max took her vacated seat.

"Leslie's having a hard time with this," she said. "And

quite honestly, I can't say as I blame her. I'm going to go help her with the flowers."

"Wait for me. I'll help." Marcy gracefully rose from the chair and followed her. Spoon in mouth, she turned back to me and said, "I'll leave you two alone."

"So." Max placed a large tanned hand on my leg. "You okay?"

I thought about it as I stared at his wedding band. I shook my head. "I don't know."

"Talk to me."

I looked into his deep brown eyes. The words were trapped in the back of my throat. I knew if I said anything, the floodgates would open. Max reached out and took my hand in both of his.

"Okay, then I'll talk. You probably want to know what happened while you were away."

I nodded, keeping my eyes on Auggie. She was dreaming, her eyes and black lips twitching like crazy. I covered a paw with my free hand. A puppy, her pads were still soft to the touch.

"Let's see if I can get this chronology right. You were supposed to meet with Kirstin Johns at five on Thursday and then pick up Leslie at six in Great Neck. Miguel had spent the day getting statements from the people in that detective's file." Max let go of my hand to push back a tuft of salt-and-pepper hair that had fallen into his eyes.

"Hickey."

"Right, Hickey. Okay, so when Leslie couldn't get through to your cell phone, she called the office . . . that would have been around six-thirty. Kerry was still there— waiting to hear from you—and as fate would have it, Miguel had just walked in. Now, no one was concerned at this point, because everyone knew you had a five o'clock in Corona, and figured you were either stuck in traffic or running late.

"Anyway, Miguel was charged up from having been a detective all day. He was feeling confident, and though he knew you'd be pissed if he interviewed Danny (because you'd said specifically that *you* wanted to talk to him), aside from Kirstin and Mazzio, Danny was the only one left on the list, and Miguel knew you were anxious to close the case. So he went against your wishes—"

"For a change," I interrupted.

"For a change, yes, but the thing is, if he hadn't done that, you might not be sitting there looking so pretty right now. Believe it or not, Miguel is completely responsible for this happy ending. You see, when he got to Long Island City—which is where Danny lives—Miguel was approaching the building from across the street, and who does he see but Mali Cajina."

"What time was that?" I asked, fighting another wave of exhaustion. I found it amazing that after having been knocked out for close to thirty hours, I was as tired as I was, but I was told that this, too, was only to be expected.

"Thursday night, about seven-thirty, eight o'clock. Anyway, this Cajina character was having an animated, in fact what Miguel referred to as an *agitated*, discussion, with a man Miguel didn't know. Now, bear in mind that Miguel didn't know Danny from a hole in the wall, but the coincidence was enough for Junior Miss to be suspicious . . . did you know that that was Miguel sitting next to you in the nightclub?" he digressed.

"Lady Lashes?" I shook my head. "I can't believe he shaved his goatee for me." I smiled at the thought of our young associate stopping crime in glorious drag. "Go on," I prodded Max, knowing that my energy was waning.

"Well, when the two men parted, Miguel made a judgment call and decided to follow Mali. He figured he now knew where Danny lived, so he could always find him there, but he was curious about Mali."

"He's learning." I tried to sit up, but my body resisted the move. Max got up off the bed and helped prop me up against the headboard. When I was set, he walked over to the windows.

"He's good, Syd. I think he's going to be a real pro. Anyway, as it turns out, Mali just went home. But now it's close to nine o'clock and everyone's starting to *really* worry about you, because it's not your style to be that late, you're usually within fifteen minutes of punctual.

"Anyway, back at around six-thirty, Leslie had called Mitch and Maddy, who picked her up at the station, so they were all together out in Great Neck. Leslie called Minnie from Mitch's house and Minnie said she hadn't heard from you in days, but she had had a bad feeling from a chat she had had with Nathan a few days earlier. She said she tried to warn you. Do you remember that?"

"I remember she left a message about Dad, but I never called her back."

"Right, well, apparently your dad had passed on the word to Minnie that something bad was going to happen to you. Mind you, it's now nine o'clock and Kerry's still at the office, hoping you'll either call there or show up. She wasn't about to leave without knowing you were okay. As a matter of fact, it was her idea to call Gil at home. He immediately had a team sent out to Corona to talk to the Johns woman. She wasn't there, there was no answer on the phone. When midnight rolled around and there was *still* no word from you, Gil went to Corona personally and had the super open the door to her apartment. That's when they found Johns's body. It's also when they called Marcy and me." He said all this to the window, and I knew the view Max was looking out on: clean old West End Avenue on a weekend afternoon . . . my own slice of heaven on earth.

"We got the first flight out of there, but by the time we landed at JFK, it was already noon on Friday. Now, right after they found Johns's body, Gil had Mali brought in for questioning. Naturally, he spilled everything.'' Max came back to the bed and sat facing me. His St. Bart tan made him look exceptionally fit. ''It was Mali who set the fire at Jake's place.''

''Mali? Jesus Christ, Miguel had him pegged right from the beginning. But why?''

He shrugged. ''Apparently Mali first met Jake when he interviewed for a job at Harriman's, but Mitch wouldn't hire him because he was illegal, and Mitch has a reputation for doing everything above board. However, when Jake was opening *his* place, Mali was one of the first people he called. He knew Mali could provide him with the staff he needed, so he made a lot of promises.'' Max turned around, kicked off his shoes, and moved so that he was sitting next to me facing the same direction. ''Essentially, Jake offered Mali and his friends a good solid future, including benefits, excellent money, and a green card for Mali. See, before Jake had even opened the doors, he was swamped with orders, so he knew he needed a dedicated staff to get the ball rolling. Mali could provide that because he had a lot of friends who needed the work, people who would go an extra nine yards for Mali. The only problem was, Jake's promises were nothing but a bunch of bull.

''Mali got a lot of his friends to work for Jake, but after the first month or so, when the initial orders were filled, and Jake had very happy clients who were putting out the word that he was good and reasonable, things started to change. It's very sad, really. He convinced his workers that he was their champion, and then, just when it looked as though money was going to start coming in, he began to back off on his promises to them.''

''So it *was* a sweatshop.''

Max nodded. ''Essentially, yes. From what Mali said, conditions got intolerable in a very short period of time. It

started with increased production, reduced staff, reduced
wages withheld, no breaks, to finally threatening workers
with deportation if they didn't comply. After a string of
disappointments, it was just the last straw for Mali. He
snapped. He had gone out on a limb, really thinking that
his life had changed, and *bam,* he's hit in the head with a
baseball bat, so to speak.'' Max took one of my pillows
and fluffed it up behind him.

He continued, ''As strange as it sounds, I think Mali's
probably a good man. He never would have started that fire
if he'd known someone was in there. He went in, in the
middle of the night, when he knew no one would be there,
but instead, as luck would have it, Danny was there.''

''So Danny *was* there. What about the woman who was
there? Who was she?''

Before he could answer, Leslie whistled at the other end
of the apartment, which bolted Auggie out of a deep sleep.
She cocked her head from side to side, looking at me with
pleading eyes, until I finally said, ''Well, go on, go check
it out.'' With that, she raced off the bed and out the door.
''There's a treat at the other end of that whistle,'' I explained. ''So, who was the woman who died in the fire?''
I asked again.

Max frowned. ''The cleaning lady, right? But you knew
that.''

''All we knew is that she was a Jane Doe at the
morgue.''

''Sorry, kid. I don't know anything about that.''

''But wait a minute—getting back to Danny, why was
he at the factory at one in the morning?''

''I do believe Daddy kept money there. It seems Danny
went to borrow from the till, the cleaning lady scared him,
he hit her, and she hit her head on a table and was out like
a light. Next thing Danny knows, Mali's turned the place
into an inferno. Danny left the woman there to die in the

fire. Mali didn't know until later, when Danny threatened to tell the police he had killed a woman." Max linked his arm through mine and took my hand. "I'll have you know, my friend, you had me scared this time."

"Imagine how I felt." I squeezed Max's hand. "He was going to sell me, Max. *Sell* me to another person." I took my hand back and folded the top sheet over the end of the comforter. Order. I needed order. "You know what really makes me sick?"

"What's that?"

"That this happens to people who aren't nearly as lucky as I am," I said to my hands. I was wearing long sleeves so I wouldn't have to look at the bruises left from the needles. "Children, women, people . . . people are still bought and sold today, made to do things . . ." My voice trailed off in a fog of thought. It felt as if Max was a statue beside me, waiting for me to continue. "Made to do horrible, awful things. It's . . . it's a terrifying thing."

"I can't imagine." His voice was as soft and loving as a caress. I am a fortunate woman in that I have my friend Max, a daily reminder that all men are not alike and I cannot therefore dismiss the gender as unacceptable because of a few rotten apples. Danny frightened me in a way that burrowed deep into the core of who I am. It made me feel vulnerable. Helpless. Incompetent. Incapable.

I changed the subject. I had to. "How did Danny get the drugs he used on me?"

"He works in a hospital in Queens." Max sighed. "The guy is charismatic, very bright, and he was able to hack into certain programs that made him a popular kind of guy. Payroll is always a superb bargaining tool. Bottom line is, Danny is totally screwed up." Max got off the bed and started to wander around the room.

"He is also in amazing shape." I knew that half of my

pain was a result of his physical manhandling and the other half was emotional.

"No kidding. If I understand correctly, once upon a time Danny had his own drug problem. When his father forced him into rehab a few years ago, Danny discovered the benefits of working out." Max took a framed photo of Leslie and her family off the wall. "Handsome family. Any news on her brother?" Max asked, referring to Leslie's brother, Lloyd, who was incarcerated in a psychiatric hospital.

"Dorothy goes to see him fairly regularly, but rehabilitation doesn't look very promising. When he snapped, he snapped."

An eerie silence descended on the room as Max and I both contemplated the similarities between Lloyd and Danny. Both men were in extraordinarily good shape, both were handsome and bright, and both had gotten stuck emotionally.

"Anyway," Max hung the photo back on the wall, "thanks to Miguel, Gil picked up Mali. Mali told him everything, including where you were and what Danny planned to do with you."

"Where was I?"

"In Danny's apartment. They transported you from Corona in a rug."

"How did they get me out of Danny's?" I strained to remember more than fractured bits and pieces.

"On your own two feet." Max sank into the club chair. "Mali's a good man. He offered to help the police without making any deals. He told them where you were and assured them you were in no immediate danger."

"Says who?"

"Well, he knew Danny had no intention of killing you." Max ran the back of his hand against his chin and stared at me. "Did he . . . abuse you?"

I knew what Max was asking, but it seemed ironic that

he couldn't say the words. Was rape worse than what I had been through? Was rape worse than a black coffin with no air and no hope? Stripped of my freedom and will, hadn't I had Danny imposed on me in a way that was emotionally a rape? Was Max hoping to heave a sigh of relief knowing that at least, thank God, I hadn't been physically penetrated?

"What do you mean?" I wasn't going to make this easy for him.

Without batting an eyelash, he kept my gaze. Perhaps after all these years he was able to read my mind, because when he finally did speak, it was an apology. "I'm sorry. It's just that none of us know what you went through, Syd. Mali said he kept you sedated in a small room, but that you were fed and you were well. Given Danny Aronson's nature, well, anything was possible." I don't know how it happened, but in a fraction of a second, Max suddenly looked old sitting there, his hair more salt than pepper, his broad shoulders hunched, and I felt myself drifting back into the safe arms of Morpheus. I didn't want to talk anymore. I didn't want to listen. I just wanted to fade out.

And that's just what I did.

Twenty-three

"What?" I looked up from the morning paper and saw Leslie casting a wary eye in my direction.

"Are you planning on dressing today?" She poured milk over a bowl of Shredded Wheat with bananas.

"The day has barely started," I said, noting that it was not yet six-thirty in the morning. It was cold and overcast, and I saw no need to rush into anything. I was quite comfortable in my sweats and flannel shirt. "Besides, I *am* dressed." I turned my attention back to the paper and my coffee.

Leslie was outfitted for a day of hands-on installation work with the boys, as she called her team of carpenters and contractors. "You are not. Dressed means that one takes the time to shower first, and then chooses fresh clean clothes. You look like shit." She sat across from me at the table and started her cereal.

"Well now, seeing as how I *feel* like shit, isn't it reassuring to know you *can* read a book by its cover?" I didn't even look up from the paper I was only pretending to peruse.

"You know, you'd be a lot easier to live with if you dealt with all this." She wiped the corner of her mouth with her middle finger.

"You know, you're very cute." I put down the paper and rested my elbow on the table and my chin in my hand.

Leslie studied me for the longest time and then turned back to her cereal without another word.

"What?" I asked as if I didn't know what.

She shook her head and reached for the Metro section of the paper.

"Okay, okay, I'll shower," I acquiesced, knowing that I couldn't risk losing contact here. As much as I might have wanted to stay cozy in my denial, I knew that what Leslie had been telling me for the last few days was right on target; I knew that sooner or later I would have to get back into the world I'd been avoiding rather successfully. I got up in search of carbohydrates. Rye toast is always a good start.

"You have to finish what you started, Sydney," she said to my back.

I turned around in one graceful movement, my hand planted firmly on my chest. "Excuse me?"

Even in my belligerent state, her smile struck me as enchanting.

"You have to finish this case," she repeated, as she scooped up a slice of milky banana. At any other time I might have taken this opportunity to note, probably with triumph, that Leslie was encouraging my career.

"The case was solved and it is closed." I rummaged through the refrigerator until I found the brie. That's the way to start the day: carbs and fat infused with a massive dose of cholesterol.

"The case is not closed, Sydney, and you know it."

"I was asked to prove that Mitch was not guilty. All charges have been dropped against him, so I'd say that was a case closed." The rye popped up, browned to perfection. A good, healthy slathering of brie and here was a meal worthy of clogging up the widest of arteries.

"There's more to it than the fire, isn't there?"

"Want some brie?" I asked, dodging her question.

"You haven't talked to your uncle since you got home. That's a week now."

I buttered the second piece of toast with brie and tried not to hear her.

"Your aunt and uncle have both called—several times— and you refuse to talk to them. You want to explain that?" God, she was persistent.

"This has been a draining experience for me." I placed the cheesy comestibles on a plate. "I've needed time to recover." Not wanting to face her directly during this line of questioning, I cleaned up my mess before I joined her at the table.

"You've had time." Still she spoke to my back. "Look, I don't know what happened, but I know you, and I'd be willing to bet anything that there is unfinished business here. Now, you can either act like a big slug and continue to just lounge around the house all day, or you can do what you do so well."

"And what would that be?" I eased onto the seat across from her.

"Confront the hard stuff head-on." She finished her cereal and downed it with a coffee chaser.

"Oh, you flatterer."

"It's not flattery, it's true. You're usually not afraid of the hard stuff. Most people are." She snatched a slice of brie toast off my plate and smiled impishly. "Thank you."

"Yeah, well, I got scared this time." I could tell this was not what she expected me to say. "I would think that would come as a big relief to you," I said, not without a hint of combativeness.

"No, no, don't lay that on me. I am the first to admit it can be very hard loving someone who puts herself in risky situations, but this time, you're wrong. How could you think it would come as a relief to me knowing that some-

one, something, took the air out of your glorious sails?''
She paused. ''Talk to me.''

''I don't know what to say.''

''Okay, then I'll prompt you. For starters, do *you* think
this case is closed? To your satisfaction?''

''Come on, *satisfaction* is an unfair qualifier.''

''Since when?'' She tossed half the toast back on the
plate. ''Listen, look me in the eye and tell me honestly that
you think this case is closed, and I'll leave you alone.''

I don't lie to Leslie. I tried it once, a silly white lie, and
I got caught red-handed. I figure it's easier to tell the truth
than hurt someone I love.

''There are a few loose ends,'' I conceded.

''Will you talk to me about them?'' She retied her shoe-
laces. Leslie is one of those women who looks as appealing
in construction attire as she does evening attire.

''Yes. Ultimately. But not now.'' I pointed to the wall
clock over the stove and said, ''Oh, my gosh, will ya look
at the time? Surely the boys will be waiting, dear.'' I
popped the last bit of toast into my mouth, pushed back
my chair, and gathered the breakfast dishes.

''The longer you let some things go, Syd, the harder it
is to deal with it. Remember that thank-you note to Barbara
last year? It took you six months and made you nuts. Deal
with it. Get it out of the way and move on.'' She came up
behind me and gave me a hug. ''I love you. Now, go
shower and do something you'll be proud of today.''

After Auggie and I said good-bye to Leslie at the door,
I took her parting words to heart. ''Get it out of the way
and move on.'' Organizing the linen closet was one of those
things that had long been neglected, and I would be so
proud of myself when I tackled it.

I did, and I was.

Which brought me to eight o'clock. The day was beginning to clear and the idea of being outside had some appeal.

I showered, changed my clothes, and put on make-up. Then I studied my reflection in the mirror. All bruising and swelling had disappeared during the week that I had been recovering, and I looked healthy, confident, and clear. I took a deep breath and memorized what I saw.

I leashed Auggie, and put several plastic bags in my jacket pocket, along with identification, money and my gun. It wasn't going to be a long walk, but my experience with Danny had changed me. I wasn't about to take any chances.

Half a block from home, while Auggie sniffed the backside of a bored basset hound, my heart started to race, and I could feel tears swelling up from deep inside. I hurried over to Riverside Park, hoping that the view of the water and sky and New Jersey would calm me.

Life was normal there. There was nothing more threatening than a handful of determined joggers, a few bicyclists, and dog walkers like myself. I let Auggie off the leash and we headed south. I didn't care if I got a ticket for giving her her freedom; it was worth it. Tugboats hauling tons of garbage sped down the Hudson and sunlight broke through the low hanging clouds. We walked past the Seventy-ninth Street boat basin and came out of the park at Seventy-second Street. Without even thinking I raised my hand and hailed a cab.

Despite our language barrier, the taxi driver, who didn't know his way around the city, hunched over his steering wheel and followed my pantomimed directions well. In no time at all, Auggie and I were standing on the median on Ocean Parkway, watching the world go by in Brighton Beach.

It is a different world in Brighton Beach, which is also known as Little Odessa. Where I live, on the Upper West Side, I can feel the neighborhood history all around me; from the time it was farmland, to shantytowns, to the wonderful rich architecture that still survives and evokes horse-drawn carriages and straw hats. But Brighton Beach is different in that it reflects not a place so much as a people. Russians and Russian Jews: a culture I feel both removed from and inextricably bound to.

Auggie and I walked two blocks south and then back again, several times over, before we finally stopped in front of a large, once elegant apartment building. Red double doors led into a musty foyer whose cracked marbled floors were protected with black grooved rubber runners. On the wall to the right, was a building directory and an old intercom system. To the left hung a bulletin board covered with building announcements; fliers, in both English and Russian, and handwritten classifieds. A video camera was mounted to the wall just inside the second set of dulled glass doors. I made it as far as the intercom and just stood there while people went in and out of the building. Everyone smiled at Auggie and most people took the time to pet her, which only confirmed my sneaking suspicion that if one wants to conduct a quiet investigation, it is best not to bring along the world's cutest dog.

I knew it was apartment number 505. All I had to do was bring my hand up to the intercom and press the buzzer. Simple. Easy.

Easy.

Simple.

I stood there, my hands flat at my side.

Familiar with building routines, Auggie waited patiently, looking from the door to me, and back again. Finally, she exhaled a deep sigh and stretched out on a cold patch of marble.

"I know, I know," I said to her arched brows, as she looked up at me. "But it's not that easy, you know. I mean, what am I supposed to say?"

I knew exactly what I had to say, and my feet weren't going to get any warmer if I continued to stand in the drafty entrance. I pressed the button to 505 and waited. It never occurred to me that I might not get a response. I rang again, impatient, now that I had found my courage.

A woman's voice came clearly over the wires and I told her that I was UPS, which in a way I was, if UPS stood for Unidentified Professional Snoop.

The woman who opened the door to apartment 505 was not what I had expected, though I really couldn't say what I had anticipated. I suppose I thought she would be an elderly, squat, overweight Russian immigrant who spoke a very broken English.

Elena Sabirova was neither fat nor squat nor elderly. Her face dropped when she saw me.

"Elena?" I asked, as I neared the open door.

The woman standing in the threshold was about 5'5", with graying shoulder-length hair and a square face. She weighed about 140 and wore black slacks and a pink angora sweater. I would have placed her in her early sixties.

"Yes." Her voice was low and she looked understandably suspicious, after all, Auggie and I hardly looked as if we were delivering anything from UPS.

I stopped less than six feet from her door, suddenly panicked that maybe Nomi was wrong about the woman standing in front of me. Seeing Elena face-to-face, I didn't know what to think, but I had come this far and I knew that if I was going to have any closure with this whole mess, she and I had to talk.

"My name is Sydney. Sydney Sloane. I'm Mitch's niece."

Much to her credit, she did a believable job at maintaining her composure. As a matter of fact, she seemed quite at ease for a woman who has just been caught, but still I knew from her reaction that what Nomi had told me was the truth: Mitch's alibi was standing right in front of me.

"May we come in?" I asked, gesturing to Auggie, who was yanking at the leash to get a better sniff of Elena.

"Yes, of course." She moved with the grace of a dancer, backing into the small foyer to give us room.

I tried to hide my curiosity as I passed through the foyer into the living room, but it was impossible. After all, I was there to confirm Nomi's assertion that Mitch had a love-nest. It was only natural that I would want to take in the details.

On the wall above a plastic-covered ornate sofa was a dark still-life, the kind you might find in a roadside motel, of fruit, cheese, and a dead chicken. The sparseness of the room only emphasized the furnishings: two quilted chairs that matched the sofa, a worn round ottoman, and a two-tiered coffee table with magazines below and nothing on top. Across from the seating area was a polished upright ebony piano, and next to that was a large TV on a rolling cart. Pots of artificial flowers sat atop the TV and framed photos covered the piano. On the parquet floor, in the center of the room, was an Oriental rug, too small for the space, but beautiful nonetheless. I moved toward the piano and photographs. There were maybe a dozen photos, mostly of Mitch, Elena, and a young woman.

"Would you like some coffee?" she asked from behind me. Her accent was actually appealing. "Or tea? I have some nice scones."

"No, thank you."

The dining room table was all but lost under stacks of banker boxes. It was from that general area that I heard a hiss. So did Auggie, who quickly positioned herself between my legs.

"That's my daughter's cat, Bella. She likes dogs."

Since the only cat Auggie knows is my neighbor's, Charlie, I couldn't guarantee how well she would behave, so without giving her leave to investigate the feline—a large orange tabby—I had Auggie come with me to the seating area. Both my pup and I seemed to be wary of what was in store for us in this Brighton Beach apartment, but of course, I could have just been projecting this on to her.

Elena sat in the middle of the sofa and folded her hands on her lap. The only jewelry she wore were a pair of hoop earrings, a watch, and a gold band on the ring finger of her left hand. She was a handsome woman who wore too much eye make-up, but her eyes were compassionate and warm. From what Nomi had said, Elena had been living in the States for twenty-five years, but she had a naïveté that made her seem almost newly immigrated.

"You are Eleanor's daughter?" she asked, leaning slightly forward.

Her question took me by surprise. "Yes," I muttered.

"Mitch has told me much about your mother. I am sorry we never met." Elena gave an almost imperceptible nod of her head. She wet her lips.

I took a deep breath. "Well, this is a little uncomfortable, isn't it?" I smiled.

She exhaled a nervous laugh and rubbed her thighs with her palms. "Mitch is not here." She looked helplessly around the room.

"I know. I suppose that's why I'm here," I said, rubbing Auggie behind ears that were standing straight up as Bella inched bravely toward us.

"I don't understand."

"I wanted to meet you."

She kept my gaze for a long time before asking, "Why? Why now, after all these years?"

"I just found out."

Her too thin eyebrows flicked up and then quickly creased into a deep furrow. "Found out what?"

"About you."

"Excuse me?"

Bella was less than three feet from my excited puppy.

"I only heard about you the other day."

"What do you mean, *heard* about me?"

"Heard about you. Knew you existed. You've been a well-kept secret. But in case you're worried, I'm the only one who knows."

Auggie stopped fussing and grew more curious as Bella positioned herself now less than a foot away from her.

Elena's mouth was set to speak but nothing came out. Finally she sighed and said, "I am confused. Maybe you have time to explain?"

"Sure."

Bella and Auggie commanded center stage when Bella placed a declawed paw gently on Auggie's nose. Elena and I watched as Auggie mimicked her gesture. Bella then rubbed her chin against Aug's side and Auggie let out a very excited puppy yap that scared the hell out of Bella, who jumped into Elena's lap and looked down at Auggie like a buzzard. Elena held Bella and introduced the pup and the cat. She then put Bella next to Auggie, and when it was clear that they would be fine, she looked up at me and said, "Now you will have coffee, yes? I just made a fresh pot."

I acquiesced and followed her into the kitchen, leaving Auggie and Bella to fend for themselves.

I stood at the doorway to her small pink kitchen with my hands in my pockets and watched as she went about preparing our drinks. It was an odd sensation, knowing that this woman had been a part of my uncle's life for so long. My uncle, who couldn't accept me for who I am because I didn't conform to the norm, obviously had a double standard that allowed for long-term adultery. Nomi had told me that she knew Mitch had been seeing his "lady friend" for at least the last twenty years. Apparently on the night of the fire, Nomi was out late for a bite with a friend at the Stolichny Deli in Brighton Beach when she saw Mitch with

Elena. "He didn't see me and I would never embarrass him." Nomi traded seats with her dinner companion so her back was to Mitch and he never saw her.

Settled at the small wrought-iron breakfast table with coffee and scones, Elena took a deep breath and said, "Now, perhaps you can explain what you mean by you are the only one who knows."

"I know about you and Mitch," I stated simply.

"Yes?" One brow arched and her face turned into a question mark.

After rummaging through all the possibilities of what could be going on in her head, I finally said, "I'm sorry, but I don't understand." I could feel a scowl tightening my eyes and mouth.

"Nor do I. Your uncle and I have been together for how many years, and you only *now* choose to introduce yourself to me? Quite honestly, if I were you, I'd be ashamed." She ladled a second heaping teaspoon of sugar into her small glass mug and stirred slowly, as if she was trying very hard to keep her composure.

"Ashamed?"

"Yes. Where I come from, family sticks together."

I was drop-jawed. Clearly something was wrong here; the last thing I expected was that my uncle's mistress would tell me I should be ashamed of myself for not having contacted her sooner.

"Elena." I paused, choosing my words very carefully. "The other day a woman you probably don't know told me that Mitch and you have been having an affair for the last dozen years or so. In all honesty, I think my aunt would find this terribly disturbing."

"Your aunt?" She glared.

"Yes, my aunt. Mitch's wife?"

She set her mug down carefully and spoke slowly. "First of all, I would think your aunt would have wanted Mitchell to be happy. Second.'' She held up her left hand, palm facing her and showed me a wedding band. ''Second, I don't know why a stranger would be talking dirt like this about me, but your uncle and I have been happily married for twenty-two years now. I wouldn't call that an affair, would you?''

''Married?'' I asked, knowing that I had heard her correctly, but hoping it was a language barrier mistake.

''Yes, married,'' she said impatiently. ''Maybe you should better explain yourself.''

Oi. Just what I needed: to explain myself to a newfound Russian relation with attitude.

Twenty-four

I learned a lot more at Elena's than I had bargained for. For one thing, my uncle was not just a bigamist, he was a bigamist with a runaway child.

By the time I got home, emotions were banging around inside me with such force, it was impossible to land on one and identify it as "this is what I am feeling." It was in this state of mind, after I gave Auggie a treat, that I called Leslie and explained that I had taken her advice and was going to finish what I started.

I knew I was angry at Mitch, yet at the same time, I felt a dusting of empathy for him. Here was a man who had spent his entire adult life enforcing an impossibly strict code of right and wrong on those around him, while he, in turn, had lived a lie, a completely bogus life that was finally about to undo him. I would have liked nothing better than to wash my hands of this whole mess and write Mitch off, but I couldn't. Whether I liked it or not, I was in.

If I was going to help find Elena's daughter, and I was determined to, I had to confront Mitch, and quickly, but how?

I called him at Harriman's and was put directly through.

"Uncle Mitch, it's Sydney. We have to talk."

"Sydney! Thank God. Maddy and I have been so worried about you . . ." It sounded like the old Mitch was back again, loving and solicitous. I heard him, but the cynic in me reduced his concern to nothing more than relief at having been vindicated and saved from life behind bars.

"I need to see you," I said coldly. "Now." We were clearly communicating on two different planes, but at that very moment, there was no room inside me to yield in any way.

"Well, that's very nice. You know, we spent a week calling you, every day, to no response, and now all of a sudden *you* get *shpilkes* and say 'Jump,' I should say, 'What? How high?' I wish I had a schedule that worked that way, kiddo, but I don't."

I said nothing.

"I can see you tonight, or I can see you tomorrow, but right now is no good."

"No, Uncle Mitch. *Now.*" I clutched the receiver with such force, my fingers cramped.

"Honey, as grateful as I am for your help, and I am very grateful, because it was nothing short of a *mitzvah,* but I'm afraid I have a meeting."

I refrained from saying, "Where? In Brighton Beach?" only because I wanted to be there, to see his face when he found out that I knew all about Elena Sabirova Gersh and their daughter, Marisha.

"Cancel it," I said, with an ease that belied my feelings.

"Excuse me?" He hiccoughed a laugh.

"Uncle Mitch, I want you to think about something." I paused. "You think about who I am and ask yourself if I would be this insistent if it wasn't *really* important." I paused again. "Now, I don't care where we meet, but we will meet today, and the sooner the better."

I could hear Mitch breathing on the other end of the line. I had an image of him standing at his desk, his fingertips tapping impatiently on his blotter. Finally he sighed and said, "Okay, if it's that important to you . . . I'll be there in half an hour."

"Where?"

"Where? Your home, where else?"

If Mitch had been to my home three times in the last twenty years, it was a lot, and yet I found myself caught between wanting it to look perfect for my uncle, and reminding myself that it didn't matter what he thought. Little Sinda was battling Big Sydney, and together all they could do was pace from one room, to another, to another.

All vestiges of the past, of the apartment Mitch had known, were either gone, or so well incorporated into the décor that I felt certain he would never notice. Gone was the heavy plastic-covered furniture. Gone were the dark floor-to-ceiling bookcases in the living room. Gone were the flocked wallpaper in the foyer and the bold orange daisies in the kitchen. Gone was Mom. And Dad. And David. Nora was in Baltimore, so all that remained of them here were photographs—and, of course, the memories that sometimes seem to fill the space.

I left a message for Minnie and continued my pacing.

Not knowing how to prepare for this sort of tête-à-tête, I soon realized that pacing would only make me nervous, so I tried meditation. When that didn't work, I settled on the floor in my office with Auggie by my side, and discovered that rubbing her sweet little puppy belly is as calming as a Valium.

By the time Mitch arrived, I was feeling centered, strong, confident, and ready.

He didn't seem to have any curiosity about the apartment beyond the living room, so I didn't offer a tour. Knowing he might easily sink and disappear into the living room furniture, I led the way into the kitchen.

"Thirsty?" I asked, as he took off his coat and threw it over the back of a chair.

"Water would be nice." He tossed his hat on top of his coat and asked, "A sofa in the kitchen? What, do you get tired when you cook?"

I brought him his water.

"So." He flattened his hands on the table. "You feeling better?" He actually sounded concerned. I wanted to believe he was.

"I'm getting there."

"I'm sorry you had to go through that. Your friend says it wasn't good what happened to you."

"Which friend, Uncle Mitch? I have so many."

"What do you mean, which friend? Leslie. Who did you think I meant? Look." He held up his hands, a passive man. "I didn't come here for you to pick a fight. And I can tell you, I think she happens to be a very nice girl. I'm an old man, Sind-ney. It's not easy to change a lifetime of seeing things in a certain way, but I'm trying."

It felt as if my stomach was wrapping around a corkscrew. I knew I had to control my breathing before I opened my mouth.

"But I tell you from my heart, I'm glad to see you up and around. And honestly, you know, you don't look so bad, not as bad as Maddy and I were thinking. As a matter of fact, personally I think you look pretty good."

"All things considered," I added for him.

He nodded. "All things considered." He sniffed and glanced at his watch. "So, what's on your mind?"

With my elbows on the table, I clasped my hands into one big fist, upon which I rested my chin.

"Yes?" he prompted.

I sat back and took another deep breath. There are all sorts of fear, and this one reminded me of what it felt like the first time I jumped into water without Mom or Dad there to catch me; I was so certain that I was doing the right thing and yet I was momentarily frozen with the fear of knowing that there was nothing between me and the water but air and the unknown.

Before Mitch's arrival, part of me had fantasized that I

would relish this moment, but I'd been wrong. I shied away from confronting my uncle the same way I avoided dissecting anything in high school biology. However, then it had been possible to let my lab partner do the dirty work. Now I had only myself to rely upon.

"I know about Elena," I finally said. It was a statement, not an indictment, but I was surprised that he reacted as if he hadn't heard me; nothing changed, he didn't go white or faint. He didn't even balk.

And this bothered me . . . a lot. As I sat there watching him, waiting for a reaction, our history appeared like a tidal wave before me, stretching from unconditional love, to his rejection, to this.

The silence was beginning to feel like a vise when without any warning Uncle Mitch burst into heaving sobs. There was only a table between us, but I knew I could no more reach out to console him than I could join the Christian Coalition. It was an odd sensation sitting there as if I was completely removed from my emotional life and viewing it from a distance.

It was several minutes before he was able to talk. I pushed a box of tissues to his side of the table and waited.

"How did you find out?" He couldn't look me in the eye.

"It doesn't matter." Despite the four thousand questions echoing in the vast space inside my head, I just sat there watching my uncle melt before my very eyes.

When Mitch found the wherewithal to look at me directly, I saw a tired old man.

"What are you going to do?" he asked. The sagging corners of his mouth were encrusted with old bits of lunch.

"What am *I* going to do?" The question took me by surprise.

"I suppose you're going to tell Maddy." He caressed

the tabletop with the palm of his hand. I didn't think it was worth mentioning that I hadn't told Elena about Maddy, whom Mitch had allegedly divorced two decades earlier. Let him sweat.

"How could you do it?" I asked. "Why?"

He wiped the corners of his mouth and shook his head. "It all happened before I could stop it. Elena was working for me. She barely spoke English back then. One day she didn't show up for work, which wasn't like her. Normally, I-I wouldn't get involved, but when a couple of days went by, and I was in Brooklyn on business anyway, I stopped by her place to see if she was okay."

"Which you do for all your employees, right? A personal call from the boss when you don't show up for work is only to be expected with you." I was baiting him, but only because I didn't have the patience to listen to a song and dance that this only happened because of his pure and altruistic heart.

Mitch paused and looked at me uncomprehendingly.

"Listen, Uncle Mitch, you call a spade a spade with everyone else. I suggest you practice it yourself for a change."

He shut his eyes, his face etched in pain. I was ashamed of myself for wanting to hurt him, especially because I knew it wasn't Elena that I was attacking him for; it was me.

He began. "In all honesty, I really did think I was going there because I was concerned about her. She was so . . . defenseless. But yes, I suppose I knew that I was attracted to her." He raked his lower teeth against his upper lip. "Also, she had her fair share of *tsores* then."

"Yes, I know. Remember, she and I met. We talked. She told me all about her troubles back then and how the man with integrity came to her rescue. She also told me what she's going through now." I shook my head. "She's a nice oman, Mitch. She deserves better than what you've given her. And Marisha.''

Here he flinched. "You know about Mari," he said, his shoulders sagging against the back of the chair.

"How come you didn't call me when it happened? I'm a detective, for God's sake."

The question dropped like an anvil between us. Of course he wouldn't have called, if for no other reason than that his secret would have been exposed.

The whole thing was unfathomable—not only that this upright, strict, unforgiving man would have an affair—let alone commit bigamy—but that he was able to carry it off for as long as he had. "Didn't you think you'd get caught?"

He shrugged. "I did. I didn't. I tried not to think about it. One minute it was a . . . flirtation and the next thing I knew, we were married, it just . . . happened. She was lonely, she adored me; I don't know. I was crazy about her. *And* I was crazy about Maddy. And then, all of a sudden, there was Marisha." Here he hung his head.

"Elena said she ran away."

Mitch pressed his lips together until his mouth was white, and nodded. "It happened . . ." He cleared his throat. "It happened around Thanksgiving."

"Why would she run away?"

Mitch shook his head. "I don't think she did. Not Mari. She's a good girl. A wonderful student. It's been unbearable."

"Yes, well, apparently not so unbearable that you couldn't reach beyond your own agenda for her. Chances are, an investigator, called in early enough, might have been able to help you."

Mitch looked as if I'd slapped him in the face, which is precisely what I wanted to do.

I knew from Elena that Marisha had been in her first

year at college, living in a dorm, when she disappeared. Apparently, Marisha had suggested to her mother that they not talk for a month because she was feeling smothered. She wanted to "test her independence," which she felt was harder because she was going to school in the same town where she had been raised. Elena, wanting to please her only child, agreed. The situation was classic for a runaway; a teenager, under the stress of leaving home for the first time, academic pressures, peer pressure . . . most runaways are kids whose problems have become what they consider insurmountable.

"The police are investigating," he said lamely.

"Elena said the police are inclined to think that she ran away," I said.

"May I have a drink, please?" he asked, his voice thin and his water glass still half full. "Vodka, if you have it. One ice cube."

I was glad for the distraction. As I poured the drinks— a gin for myself (it was early, but I figured alcohol would go down a hell of a lot smoother than my family)—the phone rang. Max's voice sailed in from the office, where we keep the answering machine. His positive energy felt completely alien in the space Mitch and I had created. It was like listening to kids laughing in one room while you are lying near death in another. "Hey Syd, listen up, pal; family night tonight, our place, seven-thirty. Minnie and EZ are coming, and Leslie says you guys are, too, so Oz has spoken, which means we'll finally get to see you . . . 'bout time. Okay, my dear, I'm at the office if you want me. 'Bye."

Back at the table, I watched Mitch: not the man I once knew, who had maintained a mesmerizing power over me when I was a child, but rather the crumbling shell of who he had been.

He downed half his drink and wiped his mouth with his thumb and index finger.

He finally said, "Mari's a beautiful girl. Stunning. She looks just like her mother, but, she's very much like *your* mother. Caring. Warm. Focused."

He took several deep breaths and the thought occurred to me that at his age, this was just the sort of thing that could cause a heart attack, not something I particularly wanted to deal with. Then again, a fatal heart attack would certainly make dealing with this whole mess a lot easier for him.

"I didn't know what to do when Mari ran away. I was terrified that once the police got involved, I'd be found out." He glanced at me as if he was afraid I might strike him at any moment. "Don't forget, I had just been arrested. Not only was I afraid that the police would find out I was illegally married, but I was scared that Elena, or one of her friends, would see the news about me in the paper."

"None of them did?"

"Most of them stick with the local Russian paper." He shrugged heavily. "But I think, in my own way, I panicked. I don't think I've handled anything very well." He finished his drink. I didn't offer to freshen it.

"You said before that you didn't think she ran away. What do you think happened?"

His face twitched through a host of emotions before he said, " I don't know, but she would have had no reason to run away."

"Often kids that age are depressed. I mean she had told Elena that she needed some space. Did you think that was odd?"

"No. I thought it was natural. I did the same thing when I was her age. So did Mark."

"What about her friends? Weren't they able to shed any light?"

"She was very serious about her studies. Her work always came first."

"What are you saying?" I asked.

"I think maybe she was a bit of a loner. But some of the girls in the dormitory said she was keeping strange hours."

"What do you mean?"

"Apparently, she would go out late at night, come back several hours later."

"Was she romantically involved?"

Mitch shrugged and shook his head.

"Well, romance could certainly take up a few hours every night. What was her major?"

"Journalism." He paused, and what little color he had washed from his face. He swallowed several times and whispered, "Mari knew. She knew about . . . she knew about Great Neck." His eyes were watery, his mouth was dry, and he seemed to be depleted of all emotions.

"She *told* you?"

His whole body was shaking.

"Oh, God, Mitch. Where *is* she?"

Twenty-five

As it turned out, Marisha hadn't told Mitch anything, and he didn't know where she was, but he did have her laptop computer, which he had taken from her dorm room. Elena didn't know or care about computers, so she never questioned him when Mitch took it.

In looking for answers to his daughter's whereabouts, Mitch stumbled onto one of her class projects, an online investigation.

"Mari knew that I had been married before, and that I had children from a previous marriage, but we never really discussed it. I told her that that life was far away from what we had together, and she really didn't seem very interested in my past. But I guess I was wrong."

"I don't know who you are," I said softly, as I sat there, my arms folded over my chest like a seatbelt keeping me locked in place.

He seemed to shrink into his chair.

"Where's the computer?" I asked.

"In my car."

"Downstairs?"

"Yes."

"Go get it."

Auggie, who had been sleeping soundly in the other room until this point, came racing to the door, hopeful to head out for a spin around the old block with Uncle Mitch.

Uttering the word "treat" was all I needed to recapture

my puppy's attention and keep her with me. Ah yes, the American lure: food. I know it works with me more often than not. Why not my dog?

When Mitch returned, I plugged in the laptop and took a look at just what Marisha had been studying at school. Mitch was right that she was investigating his *other* family for a school project (the assignment had been to get as much information from online research about another person as possible), but he was wrong about the timing. Her actual research—which looked as if it had become an obsession—had started in her senior year in high school. It looked to me as if the journalism class project seemed to fit in nicely with her own agenda. She could ace the class while conducting an investigation that had become, for her, a fixation. By mid-October, she knew just about everything concerning Mitch's life, both personally as well as professionally, and, much to her credit, it looked as though she had retrieved a lot of this information online. Mitch swore that she had never confronted him with her knowledge.

It was eerie, looking through her files. I had to respect the fact that she was absolutely meticulous, having created a database that chronologically recorded her father's life in exquisite detail. The heck with journalism, Marisha would make one hell of a detective. However, it was what was missing that was chilling. There seemed to be no outlet for her feelings. Nothing. No electronic journal or letters, no idle ramblings, no fictitious online persona. I had to assume that there was something on paper that would give voice to how she felt about all this. Something in her room at home that had been overlooked. Despite Mitch's insistence that she would never leave her parents to worry about her like this, the more I saw, the more I believed that she had run away. Now we just had to find her.

I sat at the oak table and fought the tears for what must

have certainly been an excruciatingly painful journey for this young woman, my cousin.

When I was finished with the computer, I asked Mitch to leave.

"What are you going to do?" His tone was deferential, which, if I thought about it, might have been jarring, considering his normal state of self-importance, but I just needed some time alone to think. Marisha was the last piece of the puzzle for me. When I found her, I could decide how I wanted to move forward with my family, but until then it felt like someone had left the barn door open and the pigs were running wild. As far as Mitch's marital states were concerned, I figured a fine, upstanding citizen such as he would surely be able to do the right thing . . . whatever that was.

Less than five minutes after Mitch was gone, I had Max on the phone. After I gave him the latest update, he said he'd contact the police handling the case. Since Miguel was hanging around the office, Max agreed to send him over to the college to try and find Marisha's journalism professor or fellow classmates, anyone who might have known her, known what she was going through. By one o'clock, I was headed back out to Brighton Beach, this time sans pup. There had to be something in the apartment that would point us to Marisha.

I knew Elena would be there because she had confided that ever since Marisha had disappeared, she rarely left the apartment. *What if she came home and I wasn't here?* What indeed.

She was waiting at the apartment door when I got off the elevator. Her eyes were red, her skin was blotched, and she held a fistful of tissues in her hand.

When I was no more than three feet from the door, Mitch stepped out from behind Elena and put his hand protectively on her shoulder. I stopped dead in my tracks. It made sense that he was there, yet I was completely thrown by it.

"What are you doing here?" he asked before I took another step forward.

"Looking for Marisha." I turned to Elena and added, "Is that okay?"

She pressed the tissues to her mouth and reached out to me with her free hand. Funny thing was, I didn't want physical contact with her. I wanted to help. I wanted to be done with this business once and for all. I wanted to reunite mother and daughter. But I didn't want to be touched by her in any way more intimate than a handshake.

And so I shook her hand, a prelude to an afternoon where the three of us worked side-by-side, going through Marisha's room and her personal effects. Always trusting that Marisha would return, and adamant about respecting her daughter's privacy, Elena had never rummaged through Marisha's papers or pockets, drawers or journals. Which wasn't to say that she hadn't spent a lot of time in the room, but she simply hadn't "pried."

It didn't feel like prying to me. It felt like getting to the bottom of things, which is, I guess, why I do what I do. I could have never left this room untouched had Marisha been my daughter. Hell, I couldn't leave it untouched, and I didn't even know her.

Her high school diaries revealed a lonely girl who had a crush on a boy on the debate team, as well as on her French teacher, whom she often dreamed of traveling through France with, staying only in out-of-the-way *pensions*. She liked Garth Brooks, the poet Sharon Olds, and James Baldwin, and had a small but impressive collection of books nice girls don't read, including Anne Rice's unconstrained *Sleeping Beauty* series. There was no address book, no calendar, no date book, and nothing in her journals that even eluded to "Daddy's other life." I did find one entry, in April (when she was still in high school), most interesting:

"When you have eliminated the impossible, whatever remains, however improbable, must be the truth." In the margin, beside the quote, she had scribbled, "Sir Arthur Conan Doyle, gentleman, genius." But aside from that, there was nothing that seemed to even whisper the very difficult secrets she was hiding. The more I read, the more I felt her painful isolation. I wondered if Mitch and Elena could feel her aloneness as acutely as I did, or did they need to believe that their offspring had chosen the incarceration of her solitude? The only reason a teenager chooses to be a loner is because it is an excellent self-defense mechanism.

I called Max before leaving.

"What do you guys have?" I asked.

"Nothing much. Miguel says that he actually talked to one of her professors and he said the most notable thing about the girl was how well she blended into the background. Apparently she was failing that class because she hadn't handed anything in."

"Wow. Well, she had the data. She probably just couldn't share her findings." I rubbed Bella the cat, who had jumped onto the kitchen table for a shot of affection.

"Yeah, well, I talked to one of the officers handling the case. He said they're doing it by the book, but that his gut feeling was that she ran away. Quite honestly, it has all the earmarks of a runaway. But regardless, the police are continuing to stay on top of it. He said that he does a weekly Jane Doe search."

"From what date do they have her missing?"

Max sighed and I could hear papers rustling on the other end of the line. "The day after Thanksgiving, which would have been the twenty-second."

"But they don't know how long she was missing *before* that," I said, lifting Bella off the table and putting her on the floor.

"No. From what the police and Miguel said, no one re-

membered when they last saw her. Can you imagine that?
People just didn't seem to notice her, not even the girls
who lived in the room right next door.''

''What about a roommate?''

''The girl was living with her boyfriend ninety-eight percent of the time. They didn't even know each other.''

Before I left Elena and Mitch, I asked if I could take a
few diaries and school notebooks, just so I could take my
time with them and see if something jumped out at me. I
also asked for a photograph of Marisha. Mitch was in the
other room on the phone (I couldn't help but wonder if he
was talking to Maddy), and as Elena put the books into a
manila envelope, I poked one last time through the scattered
bits and pieces of paper on the girl's desk. I picked up the
stub to her driver's license.

''Marisha drives?'' I asked.

''Oh yes. She's an excellent driver. Mitch taught her.''
Elena handed me the package of journals. ''You will bring
this back when you're finished?''

''I will.''

''You think you will find her?''

''I hope so.''

Elena walked me to the door.

''Do you have a car?'' I turned and asked, halfway to
the elevator.

''No, I don't. But Mari does.''

''She does?'' I stopped in my tracks. ''Where is it?''

Elena bit her lower lip and shook her head. ''I don't
know.''

''She had it at school?'' I asked, walking back to the
apartment. Why hadn't they told me this before?

''Yes. Of course.''

''What kind of car?'' I went back in with Elena and got
all the information about Marisha's 1989 Honda Civic. No
doubt the police had run a check on her car and come up

empty-handed, which increased the likelihood that she had driven to the West Coast or some other place where she could get lost.

When I jumped on the Q train headed back into the city, it occurred to me that I had just spent the afternoon with my intolerant uncle and his other wife. It was only now that I wondered why Elena had been crying when I arrived. Had Mitch confessed to his years of deception and my un-announced arrival pushed everyone into another headset, one that had us working together? I didn't know. I didn't want to care.

Why I cared about this Maria was another thing alto-gether . . . no, not Maria, Marisha. But now that I thought about it, Maria was the name on her driver's license.

On the jacket of one journal, scratched into the laminated cardboard cover, was a quote attributed to James Baldwin: "Ultimately power without morality is no longer power." I pored over her journals from Brighton Beach all the way to Eighty-sixth Street, where I picked up a falafel on my way to the office. It was four o'clock and I hadn't eaten since breakfast, which had been at dawn. I was starving.

Max was back from his honeymoon, all right, proved by the picture hanging on his dartboard; this week it was a newspaper photo of three men standing at a table, all look-ing somewhat amused at something happening off camera. When I asked who the trio was, I was told that these three *yatzes* had single-handedly raped and tortured hundreds and hundreds of people in Bosnia during the war. I like this about Max. His Dartboard Hall of Shame might have seemed silly and childish to some, but in his own way he was venting his feelings toward injustice and inhumanity. With the Hall of Shame, he thinks about the things he finds offensive every day, which affects his approach to every-thing he does. He says it keeps him on target, so to speak.

As soon as I gave him the data on Marisha's car, he had

his lovely police officer wife Marcy on the line. Her shift was just ending, but that didn't matter. She said she'd get something for us within an hour or two.

"Good thing I'm cooking tonight." Max leaned back in his chair and put his feet up on his desk. "And it's a good thing you're eating now, because, by golly, you won't eat nearly as much of my cooking. Or is that the idea?" He raised a brow in my direction.

"I'm starving," I said with a mouthful. "Want some?" I offered the falafel.

"No. I'll wait for an epicurean delight, constructed by these very hands." He wiggled his fingers in the air. "So. It's good to see you in the office, my dear. The place has been way too quiet without you."

Kerry poked her head in and said, "Knock, knock."

"Who's there?" Max asked.

"Ha, ha." She made a sour face at him and joined me on the blue-and-white-striped sofa.

"Ha, ha, who?" Max pressed it.

"Fine, thanks. How are you?" She stuck out her tongue at him and posed the same question to me, giving my arm a quick squeeze. "You sure look better than when I last saw you."

"I should hope so." I smiled. The last time I had seen Kerry was a week earlier at the nightclub, when, come to think of it, I was wearing something that could have easily come from her very own wardrobe. "I think I'm back on track," I said.

"This is crazy about your uncle, eh?" There are times when, given what Kerry is wearing, it is hard to take her seriously. For example, at that moment she was wearing an oversized Tartan jumper, a red sweater with puffy red frou-frou balls sewn all over it, black tights, white anklets, and clunky saddle shoes. Miniature boxes of Purina dog chow hung from her earlobes.

"What's he going to do?" Max asked.

"I don't have a clue." I polished off the falafel as I told them about my bizarre afternoon in Brighton Beach. "There we were, my bigamist uncle who can't *morally* accept that fact that I'm gay, his Russian wife, and me. And all of us barreling through their daughter's private life, not knowing what the hell we're looking for."

"Hadn't they done that already?" Kerry asked.

"Apparently not. Elena said she respected her daughter's privacy."

"Un-huh," Kerry said, like a true disbeliever.

"Did you find anything useful?" Max asked.

"Not that I'm aware of. Oh, but here . . ." I pulled the picture of her out of the file folder and showed it to Kerry.

"Oh, wow, great glasses. So, like, everything she knew about her dad was on the computer, and that's it?" Kerry chewed on a wad of gum far too big for her mouth.

"Yeah, that's the strange thing," I said, feeling exhaustion creep through my entire body. I got up to give Max the picture and could feel in my bones that it had been a long day, after a week of doing nothing more taxing than reading books by women named Margaret (Atwood, Drabble, Lawrence).

I continued, "I looked through her journals, and her notebooks, and she has never mentioned what she knows, or, more important, how she feels about it. And the database, which is amazing, is just the cold, hard facts, nothing to let on what she was feeling, emotionally."

"*That alone* tells you what she was feeling," Kerry said, as she got up from the sofa. She walked to the dartboard and extracted the six darts.

"That's true." I handed Max the picture and sank into the chair across from his desk. It didn't take Dr. Joyce Brothers to understand that Marisha was so far into denial she was probably stone.

He slipped on his glasses and studied the photo. "Cute kid." He put the picture down and asked, "What kind of data did she have?"

Kerry's first dart hit one of the trio square in the face.

"She knew everything from the state of his business to his credit card status. She knew his property taxes, his frequent flyer miles, she knew everything about the situation with Jake and the impending lawsuit. I mean, the kid had done her research and done it well. I'm telling you, she could be a great detective—thorough, meticulous, and able to view it with a detachment that . . ."

"A detachment that's *nuts!*" Kerry finished for me, as her second dart hit the middle man right between the eyes.

"Well, yeah, there is that," I muttered, just as the phone rang.

Max answered and we all knew right away that it was Marcy.

"That was fast," he said, planting his feet firmly on the floor under his desk. He reached for a pen. "Un-huh. Un-huh. When was that?" He scribbled something on a piece of paper. Both Kerry and I watched him intently. "How come they didn't . . . ? Oh, I get it. Okay. Okay. Excellent. Thanks, babe. Listen, do you mind getting things started at home? I'll stay here with Sydney and hook up with you in a little while, okay?" He looked up at the two of us and nodded. "Me too, you. Good-bye." He put the receiver in the cradle and looked from Kerry to me and sighed. "Her car is in the pound." The news fell on the room like a lead weight.

"Since when?" I asked.

"November *eighth.*"

"How could the police have missed that?" Kerry asked, putting the last few darts on Max's desk.

"Their investigation didn't start until almost a month later." He shrugged. "It was an easy enough thing to miss.

It was abandoned, and towed, from the Lower East Side.''

I rubbed the back of my neck, trying to ward off the sense of foreboding I was feeling. ''That witness, Billy Mazzio, he lives down there,'' I said.

The three of us looked at each other, knowing perfectly well that no one had seen hide nor hair of Mazzio since my breakfast with him at Sado's.

''You think this girl knew Mazzio?'' Kerry asked. ''Why would she know him? That doesn't make any sense. Maybe she left her car behind deliberately when she ran away, so no one would follow her. Throw everyone off her scent, so to speak.''

''Nothing was found in the car. Nothing. Marcy's already informed the officer heading the investigation. My guess is they'll check for prints now, just as a precaution.'' Max massaged his jaw.

''They won't find anything,'' I said.

It felt like all the air was being sucked out of the room.

''What are you thinking, Sydney?'' Max asked, suspiciously.

''I'm thinking I need to go out to Bay Terrace, Queens. You in?'' I asked Max.

''Yes.''

''I have to pick up Auggie,'' I said.

''I can walk her,'' Kerry volunteered. She cocked her head to the side and explained, ''Max invited everyone for dinner tonight. I think it's a coming out party for you. But this way, I don't have to go home first. Is that cool with you?''

It was cool indeed. It was also cool that I didn't have to drive, especially since it had started to snow. Max, whose old Chevy had finally, thankfully, died in December, was now the proud owner of a brand new Saab he liked to drive. I gave Kerry the keys to my apartment and asked her to find Leslie and tell her I'd meet her at Max and Marcy's for dinner.

"You guys will never be back in time for dinner." Kerry pointed out that our departure coincided with rush hour.

"Never underestimate my skills as a driver," Max said, as he covered his tanned self with a scarf, beret, down jacket, and gloves.

I wrote out explicit instructions for feeding Auggie, but I knew Kerry well enough to know that when I next saw my puppy she would be overfed and look like a roly-poly toy.

I made one phone call before leaving. It would be a shame to drive all the way out there and find no one at home.

By five-thirty thick snowflakes were sticking to the windshield and the sidewalks and traffic was heavy.

"What's in Bay Terrace?" Max finally asked, as we crossed the Triborough Bridge.

"A man with the answer." I shut my eyes and leaned my head against the leather headrest. The seat was warm and Max had tuned in National Public Radio.

An hour later, Max and I were walking into Florida by the Sound. The same snooty doorman was posted at the entrance, the same bad Muzak was playing in the elevator, and Jake's apartment still looked like a harem.

Jake greeted me cautiously, as if suspecting I had brought Max along to beat him senseless for having begot such a sick son. I introduced Max and Jake, though they had met one another years earlier.

I suppose part of me expected that Jake would say something about all that had happened since we had last seen one another; after all, his life had essentially unraveled in the last week, his archrival had been vindicated, his ex-employee Mali had admitted to setting the fire, his son had been arrested on various counts, including manslaughter for his role in the death of the cleaning lady at the factory, and the insurance company was, as I understood it, reevaluating his claim.

"What do you want?" he asked flatly, watching Max out of the corner of his eye.

"I have a picture I want to show you." I pulled Marisha's photograph out of my bag and handed it to Jake.

He took the picture, but stared up at me for a long time before pulling his glasses out of his pocket and slipping them onto the bridge of his Roman nose.

"Yeah, so?" he said, after taking a good look at the picture.

"Do you know that girl?"

He thrust out his lower lip, frowned, and nodded. "Sure I do. It's Maria, the cleaning lady, why?"

I couldn't respond. By this point it was common knowledge that the cleaning lady had caught Danny with his hand in his father's till. Danny panicked and punched her. Maria went flying and hit her head on a table, which knocked her out. It was at precisely that moment that Mali had come in, tossed the gasoline without even looking, and started the fire that would eventually kill the woman. Danny left her there to die in the fire. At first it was simply a matter of there being no witness to his theft, but after he had taken her purse, which had her car keys (which he also took and dumped downtown when he was done with it), Danny had a chance to think about it and the idea of framing Mitch took shape. He could enlist Mali's help easily because all he'd have to do is threaten the little spic with telling the police that Mali had murdered that cleaning lady.

I took the picture and wondered what Marisha had been doing at Jake's, working as a cleaning woman. That, of course, accounted for her odd hours late at night, but the sheer coincidence of it made me uncomfortable. I remembered one of the quotes in her journal, "When you have eliminated the impossible, whatever remains, however improbable, must be the truth.'' I nodded my thanks to Jake. Max followed me to the front door and we both stopped when Jake called out my name.

''Sydney.'' He paused. ''I'm real sorry about what Danny did to you. You're family. You didn't deserve that.''

''Neither did she.'' I didn't turn around. I simply held up the picture and continued toward the elevator with the bad Muzak.

You're family, you didn't deserve that. I wondered if I'd have deserved it had I not been family.

In the elevator, I finally looked up at Max and said, through the chorus of perky singers hammering away at ''On Broadway,'' ''*She* was family.''

He nodded.

''Why was she there, Max? Why was she at Jake's?''

He shook his head. ''I don't know, but we'll find out.''

And I knew he was right. I wouldn't be content without an answer. But right then, all I could do was cry for the loss of an intensely lonely girl who might have one day been a very fine detective.

Epilogue

There are those who will argue that since polygamy is recognized in the Bible, it should therefore be accepted both socially and legally. Aunt Maddy, however, does not share that belief, nor, it seems, does Elena. And while it is true that once upon a time in the annals of Jewish history there was a spell when polygamy was tolerated by Mosaic law, the State of New York currently considers bigamy a class E felony, punishable by up to four years in prison.

Fortunately for Mitch, no one has pressed charges. In fact, both Maddy and Elena want to keep this whole episode as quiet as they possibly can.

Max says he thinks both women want to keep it private because they're embarrassed. Leslie says she thinks Maddy wants to keep it under wraps to protect Mitch. Minnie agrees with Leslie, but includes Elena and says she probably wants to protect him as well, because people have protected Mitch all his life (which really pisses her off). On the other hand, Kerry firmly believes that despite the fact that Mitch is now living in the basement of his Great Neck home, things probably haven't changed much; she's convinced that both women are probably still seeing him without the other one knowing it. My sister Nora has reduced the whole ugly thing to its most basic aspect: money. She thinks both women should sue him for every cent he's got. Marcy seems to be the only one who feels sorry for

Mitch, and Miguel just wants to know which one is going to divorce him.

One thing I will say for Mitch is that he chose two extraordinary women to embrace the central part of his life. Whether either, or both, will be there at the end of his life, I can't predict. The last time I saw him was at Marisha's funeral, a sad affair where Mitch and Elena were joined by a meager handful of Brooklyn friends, as well as Max, Marcy, Miguel, Kerry, Leslie, and me. Elly, who had suspected that her father had a mistress for a long time and kept it to herself, came to the cemetery, but kept her distance. Apparently, the night Elly had called me at Minnie's, she had wanted to tell me her (correct) hypothesis about her father's alibi, but Paul came in while we were on the phone and she took it as an omen to keep her mouth shut.

Between Max, Kerry, Miguel and me poring over everything that Marisha had left behind as evidence to her obsession, there came the general agreement that a cryptic note in the database was the clue as to why she had taken a job with Jake. *Deliver him from evil,* was all it said, written on the day she had taken the job with Jake. No one will ever know for sure, but the four of us have concluded that Marisha probably believed she could get evidence against Jake, evidence which would help her father. I was reminded of Minnie's warning, early on in this case. ''This is about you wanting to ride in on a white horse and make everything better. I know you, Sydney, you think if you save him now he'll *really* love you.'' I couldn't help but wonder if Marisha and I had this in common.

Not long after the funeral, I sent Miguel to Nomi's apartment with a check and a note vaguely explaining that had she not confided in me, I would have never found a missing child, and isn't it strange how things connect. Though she could really have used the money, Nomi sent Miguel back with the check, torn to resemble confetti. Miguel was nearly in tears when she did it, but I understood, and I didn't push. It was hard enough for her to be disloyal to Mitch, as she felt she had, but to be paid for it was unthinkable.

In the end, there's really only one person I feel bad for, and that's Jake Aronson. Not because he wears a bad toupee or lives in a very red apartment, but because when all the dust settles, he is utterly alone.

There was no family there to support him when he had to sit in the courtroom and listen to the uncontested case against his son, a very sick man who sincerely believes that he did what he did out of love for his father. There was no one there except me (having refused to press charges to avoid testifying against him), hiding in the shadows until the last day. When the courtroom had emptied, Jake sat alone crying, a frail man in a cheap suit. I came out of the shadows then and sat silently beside him, my hand resting gently on his back. There were no words of comfort I could offer. Instead, I helped him out of the courthouse to where he had parked his car, and asked if he would be all right. That's when he looked up at me and said, "He didn't mean to hurt you."

No. He just meant to sell me, which was much better than what he had given Hickey and Kirstin, and probably Billy Mazzio, too, though no one's ever found his body. Danny wouldn't confess, but the general consensus is that he killed Mazzio. He did, however, admit to having met Billy at Sado's, and paid the actor to lie on the witness stand. As far as Kirstin's connection to the whole thing, from paraphernalia found in her apartment and pictures discovered at Mazzio's, it's safe to assume she had simply done as she was told.

Just as Isabel Wang had done as she was told, until she met Hickey. I haven't seen her again, though I do have a floppy disk with her pictures, in case I ever feel the need to reminisce. The week I was out of the office, Kerry played a significant role in helping her start a new life, from setting her up in a women's residence, to getting her a therapist and a job at a health food store in Soho. She also gave Isabel the envelope Hickey had left her. True to Hickey's wishes, Isabel took ten crisp one-hundred-dollar bills out and left them for me. Max and I agreed to donate the money to a women's shelter, where some good would come of it.

I have steered clear of my mother's family, though we recently received an invitation to Paul and Elly's son's bar mitzvah. Leslie asked if Mitch would be there, and Max, of course, wanted to know if Elena would be invited. We all joked about it, but the bottom line, I told them, is that we won't go.

"Not go? How can we not go? This is your family. This is important," Leslie insists.

"*This* is my family." I hold up a photograph taken at Gil and Jane's anniversary party.

"So is *this*." She holds up the invitation. "Elly is reaching out, Sydney, and I, for one, plan on reaching back, even if you don't."

Suffice it to say, we will find out, firsthand, who's on the guest list. Miguel and Kerry have already started taking bets.

As far as my old friend Ned is concerned, much to Auggie and Leslie's chagrin, since I have not found a suitable candidate for his trumpet, I have decided to take up the instrument myself. Maybe, just maybe, I'll give up this crazy business and become the new Louie Armstrong. Hey, you never know.

Yiddish Glossary

Alter kocker	a lecherous old man
Balebosteh	capable housewife, hostess . . . a compliment
Bubeleh	endearing term for anyone you like, young or old
Bobbeh	grandmother
Chozzer	pig
Dreck	feces
Faigeleh	homosexual, fairy
Genug iz genug	Enough is enough
Goniff	thief
k'velen	glow with pride
Mamzer	bastard
Mentsh	special man/person; someone with worth and dignity
Mishegoss	craziness
Mieskeit	ugly person or thing
Mitzvah	blessing
Oi	exclamation to denote disgust, pain, suffering or excitement
Oi vai iz mir	Woe is me
Pisher	a little squirt
Putz	same as *schmuck*

Courtesy of *A Dictionary of Yiddish Slang and Idioms* by Fred Kogos.

Schlemiel	fool, simpleton
Schmuck	penis
Shaineh maidel	pretty girl
Shmatte	rag
Shmuts	dirt
Shpilkes	ants in the pants
Tsores	sorrow, troubles
Zaftik	pleasantly plump and pretty (woman)
Ziskeit	sweetness; an endearing term for a child

Nationally Bestselling Author
of the Peter Decker and Rina Lazarus Novels

Faye Kellerman

"Faye Kellerman is a master of mystery."
Cleveland Plain Dealer

JUSTICE
72498-7/$6.99 US/$8.99 Can
L.A.P.D. Homicide Detective Peter Decker and his wife
and confidante Rina Lazarus have a daughter of their
own. So the savage murder of a popular high school
girl on prom night strikes home . . . very hard.

SANCTUARY
72497-9/$6.99 US/$8.99 Can

PRAYERS FOR THE DEAD
72624-6/$6.99 US/$8.99 Can
"First-rate. . . fascinating. . .
an unusually well-written detective story."
Los Angeles Times Book Review

SERPENT'S TOOTH
72625-4/$6.99 US/$8.99 Can

And Coming Soon
MOON MUSIC

Buy these books at your local bookstore or use this coupon for ordering:

Mail to: Avon Books, Dept BP, Box 767, Rte 2, Dresden, TN 38225   G
Please send me the book(s) I have checked above.
❑ My check or money order—no cash or CODs please—for $_____is enclosed (please
add $1.50 per order to cover postage and handling—Canadian residents add 7% GST). U.S.
residents make checks payable to Avon Books; Canada residents make checks payable to
Hearst Book Group of Canada.
❑ Charge my VISA/MC Acct#_____Exp Date_____
Minimum credit card order is two books or $7.50 (please add postage and handling
charge of $1.50 per order—Canadian residents add 7% GST). For faster service, call
1-800-762-0779. Prices and numbers are subject to change without notice. Please allow six to
eight weeks for delivery.
Name_____
Address_____
City_____State/Zip_____
Telephone No._____   FK 0998

Explore Uncharted Terrains of Mystery
with *Anna Pigeon, Parks Ranger* by

NEVADA BARR

TRACK OF THE CAT
72164-3/$6.50 US/$8.50 Can

National parks ranger Anna Pigeon must hunt down
the killer of a fellow ranger in the Southwestern
wilderness—and it looks as if the trail might lead her
to a two-legged beast.

A SUPERIOR DEATH
72362-X/$6.99 US/$8.99 Can

Anna must leave the serene backcountry to investigate a fresh corpse found on a submerged shipwreck
at the bottom of Lake Superior.

ILL WIND
72363-8/$6.99 US/$8.99Can

FIRE STORM
72528-7/$6.50 US/$8.50 Can

ENDANGERED SPECIES
72583-5/$6.99 US/$8.99Can

Buy these books at your local bookstore or use this coupon for ordering:

Mail to: Avon Books, Dept BP, Box 767, Rte 2, Dresden, TN 38225   G
Please send me the book(s) I have checked above.
❏ My check or money order—no cash or CODs please—for $_____is enclosed (please
add $1.50 per order to cover postage and handling—Canadian residents add 7% GST). U.S.
residents make checks payable to Avon Books; Canada residents make checks payable to
Hearst Book Group of Canada.
❏ Charge my VISA/MC Acct#_____Exp Date_____
Minimum credit card order is two books or $7.50 (please add postage and handling
charge of $1.50 per order—Canadian residents add 7% GST). For faster service, call
1-800-762-0779. Prices and numbers are subject to change without notice. Please allow six to
eight weeks for delivery.
Name_____
Address_____
City_____State/Zip_____
Telephone No._____   BAR 0398

Nationally Bestselling Author

J·A·JANCE

The J.P. Beaumont Mysteries

UNTIL PROVEN GUILTY	89638-9/$6.50 US/$8.50 CAN
INJUSTICE FOR ALL	89641-9/$6.50 US/$8.50 CAN
TRIAL BY FURY	75138-0/$6.99 US/$8.99 CAN
TAKING THE FIFTH	75139-9/$6.50 US/$8.50 CAN
IMPROBABLE CAUSE	75412-6/$6.50 US/$8.50 CAN
A MORE PERFECT UNION	75413-4/$6.50 US/$8.50 CAN
DISMISSED WITH PREJUDICE	
	75547-5/$6.50 US/$8.50 CAN
MINOR IN POSSESSION	75546-7/$6.50 US/$8.50 CAN
PAYMENT IN KIND	75836-9/$6.50 US/$8.50 CAN
WITHOUT DUE PROCESS	75837-7/$6.50 US/$8.50 CAN
FAILURE TO APPEAR	75839-3/$6.50 US/$8.50 CAN
LYING IN WAIT	71841-3/$6.99 US/$8.99 CAN
NAME WITHHELD	71842-1/$6.99 US/$8.99 CAN

Buy these books at your local bookstore or use this coupon for ordering:

Mail to: Avon Books, Dept BP, Box 767, Rte 2, Dresden, TN 38225   G
Please send me the book(s) I have checked above.
❑ My check or money order—no cash or CODs please—for $_____is enclosed (please add $1.50 per order to cover postage and handling—Canadian residents add 7% GST). U.S. residents make checks payable to Avon Books; Canada residents make checks payable to Hearst Book Group of Canada.
❑ Charge my VISA/MC Acct#_____Exp Date_____
Minimum credit card order is two books or $7.50 (please add postage and handling charge of $1.50 per order—Canadian residents add 7% GST). For faster service, call 1-800-762-0779. Prices and numbers are subject to change without notice. Please allow six to eight weeks for delivery.
Name_____
Address_____
City_____State/Zip_____
Telephone No._____   JAN 0898

Blackboard Bestselling Author
VALERIE WILSON WESLEY
The Tamara Hayle Mysteries

NO HIDING PLACE
72909-1/$6.99 US/$8.99 Can

WHERE EVIL SLEEPS
72908-3/$6.50 US/$8.50 Can

"A dozen or more top-notch women writers have roared onto
the mystery scene in the last five years, but Valerie
Wilson Wesley has her signal light on and is already edging
into the passing lane."

Margaret Maron, Edgar Award-winning author of *Up Jumps the Devil*

DEVIL'S GONNA GET HIM
72492-8/$5.99 US/$7.99 Can

"Move over, Kinsey and V. I., to make room for Tamara."

Carolyn Hart, author of *Death on Demand*

WHEN DEATH COMES STEALING
72491-X/$6.50 US/$8.50 Can

"Grips you by the throat and doesn't let go until the
last spine-tingling word."

Bebe Moore Campbell, author of *Brothers and Sisters*

Buy these books at your local bookstore or use this coupon for ordering:

Mail to: Avon Books, Dept BP, Box 767, Rte 2, Dresden, TN 38225   G
Please send me the book(s) I have checked above.
❏ My check or money order—no cash or CODs please—for $_____is enclosed (please
add $1.50 per order to cover postage and handling—Canadian residents add 7% GST). U.S.
residents make checks payable to Avon Books; Canada residents make checks payable to
Hearst Book Group of Canada.
❏ Charge my VISA/MC Acct#_____Exp Date_____
Minimum credit card order is two books or $7.50 (please add postage and handling
charge of $1.50 per order—Canadian residents add 7% GST). For faster service, call
1-800-762-0779. Prices and numbers are subject to change without notice. Please allow six to
eight weeks for delivery.
Name_____
Address_____
City_____State/Zip_____
Telephone No._____   VWW 0898

Discover the
Deadly Side of Baltimore
with the Tess Monaghan Mysteries by
LAURA LIPPMAN

"Laura Lippman deserves to be a big star."
Julie Smith, author of *Crescent City Kill*

BALTIMORE BLUES
78875-6/$5.99 US/$7.99 Can
Until her newspaper crashed and burned, Tess Monaghan
was a damn good reporter who knew her hometown
intimately. Now she's willing to take any freelance job—
including a bit of unorthodox snooping for her
rowing buddy, Darryl "Rock" Paxton.

CHARM CITY
78876-4/$5.99 US/$7.99 Can
When business tycoon "Wink" Wynkowski is found dead
in his garage with the car running, Tess is hired
to find out who planted the false newspaper story
that led to his apparent suicide.

BUTCHER'S HILL
79846-8/$5.99 US/$7.99 Can
"Lucky Baltimore to have such a chronicler
as Laura Lippman."
Margaret Maron, Edgar Award-winning author of *Killer Market*

Buy these books at your local bookstore or use this coupon for ordering:

Mail to: Avon Books, Dept BP, Box 767, Rte 2, Dresden, TN 38225   G
Please send me the book(s) I have checked above.
❏ My check or money order—no cash or CODs please—for $_____is enclosed (please
add $1.50 per order to cover postage and handling—Canadian residents add 7% GST). U.S.
residents make checks payable to Avon Books; Canadian residents make checks payable to
Hearst Book Group of Canada.
❏ Charge my VISA/MC Acct#_____Exp Date_____
Minimum credit card order is two books or $7.50 (please add postage and handling
charge of $1.50 per order—Canadian residents add 7% GST). For faster service, call
1-800-762-0779. Prices and numbers are subject to change without notice. Please allow six to
eight weeks for delivery.
Name_____
Address_____
City_____State/Zip_____
Telephone No._____   LL 0798

Get A Clue

at
http://www.AvonBooks.com

Solve a "60 Second Mystery" and win some books.

Look up your favorite sleuth in "Detective Data."

Meet new authors in "First Edition."

Subscribe to our monthly e-mail newsletter for all the buzz on upcoming mysteries.

Browse through our list of new and upcoming titles and read chapter excerpts.

MYS 0898